Honeymoon Suite

Jennifer Blake
Margaret Brownley
Ruth Jean Dale
Sheryl Lynn

SMP

ST. MARTIN'S PAPERBACKS

HONEYMOON SUITE

"Reservations" copyright © 1995 by Jennifer Blake.
"Checkout Time" copyright © 1995 by Margaret Brownley.
"Wake-Up Call" copyright © 1995 by Betty Duran.
"Lost and Found" copyright © 1995 by Jaye W. Manus.

ISBN: 0-312-95480-8

Printed in the United States of America

St. Martin's Paperbacks edition/June 1995

10 9 8 7 6 5 4 3 2 1

What do you get when you fill a van with romance writers and send it trekking across Kansas and Missouri during the flood of '93? You get a book about a hotel in Dallas. Someday we plan to go to Dallas and write a book about Kansas . . . .

—Jennifer, Margaret, Sheryl and Ruth Jean

Reservations

Jennifer Blake

Chapter One

The knock that fell on the door of the honeymoon suite was firm and commanding. Gina Madison swung toward the sound with her nerves rattling like Mexican jumping beans.

She was alone and not expecting company. It had been at least a half hour since Chad, the breezy, fresh-faced bellman, had deposited her suitcase and whistled himself from the rooms. She had put out the Do Not Disturb sign the minute the door closed behind him.

No person with any decency would ignore the message on the doorknob sign. That meant it was probably her ex-fiancé waiting outside in the hall.

Gina turned back to her contemplation of the Dallas skyline which lay before her, half hidden in the gray-blue haze of distance and June twilight. Giving her chin a defiant tilt, she willed herself to relax while she enjoyed the last rays of sunset glinting across the fourth-floor balcony where she stood. She was not going to open the door. Bradley Dillman could wait out in the hall all night. Or forever.

Her former fiancé just wanted to snoop; she would bet her life on it. He didn't believe she could possibly be tucked into the honeymoon suite of the Glass Garden Hotel with a substitute for his own conceited self. That kind of thing was his game.

He was right, of course. She had no groom.

Oh, but how she wished she did. She would dearly love to be able to flaunt a drop-dead-handsome, outrageously sexy new husband in front of Bradley. How grand it would be to have someone with her for the next week, someone to watch her with love and joy in his face, to reach out and touch her as if he couldn't keep his hands off her. That would show Bradley a thing or two.

Depression welled up inside Gina and she clasped her arms around her waist. The loving closeness of marriage, the warm affection and sweet, unending desire, had been a major attraction for her. She had looked forward to it with bone-deep yearning. Now it was gone. She was beginning to think she missed its promise more than she missed Bradley.

It was the doorbell for the suite that pealed out a summons next, playing the first bars of "Lara's Theme" from Dr. Zhivago, of all things. The music lingered in the air as if the button had been pressed with extra strength. Bradley did not give up easily.

In fact, her ex-fiancé was perfectly capable of camping outside her door until the place fell down around his ears. Or else he just might call on the hotel staff for a pass key, pretending he thought she was in trouble inside. She wouldn't put anything past him; he was addicted to having his own way. It was one of the things about him that had always bothered her.

Once more the bell pealed out its tune. With a sharp exclamation, Gina turned and marched through the open French doors into the sitting room. Crossing the foyer to the suite's outer door, she applied an eye to the peephole.

Gina caught her breath. The man standing outside was not Bradley, not by a long shot.

This guy was taller by a good six inches, and his wide shoulders strained the seams of his faded chambray shirt in a way her ex-fiancé had never come close to matching. His hair gleamed silver-blond instead of Bradley's dusty brown, and his skin was glazed with the rich bronze that came from healthy outdoor labor. The blue of his eyes was as fathomless as a cobalt sea, a tint both darker and richer that Bradley's pale aqua.

The man outside the door was, in fact, a knock'em-dead gorgeous hunk. A hunk who looked tired, grimy, and in no mood to wait for anything or anybody. A hunk who was about to give the doorbell a knockout punch.

Pure instinct made Gina reach for the handle and open the door a few inches. She saw now that the man, confident in his poise, was wearing stained jeans and rough work boots that her ex-fiancé would not have touched with a ten foot pole.

"Yes?" she said, as she made certain the safety latch remained fastened.

"Eugenia Madison?"

She gave a wary nod. The more formal version of her name appeared only on her birth certificate and driver's license. How had this man come by it?

"Evening, ma'am. I'm Race Bannister, and I understand you're in need of a groom."

Gina blinked, stunned by both the effect of a smile on the man's strong, classical features and what he had said. As he reached into his shirt pocket for a business card then handed it through the crack of the door, she accepted it automatically.

Rent-A-Gent.

The name was emblazoned in bold letters on the thick white paper. In the lower left-hand corner was the tiny silhouette of a gentleman in a tailcoat bowing low, sweeping off his top hat while holding a cane under one arm. In the upper right corner was a street address and phone number. Dead center was the business name. Underneath was a line of explanation: Model and Escort Agency.

This Race Bannister was an escort.

"I'm think there's some mistake," she said, the words cool as she pushed the card back toward him.

Race made no move to take the piece of white cardboard. Voice quiet, he said, "No mistake, ma'am. The contact was made by a third party. They said you needed somebody to escort you to dinner and make a fuss over you to throw some guy off track who's been giving you a hard time. The fee has already been paid. I'm your man."

Her man. The words ignited an odd, glowing warmth around her heart, one that threatened to spread.

This would not do. Logic was what she needed here.

Diane, she thought with relief; it had to be Diane who

had sent him. Her friend in the next apartment was the only person who knew Gina was checking into the hotel, the only one she had spoken to after Bradley called to say he was getting married and wanted the suite still reserved in her name. Still, Diane was more than a little distracted at the time; their conversation had been interrupted several times as she ordered her five-year-old son Corey to stop playing with her new camcorder. That her friend had even heard her as she laughed and moaned over her stupidity in telling her ex-fiancé she meant to use the suite herself was a surprise. The fact that Diane had actually sent the rent-a-groom she had wished for so fervently was nothing short of amazing.

It was also the last thing Gina would have expected. She had only known Diane a few months, since she herself moved in next door, but she thought of her neighbor as the epitome of level-headed practicality. More than that, she had been sure Diane understood she was only kidding.

"Look, I'm sorry," Gina said in some embarrassment to the man on the other side of the door. "But I really don't think I need you—your services."

"Neither do I." He flashed her a wry glance before his gaze moved from the burnt-sienna brown of her eyes to the smooth oval of her face, then brushed over the shining autumn-bronze of her hair and down her slender shape. "No woman who looks like you do should ever have to hire an escort under normal circumstances. But there's a first time for everything."

"I didn't mean it that way. I just—"

He lifted a hand to halt her refusal. "If it's me personally that's bothering you, please don't make up your mind just yet. I know I look rough, but I came straight from the ranch; what you see is not necessarily what you get. I brought a tux and a few other things with me. If I could use your bathroom for a quick shower, you'll see I clean up fairly decent."

She could just imagine. Seizing on the one word he had spoken that was not loaded, she said, "Ranch?"

His smile was immediate. "That's my real line of work. Jobs like this help pay the vet bills."

Looking down at the card she still held, Gina gave the

idea of hiring this cowboy two whole seconds of serious consideration. Then she shook her head. "I hate to do you out of a job, but I really don't think it would work."

"It's just a single evening, not a lifetime commitment." His voice dropped to a note of husky persuasion as he braced a hand on the door frame and leaned closer. "I don't bite, I promise. I'm no sex fiend or axe murderer. You'll be safer than at a Sunday morning church service. We'll have dinner down at the Terrace, talk a little, get to know each other. Afterward, maybe we'll dance or stroll around the Glass Garden. I don't say it will be a dream date, but it should be pleasant. At least, I know it would be for me."

He was good at the charm stuff, she had to give him that; the sincerity in his voice was totally convincing. Moreover, the evening he had outlined sounded much better than the one she'd planned, which included ordering room service and going to bed with a murder mystery. And she would dearly love to see the look on Bradley's face if he should happen to catch sight of her with this male model.

Still, Gina hesitated. The falseness of the whole thing bothered her. On top of that was the expense, a major consideration to her frugal accountant's soul. Diane might have made the arrangement, but she couldn't let her friend foot the bill.

Down the hall and around the corner there came the discreet chime that announced the arrival of the elevator on this floor of the West Tower. Race Bannister glanced in that direction, then swung back to her with some urgency. "When I passed the registration desk down below, there was a man and a woman checking into the Emerald Suite next door. I'm not sure it's the guy giving you problems, but the name sounded about right. You want to take this up inside, just in case?"

Gina reached quickly to release the brass safety latch and pull the door wide. Race picked up the black duffel and suit bag at his feet, then stepped smoothly into the foyer. She shut the door and turned to face him.

Race was standing in the middle of the floor with a stunned expression on his face as he took in the pink marble under his feet, the mirrored walls, and the luxuriant fern on an antique brass stand that filled one corner. He eyed the bronze bust of Mitsy Packard, the lady for whom the three-story conservatory-atrium that gave the Glass Garden Hotel its name had originally been built. Then he looked toward the Victorian rose bower of a sitting room, with its wallpaper on which flowers bloomed in profusion. He took in the flowing chintz, the rococo extravagance of gilded picture frames, the carved wood, porcelain clocks, and fringed cushions.

"Good Lord," he said in blank tones.

Gina gave him a defensive look. "It's supposed to be romantic."

"Right." The word was laconic, but the glance that went with it carried a spark of interest.

"I've heard about this suite for years, read about it in *Bride's* magazine—and also about the hotel built by a tough cattle and oil millionaire for his fragile flower of a wife. I always wanted to spend my honeymoon here."

Race studied her while warm appreciation gathered in his cobalt eyes. "Yes, and I'll bet you picked out one of those old-fashioned nightgowns to match the place, didn't you? White silk, maybe, and down to your ankles. Ruffles and lace—and a thousand buttons somebody should have the fun of opening one by one." He smiled with a slow shake of his head. "The guy who disappointed you must be a terminal idiot."

She could get used to the way this man thought. He was right, of course. He knew it, too; that was obvious from the way his grin widened as he watched a flush climb to her hairline.

She cleared her throat. "Look, I—"

"No, you look," he said, leaning to put his bags down before he straightened and set his hands on his hips. "This is not a big deal. I'm here, you're here, and it's just a few hours out of our lives. We'll have a good time showing off for the idiot's benefit, then I disappear. Mission accomplished. You can spend the rest of your week holed up in here letting empty room service trays pile up outside the door."

"But I've never done anything like this before," she

said, and closed her eyes immediately as she realized how that sounded.

"I didn't think you made a habit of it," he drawled with a wicked undercurrent of suppressed humor.

"What I meant to say is, this isn't the kind of thing I would ever consider in my wildest—" She stopped, realizing she was making matters worse.

"So try it for a change. Live dangerously. Step out and do something a little reckless—or maybe a lot reckless." His voice dropped to a lower note. "Who knows? You might enjoy it."

"I don't think that's likely," she said with an effort toward firmness. "I dislike jumped-up decisions or awkward situations. When I do something, I want it planned and organized down to the last detail."

"Like your wedding? Not to mention your honeymoon?" There was a shadow of sympathy in the dark blue of his eyes, but no relenting in his voice.

Her embarrassment shifted into resentment. "What can you possibly know about it!"

"I know you made the reservation for this suite in your name, on your personal credit card, then neglected to cancel it when you canceled the wedding. I know you wouldn't give the place up to your former bridegroom when he had the nerve to get himself hitched to a new bride on your original wedding date. What I'm not sure about is whether you're here now to spite him, or only because you hate to let the suite go to waste since you'll have to pay for it anyway."

"And it's none of your business!" The words were so sharp they seemed to scrape her throat.

"No? Not even if I'm supposed to be helping you out of a fix?"

"I'm not in a—" Gina stopped as she realized what she'd been about to say was patently untrue. At the same time, her annoyance seemed to drain away before the quiet reason in his voice. "You must be good at what you do," she said evenly. "You certainly have the gall for it."

He lifted a gold-dusted brow. "I'm not afraid of taking a chance for something I want, if that's what you mean."

She could believe it. There was an edge of daring about

him, plus a hint of well-honed competence that did not quite mesh with her image of a male model.

He was also correct about her erstwhile wedding. Nothing about that dismal affair had gone as it should; she had been plagued by problems and doubts even before discovering that Bradley was cheating on her. In truth, she'd gone to his apartment to talk about breaking it off when she found him in bed with Sandra, her maid of honor.

For the two weeks since then, she'd been doing her best to discover where she went wrong, how she could have been so blind. Maybe she had been using too much logic and not enough impulse, too much calculation and not enough emotion. Maybe there had been too much planning and not enough going with the flow.

Could be time for a change, after all. Hadn't she just been fantasizing about parading a good-looking groom in front of Bradley? What was she thinking of, turning down such a perfect candidate?

She closed her eyes tightly, then opened them again. Her lips parted as she tried to find the words to tell Race Bannister she would go through with it, would pretend to be his bride.

They wouldn't come. Her shoulders slumped and she sighed. "I can't."

"Why?" he said softly. "What are you afraid of? It isn't me. Or at least I don't think it is, since you let me in here."

Was he suggesting she was afraid of herself? That was ridiculous. "I'm not afraid," she said defensively. "It's just—oh, it wouldn't work."

"Why not?"

"Bradley will find out eventually that we aren't married."

"Marriage isn't the only reason two people take a hotel suite together. A man doesn't have to be a groom to act like a lover."

The low timbre of his voice, his choice of words and the images they evoked, muddled her thinking and did peculiar things to the rhythm of her heartbeat. Her voice not quite steady, she said, "Call it a matter of principle."

"Principle is a lovely thing," he said, tilting his head, "but not a lot of comfort."

"Yes, well, it's all I've got."

He shook his head in a definite negative. "You've got me, if you want me." He paused. "Tell you what. I'll make it easy for you. Say the word, and I'll go without a whimper. But if you have any use for my support, if you think you can stand an evening with me, then all you have to do is point the way toward the shower."

He faced her in relaxed ease. A near-overwhelming presence there in the close confines of the foyer, he waited for her approval.

She did approve. It was possible she approved too much.

He made the situation sound so simple. It wasn't, and she knew it. Still, to resist the steady light in his eyes and the force of his personality was beyond her. She should never have let him inside, never have spoken to him at all.

She was going to regret this; she knew it beyond a doubt. But she couldn't help it. Both the man and the opportunity were too good to resist.

Lifting a hand, she waved vaguely toward the door between the sitting room and sunken bedroom. Voice barely above a whisper, she said, "In there."

His smile was slow in coming, but worth the wait. "Good decision," he said, then picked up his belongings and swung in the direction of the bathroom. "You won't be sorry."

She was sorry already. She just couldn't quite find the words to call him back.

Her nerves were so on edge that she couldn't sit down, couldn't relax. All she could do was think about the man taking off his clothes in her bathroom, stepping into her life as he stepped into her shower. All the mirrors behind the vanity and along one side of the raised Jacuzzi tub would reflect his hard, lean form with its acres of sun-burnished muscle. He would see all her cosmetics and other personal articles scattered across the marble-topped vanity, emptied from her travel bag as she searched earlier for something for a throbbing headache.

She could feel the pain in her head returning now.

A hired escort. She must be losing her mind.

And yet he was so right. She could not have found a better groom if she had constructed him herself. No, nor one more likely to make Bradley sit up and take notice.

At the same time, it was completely unreal that he was there. It almost seemed she must have summoned him with her pure, unadulterated need.

But no, Diane had sent him. She really should thank her, Gina thought. More than that, her friend and neighbor deserved to know how well her idea had worked out, what a great groom the Rent-A-Gent agency had sent.

Moving to the wicker love seat that took up one corner before the sitting room fireplace, Gina dropped down on the cushions and reached for the phone on the end table. As she dialed and waited for Diane to answer, a mischievous smile tilted the generous curves of her mouth.

"Diane? You will never guess who's taking a shower in my bathroom," she said as soon as her friend answered. Without waiting for a reply, she began to fill her in on the details.

"Wait! Gina, stop!" Diane exclaimed. "You mean this man is there now? Right now?"

Her friend's voice sounded strange. Gina thought she was probably in shock at the idea of her going along so easily with the deal. On a low laugh, Gina said, "You got it."

"Get out!" Diane screamed. "Get out of the suite right now!"

"But Diane—"

"Listen to me," her friend interrupted in tense command. "I didn't send this man, Gina. I didn't send anybody. I never called this Rent-A-Gent place! You've got to get out of there."

"But this guy must know you," Gina protested. "There's no other way he could—"

"I never heard of him, I swear it! It's some kind of scam, or else a trick to get into your room. If you don't get out of there right now, you're going to wind up a statistic in the Dallas police file."

The more Diane tried to warn her off, the more stubbornly attached Gina became to the idea. "But Diane, he has a business card and everything; I'm looking at it right now. And he's perfectly normal—except for being a cross between the angel Gabriel and Robert Redford as the Sundance Kid!''

"Honey, you're not making sense. Business cards can be faked, made up at any print shop. Mass murderers who prey on women have to be at least semipresentable or they wouldn't be able to get to their victims. What has this guy done to you?"

"Nothing!" Gina, hearing the rising note of her own voice, glanced around toward the bathroom where the shower was running. Speaking more quietly, she said, "But he knew I was here and in the honeymoon suite, knew about Bradley and the canceled wedding. Explain that."

"I don't know," Diane cried in an agony of apprehension. "Maybe Bradley put this escort on to you as a sick joke."

"Come on! The last thing Bradley would do is fix me up with another man."

"All right, whatever; it doesn't make any difference. Just get out of there, will you? Don't stop to hang up, don't try to take your suitcase, and for God's sake don't wait for explanations. Just make a run for it. Drop everything this minute and run like hell!"

In the bathroom, the shower was abruptly turned off. Race would be reaching for a towel to dry himself. He would be naked. Oh, God, an unknown naked man in her bathroom. Gina swallowed hard before she spoke quickly into the mouthpiece, "Yes, all right, I'm going. Don't worry."

"Call me again when you're safe." The phone clicked as Diane hung up.

Gina's purse was lying on the cabinet of polished cherry that anchored the sitting room's back wall. The ornate room key was beside it. She scooped both of them up and moved quietly toward the foyer.

The knob of the bathroom door rattled, then turned. As it opened a crack, Gina spun around with the blood leaving her face.

"Hey, I forgot to bring a razor," Race called. "I see you have a pack of disposables. Mind if I borrow one?"

"Be my guest," she called in a strained voice. At the same time, she whipped the purse she held around behind her back.

"Thanks." He put his head out the door to give her a quick grin. As he withdrew, the door closed once more.

Gina exhaled the air trapped in her lungs. Skimming across the foyer's marble tiles on tiptoe, she let herself out of the suite and closed the door carefully behind her. She ran for the elevator then, and stood pressing the down button again and again as she waited for it to appear. Only when she was safely inside the compartment, sinking in silent efficiency toward the lower level, did she breathe more easily.

She was okay. She had done the right thing. She was out of it.

What now? Hotel security, that was it. She would dump this in their laps and let them deal with Race Bannister. A guard or hotel official would see that he was conducted from the premises. Afterward, she could regain possession of her suite and her belongings. That would be the end of it.

She had escaped unscathed from a potentially dangerous situation. She should be congratulating herself. She ought to be delighted, even ecstatic, that nothing whatever had come of her brush with this Rent-A-Gent.

Why, then, was she suddenly sick with disappointment?

Chapter Two

Race Bannister stood with his hand on the bathroom door and his head tipped forward as he listened. He winced as he heard the outer door of the suite close behind Gina Madison.

Second thoughts, he suspected, and who could blame her? He must have scared her off. How? he wondered. He had played his part as smoothly as he could manage, and really thought he convinced her. Well, nothing was ever as easy as it seemed.

No, wait. There had been a sound, a click just after he

turned off the shower. She'd phoned somebody. Whoever she spoke to must have spooked her. That was it.

Should he go after her, or let it be and see what happened? She would probably come back with a cop in tow, but that didn't worry him. He hadn't even bent a law, much less broken one.

He might have to come clean, of course. Could be he would prefer it that way; playing tricks on this particular woman was a raw deal. The way she looked at him with her deep brown eyes made him feel as if she could see right through him.

Turning from the door, he caught a glimpse of himself in the mirror. Slicking back his wet hair with the splayed fingers of one hand, he grimaced in disgust. His opinion of the man reflected there wasn't particularly high just now.

Gina hadn't been what he expected, not by a long shot. Oh, she had her defenses, her cool, well-glazed outer shell, but there was something fine and sweet and entrancingly soft underneath. Something that brought out his protective instincts. Which was probably just as well under the circumstances.

Or dumb. She was probably nothing like that.

It wasn't like him to be influenced by a pretty face. All right, a beautiful face. But still.

Women didn't faze him; he'd been fending them off for years. No credit was due on that score, since he couldn't help the way he looked and most women only cared about what was on the surface. It wasn't often that he came across a female person who could see past the outside wrapping to what was underneath, what he was inside. When he did, they were usually attached already. It had been his experience that the best were taken.

Gina Madison had almost been removed from the market. Almost but not quite, and that was what intrigued him. That was why he was here.

It was possible she would come back to the suite alone, if only from curiosity. Or maybe out of fairness, because she seemed that kind of person, and had no proof that he was anything other than he'd said. She might also return for the sake of revenge against Bradley Dillman. She did seem to have a grudge against the man.

Maybe the best thing he could do was shave, get dressed, then wait for developments. If she didn't come back, he could always leave. If she did, he would play it by ear.

But first there was a little task that needed doing, he thought as he set his lips in a resolute line and reached for the bathroom phone. He had a good idea who Gina might have called. That interference had to be blocked before it made a mess of everything.

Then he would wait and see.

"How may I be of service, ma'am?"

Gina bit down on the inside of her lower lip as she studied the concierge who had posed the question. Identified as Tyrone by the name plate on his mezzanine-level desk, he was wearing a perfectly tailored suit with a stripe that matched his silver hair. He appeared poised and capable, discreet and unflappable; it seemed he might well be the person to handle the peculiar situation in which she found herself.

At the same time, she was struck by sudden doubt. What if Race was exactly what he said, a rancher who modeled part-time? What if he was an innocent pawn in all this, or else there was some reasonable explanation for everything? She would feel terrible if she brought the authorities down on a hardworking cowboy who was only trying to make a living. Never mind that she was doing him out of a job.

Nothing about Race Bannister had appeared sinister. He'd looked her straight in the eyes and gone to great lengths to reassure her. He couldn't be dangerous. Could he?

And if she ran away now, she would never find out what was going on. That seemed a shame.

The smile on the concierge's face faded, to be replaced by a frown that mirrored her own. "What seems to be the problem, ma'am? Is it something here in the hotel? Is there any way I can fix it?"

Gina gave him a rueful smile. "I don't know; I can't quite make up my mind. You—You haven't had any reports of a strange man finding excuses to get into the rooms, have you?''

''Good heavens, no!'' The concierge's eyes widened. ''Don't tell me you've had someone like that?''

''That's the problem; I'm not sure whether he's legitimate or not. And I don't know how to get him out again.''

Her uncertainty was not like her; she was usually so sure of most things. For instance, she'd been certain she and Bradley were compatible.

. The two of them had liked the same food, music, and cars, had the same ideas about work and leisure, shared many of the same political convictions. True, their senses of humor were totally opposite: Bradley roared at slapstick, and she thought it totally dumb. Their ideas about ethics had turned out to be different, too. The truth was, she had been wrong about Bradley, and now she was half afraid to trust her judgment.

Tyrone was looking at her with doubt in his face. ''Let me be sure I understand you, ma'am. There's a strange man in your room, and you don't know if he's what he claims?''

She gave a small shrug. ''That's about the size of it.''

''And which room are you in?''

''The honeymoon suite . . .'' She trailed off as she saw how it was going to look. The abrupt lift of the concierge's eyebrows was perfectly understandable, given the circumstances.

Tyrone cleared his throat. With great delicacy he said, ''I assume he isn't the groom?''

''Not exactly.'' Gina could feel the heat of her swift flush.

''I . . . see.'' The man behind the desk took a breath that swelled his deep chest. ''If I might ask, how long has he been—uh, on the scene?''

Gina glanced at her watch. ''About fifteen minutes. Long enough to take a shower and shave.''

''Of course. A shower. And a shave. And you have reason to believe he will be there when you return?''

She nodded without quite looking at him. ''Unless he's discovered that I left.''

"Hmm." The concierge hesitated, then said anyway, "Just what was it you had in mind to do with him?"

"I don't know," she said with troubled frankness. "What do you suggest?"

Tyrone tilted his head. "Well, I suppose it all depends."

"Meaning?"

"He didn't force his way into your suite?"

"Oh, no!"

"He made no move to harm you?"

She shook her head.

"He made no threats, no demands?"

"None at all." The words were spoken with emphasis.

Tyrone pursed his lips. "It doesn't seem to be a matter for the police, then."

"Of course not," she said sharply, then closed her eyes as she sighed. Since there seemed no other choice, she explained the situation as fully as she was able.

"Well," Tyrone said briskly when she had finished, "I can certainly have someone from security speak to this gentleman. If he doesn't leave quietly, we can call in a couple of strong-arm guys to take care of him."

"Oh, surely not! I mean, I don't think any rough stuff is necessary."

The concierge studied her. "I pride myself on my ability to take charge of any situation, Miss Madison, but are you quite sure you want this man removed? I mean, most young women in your place would be screaming bloody murder and demanding someone throw the bum out instead of worrying about him."

"Well, but there's really no other choice, is there?" she said with a rueful smile.

The concierge reached to pat her hand, which rested on the counter. "Not unless you are in the mood for a little adventure."

Live dangerously. Race had said that; she could hear the words echoing in her head in his deep, seductive tones.

All her life she had been sensible, conscientious, and law-abiding. Her clothes had always matched as a child; her closet had always been tidy. She never walked on the grass, never crossed against the light or exceeded the speed limit. She always made and finished her To Do lists, and double-checked her addition without fail. Her bank account balanced to the penny, not to mention the books she kept for others.

She had played it safe, and look what it got her: a fiancé who was a cheat, and a solo honeymoon.

She was tired of it. She had also had it with men who thought they could move in on her as they pleased, treat her as they liked, while she did nothing about it.

Her gaze narrowed as she stared at Tyrone. "You think I should risk going back up there?"

"Here, now, that's not exactly what I meant," the concierge said in alarm.

"But you said I might enjoy the adventure."

"I said—What did I say? No matter. You must realize, Miss Madison, that I am here only to serve you, not to advise you."

"Thank you," Gina said, a slow smile lighting her face. "You've really been very helpful." As she turned and walked away, she suspected the concierge stood staring after her.

And why not? She must be nuts. She could not be thinking seriously of going back upstairs and playing along with the man in her shower? Could she?

She could.

To give herself a little more time, she turned to make a circuit of the mezzanine balcony that overlooked the Glass Garden. Though she glanced over the railing, she scarcely saw the luxuriant palms and bromeliads, the sparkling fountain, or the fairy lights twinkling along the limbs of the ficus trees. The music drifting up from below was a Caribbean rhythm that put a lilt in her steps and provided a reckless undertone to her thoughts.

Race Bannister had not seemed threatening, she told herself. In fact, he'd looked like the cowboy-rancher he pretended to be. He even smelled like one; there was about him the scent of horses and the honest sweat of a healthy male who had been working in the great outdoors. You couldn't fake that, surely.

So there was a mix-up. She could find out what it was, couldn't she? He would explain, then everything would be fine. She and Race would spend the evening together, and that would be that. It was no big deal, not really.

All things considered, she loved the idea of being seen in Race's company. Bradley would be flabbergasted. He seemed to think she must be miserable without him; he'd been so careful when he talked to her on the phone, as if afraid she'd descend to hysterical tears and pleading.

He needn't have worried.

She was ready for something different in her life, for someone different. She should be thanking her lucky stars that Race Bannister had shown up, instead of getting ready to send him packing. If he came with a little mystery attached, well, that could be a good thing. Maybe it would get her out of her rut, away from her dull, too safe life.

Change, excitement, and yes, adventure. That was what she needed. She was going to live dangerously.

Yes, she was indeed.

Gina shivered, and could not be sure if it was caused by the thrill of it all or sheer, undiluted terror. In any case, it was banished an instant later by another consideration altogether.

Race was getting into a tuxedo. Where did that leave her?

True to her usual organization, her honeymoon trousseau had been packed weeks in advance. She had only to grab the suitcase on the way out of her apartment. Regardless, nothing in it remotely resembled an evening dress. With Bradley, the most she had expected to need was an understated outfit of the kind she wore to church. Something told her that more would be required to keep up with Race. Besides, being an adventuress seemed to call for a drastic change of style.

She'd noticed a boutique tucked into a corner near the hotel gift shop. That was her only hope. If she gave them her gold card and an option on her firstborn son, they might let her take a few things up to her room on approval. Face set in determined lines, Gina turned in that direction.

Race was standing in the middle of the sitting room when she let herself back into the suite. Dressed in a pleated white shirt that hung open over black tuxedo trousers, he was struggling with a cuff link.

He looked up with a flashing smile. "I wondered where you got off to."

Gina tore her gaze away from the section of muscle-wrapped chest revealed by his unfastened shirt. It was gilded with curling hair the color of old gold. A little breathless, undoubtedly from her haste, she gestured toward her burden of dresses draped in mint-green plastic. "Would you believe I didn't have a thing to wear, at least anything formal?"

"We could have gone more casual." There was a trace of concern in his eyes.

"No way," she returned as she headed toward the bedroom. "I'll try not to take too long. When you're done, help yourself to a drink at the wet bar."

Intent on watching her, he fumbled the cuff link in his fingers, dropping it. As he bent in a swift, lithe movement to pick it up, he said, "Could you give me a hand here first? I never have been any good at fastening these things."

To come that close to him didn't seem like a real bright idea, but Gina could think of no way to avoid it. Draping the dress bag across the arm of a chair, she moved toward him. She took the plain gold link he held out to her and reached for his arm.

His wrist was taut and strong, with its molding of muscle and sinew. He held it rock steady while she guided the post of the cuff link through the holes in both sides of his silk shirt cuff. It was her fingers that had a tendency to tremble.

Standing so close, she inhaled the soap freshness of him, also the scent of a subtle aftershave that hinted of wild canyons and desert nights. The warmth of his body reached out to her like an invisible caress. Feeling it, her own skin prickled with the sudden rise of goose flesh.

"I called down for reservations at the Terrace," he said, his voice slightly husky. "I hope that's all right."

"Fine. I'm glad you thought of it."

"That's my job, to make things easier for you."

She swept her lashes upward, searching his face. He was

watching her, his dark blue gaze intent in its measuring curiosity. His pupils widened slightly, as if to better absorb her, while a pulse began to throb in the strong column of his neck.

His hair, still damp from his shower, curled a little across the tops of his ears. The dark gold stubble of his beard was just visible under his smooth-shaven skin. A thin scar above the center of one brow gave it a small quirk that saved him from vapid perfection, lending an air that was quizzical and cynical by turns.

The firm contours of his mouth were finely molded, and finished at the corners with the small indentations of omnipresent humor. They deepened, reaching toward the crinkles at the corners of his eyes, as his lips curved in a slow grin. Voice soft, he said, "Think you'll know me next time you see me?"

"Maybe," she said, lowering her lashes like dropping mini-blinds in a single, swift fall, "if I ever do run into you again after tonight."

"Oh, you will. I'll see to it. Personally."

The words were simple. Still, spoken in his quiet, even drawl, they had the sound of a vow.

Or a threat.

Chapter Three

The dress was like nothing Gina had ever worn before in her buttoned-up, buttoned-down-collar life. A black knit with a bolero jacket set off by jewel-colored beading sewn in Arabesque patterns, it was a shade too form-fitting, a bit too revealing at the top, a little too short, and a great deal too sparkly. It made her look like Dolly Parton, Madonna, and Mata Hari rolled into one. But it made her feel like the Queen of the Night.

She must have a heretofore undiscovered split personality, she decided with an ironic twist to her lips. She usually preferred simple, comfortable styles, though she had a hidden romantic streak that showed up in things like her Victorian nightgown and the lacy nothings in rich colors that she wore under her business suits. Yet this outfit with its hint of drama seemed right for the moment. She felt daring in it, daring and sexy. It was just possible, of course, that her mood had something to do with the man waiting in the sitting room.

It was also possible she was overreacting by even considering such a thing. Feelings did not come into this, not at all.

Regardless of the reason he was here, the time with Race Bannister was limited. One evening, and he would be gone. Finis. Which made it all the more necessary to find out as soon as possible just who had sent him and why. If a new dress would help the situation, then she didn't begrudge the price of it.

More than that, it would show Bradley what he had missed. She mustn't forget the original purpose for this charade.

"Wow," Race said as she walked into the sitting room. Rising to his feet, he allowed his gaze to move from the shining waves of her hair, which brushed the tops of her shoulders, to her slender waist, emphasized by the bolero jacket, and the length of shapely leg exposed by her skirt. With a slow shake of his head and a bemused look in his eyes, he added, "Stunning."

His reaction was so gratifying that she gave a low laugh. Suddenly a little light-headed, she said, "I could say the same for you. If men only realized how absolutely fine they look in black tie, they would never wear anything else."

"Yes, well," he said as a hint of color rose under the bronze of his skin, "but it isn't too practical for riding a horse." Swinging away, he moved into the foyer, where he opened the door and held it for her.

She had disconcerted him, she saw; the fact that she could did odd things for her confidence. She walked a little taller as she passed in front of him on her way from the suite.

It was almost possible to forget, as the evening advanced, that theirs was not a normal night out. Conversation was easy; they talked with hardly an awkward moment from the time they left the room until their entrées were placed in front of them at the restaurant table.

The major credit for the sense of ease was due to Race. He seemed genuinely interested in her thoughts on any and every subject under the sun, in her likes and dislikes, her opinions and convictions. Discovering her ready sense of the ridiculous, he exercised a droll wit and a wicked talent for observation, which made her laugh. His comments were not vicious, however; in fact they indicated a bedrock of tolerance that was amazingly attractive.

At the same time, he was attentive. To hold her chair for her, inquire about her taste in wine, offer whatever she might like in the way of condiments or hot breads—even the black olives from his salad when he discovered she loved them—seemed natural to him. He set his pace to hers, seemingly in no hurry whatever to have the evening end. Since she did much the same, the time between the courses stretched longer and longer.

Race Bannister, Gina had to acknowledge, was a captivating companion. But then, he would be, wouldn't he? It was his stock-in-trade. She should not need to remind herself of that last fact, yet she did.

They were halfway through their broiled shrimp with white asparagus and baby carrots when she noticed Bradley. How long he and Sandra—the new Mrs. Dillman—had been at the table on the far side of the room, she didn't know. Since the tables were set within booths with high backs that provided a great deal of privacy, she'd managed to forget the other diners, even those visible across the room. It was actually the way her ex-fiancé stared in her direction that drew her attention.

For Bradley to finally show up felt like an intrusion. It gave her a start to realize she was annoyed with him for it.

"What is it?" Race said, his expression alert as he watched her face.

"The idiot," she said with a stiff nod in the direction of the other couple. "Otherwise known as my former fiancé, Bradley Dillman. The woman with him is his wife, of course."

"Right," Race said, reaching out to cover her hand with his own while his lips curved in a smile of infinite appreciation. "Curtain going up."

It did, too, at least in a manner of speaking.

If she had thought Race Bannister was attentive before, it was nothing compared to the sudden acceleration of his concentration upon her. Eye contact was increased. No opportunity was lost to touch her. He made her laugh with his intimate comments. He even fed her bites of the cherries jubilee he ordered for dessert. When she used her a fingertip to catch a vagrant drop of melted ice cream, he reached for her hand and took away the stickiness with a flick of his tongue.

The firm grasp of his hand, that warm, wet-velvet abrasion, made her feel a little dizzy. Or perhaps it was the wine; she couldn't tell. All she knew was that she could easily drown in the liquid sea-blue of his eyes. On top of that, if he licked her finger one more time, she might well dissolve into a puddle like the melting ice cream of his cherries jubilee.

This would not do. "I think," she said with some difficulty, "that we had better call it a night."

The small triangular scar above his left eyebrow arched diabolically. In soft tones he said, "Why? The evening has just started."

"Yes, but this—it could get out of hand."

"Could it?" The question was innocent, but the look in his eyes was not.

She moistened her lips. "What do you think you're doing?"

"Playing bridegroom," he said, still smiling. "And looking forward to dancing with you. On the patio, maybe, in the moonlight."

"I'm not sure that's a good idea."

"And here I was thinking it was one of my best." His smile was whimsical before he added, "For Dillman's benefit, of course. It should convince him that he's the farthest thing from your mind."

He was, which was what worried her. To call it quits now, however, would mean that she might never discover who Race Bannister was or how he had found out so much about her. She had somehow lost sight of that aspect of the situation in the last hour or two.

"You're right," she said, her tone abrupt as looked

away from him to glance around room. "What became of our waiter, and the check?"

Race's smile faded. Glancing behind her, he signaled, then indicated that the check would be forthcoming in a few minutes. He leaned back in his chair before he said, "Have you known Dillman long?"

"Long enough," she replied, her attention on the last bite of the chocolate indulgence that was her chosen dessert.

"How did you happen to meet him?"

"He was a client at the firm where I work when I started there. I was assigned his account, but had trouble getting the information to keep his books properly. When I chased him down at one of his fast food places to discuss the problem, he took me to lunch."

"And you worked things out from there."

"More or less," she said with a small shrug. To change the subject, she said, "What about you? I suppose you're involved with someone?"

Race's brief smile said he recognized the evasive tactic; still, he answered easily. "Not right now. My job doesn't exactly encourage it."

"I can see how it might make things a little difficult if many of your evenings wind up like this."

"Not many do." The words were short and a little cryptic. An odd expression flitted across his face, as if he might have surprised himself with his answer. It was gone a moment later as he said, "You enjoy being an accountant?"

"Most of the time. It's one of the few jobs where you can line things up in neat rows and columns and always have the answer come out as it should."

"But it doesn't always, does it? Isn't there sometimes a discrepancy in the figures?"

She gave him a sharp look. There was no time to answer, however, as the waiter materialized beside their table and placed a leather folder at Race's elbow. He flipped the folder open with a practiced motion and glanced over the check while reaching for his wallet to extract a credit card.

"No, wait," Gina said in haste. "Let me sign for it." She reached out for the check.

Evading her grasp, Race tucked his card inside the folder before handing it over to the waiter. Voice firm, he said, "My treat."

"What about the ranch's vet bill?" she demanded, a frown between her eyes, as the waiter turned smartly and walked away.

"I can stand it this once."

"But things aren't supposed to work this way."

"How do you know? Maybe it's part of the deal, maybe I send you a bill later for all the extra services."

There was a lazy, half-insinuating tone in his voice that struck a note of caution in her mind. She drew back a little. "All of what extra services?"

His eyes took on a silvery, slumberous glint while his smile deepened. "Whatever you please," he said simply. "For you, there are no limits."

Did he mean what she thought? Her breath caught in her throat.

No. No, he couldn't have been indicating such a thing. That would be like saying he was a hustler, that he hired out as a—well, a gigolo was the polite term for it. She wouldn't believe that. She just plain refused.

Nevertheless, Dallas was a town with more than its share of wealthy widows—lonely older women who might be willing to pay for the attentions of an attractive, entertaining, virile man. Race Bannister could certainly command any price he chose if he decided to make a career for himself that way. What woman could resist an evening with him that included a passionate finale in a darkened bedroom like the one upstairs in the honeymoon suite?

As he watched her face, his smile deepened. "My sweet Gina," he said softly, "what are you thinking?"

"Nothing!" She drew air into her lungs with a small gasp before she repeated more quietly, "Nothing important."

He didn't believe her; the look in his eyes said so. But at least he had the decency not to call her on it.

"Dancing was next on our agenda, I think," he said in a deliberate change of subject. "Or maybe that walk around the garden. Which shall it be? It's up to you. Lady's choice."

The Terrace, where they had eaten, located on the lower level of the hotel's East Tower, was dedicated to serious dining. It had a Steinway tucked away in one corner, where a pianist in black tie sometimes played show tunes and classical pieces as an aid to digestion, but there was no dance floor. Dancing, then, took place at the hotel's other eating place, over beneath the West Tower. Montague's, as it was called, catered to the steak-and-potatoes, hats-and-jeans, two-stepping crowd, with a live band featuring twin fiddles and electric guitars. The atmosphere there was lively, and the music loud.

To Gina's mind, it was a little too much of both. She and Race in their evening clothes didn't fit in. Though they wandered through, they kept right on going until they were on the patio outside.

That cool, open space was an excellent compromise between the formal and informal. A night wind rattled the green-black leaves of the magnolias overhead and wafted the scents of gardenias and nicotiana that grew in raised beds. Beyond the paving of Mexican tiles lay the walkway leading to a small ornamental lake and the gazebo that centered it. Somewhere among the cypress trees and weeping willows that edged the water, a peacock cried in raucous shrillness, a counterpoint to the music drifting from inside.

Among the shifting tree shadows cast on the patio by a high-riding moon, Race turned to her and held out his arms. It was a moment before Gina realized that it was only an invitation to dance.

They moved together across the tile floor to a slow tune of aching nostalgia. Race hummed snatches of it in a rich baritone. He moved well to the music, which wasn't surprising, all things considered. Gina almost wished he had been a little less smooth, a little less assured. A little less professional.

All the same, it was necessary to keep reminding herself that he was holding her so near for the sake of appearances. That the way he gazed down at her, as if she were the most lovely thing he had ever seen, was just one of his bag of tricks. That the firm circle of his arms was not meant to feel protective, nor was the taut musculature of his thighs moving against her intended to ignite the flare of response inside her.

Of course, Bradley was nowhere around. As far as she knew, he was still inside stuffing himself. It was possible, however, for him to appear, and that was enough.

The song playing was one she knew well. Called "The Dance," it was a country-western paean to love that had been recorded and made popular by Garth Brooks. To chance the pain that could come of loving was a choice, according to the lyrics; the pain could be avoided, but only if you missed the dance of love itself.

It came to Gina, as the evening wind blew around her and she breathed the hidden scents of the night while moving in Race Bannister's arms, that this was one particular dance she was glad she had not missed. There was a subtle magic in it, a magic that ran swift and beguiling in her veins.

She was alive, wonderfully alive, and she was whole within herself in spite of a near miss at the altar and Bradley's betrayal. She had taken a wrong turn on the way to romance, but it was only a detour, not the end of the road. There was nothing wrong with her; she was eminently capable of feeling love and desire again. Someday, somewhere, she would find a man who was worthy of her trust and devotion, and he would love her in return.

Race had given her that sense of confidence and hope by the simple act of being himself. In a few short hours, he had made her feel attractive again, had shown her that she could respond to the right man, at the right time and place. He could not know it, of course, and she didn't mean to tell him. Still, she was grateful.

But it could go no further. Seeing that it did not was something she must do for herself, from sheer self-protection. She was too vulnerable just now to risk an entanglement. Gratitude, however sincere, was no substitute for real caring.

At the same time, it was difficult to believe that she could be so affected by a caressing manner and a handsome face; it seemed there had to be something more behind it. Or perhaps she only preferred to think so.

Drawing back a little in his arms, she said, "You mentioned that a third party contacted you about this job, I think. Who was it?''

"I didn't get a name," he said easily. "The office took the call and passed the information on through my answering service."

Was he telling the truth? His face was open, he met her gaze without evasion, and yet she could not tell.

"So you showed up at my hotel room," she said. "Isn't that a little dangerous? I mean, what if it turns out to be somebody's idea of a joke, and an irate husband meets you at the door with a gun?''

"Then I'd do some fast talking, I expect. So far, it hasn't happened."

She thought it likely he could take care of himself in any case; certainly she had no call to worry about him. Reverting to the first subject, she said, "Since the Rent-A-Gent office made the arrangements, they must have the name of whoever called on file. I imagine they would give it to you if you asked."

"Probably," he agreed, his gaze resting on her lips, "But why should I bother?''

"I'd like to know, even if you wouldn't."

"You want to take all the mystery out of life," he complained, humor shifting in his face. "There are some questions that should go unanswered."

"Not this one," she said with determination. "I intend to find out exactly—"

She got no further. One moment Race was moving with her to the music, the next he was sweeping her against his hard form. He hesitated a bare instant, then bent his head and pressed his lips to hers.

Shock rippled over her in a tingling wave. She stiffened against it with her lips parting in surprise. Then she was caught in a rushing moontide of fervent impressions. The surfaces of his mouth were smooth and vibrant upon hers, setting off a delicate pulsing between them. He tasted of sweet-tart cherries and the richness of cream and desire. The swirl of his tongue into her mouth was a heated invasion that changed to achingly deliberate exploration. Their breaths mingled, increasing in tempo. His hold tightened as he probed deeper.

Then she felt a shuddering reflex run over him. Suddenly, she was free. He whipped away from her with lithe and dangerous grace, though he retained an arm around her as she swayed in the effort to regain balance. Narrow-eyed, he faced the man who had approached from behind him.

"Hey, now!" Bradley said, throwing up his hands. "I didn't mean to startle you." Beside him, Sandra, Gina's former friend and the woman who was supposed to have been her maid of honor, looked everywhere except at Gina.

"What did you mean to do?" Race demanded. There was no compromise in his voice, no relaxation of his taut stance.

"I just wanted to meet the guy who's man enough to sweep Gina off her feet in two short weeks. My hat's off to you, pal. We were engaged over a year and she never let me lay a hand on her in public—and hardly in private, come to think of it."

"Your loss," Race said succinctly.

Gina sent the man at her side a sharp look, her attention snared by an undertone of fierce dislike in his voice. His eyes were as hard as polished turquoise, his jaws taut. As he stared at Bradley, it almost seemed that the challenge and enmity stamped on his features was personal.

Collecting her wits with an effort, she stumbled through the necessary introductions. At the same time, she puzzled over the fact that Bradley and Sandra had sneaked up behind them from the direction of the Terrace, the opposite direction from which they should have appeared. She had assumed that Race's kiss had been a part of the act, brought on because he had seen Bradley coming. That could not be.

Either Race had kissed her as part of the services he'd mentioned, or else he had reasons of his own. It would be foolish to assume it was the last, but she wished with sudden fervor that she could.

There was another thing. Though Bradley did not look happy at seeing her in Race's arms, Gina herself didn't care that he had discovered them. In fact, there was a heady freedom in that discovery, which was something else she owed to the man standing next to her.

Her voice suddenly clear and cool, she said, "Tell me something, Bradley. Why in the world did you choose this hotel for your honeymoon?"

He glanced at his new bride, then shrugged. "Sandra remembered all the stuff you spouted about the special suite, so I called. When I found out you still held the reservation, I thought I might as well take it off your hands. You could have knocked me over with a feather when you said you meant to use it yourself."

His tone was a shade glib, making Gina wonder if there wasn't more to it than he was telling. "Why not go somewhere else, then?"

"I have as much right to be here as you do," he said defensively. "Anyway, I was curious. Like I said, I wanted to see this new husband of yours."

He wanted to spy on her. Made reckless by the surge of anger, she gave him a blithe smile as she said, "Oh, Race and I aren't married."

Bradley's eyes bulged. "You've got to be kidding!"

"Not at all. Now I'm sure you'll excuse us if we say good night." She threaded her hand around Race's arm, clasping it as she eased closer against his lean form. Lowering her voice to a more intimate note, she raised her gaze to his in limpid invitation. "I think I've danced enough, darling, don't you? Isn't it time we headed up to bed?"

Chapter Four

*D*arling . . .

Race felt the shock of Gina's endearment and the suggestion that went with it clear down to his heels. She was playing up; he knew that had to be it. Still, it took every ounce of self-control he possessed not to show his amazement.

God above, but what would it be like for her to say those words and mean them? He would risk much to find out.

"Good idea," Bradley said. "My bride and I will walk along with you, if you don't mind the company."

The man's smile was affable, his manner suggestive of civilized acceptance of an awkward situation. Race didn't believe it for a minute. The guy wasn't the type.

Gina's ex-fiancé had a polished look to him that might appeal to some women. His brown hair was carefully barbered to suit his thin face, a skinny mustache made a wing under his nose, and his clothes were custom-made and expensive. Of medium height, his body shape had the artificial contours that came from working out instead of working for a living, and his tan was straight from a sun bed. To Race it all added up to fake. His dislike for Bradley Dillman was instant.

It was also mutual, he thought. Somewhere in the back of the guy's ice-blue eyes was a look that said he thought he could take Race Bannister. Yeah, well, he could try. Any time.

And Race definitely did mind the company. He minded more than he could have imagined. At the same time, he recognized the advantage for himself in the situation. There was no way Gina could dismiss him at the door of her suite while the idiot and his bride tagged along with them, not and still pretend they were a couple. It might even be possible to parlay these peculiar circumstances into an invitation to stay the night.

To start with, though, this meeting was a chance to ask a few pointed questions. He couldn't forget that angle, no matter how easy it was becoming.

Gina's greeting for the new wife, Sandra, had been cool, he noted, which was not surprising, considering she was the Other Woman in the case. If the two women had been on closer terms, no doubt they would have taken up more of the conversational slack. Since they were not, he was left with room to maneuver. Turning with Gina, he strolled in the direction of the rear entrance to the Glass Garden. As the other two fell in beside them, he launched his attack with what he hoped was offhand casualness.

"So, Dillman, what do you do for a living?"

"This and that," the other man answered in the same tone. "Couple of pizza franchises, one in Shreveport and another in Longview. Some import and export out of Houston. You?''

"Beef cattle. A spread north of town.''

"Prime acreage up there. Must be nice.'' Dillman gave him a sharp glance.

"Might be,'' Race answered with a smile meant to be both disarming and deprecating, "if it ever pays its way.''

"I'm sure,'' Dillman said in dry tones.

The other man didn't buy the poor-mouth routine. Race didn't mind. The family fortune hadn't been based on beef cattle alone for a couple of generations now. The ranch still produced purebred Herefords, but was dedicated primarily to a rare breed of cattle from Britain that were solid white, had lyre-shaped horns, and weren't for sale.

Reaching for the heavy glass door into the garden, he held it for the others to enter. The quick, conspiratorial grin Gina gave him as Dillman and Sandra went on ahead sent a shaft of purest pleasure zinging through him. That tingling lodged just under his pants zipper, where it became a troublesome discomfort that warned of a tough night ahead. He drew a deep, silent breath and let it out with slow care.

The water music of the fountain filled the soaring three-storied Glass Garden. Lights twinkled among the foliage and turned the spray from the cascading water to atomized diamonds. Hibiscus and impatiens glowed in broad, curving strips of color, while the white perfection of peace lilies waved like magic wands in the air currents wafting through the open space.

On impulse, Race took the winding pathway that went through the center and past the fountain, instead of the faster passage around the outer rim. He recognized his need to prolong the evening, and didn't even try to fight it. It would be convenient, however, to know how long he might have to keep up his act.

Closing in on the Roman extravaganza of a fountain imported by the old cattle baron Packard, Race said to Dillman, "You two here for the weekend, or are you making a week of it?''

"Depends,'' the other man said. "We reserved for the

weekend, but might extend it if we're having a good time.''

Gina and Sandra had moved ahead on the narrow path and were exchanging comments about the coins shining in the fountain's basin. Gina reached for the small evening bag she carried. "It looks as if making a wish must be tradition," she said with a smile. "We may as well give it a try."

Dillman, catching the comment, shot her a cynical look. "It's throwing your money away, you know. Must amount to a hunk of change, all the coins people like you drop in there. Nice extra take for the hotel."

Race, seeing the light of enjoyment fade from Gina's face, felt irritation rise inside him. The words clipped, he said, "The money goes to a list of different charities."

"Yeah, I'll bet." The other man gave a short, sarcastic laugh.

Race wanted to nail Bradley Dillman right then and there. It startled him how much he wanted it.

Coins were something Race never carried if he could help it; he had none in his pocket at that moment. It was a real shame. He just might have to change his ways.

"Go ahead and make your wish," he said, his voice quiet as he met Gina's gaze. "We'll wait."

"Never mind," she answered as she turned to walk on. "I—I'm not in the mood anymore."

Watching the straight set of her shoulders and proud, defiant tilt of her head, Race cursed to himself. And he was suddenly afraid.

As the four of them went up in the elevator, he felt the grip of Gina's fingers as she took his arm again. Meeting her gaze for a strained instant, he saw that her face was set and pale.

What was she thinking that had her so tense? Race would have given much to be able to read minds just then, because he didn't have a clue.

For a fleeting second he considered the possibility that she was on to him. He dismissed it at once; there was no way she would still be around if she knew.

Unless she had something to prove? Unless, God help him, she wasn't as innocent as she seemed.

No, she must be worrying about what Dillman was going to say or do when they reached the suite. The other man had chased them down on the patio when he could have avoided them; he must have a reason. More than that, seeing the idiot here like this had to be upsetting for her. She had almost married the guy, after all. That was it; it had to be.

What if it wasn't? Race frowned as the elevator doors slid open. He couldn't afford to ignore this kind of gut instinct. Careful attention to such things had paid off more times than he could count. What he needed was a way to put it to a test.

He could think of one, but was afraid to try it, afraid he might enjoy the experiment far too much. Besides, he had made himself an ironclad promise that he would not take advantage of this deal.

Of course, Gina Madison could take any advantage she wanted. She wouldn't hear a whisper of objection from him.

The doors for their two respective suites were placed almost at right angles to each other at the far end of the main hall. As the four of them walked along together in that direction, drawing closer to the doors, Bradley cleared his throat. "You two may as well come in with us for a nightcap," he said expansively. "I ordered champagne and left it chilling on ice."

"Thanks for the invitation, but we'll pass," Race said before Gina could answer. "We have champagne of our own, compliments of the management. It would be a shame to let it go to waste."

"Well, then, we could pool our resources and—" Bradley began.

"Oh, I'm sure you don't want to do that, not tonight of all nights," Race interrupted in dry tones. "And frankly, neither do we." He ignored Gina's soft gasp and the sudden bite of her nails into his biceps. "We'll say good night here. See you around. If we decide to get out of bed."

Without allowing Dillman time to comment, he clamped Gina's arm against his side and moved on. Gina had given him the room key to carry, and he dug it out of his pocket.

Inserting it, he pushed the door open in a smooth movement, then swung Gina inside.

As the heavy door closed behind them, she turned on him and opened her mouth to give him the hiding he deserved. He reached to place his fingers on the soft surfaces of her lips, then stood listening with his head cocked toward the hall outside.

Nothing. Not a sound.

He glanced down at Gina, then took his fingers away. She was quiet for the moment, but there was mutiny in her face. He had about five seconds, he thought, before she started throwing things.

The Do Not Disturb sign hung on the doorknob, where it had been taken in as they went down to dinner. He opened the door and put it out as an excuse to check on Dillman and his wife. The two were just disappearing inside the Emerald Suite.

That was good. In fact, that was perfect. Drawing back into the foyer, he closed the door once more and swung to face Gina.

"I hope," she said distinctly as she crossed her arms over her chest, "that you don't think you're really staying here with me."

He leaned his shoulders against the door panel behind him for support and folded his own arms. "What? You mean we aren't going to—what was the phrase—head to bed?"

"You know that was part of the act!"

"And a very nice part, too," he said softly as he remembered the sweet incitement of her breast and thigh pressed against him.

"But you didn't have to pick up on it quite so fast." There was a flash of gold in the dark brown of her eyes.

He lifted a brow. "What was I supposed to do? Shake your hand and say a polite good-night at the door? I thought the idea was to convince your old flame over there that we're using this place for the purpose intended."

Her face turned pink; it was amazing. It was also incredibly sexy. Which just went to show how fast he was losing it.

"Whatever the reason may have been," she said

through her teeth, "it's over. You're supposed to be out of here."

She had him there. Because he knew it, he answered with great reasonableness. "But since you didn't throw me out when I first showed up, and since the idiot over there saw me and now thinks we're a couple, don't you agree it makes sense for him to believe I'm staying?"

"What he believes and what is going to happen are two entirely different things. You are going out that door in about two seconds flat, and that's final." She moved away a few wary steps, pausing in the doorway that led from the foyer to the sitting area.

"What if Dillman checks up on you?"

"Why would he?" she countered in sharp distrust.

"How should I know; he's your old boyfriend," he said. "All I can tell you is that he looked mighty worried just now. Maybe he's a weirdo. Maybe he still has the hots for you. Or maybe he didn't find our little performance all that convincing."

She shot him a look of virulent annoyance from under winged brows. "I can't imagine why he wouldn't after all your disgusting innuendos."

"Is that right? What about yours? Not to mention you wrapping yourself around me like a—" He stopped, took a quick breath.

"Like a what?" she demanded instantly.

"Forget it." Looking away from her, he unfolded his arms and shoved his hands deep into his pants pockets.

"I want to know what you were going to say!"

"No, you don't."

She only stared at him with set features while she waited.

He compressed his lips, then gave up. "All right, like a pea vine around a bean pole, as my churchgoing grandmother used to put it. The description didn't seem like such a good one to come out with just now."

"Why not?" She tilted her head, frowning in puzzlement.

Exasperation allied to a kind of embarrassment he hadn't felt since he was in high school made him reckless.

"If I have to tell you, then you must need a lesson in basic male-female anatomy."

She stared at him, then blinked. "Oh."

He removed a hand from his pant's pocket and pushed his fingers through his hair. "Yes, well, never mind. All I meant to do is help out here. There's no reason why I should have to invade your privacy or your bed to do the job, and I never intended either one. We can drink champagne to all hours if you want, maybe dance, play a few hands of cards. Or you can shut yourself up in the bedroom and I'll bed down on the love seat in the sitting room. Whatever. Dillman gets the impression that you're occupied in the appropriate manner. You make your point in spades, which is—correct me if I'm wrong—that you're through with him."

"No, you're not wrong," she said slowly, then stood staring at the floor while she chewed the inside corner of her bottom lip. At last she spoke again. "I don't understand why you're doing this. I mean, what's it to you?"

The truth was sometimes the best weapon, he thought. "I was sent to do a job, and I like to finish what I start. Besides, I don't much like the man you meant to marry."

She shook her head, swinging away from him to move into the sitting room. He really thought he was sunk. Then she made a small, winded sound, as if she'd taken a hard hit to the stomach.

He was beside her in two swift strides. She seemed okay. Then he followed her gaze toward the far wall with its tall French windows.

The drapes had been left open for the view of the lights of Dallas, which stretched toward the horizon like a gray blanket sewn with gold and green stars. Beyond the glass panes of the double doors could be seen a portion of the balcony that wrapped around the fourth level to connect the three tower suites. Bradley Dillman was standing out there, looking in. As he saw them staring in his direction, he gave a nonchalant wave and strolled from view.

Race turned his head to meet Gina's disbelieving gaze. Voice taut, he said, "See what I mean?"

She closed her eyes, then pressed her hands to her face and rubbed hard, as if getting rid of something clinging and unpleasant, like an old spiderweb. When she let them drop again, she looked tired and somehow defeated, so that compunction stirred uncomfortably inside him.

After a moment she released her breath in a long sigh. She said finally, "No man your size could possibly sleep on a love seat, and the bedroom is definitely off limits. That leaves the bathtub, or maybe a pallet."

"I'll stretch out on the sheepskin rug in front of the fireplace," he replied in quiet tones. "I've slept on worse." She was silent so long, watching him with wide, questioning eyes, that he added, "You'll be safe, I promise. Scout's honor."

She gave a slow nod. Voice not quite steady, she said, "Well, I suppose I can let you have one of the bed pillows. And maybe there's an extra blanket around here somewhere."

His satisfaction seemed obscene somehow; he hid it as well as he was able. It was short-lived, in any case. The night was not going to be easy, much less exciting. Before it was over, he might discover he had outsmarted himself.

The bed he made was comfortable enough, all things considered, once he pushed the love seat out of the way. Regardless, he had never been more restless, never felt less ready to sleep. He could not seem to wrench his stupid mind away from visions of Gina in a long, white gown with ruffles and lace. Nor could he prevent the memory of her kiss. The sweet nectar of her mouth seemed to linger on his tongue, and he could almost feel her close against him. He ached like a teenager with the need to wrap his arms around her warmth and fragrance, her firmness that was so soft, her softness that was so firm. Her face floated in the forefront of his mind, with a smile curving her lips and promise in her eyes.

It was pure torture. And he deserved it, no doubt about it.

The hours advanced, and all he did was twist the blanket around him with his tossing and turning. He thought of getting up and finding something to read in the well-stocked shelves beside the fireplace, but was afraid he might wake Gina. That wouldn't do, because he had been forced to sleep in his briefs. Pajamas were not a part of his life; he had failed to throw a pair into his bag.

It was toward dawn when he finally began to feel drowsy. With the usual timing of such things, he was just at the edge of sleep when he remembered he hadn't turned the dead bolt or flipped the safety latch when he shut the outer door. There had been too many other things on his mind.

The door locked automatically, of course, but he really should get up and secure it as a security precaution.

There was no real worry; he was a light sleeper. If anybody tried anything he would be up before they could get both feet across the threshold. At least the balcony doors, both in sitting room and bedroom, were locked tight; he had managed to retain that much presence of mind.

Turning to his back, Race kicked the blanket away from him, then flung his arms out on either side. He breathed deep once, then made a conscious effort to relax. Sleep came down like the fall of an auctioneer's hammer.

It might have been hours later, or only minutes, that he heard the rattle of a key in a lock. The sound brought him surging up through deep fathoms of unconsciousness. He rolled from the sheepskin in a fluid movement before he was fully awake.

Gaining his feet, he plunged toward the foyer. He stopped so fast his bare feet squeaked as he skidded on the pink marble floor.

The woman just opening the door came to a halt with her mouth open. Her hand went to the breast of her pink uniform, holding her heart.

"Oh, my stars!" The maid's startled gaze flickered over him, touching the width of his shoulders, the breadth of his chest, the low-cut briefs and the naked thighs under them. She looked beyond him to the twisted blanket and rumpled rug before the fireplace. Rosy color flooded her cheeks, though her eyes began to sparkle.

"What the devil do you want?" Race demanded in a low growl.

She rubbed her hands down the front of her frilly white apron, then clutched its folds. "I'm Etta, and this is my floor. I—well, the gentleman next door said you and your bride had gone to breakfast. Oh, my goodness, I'm so sorry. I'll come back later!''

Chapter Five

Gina woke to the aroma of fresh-brewed coffee. It wafted around her in a rich and enticing cloud. She opened one eye to a slit without lifting her head from where she lay on her stomach, hugging her pillow.

There was a man down on one knee directly in front of her. He held a cup of coffee in one hand while he waved the steam from it toward her with the other.

Her eyes snapped wide. She pushed up from the pillow so fast she almost jerked a crick in her neck. Then she remembered. Exhaling in a rush, trying to control the staccato thumping of her heart, she rolled to support herself on one elbow.

Race's mouth tugged in a slow and entirely too confident grin. ''Morning.''

''What,'' she said in hollow tones, ''are you doing?''

''Finding out whether you're a morning person.''

His tone and the words were genial, yet unencroaching. She said after a moment, ''The answer is maybe. Sometimes.''

''I figured. So the coffee is a peace-offering, in case it might be what makes the difference.''

His hair was damp and still had comb marks in it. His shirt of madras plaid was left unbuttoned over a pair of cutoff jeans, and his bare feet were pushed into canvas deck shoes. He looked altogether too fresh, too cheerful, and too casually attractive to be true. Gina closed her eyes to recruit her strength, then turned to her back and pushed herself up in the bed. Propping pillows behind her, she leaned against the ornate headboard of black lacquer painted with roses and gilt ribbon, then reached wordlessly for the coffee cup.

He had the decency, or maybe it was the good sense, not to try to talk to her immediately. Pouring himself a cup of coffee from the carafe on the tray beside him, he moved to the end of the mattress, where he settled himself, reclining against the footboard.

Gina thought of ordering him off her bed, but it was too much effort. Instead she watched him from under her lashes as she sipped the reviving brew she held. He made such an incongruous picture, so obviously masculine against the background of the ultrafeminine room.

The atmosphere didn't seem to bother him, however; she had to give him that. It wasn't that he was superior or impervious to it, but rather so secure within himself that it made no difference. It was an attractive quality.

To wake with a man around was a new experience. If this was the way it was going to be, she thought she might get used to it. Easily. Too easily.

Something about the way he was watching her made her abruptly self-conscious. She glanced down at the front of her white silk gown, wondering if the material was more transparent than she had thought, if maybe the darker aureoles of her nipples were visible through the soft cloth. She could see nothing. Regardless, she crossed her arms over herself as best she could without being too obvious about it.

At the same time, she could not help wondering what it would be like if the two of them really were honeymooning. How would it be to have him lounging at her feet in whatever he wore to sleep? What would happen if, when they finished their coffee, she shifted to stretch out beside him, reaching for him, pressing close? What would it be like to fit herself to the hard musculature of his body? Would he wrap his arms around her to pull her nearer before he pressed her down into the softness of the bed? How would it feel to know that all barriers between them had been set aside, that they had all day, all week, to make love?

A warm and turgid longing flooded over her, cresting somewhere deep inside. Painful in its pressure, it threatened to swamp her good sense, never mind her better intentions. She held her breath against it, and against the ache of need for that kind of deep, enduring acceptance, that human connection.

This would not do. It would not do at all.

Clearing her throat, she said, "Is there some reason you're so bright-eyed and busy this morning?"

"Not exactly. Except that I've already shocked the maid out of her pink socks, started a feud with Bradley-the-idiot, and splashed half the water out of the hotel pool. I thought it was time to let you in on some of the fun."

She stared at him. "Come again?"

He explained, and was so droll about it she couldn't help laughing. She conquered her amusement by taking quick swallows of coffee. When he finished, she said, "You think Bradley sent the maid in on purpose?"

"What else? He sure didn't see us going out."

"True," she said, then narrowed her eyes. "We really ought to retaliate."

"We could nail his door shut," Race suggested hopefully.

She gave him a considering look. "The hotel might not appreciate the nail holes. But maybe we could send people to his room as he did ours, order towels and ice and a TV repairman. Or we could call room service and have a huge breakfast sent to them—Bradley doesn't eat breakfast."

"You have a diabolical mind," he said with a slow smile. "I love it. And it would be a great plan, except that your late groom and maid of honor are having lunch even as we speak."

"Lunch!"

"Exactly." Irony crept into his eyes. "It is that time of day."

"You're joking." She gazed at him with her cup suspended halfway to her lips.

"You must have needed the rest," he said, tipping his head a little as he watched her.

"Yes, I—must have," she echoed. That she had slept so soundly and long while he was close by was amazing. It seemed having him in the next room had made her feel more secure rather than less.

"Overwork leads to sleep deprivation," he suggested. "Ditto worrying. And stress. Depression. You have something on your mind lately? Other than a canceled wedding, I mean?"

"Nothing special," she answered, though she looked

away from him toward a table draped in ruffles and the window behind it, where daylight made a bright noon glow at the edges of the draperies.

He was quiet a long moment, staring at nothing while he drank his coffee. Then his gaze focused on her once more. "So what's on the agenda for the rest of the day? A leisurely brunch on the balcony? A walk around the lake? Golf? Shopping? Museums? You choose, and I'll make the arrangements. Or the other way around. I'm easy."

So was she easy, or so it seemed, since she did not refuse immediately to go along with him. The agreement had been that he stay the night to throw Bradley off the scent. Nothing had been said about the morning after, or the afternoon.

Still, what was a few more hours after spending the night together? How much difference could it make?

Race Bannister had kept his word: he had not tried anything during the night. If he wanted to forget that they had a deal, then so could she. For a little while. Just a little while longer.

They ate on the balcony while sharing the Sunday paper. The warm breeze rustled the masses of ivy and the leaves of the potted shrubs in glazed pots that created islands of privacy along the open space. It lifted the edges of the pink linen tablecloth and brought the scent of new-mown grass drifting up from below. Sparrows winged to join them, hopping around under the table or perching hopefully on the railing. The food was delicious; the coffee perfect. Peace and tranquility and an odd sense of comfort flowed between them.

Gina had not bothered to dress, but only thrown one of the hotel's white terry-cloth courtesy robes on over her gown. She tried at first to keep it securely belted and closed over her chest and knees, but finally gave up the struggle. Once, she caught Race's gaze resting on the lace and tiny pearl buttons revealed between her breasts as the heavy robe fell open. The smile he gave her then seemed lazy, almost sleepy, yet she glimpsed hypnotic intensity in its depths before his lashes flickered down to conceal it. He looked away, and did not make the same mistake again.

Talk between them was sporadic and based mostly on bits and pieces culled from the paper. The easy comments were punctuated by long periods of silence broken only by the rustle of pages and the clink of a cup on a saucer.

It was the Sunday comics, after they had pushed back their plates and were finishing the last of the coffee, that brought up the subject of cartoon movies. They fell into a mild argument about the effects of cartoon violence, with Gina maintaining that movies such as *Beauty and the Beast* or *Aladdin* were far better for kids than simplistic kick-and-slash shows with heroes like the Ninja Turtles. Race would not be convinced. While admitting the excellence of Disney productions, he claimed that the values of loyalty and cooperation portrayed in the turtle movies made up for their emphasis on action. Besides, he said, nobody ever stabbed the turtles in the back, and no giant tiger's head opened up with a roar and swallowed them whole, as happened with Disney animation.

Gina had to laugh and agree. At the same time, she was struck by his knowledge of children's cartoon fare. The only reason she was familiar with the stories was because of Diane's son Corey, a pint-sized genius with a passion for electronic gadgets who was usually watching a kid's movie or cartoon on his portable TV-VCR while Gina visited her friend. What excuse could a man like Race have? Unless he was married and had children?

But no, he had said he was unattached. That didn't make it the truth, of course; men had been known to lie about such things.

As Gina thought of Corey and Diane, she realized with a start that she hadn't phoned her friend again, as promised the night before. Diane would be frantic. It was a wonder she hadn't called the police, or at least sent someone from hotel security to check on her.

Gina set her section of paper aside as she got to her feet. "Excuse me a second, if you don't mind. I need to make a phone call."

Race looked up, then nodded toward an extension half hidden by a pot of greenery. "There's one over there."

"That's all right, I'll just make a pit stop at the same

time," she said in hasty improvisation. Before he could reply, she opened the French door and stepped inside.

Diane answered on the second ring. Gina rushed into explanations, since she was half afraid she might have to cut her call short if Race decided to move back in from the balcony. Diane heard her out without interrupting. When Gina stopped speaking, a small silence fell.

"Well," her friend finally, "I hope you know what you're doing."

"Actually, I'm not so sure," Gina said on an uneven laugh, "but I don't care. Race is so fine, you wouldn't believe it—even I don't believe it. And you should have seen Bradley's face when he met him! He was dumbstruck. I mean that literally. And he sounded so two-faced. I don't know what I ever saw in him."

"Praise be," Diane said. "At least some good seems to be coming of all this. But you won't do anything silly like falling for this Race character, will you? I mean, you've had enough of men who aren't exactly marriage material; the last thing you need is another one."

Gina couldn't help a quick laugh. "How do you know Race wouldn't make an excellent husband? Stranger things have happened."

"Don't say that!" Diane's tone was sharp. "You don't know a thing about this person. I mean, a male model, for heaven's sake!"

"He's more than that," Gina protested. She went on to tell her friend about the ranch.

"I don't care if his spread covers half of Texas, it still doesn't make him a good risk. I just don't want you to get hurt."

"Oh, Diane, he's a nice person, really he is."

"I'm sure his mother would be happy to hear you say so, but that doesn't make it right. The thing you should do is get rid of him pronto."

"Well, I meant to, but we both seem to be at loose ends. It's just one more afternoon."

Diane made a sound that was both disgruntled and despairing. "Well, if you won't, you won't. At least be careful."

"Diane—" Gina began, troubled by the other woman's doubts and strictures.

"I gotta go," Diane said. "Corey was saying something just now about hooking up the CD-ROM on my computer to the stereo speakers, and now he's entirely too quiet. But you take care of yourself, you hear? And don't believe a word this Race character has to say, because you can bet your boots it doesn't mean a thing!"

Gina hung up, then sat staring at the cold gas logs inside the fireplace. It wasn't like Diane to be so brusque or so edgy. She was usually the most laid-back of women, never in a hurry, infinitely tolerant of people's little quirks and always ready to look for the best in them. At the same time, she was open and plain-spoken to a fault.

Her friend had been most of those things this time, of course, yet something had been different. She had asked almost no questions about Race, for one thing. For another, she had condemned him sight unseen. And she really hadn't wanted to talk about the whole thing except to issue warnings.

Something was wrong. What was it?

Gina realized, after a moment's thought, that the few months she known Diane were not enough for an educated guess at the problem. Diane was originally from the Dallas area; she spoke of it often and had actually stayed at the Glass Garden Hotel for her own honeymoon. Near Gina's own age, Diane was a widow whose engineer husband, her childhood sweetheart, had been killed while working on an offshore oil rig. Diane had little family other than her young son. There was only an elderly aunt, an older brother who was in politics, and a younger sister she worried about because she was mixed up in some kind of ultraconservative high-achievement cult in California.

Gina's own family were country people who seldom left their delta-land farm. Because she and Diane were both virtually alone, they had established an instant rapport. More than that, something had clicked between them in the way it sometimes did with two people; they simply liked each other on sight.

On the strength of that affection, Gina had somehow expected more alarm and concern from Diane, more of the kind of panic she had shown last night. It hadn't been there. In some peculiar fashion, Gina felt cut off, even abandoned. It was disturbing.

It was also appalling, because she could think of only one reason Diane had stopped caring what happened to her. That reason was directly connected to Bradley Dillman. Yet if Diane had discovered it, then any number of other people could know about it also.

Any number. Including Race.

Yes, but how? And why would he care? He was a rancher and a part-time model.

Wasn't he?

Beside the phone was the business card he had given her the night before, lying where she had put it before she called Diane the first time. Gina glanced at it, her gaze focusing on the number printed across the bottom. She looked at the phone again, then reached out to take up the receiver. She punched in the number.

The model agency seemed to be legitimate; the phone was ringing on the other end. Once, twice, three times. Nobody was going to answer.

Of course they weren't going to answer. It was Sunday. She should have remembered.

She started to hang up. Abruptly, the fourth ring ended and there came the familiar hollow noise of a line open to an answering machine. Gina snatched the receiver back to her ear.

"Thank you for calling the Humane Society of Greater Dallas-Fort Worth. Please leave your message at the tone—"

She had made a mistake; that had to be it. She broke the connection. She dialed again.

Four rings. An answering machine. The same announcement.

Gina slammed the phone into its cradle. She snatched her fingers away as if the molded plastic were white hot. Her heart was pounding so hard she could hear it in her ears, see it vibrating the thick terry-cloth of her robe over her chest.

"Gina?" Race stepped through the door from the balcony that she had not heard him open. He came toward her with concern in his face. "Is something wrong?"

Everything was wrong. Every single thing in her life had turned out totally, impossibly, unforgivably wrong.

It wouldn't do to say so, not now. She couldn't afford to be that forthright. Or that honest.

She looked up, her gaze open and vulnerable as she met the blue darkness of his eyes. She moistened her lips as she tried to find some answer that might satisfy him, at least for a little while. Then she had it.

"Nothing," she said. "I just hate answering machines."

Chapter Six

"Oh, my stars, was I ever embarrassed! I must have turned three shades of red. But such a man, honey! Not too many strip that well, I expect, though I shouldn't be sayin' such a thing. And makin' his bed on the rug like that is so romantic, like *Desire Under the Stars,* where the hero sleeps on the floor for seventy-five whole pages. Oh, but then! Let's just say he makes up for it."

The maid rattled on while she cleaned the bathroom with quick, practiced motions. Gina glanced at her from the corners of her eyes as she applied mascara at the dressing table. This Etta was quite a character, with her spun-sugar hairstyle, a pin on her breast pocket in the shape of a giant pewter heart, and a proprietary air as if she were straightening her own home. Her comments and snatched looks in Gina's direction indicated curiosity, but were robbed of offense by their warmth and down-home frankness.

Gina had reached the makeup stage in her dressing when the maid checked the room the second time. Since Race had gone downstairs to reserve a court for tennis and she would be leaving in a few minutes to join him, she had told Etta to go ahead with her job.

In a carefully offhand manner, Gina said now, "The—uh, sleeping arrangement is only temporary."

"I should hope so," Etta said with a quick grin as she

smoothed bed covers. "You wouldn't want to keep a man like layin' around on the floor too long. I noticed him bringin' coffee up a while ago, too, you know. Now, I like a strong, take-charge type as well as any, but the man who sees to his woman's comfort like that is something special."

"You think so?" Gina reached for her lip gloss and applied it with more quickness than precision.

"You'd better believe it. Yes, and another thing. Heaven help me if I had been up to no good when I walked in on him earlier. I expect I'd still be picking myself up. Protecting his own, that's what he was doing."

"Oh, I don't think it was anything quite that dramatic," Gina said uneasily.

Etta stopped in the middle of fluffing pillows to give her a straight look. "You didn't see his face before he cottoned to who was comin' in on him."

No, or the rest of him, either, Gina thought. Which seemed a shame. She said, "That's all well and good, but some men just aren't cut out to be good husbands."

"No, but this one will be— Oh!" Etta straightened with a hand to her lips. "I shouldn't have said that; now I've gone and done it. Tyrone—the concierge, you know—told me that you and this watch dog hero of yours don't know each any too well. But he wasn't gossiping. He just wanted me to keep an eye on you since he was worried he led you to do the wrong thing."

"Because of his advice, you mean." Gina could not be surprised, somehow, that Etta knew what was going on. It seemed typical.

"He's a great one for solving guest's special problems," Etta allowed, lowering her voice to a confidential mutter. "That's so long as it's arranging for limos, having major jewelry delivered, or filling a Jacuzzi with champagne. But he can't get it through his head that some things are not that easy."

"I appreciate the concern," Gina said, "though it really isn't a problem. A few hours more and that will be the end of it."

Etta paused in her task of dumping the bedroom wastebasket. "You mean you'll be leaving the hotel? I thought I had you down on my list for a week?"

"Rather, my—that is, the gentleman will be leaving."

"But why? What did he do?"

He had tricked her, betrayed her, mocked her, made her feel things she did not want or need. What had he not done? should be the question.

"Nothing, nothing at all," Gina answered as she zipped the few cosmetics she had used back into their bag. "It's just that—some things don't work out."

"Don't you like him?" the maid said, then gave a shake of her head. "Silly question, of course you do; what's not to like? So what is it with you?"

"How do you know it's me?" Gina's tone was defensive.

"Don't look to me like it's him." The words were positive. "Men don't rise up like that to protect women they don't care about. And they don't swim laps like the devil's after them unless they got troubles on their minds or they're trying to forget their manly frustrations."

Manly frustrations.

"Maybe he has troubles, all right," Gina said with grim emphasis.

Etta tipped her head like a wise sparrow. "I see what it is; you just don't trust him."

"That about covers it." Gina avoided the maid's gaze as she ran a hairbrush through her hair.

"Now that's a real bawler," Etta said with a woeful look. "I never saw a handsomer couple than you two. There's got to be something somebody can do."

"I wouldn't count on it." Gina reached for a headband, holding it in her hands a blind instant as depression washed over her. Then she pushed the band in place with determination and gave a final glance in the mirror at her aqua T-shirt and turquoise shorts. She looked neat and cool, if not particularly exciting or glamorous. Her steps firm, she headed toward the door.

The maid shook her head as she watched her go, but the look in her eyes was thoughtful.

A pair of peacocks were strutting and screaming outside the fence of the tennis court when Gina reached it. Race was waiting at the gate. Sunlight made a golden sheen in his hair and slanted across his features to reveal his barely controlled impatience. He was not alone.

Bradley and Sandra, in spiffy, regulation tennis whites, stood next to him. Bradley looked around as Gina approached, and flashed a cocksure grin.

"Gina, love," he called, "tell this man of yours that you don't mind a foursome. Last night was one thing, but he seems to have some crazy idea you'd rather avoid us this morning, too."

"Maybe he's right," Gina said as irritation rose inside her. The last thing she wanted was to be forced to deal with Bradley and Race at the same time.

"Oh, sure," her former fiancé said. "If you wanted that, you'd have checked out by now."

"Why would I do that? This was always my choice, if you recall."

"Yeah," Bradley said as he lowered his voice to an intimate note. "I remember we were supposed to be here together."

That blatant attempt to disconcert her, and in front of Sandra and Race, made her temperature rise. It was only fire added to the anger that had been simmering inside her since she learned Race was not who he claimed. The combination fueled the impulse that made her walk right up to Race, put her hand on his shoulder and stand on tiptoe to press a kiss of greeting to his lips.

His chest swelled as he caught his breath in surprise. Then he circled her waist with one arm and pulled her close.

His lips were smooth and warm, their firm touch beguiling. Her own lips parted in startled surprise at the transfer of initiative. The careful sweep of his tongue just inside the sensitive lining of her mouth sent an unwanted tremor of pleasure along her nerves. She met his entry, delicately defending against it, fighting the captivating sweetness and tender skill of his incitement.

But the battle was provocation in itself, a warm clash of tastes and textures and inclinations that routed thought, leaving only intuitive response. Before its force, she felt her hostility draining away against her will, being replaced by the despairing need to be held close and closer still.

Exhilaration swept in upon her in a surging flood. She lifted her arms to link them behind his head. Race drew her closer. Molded to him from breastbone to knees, she felt time slow to a standstill. Almost, she forgot what she was doing and where, who was watching, and why. Almost.

"God," Bradley said in tones of disgust, "are you two sure you want to play at all?"

Race lifted his head, releasing her lips but not his grasp. Dark concentration in his face, he spoke without looking at the other man. "Yes, we're sure, or rather I am. Though tennis may not be the right game."

"Come on, just a friendly little set or two."

Race let Gina go, though there seemed to be the tension of reluctance in the muscles of his arms and he retained a hand at her waist. Turning with her, he began to walk away, back toward the hotel. His smile oblique, he said over his shoulder, "Sorry, Dillman. I don't feel friendly."

What did he feel? In that moment, Gina would have given a lot to know. But she could not ask.

The reason she could not was because the answer was too important. How that happened, she was not entirely sure. She only knew that it had, and senseless as it might be, she could not deny it.

The maid Etta had nothing on her, Gina realized with an ache deep in her chest. She was also a sucker for a protective man, not to mention being a hopeless romantic.

Totally hopeless.

Chapter Seven

She caught him.

Race could hardly believe it; he usually had more finesse. But there Gina was, standing on the balcony, when he stepped out of Dillman's room. By the time he noticed her, it was too late to retreat.

He was royally ticked-off, though not at her. He had made the mistake of thinking she was like other women.

He figured he had at least another half hour before she was finished dressing for dinner. She had beaten the estimate by a good twenty minutes.

There was only one thing to do and that was brazen it out. Since a lie was in order, he might as well make it count. With as much practice as he was getting, he ought to be expert at it before long.

Sauntering toward her with a whimsical smile and more nonchalance than he felt, he said, "Our neighbors left their door open when they went down to dinner. You know, I'm not too sure those two are married, after all. Shocking, don't you think?"

She did not find his comment humorous. "What makes you say that?"

"No loose grains of rice—or the bird seed that's become the environmentally correct substitute. No monogrammed champagne glasses or wedding cake crumbs. No wrinkled dress clothes." He stopped beside her and turned to rest his spine against the balcony railing. "Of course, they could have made a quick trip past some judge. But then, I wasn't too impressed by the wedding ring on your friend Sandra's finger, and she doesn't look much like a happy bride. What do you think?"

"The ring looks like a Cubic Zirconia," Gina said with a shake of her head. "And in a gold-plated mounting, at that."

Relief that she was going along with him made the blood feel hot in his head. "My thoughts exactly," he said. "So what gives? Is the idiot that cheap, or is he here for a little hanky-panky? Or could it just be a smoke screen while he keeps an eye on the woman he almost married?"

"What do you think?" Her gaze was direct.

He tried for a careless shrug. "Hard to say since I don't know the guy. I was asking you."

"Any of the above," she replied with a rueful twist of her lips. "Though I'm not too sure Sandra would go along without the ring. I'm only surprised she isn't wearing the solitaire I gave back."

"That would bother you?"

She studied him, her gaze dark. "You want to know if I

have any regrets? The answer is only one: I regret it took me so long to see through Bradley.''

''No righteous indignation that he's here with another woman? No heart-burning over the way he treated you?

''Not really, not anymore.''

He made a soft sound of wonder. ''You aren't normal.''

''Maybe what I am is relieved.'' She directed her attention beyond him, to the high rise on the Dallas skyline that looked like a giant golf ball on a tee.

''Or in shock?'' he suggested.

''If I'm shocked,'' she said, ''it's because you seem to care one way or the other.''

He allowed his gaze to wander over her, from the auburn sheen of her hair and delicate planes of her face, tinted with soft, fresh color, to the gentle curves of her body under a simple shirtwaist of blue chambray worn with a belt of silver conchas. A wry smile tugged at his mouth.

''You're a beautiful and intelligent woman who deserves to be happy,'' he said. ''The last thing I want is to see you get hurt.'' Which was, he saw, the exact truth, though it was a little late to worry about it.

''Why?'' she said baldly as her gaze met his.

He ought to tell her. Here and now. He felt his heart begin to hammer in his chest at the mere thought. But he couldn't do it; he had no right.

He said quietly, ''Why not? I may be a paid escort, but I'm still a normal man, with normal impulses.''

Her smile held a shade of weariness. ''I never thought otherwise.''

That deserved some reward. He said in gruff tones, ''Would you like me to get rid of Dillman?''

''Could you?'' Her gaze sharpened as she studied his face. ''No, forget that I said that. It isn't worth the trouble.''

Her words finally answered one question for him, he saw; she didn't care enough about Dillman to work up a good sweat over being free of him. Regardless, he should never have made the suggestion; she was suspicious enough already. One more mistake to go with the others.

Or rather, one more stupid macho gesture brought on by tried temper and self-disgust.

This charade was getting to him. More than that, it was beginning to break down, and he didn't know how much longer he could hold it together. During the long afternoon just past, he had talked more than he should have about the ranch, his views on farm subsidies, Texas politics, and a thousand other things. As he and Gina strolled around the lake earlier and sat enjoying the breeze in the gazebo, he had caught himself reaching out more than once to take her hand, touch her arm, brush her hair away from her face. Later, watching a movie with her while stretched out on the sitting room floor in a nest of pillows, it had been all he could do not to roll over, pin her under him, and do all those things that had haunted him the night before. Suggesting that they change clothes for an early dinner as a follow-up to their late brunch had been a desperate attempt to remove them from the suite before he made a fool of himself.

Lying, hiding, pretending: he should have known he couldn't pull it off. Of course, the act had never been intended to last so long. An hour or two, an evening at the most, then it should have been over. He was supposed to have passed the whole thing off as a bad joke, or else made a polite bow and skipped out without a word.

Instead he had gone all gallant. His motives had been the best, or so he had thought at the time. Now he wasn't so sure.

Gina deserved better. It was time he did what he had come to do, then was on his way. If he could bear to go.

He gave a dismissive nod by way of agreement with her last comment. Indicating the door behind her with a quick gesture, he said, "Hungry? I'm ready to head down to Montague's if you are."

Gina glanced at Race as they waited to be seated in the hotel's western-style restaurant. There was a forbidding cast to his features as he stood glancing around impatiently for the hostess.

He had been something less than approachable the entire afternoon. More than once she had searched for words to ask him who and what he was, and what he wanted with her, but none had seemed right. It had occurred to her, after a time, that it would be dumb to force a showdown while they were alone. What would she do if took violent exception to her questions? What if he told her he was a jewel thief, a hit man, a CIA operative, or something equally exotic and dangerous?

No, it would be best to wait until there were people around before she forced the issue. This evening in the restaurant should do nicely. Now that time had come.

The turmoil in her mind was more effective than a diet pill for curbing her appetite. No matter; she would be delighted to get the meal out of the way, to get everything out of the way. She was grateful when they were finally shown to a table in one corner.

To say the atmosphere in Montague's was relaxed was a vast understatement: half the male customers were eating with their hats on, and a soccer game was in progress on the big-screen television. The drink of choice appeared to be beer in long necks, and barbecued ribs and beans was the house specialty. Of the four guys in the band, only one wore a real shirt, while the rest made do with some form of vest over their bare chests.

One reason for choosing Montague's instead of the Terrace was the casual atmosphere, since neither she nor Race had felt like getting into formal wear again. They had both settled for comfort instead, though Gina thought there was a certain Texas elegance in the open-necked white dress shirt that Race wore with his jeans. The main purpose for changing restaurants, however, had to do with Bradley and Sandra. The best way to avoid a meeting seemed to be to steer clear of the Terrace, where they had all eaten the night before.

For the first part, they were fine. The second didn't pan out.

They had just filled their plates from the buffet and sat down with them when they heard a hail. Bradley, with Sandra in tow, was winding his way through the tables toward them.

"Hi guys!" her ex-fiancé said, teeth flashing as he

smiled. "I looked in and saw you two as my bride and I were walking past. Mind if we pull up a chair?"

Bradley didn't wait for a reply, but seated Sandra, then plopped down himself. Gina fully expected Race to put a stop to the intrusion since he had not been bashful about it earlier, but he did no such thing. After a curt greeting, he only signaled for the waitress to bring two more place settings.

Sandra was less than happy, that was easy to see. Gina felt sorry for her. Because of it, she was as pleasant as she was able as the other two settled in and placed their orders. At the same time, she glanced at Race, wanting to share her discomfort and also her entertainment at the odd picture they presented: the jilted bride, guilty bridegroom, substitute wife, and sham lover all sitting down to dinner together. So modern, so false, and such a farce.

He avoided her gaze, or so it seemed. Face impassive, manner perfectly polite, he began to talk about soccer, sliding easily from that into football, then making brief forays into other realms of manly sports. She would have been impressed if she had not been half convinced that his interest was genuine.

The conviction grew as the minutes ticked past. The two men seemed to be getting along splendidly, comparing teams and players, capping each other's stories of great games, arguing amiably about scores. They might, in fact, have been buddies. It was a peculiar phenomenon, a man thing, no doubt, using sports to form a bond of mutual interest. They did it by instinct, it seemed, even when a bond was the last thing that was needed. Or perhaps it was only a method of defusing unacceptable aggression.

Whatever the reason, it was irritating.

Gina began to feel the beginnings of a tension headache behind her eyes. There was a time when she could have laughed and talked with the woman who sat next to her at the table, a time when they had been close. They both knew that time was over, and nothing was ever going to make it possible for them to communicate on the same level as the two men across from them who barely knew each other.

"What do you think?"

It was Race who broke into her preoccupation with the question. His gaze was so intent that it seemed the fate of mankind waited on her answer. She was in no mood for such games. "I wasn't paying attention," she said shortly. "What were you saying?"

"Is accepting money for making commercials a violation of an athlete's amateur status? Should American athletes be penalized for it in international competition, for instance, when other countries subsidize their athletes—in effect paying them for their ability?"

"Good grief," she said. "How on earth did you get on that subject?"

Bradley let out a bark of laughter. "Where has your mind been, sweetheart? Never mind, Bannister; I can tell you exactly how Gina will answer." A sardonic smile curled his mustached upper lip. "She'll tell you that anybody who knows the rules and doesn't follow them ought to pay the price, no matter what everybody else is doing. No shades of gray for her, no sir. Black or white, right or wrong; that's the way she sees it and the way she calls it."

"That right?" Race asked. He leaned back in his chair, his eyes dark blue and steady as they held hers across the table.

"I suppose so," Gina said slowly. There was something here she did not quite understand; still, she could not deny her basic beliefs.

A shadow crossed Race's face. His voice low, he said, "I should have known."

"So should I, right from the start," Bradley agreed. "No second chances, huh, Gina? No forgiving, not from you."

She looked at the man she had almost married, noting the weakness in his face and, just possibly, a faint trace of regret. In spite of the last, there could be only one answer. "No, not often."

Bradley looked at Race. "See what I mean?"

It seemed to Gina's heightened imagination that some flash of understanding passed between the two men. Her head began to throb. What if Diane had been right? What if it was Bradley who had hired Race, had instructed him to wine her, dine her, flatter her silly, then find out just how much she knew?

With the months of their engagement to give him insight, Bradley must have guessed there would be no groom eloping with her to the hotel. He had decided to use that fact for his own ends, plus have a little fun at her expense.

And she had fallen for it. She had let Race into her suite and into her life. The mistake was going to cost her; she knew that already. The only question was how much.

Earlier, when she had seen Race coming from Bradley's rooms, he had not just stepped inside the open door from idle curiosity as he had implied. No, he had gone to talk to his employer. The two of them must have been setting up this restaurant meeting.

Bradley could not be sure she knew of his illegal operations; she had never told him, since he had presented her with such a fine alternative for calling off the wedding. But possibly he had suspected it. That was what Race's innocuous question about amateur athletes had been about, then; it had nothing to do with sports, but was a test of her scruples. It had been a trap.

Gina put down her fork and pushed her plate away. Her eyes were steady as she looked from Bradley to Race, then returned her gaze to the man she had almost married. "What other answer could there be?" she said. "Right is right and wrong is wrong, and I could never remain in a relationship of any kind with someone who doesn't recognize the difference. A person who ignores the rules should look out for the consequences. That's the way I see it, and I refuse to apologize for it."

Bradley gave a short laugh. "Sweet and simple, but not very practical. You may get lonesome out there on a limb by yourself with nothing but your principles."

"Could be," she said quietly, "but I'll chance it."

What now? Bradley had his connections, some of them dangerous ones. If she had ever doubted it, she had only to look at the man across from her. Still, this was a public place. She could hardly be taken out of it without someone noticing. Could she?

Race was watching her with his face set in taut, unrevealing planes. She wondered what he was thinking, wondered if he knew how fast her heart was beating. Did he have any idea of the pain inside her? Could he even begin to guess how much it hurt to think of what he had done?

He could do no more harm. She wouldn't give him the chance, not if she could prevent it.

Yes, but could she?

He was supposed to be her lover, if not her husband. She had told the concierge otherwise, and the maid Etta also knew, but everyone else who had seen them coming and going from the honeymoon suite would naturally assume they were a couple. He could take her anywhere he wanted; he had the strength, and then some. Who would interfere? Who would prevent him from leading her upstairs and doing whatever he pleased with her?

Diane had been right about everything; Gina saw that with sudden, blinding clarity. She really should have run like hell while she had the chance.

Chapter Eight

At that moment, Sandra caught Gina's eye. "I'm going to the ladies' room," she murmured. "Come with me?"

The invitation seemed to have a special intensity. Was it possible that Sandra realized what was happening and was trying to help her? If she was, what would the two men do about it?

There was only one way to find out. Moving with care, Gina got to her feet.

No one objected, no one tried to stop them. Neither Bradley nor Race said a word. Gina's knees felt weak as she followed the other woman. At the same time, she was puzzled. Was it possible she had been wrong? Had the whole standoff between Bradley, Race, and herself been a figment of her overactive imagination?

The rest room was behind the main lobby, convenient to both Montague's and the Terrace. An extravaganza in cream marble with warm gold tracery, it featured free-standing sculptured-marble basins, crystal chandeliers, scented soaps, and a pink rose in a holder attached to every mirror. The vast space was virtually empty; a woman drying her hands at the electric air dryer nodded and left as Gina and Sandra entered.

"Look, Gina," Sandra said as she turned to face her in front of the basins, "I just wanted a chance to say I'm sorry. I know you don't care for me much anymore, and I don't blame you. But I never meant to make a mess of things for you with Bradley. It just . . . happened, and I feel so bad about it."

"Not to worry," Gina said. "I expect I should be thanking you."

The other woman's face lightened a fraction before she looked down to study her plastic nails. "I don't think Bradley's overjoyed with how things worked out."

"I can't help that."

"It's driving him nuts, you know, you being next door with this guy Race."

Gina allowed a grim smile to curve her lips. "I'm not so sure of that, but if so—well, fine."

A surprised laugh left Sandra. "Lord, Gina, I never knew you had it in you."

"No?" Gina considered an instant. "You know, neither did I."

The other woman gave her a strained smile, then said abruptly, "I'm leaving right after dinner, going back to Shreveport. I have to be back at work in the morning, and I need the job because I don't think this marriage is going to work. Bradley only proposed to get back at you, because you walked out on him."

Sandra was in pain not so different from her own, Gina saw. That was cause enough to be kind. "Oh, I doubt that was the reason. The two of you were already involved."

"Last fling stuff." Sandra tapped her nails on the marble basin. "You scared him, you know, Gina? You ask a lot from a man."

"No more than I'm willing to give." The words were soft and fretted with pain.

"That's just it, don't you see?" Sandra said earnestly. "With you it was all or nothing, and Bradley wasn't sure he could live up to that."

"So he proved he couldn't."

"Yeah, well, maybe it was easier than trying to change. But I know he wishes he had made the effort."

Gina stared at the other woman. "You aren't suggesting he's here because—because he wants to get back together?"

Sandra scrubbed at a nonexistent spot on the marble. "Maybe not that, exactly. But he was worried about you, afraid of what you might do."

"Oh, come on!"

"No, really," Sandra said, looking up with worry in her eyes. "Going off like this isn't like you. You're practical, solid; you always do the right thing. You would never go running off to a high-class love nest with some guy you don't know from Adam."

Gina all but snorted. "Give me a break, Sandra! How am I supposed to believe Bradley is all worked up because I'm here with Race when he's the one who sent him?"

Sandra snapped her head back in amazement. "You've got to be kidding. Bradley's frothing at the mouth because he's here; he really expected to find you alone."

Gina stared at her former maid of honor, then gave a quick shake of her head. "That's just what he wants you to believe."

"I swear it's exactly what he thought. He was laughing all the way out here about how he planned to make you admit there was no other man. When he saw you with Race in the Terrace last night, he nearly passed out."

It didn't make sense, Gina thought in confusion. Yet, if Sandra was right, she was going to have to readjust her thinking. The only trouble was, she couldn't see how.

She said finally, "This hasn't exactly been a wonderful honeymoon for you, has it? I'm sorry."

"Yeah," Sandra said with weak smile as she turned and started toward the toilet stalls. "So am I."

Race saw them returning to the table well before they reached it. The smile he gave Gina sent a small shiver down her spine. She suppressed it with determination, but it was a real effort.

"Did you want dessert?" His gaze upon her was intent, though infinitely polite.

She shook her head. She had barely touched her barbecue and beans. The thought of anything sweet was positively nauseating.

"Then it must be about time to call it a night," he said, and signaled for the check.

She should have asked for ice cream, cake, pie, coffee, anything. Her time, she saw, had just run out.

Bradley protested, suggesting they take his car, head over to the West End tourist haunts and wander around. Race was polite but firm in his refusal. Gina didn't know whether to laugh or cry when her ex-fiancé subsided without a fight. It really seemed unreasonable to be inclined to do both.

She could have refused to leave the restaurant, of course. But that would have meant forcing a confrontation. She wasn't ready. She had no idea what to say, what to think; she could not even decide what were the right questions to ask. She was afraid of looking dumb by jumping to the wrong conclusion, but just as terrified of being a bigger fool by not standing up for herself. Paralyzed by the clamor of doubts and possibilities that whirled in her brain, she allowed herself to be escorted toward the elevators.

She didn't want to know the truth.

That was it, she realized as they left the elevator and moved along the hall toward their suite. She didn't want to listen to Race saying it had all been a sham, that none of it had meant anything to him. Whether he was Bradley's hired hand or just a hustler, she just didn't want to hear it.

Was this the way it was for all those women who wound up victims of violence from lovers and friends? Could they not believe in their melodramatic fears? Did they not run for safety because they could not bring themselves to accept that someone they loved would hurt them? Or because the wound inside from that betrayal, when it came, would be worse than anything that might be done to them?

Love. It was a simple word, yet so complex.

She didn't love Race; why, she barely knew him. You had to know someone to love them, didn't you? That sure knowledge took time, the careful exploration of feelings and ideas, the diligent search for compatibility. It didn't come in an instant, with a look, a touch.

Did it?

There were small heart-shaped candies lying on the pillows where Etta had turned down the bed. Gina was touched by the maid's small hint at romantic possibilities. Etta had certainly been taken with Race. And she had been so sure that he was being protective by sleeping on the sitting room floor. No doubt he was—protective of himself, that is.

Gina wished with sudden fervency that Etta could have been right. What a difference it would make. But she didn't believe in romance, not anymore. After this, she would never be romantic again.

"Are you all right?" Race spoke from behind her, his voice deep and a little rough.

She turned her head to see him standing with one hand braced on the bedroom door frame. The frown of concern between his brows looked genuine. He was a good actor.

"Yes, fine," she said.

"I'll lock up." He waited an instant, but when she made no reply, moved back inside the sitting room. After a moment she heard the click of the dead bolt on the outer door.

He had been waiting, she realized, for her to protest, or at least question, his presence in the suite for a second night. She hadn't the time or energy; there were other decisions to be made that were far more important.

She didn't want to be locked in, suddenly couldn't bear it. Moving to the French doors to the balcony, she pushed the draperies aside and let herself out. Walking to the railing, she clung to it while she stood breathing fast and deep in the darkness.

"Gina?"

The darkness lightened then dimmed again as Race swept the drapes open and let them fall into place behind him. She refused to look at him, though he moved to stand beside her, his hands thrust into his pockets.

The night air was soft and cool. The arc of the sky overhead was gray-black and starless, washed out by the city lights that lay like fallen planets in the distance. Race was silent. There was something calming in the size and solidity of him there, so near yet so undemanding. As strange as it seemed, his very presence gave her courage.

Her voice not quite natural, she said, "Who are you, really?"

His sigh was quietly accepting, a tacit admission. "Just a man who wishes that things had been different—that he was different. Or that you were."

She had known, yet had still hoped she was wrong. She began, "You aren't—"

"I'm a lot of things," he interrupted, turning to put his back to the railing, "some of them even legitimate. The part about the ranch is true; I run it, work hard at it."

"That's something, anyway."

He glanced away, his face stiff, before he turned back and concentrated his attention upon her once more. His voice lower, he said, "Do you know anything about the rodeo?"

"A little." She waited, knowing there was more to come.

"I used to follow it, riding the bulls, years ago when I was young and stupid and full of vinegar. I loved the challenge and, yes, the death-defying charge of the danger. You have only eight seconds to prove yourself, eight seconds that can be a lifetime. The ride is dangerous and soon over, but it's a heart-pounding glory. And if you can stay on, if you can make the bell, then you win the day and the silver buckle that says you're a winner. You take home the prize."

"And what," she said quietly, "if you fall off?"

"Then you hit the hard ground and the bull puts his foot in your ribs or your face and—well, you have the pain and the defeat." His voice turned rough. "But, God, you also had the ride."

"Yes, I see," she said, and she did, somewhere inside where logic could not reach and instinct took over. Where the mind stopped and the heart began.

They were quiet, while from the restaurant far below them music floated upward. It was an old sweet ballad, one about love and loss.

Race tilted his head, listening. Then he removed a hand from his pocket and held it out with his gaze unwavering on the pale shape of her face. His voice deep and steady, he said, "Dance?"

She could not refuse, nor did she want to; that much was suddenly clear. To accept the dance, to ride the bull, to take a chance on love—for all these things you had to be willing to risk the pain.

Some people never managed it. They preferred to play it safe, to avoid being hurt at all costs. But to avoid being hurt was to avoid living. And life, like bull-riding, was a heart-pounding glory too precious to be missed.

She had vowed to live dangerously, and she would. There was no other way.

She turned to gaze at him there in the dimness. He was a warm shadow, yet solid. Real. She put her hand in his, then went into his arms. They closed around her, drawing her firmly against the muscle-clad planes of his chest. Accepting, absorbing his hard strength, she closed her eyes.

Together, body to body, they shifted, drifting slowly around the narrow space of the balcony. It was an ancient instinct, that urge to move in seductive rhythm. They accepted it, sustained, used it. They held each other until nerves and sinew sang to the music and the moment, until flesh and blood could stand no more. Until the music ended.

Race brushed the silk of her hair with his lips, grazed her forehead, sought her lips as she lifted her face blindly for his kiss. Inside, she felt a sweet, warm yielding. With infinite courtesy, she let him see it, allowed him to feel it.

His chest swelled on a deep-drawn breath, then he bent to place his arm under her knees, lifting her against his chest. In that close embrace, he moved inside, where he placed her on the wide, soft surface of the bed. His knee dented the surface beside her, then he joined her in a smooth, controlled glide.

She made a soft sound of pleasure as he reached to touch her breast, cupping it in his warm grasp. It was only a prelude, however, to his gentle, yet thorough exploration of the curves and hollows of her body. He stroked her, holding, pressing with shuttered eyes and widespread fingers, as if he meant to memorize every inch of silken skin and each muscle and finely turned bone beneath it.

He unbuttoned her shirtwaist, following the opening line with heated kisses as the edges parted. Exposing the lace cups of her bra, he brushed the firm swells under them with his mouth, letting her feel the heat of his breath, the wet lap of his tongue around the nipples. Taking the straining peaks between his lips, first one then the other, he teased them gently to berrylike tautness.

Barely breathing, she slipped the buttons of his shirt free and trailed her fingertips through the silky thicket of hair on his chest. Finding his pap, she rubbed it with the ball of her thumb. So enthralled was she by its abrupt contraction into nubbed hardness that she hardly noticed as he slid a bra strap from her shoulder.

Then the hot wetness of his mouth covered her bare nipple. She inhaled with a soft gasp that grew deeper as he applied delicate, deliberate suction.

His hands, oh, his hands were sure. She tried not to think why, tried not to think of other women he might have known. And succeeded, at least in part. By degrees the suite, the bed, the night faded, to be replaced by the touch and taste and scent of the man who held her, drowned out by the thunder of the blood in her veins.

She was on fire inside, lost in a world of hot, consuming sensation. Flushed with need, she reached out for him, giving him in full measure the pleasure he was extending with such care and generosity. Clothing was loosened and pulled away, then dropped from sight. The smoothness of silken percale sheets soothed their skin as they turned and stretched, sought and held, while supporting themselves on an elbow or a knee.

Licking, tasting, they learned about each other, imprinting the exact pattern of the molecules of their bodies on the circuits of minds and souls. He held the apex of her being in his hand, and she gave him unrestrained access. As he pressed deep, she contracted around his fingers in fervent internal embrace.

The intrusion stung, burned, in spite of its inciting glory. She closed her eyes tight as she pressed her face into his shoulder.

A soft sound left him. His every muscle stiffened, and

he tried to draw back as he recognized the barrier he had reached. She would not release him.

"No," he whispered against her hair in strained tones. "I can't. You—"

"It doesn't matter. Please," she answered in low entreaty while she pressed closer.

A shudder ran over him as he reined in his ardor. He took her mouth in a kiss of plundering, near-desperate need. Then slowly, carefully, he began to ease the way for her with deliberate stretching movements. At the same time, he centered the ball of his thumb on the tiny peak of her femininity so that his every effort compounded the waves of pleasure rippling through her.

Her muscles tensed. Her chest rose and fell in increasing tempo that kept pace with the hot rush of her blood. Their damp skins clung. She smoothed her hands over his arms and shoulders, clasping, holding. Reaching lower, she closed her fingers around the vibrant, fevered hardness of his silken length. It pulsed against her palm, straining in bold power toward the inevitable union.

Desire burgeoned, hovered, erupted into sudden, bright ecstasy. She gave a soft cry as she arched against him. He shifted at once to cover her, fitting himself between her thighs. At the towering crest of her pleasure, he pressed into her wet, hot softness. He held the joining while he tasted her mouth once more, sounding it, drinking its sweetness. Then he drew back a little. Watching her face, holding her gaze in the dimness, he eased deeper, penetrating her internal constriction so carefully there was only an instant of aching strain before she was swept into beatitude.

At that extreme he stopped, and with a slow twist of his hips he tested the tight, resilient walls of her most secret self. She met the glistening darkness of his eyes while her heart swelled with fullness. She held nothing back then, but let him into her utmost depth, opening it to him like swinging wide the gate of a fenced enclosure.

The breath he took had a soft hissing sound. His arms, which held her, quivered with the effort of his control, the restriction of his need.

Then he began to move.

The loving was a dance, fast and slow, lurching now and then, but gaining a steady, throbbing cadence that increased in strength, swelled in tempo and vital intensity. It was a melody both old and new, strange and familiar, wild and gentle in its piercingly sweet refrain.

And unending. It beat in their blood, gaining force, rising, ever rising. It spread, building in volume, gathering speed, spawning variations. Advancing, retreating, ascending, plummeting, they followed its lead with panting breaths and moisture-slick bodies, with raging hearts and fierce minds. It surged around them, a song of wonder that rushed into a sudden, incomparable crescendo ringing to a single note held long and strong. It burst in their minds with unimagined splendor, flooding their bodies with life and grace and delicate, merging wholeness.

It did not fade, but was sustained, held pure and true and clear as they held each other afterward. Gina could hear it still even as she fell asleep as if hit with a stun gun, lying with her head nestled into the curve of Race's neck, his arms wrapped around her.

Much later in the night she felt him ease away from her. Murmuring in distress, she reached out. He returned to her at once, kissing the tucked corner of her mouth so she smiled even in semiconsciousness. He brushed her hair aside to stroke her cheek with his own, letting her feel the slight abrasion of his beard stubble, the smoothness of his eyelids with moisture at their tight line, the sweep of his lashes. Satisfied, she settled deeper into her pillow.

Yet she was alone in the great black-lacquered romantic fantasy of a bed when morning came. Alone in the suite.

Race was gone.

Chapter Nine

The doorbell pealing out its syrupy theme was the last thing Gina wanted to hear. Exclaiming under her breath, she reached for the hotel robe. She knew she should have got up and put on her clothes when she first heard the commotion next door. She would have, if it hadn't seemed like more effort than it was worth.

Coffee was the most that she had been able to manage so far. She knew that moping around the suite with a tissue clutched in her hand was going to get her nowhere. But what did it really matter? There was nowhere she wanted to be, nothing she wanted to do, even if she had the heart for it.

As she moved to answer the door, she glanced at herself in the mirrored wall of the foyer. Her hair was a mess, her face pale, and there were lavender shadows under her eyes. Her lips, red and swollen from Race's kisses, were a perfect match for her eyes, red and swollen from crying. She didn't care. Anyone who objected to her appearance didn't have to look.

The two men at the door were policemen, though they were in plainclothes. One was grizzled and had bags under his eyes, the other was crew-cut, polished, and polite, but both had the indefinable edge of their kind. They presented their credentials and were allowed inside, then the older man came straight to the point.

"We understand, Miss Madison, that you were the accountant for Bradley Dillman until recently. Is that correct?"

The chill of shock ran down her spine, and she clenched her hands together in front of her. "The accounting firm where I work was retained by him, yes."

"You kept the books?"

"That's right."

The older policeman took out a notepad. "We would like you to tell us what you can concerning the flow of money through the various enterprises belonging to Mr. Dillman."

The brisk, businesslike air of the two men was calming to a degree. She could not be too surprised that they wanted to talk to her; she'd been afraid of a visit like this for some time. It even seemed appropriate for it to come now. Moistening her lips, she said, "You are—investigating Bradley's business activities?"

"Mr. Dillman was taken into custody this morning on the charge of money laundering."

Arrested. Bradley. She had half expected it, yet it still

seemed oddly providential, like wishing someone bad luck and having them fall down a well.

The older man gave her a keen stare as he said, "We should make it plain that this visit is an informal inquiry only, Miss Madison. You have been cleared of involvement in his illegal actions. However, any information you can give us will be invaluable in obtaining a conviction, and we would appreciate your cooperation."

"Yes, of course." Gina moved to the wicker love seat in the sitting room and dropped down on it as her knees threatened to give way. Indicating that the men should be seated, she said, "Was—Was Bradley the only person taken into custody?"

"For the time being. He was alone in the suite. I understand his wife left the hotel at an early hour."

She wanted to ask about Race, but the words wouldn't come. It was just as well. If they didn't know he might be implicated, then she must not drag him into it.

"And you really don't suspect me? I'm not under arrest?"

The younger man smiled at her. "We have it on good authority, ma'am, that you didn't know what the guy was up to at the time you took over his bookkeeping. When you found out, you apparently broke off both the business relationship and a personal one. That's enough for us."

"Good authority," she repeated, her voice not quite steady. "What does that mean?"

The two men looked at each other. It was the older one who answered. "We'd rather not go into that just yet. Now, if you could start at the beginning and tell us everything you can about Dillman?"

The questioning that followed was exhaustive and detailed. Gina gave the two men the facts as she knew them, plus as much background on Bradley's activities as she'd managed to discover. The confidentiality of client transactions was one thing when it was a matter of simple business principle, but a man who deliberately broke the law placed himself beyond ethics, so could not expect to be protected by them. She might feel some compunction about exposing him, but her responsibility was clear.

Still, she was not used to dealing with the police. By the

time she finally saw the two men out of the suite, she was shaking with nerves. She closed the door, turned and leaned against it with her eyes shut.

Her throat ached with unshed tears and her mind felt as if it had been put through a meat grinder. The pain of loss moved through her with the slow force of a glacier that destroys everything in front of it. She wanted either to scream out loud or else run away and hide in mute misery.

Race. Where was he? What was he doing? Had he guessed Bradley was going to be arrested? Was that why he had left her?

She should have told the police about him. Keeping silent made a mockery of her fine, upstanding principles. But she couldn't do it. She just couldn't.

Still, why not? He had tricked her, used her, taken everything she had to give, then vanished like the proverbial thief in the night. Which was exactly what he was, more than likely, or else a con man. She ought to be enraged. She would like to feel that kind of self-righteous, soul-freeing violence of emotion.

She couldn't; she hurt too much. Besides, she had gone into the one-night stand with her eyes wide open. There was no one to blame except herself.

She could take some minor comfort from knowing she'd been cleared of suspicion in Bradley's operation. It had been nice of him to see to that in the midst of his problems. She would not have expected it of him; possibly, he had cared a little about her, after all. Maybe he had proposed simply because he needed an accountant, as she'd thought once or twice, one who could not be required to testify against him.

Looking back, she knew she'd accepted his proposal because she had given up on love. She'd stopped expecting to find a man she could care about with all her heart, one who would love her in return on the level they wrote about in the kind of books that the maid Etta read.

She had actually accepted that love like that was a myth. It wasn't. She knew that now, for what good it did her.

Tears rose to blur her vision. She wiped them away with a quick, almost furtive gesture. She would not cry anymore. No, she wouldn't. She would shower and get dressed, then pack up and go home. If the police wanted anything more from her, they knew where to find her. There was nothing left for her here except memories—memories that were only another reason to go.

Gina was slipping her cosmetics into her suitcase when the doorbell chimed again. It was Etta, pushing a wheeled serving table before her.

"Just as I thought," the maid said as she caught sight of the bag on the bed. "I told Tyrone you would be packin' to get out of here. I feel so bad, you havin' such a terrible time of it, like I should have taken better care of you, done something to make things turn out right."

"You know Race is gone," Gina said without real surprise.

"Saw him leavin' myself, early this morning. He didn't look proud to be goin', I can tell you that. Truth is, seemed he had the weight of the world on his shoulders." Etta rolled the table in front of the sitting room windows and whisked aside the cloth that draped it. "Anyway, I know you didn't have any breakfast, so I brought you a little lunch, just a nice salad along with a little piece of roasted chicken and a tad of cheesecake."

"That's very kind of you, but I'm honestly not hungry."

"I know, I know, but you'll feel better after you've had a bite to eat. I promise you will."

"No, really—"

"Please. Just try it. Let us do this little thing to make up for everything, especially that commotion next door this morning. I think you knew Mr. Dillman, didn't you?"

Gina gave a resigned nod as she moved to seat herself at the table. That response, minor as it might have been, was enough for Etta.

"I thought so. You must be upset about him being arrested and all, then. 'Course the hotel is tryin' to keep it quiet. But as Tyrone said, the police had to catch him while he was in Texas since he was doing most of his criminal stuff here. Reckon as how we should be honored."

It was an aspect Gina had not considered. She said slowly, "I see what you mean."

Etta directed a shrewd glance her way, one that lingered sympathetically on her red-rimmed eyes. "Must have been excitin', being in the middle of everything. Still and all, I imagine it wasn't exactly what you expected."

"Not exactly." The admission was wry.

"No, well, anyway, we don't want you to go away with a bad impression of the Glass Garden Hotel. We sure hope you come back again sometime, maybe use the suite the way it was meant."

On a ragged laugh Gina said, "I don't think it's very likely."

"No?" The glance Etta gave her was wise. "I'd say there was nothing more likely in the world, honey. Women like you don't get left behind. That man of yours will be back, you just wait and see."

"I'm not so sure I want him back."

"Now, don't say that; he'll have a good reason for what he did. And when he tells it to you, you'll want to cut him some slack if you care at all about him. The golden rule of loving, you know, is always believing that the one you care about means the best by you."

"What if you're wrong?" Gina said in subdued tones.

"Well, it's like this," Etta said, with one hand on her hip. "If you lose a man because you thought the best but were all wrong, then that's his fault. If you lose him because you thought the very worst and were wrong, then that's yours. And there's nothing so sad as missing out on love for lack of a little faith."

"I just don't know," Gina said without looking at the maid.

Etta gave her a bright smile. "I do. You'll do right when the time comes, you just mark my words."

Etta was right about one thing at least—eating did make Gina feel some small bit better. Afterward, the four-hour drive back to Shreveport that lay ahead of her no longer seemed quite such an ordeal.

Gina was ready to go at last; all she needed was to call for a bellman. She was reaching for the phone when it rang under her hand. She jumped and snatched her hand back, reluctant to answer. Only the thought that it might be the police with some further question made her pick up the receiver.

The voice on the other end came through loud and clear and familiar. Diane, only Diane. Gina let out a breath she had not realized she was holding.

"Gina? Is that you?" Her friend's voice was taut with concern. "Thank God I caught you; I was so afraid I wouldn't."

"I decided this morning to come on home, and was just getting ready to check out," Gina said quickly. "I'll see you in a few hours."

"No, no, I'm downstairs. Do you mind if I come up? There's something I've got to show you."

"You mean you're here at the hotel?"

"In the flesh," Diane said with amusement, apparently over Gina's blank tone. "I'll be there in a minute."

As the phone went dead, Gina replaced the receiver. What in the world was Diane doing in Dallas? More than that, what was so important it couldn't have waited until she got home?

There was not a lot of time to wonder. It seemed to Gina that she had hardly turned from the phone before her friend was at the door.

Diane was breathless from haste as she stepped into the suite. With her was a young, towheaded boy. She ushered him in ahead of her with one hand in the middle of his back, while under her other arm she carried a small-screen TV.

"Corey!" Gina said with quick pleasure as she reached to give the child a hug. "I didn't know you were here, too."

"We rode forever and ever," Diane's son said as he walked on ahead of them into the sitting room, taking in the wonders of the suite with his bright, intelligent gaze. He stopped, then turned with his hands behind his back. "Miss Gina, am I in trouble?"

"I don't think so," she answered, smiling a little at his solemnity even as she lifted a brow in Diane's direction.

"Wait before you answer," his mother said. "You might want to look at what I've got here first."

The television under her arm was Corey's set with its

built-in VCR, which he used to play his cartoon movies. Diane set it up with quick efficiency, then pushed a tape into the opening under the screen. Within seconds the title and music of a cartoon began to play, unreeling *The Adventures of Jonny Quest*.

Gina sent Diane a puzzled frown. "Am I missing something? I don't get it."

"You will."

Her friend was right. Within a few seconds the cartoon on the screen vanished, replaced by what appeared to be a bad home movie. The lighting was dim, the action jerky, and the camera angle too low. The voices of the two women who sat talking at a dining room table had a hollow, indistinct sound.

An instant later Gina realized that she was looking at the inside of Diane's apartment, and the two women were Diane and herself. There, on the television screen, she was laughing a little as she talked to Diane, saying in annoyance laced with mock despair, *"What I really need, you know, is a rent-a-groom . . ."*

As the home movie played on, Corey walked quickly to sit on the wicker love seat with his knees together and his head bowed. Gina glanced at him before she turned back to the TV, transfixed by what she was seeing.

Diane said, "You remember Corey was playing with my new camcorder while we talked Saturday morning? I told him at least a dozen times to leave it alone, but you know how he is, a concentration so total only the voice of doom penetrates."

"Yes, I remember," Gina said with slow, dawning comprehension.

"Right. I was too interested in what you were saying to make him mind, and I really thought the camera was empty. Apparently he had popped in this videocassette and was recording over the cartoon. He took it out later and never said a word, the little fink."

Corey turned liquid blue eyes in their direction. His voice small, he said, "I just wanted to make the camera work."

"I know, sweetie," his mother said. "It was my fault for not paying more attention." Diane crossed her arms over her chest as she looked back at Gina. "Anyway, I think I've mentioned my brother who lives out here? Well, he came to see me in Shreveport later in the morning, after you left. I found him on my doorstep when I came back from the supermarket."

"You're saying that—" Gina stopped, unable to go on.

Diane inclined her head in a short nod. "While I was putting the groceries away and making a quick lunch, my brother and Corey were busy in the living room. Apparently, Corey put this tape on for him. My brother left as soon as he downed his lunch, saying something about chores on the ranch he had to get out of the way before a special meeting. I thought at the time that his visit had hardly been worth his long drive both ways."

"Uncle Rory said you were gorgeous, Miss Gina," Corey piped up. "He rewound the tape three whole times just to watch you. And he said he'd sure like to meet Mama's neighbor."

A frown pleated the skin between Gina's eyes. "But what does this have to do with me being here?"

"Watch this part," Diane instructed. "It's where you say you refuse to give Bradley Dillman the satisfaction of using the honeymoon suite, then I tell you what a phony the man is, how I never liked him, and how much better off you are without him. I think that's what did it."

"I'm not sure I understand." But she was afraid she did.

"Yeah, well, when Rory isn't out on the ranch, he spends a good bit of time in Austin as a special adviser to the governor on farm and ranch issues. Here lately, though, he's been closely involved with the governor's task force against organized crime."

"A politician, I think you told me once."

"In a manner of speaking. It isn't a career; he just helps out when he's needed. He works best behind the scenes since he doesn't much care for the limelight."

It made a terrible kind of sense as Gina thought of it: a task force against organized crime, and an arrest for money laundering. Her job as Bradley's accountant, and a need for information to convict him. A man who had seen her mention a rent-a-groom, and a card that said Rent-A-Gent.

"Why didn't you tell me when I called?" Gina asked, her voice tight.

"I didn't make the connection or I probably would have blurted it out," Diane said with a quick shake of her head.

"Oh, come on; I gave you his name, told you what he looked like!"

"My brother's name is Rory, Rory Donavan. As for the description you gave . . . now how did it go? A cross between the Sundance Kid and the angel Gabriel? Sisters don't usually think of brothers in anything like those terms, believe me. But then Rory called at the crack of dawn this morning. I got this tape out and watched it. And here I am."

On the television screen the home movie came to an end and the cartoon tape picked up again. Jonny Quest was talking with great excitement to a good-looking hero type with silver-blond hair, telling him something about a diving bell being used by the boy's father, Dr. Quest. Even before Jonny called the man by name, Gina knew. She had watched Jonny Quest cartoons herself when she was Corey's age.

Jonny Quest's companion, like Corey's uncle, was an undercover man of sorts. And his name was, and always had been, Race. Race Bannister.

Race had not been hired by Bradley.

Race was not an escort.

There was not and never had been a real Race Bannister.

Diane's brother was the Rent-A-Gent.

Chapter Ten

"He's waiting downstairs."

Gina brought her head up to stare at Diane as if she had grown horns. "Race—I mean, your brother?"

"He asked me to come and show you this tape, insisted on it, in fact. He wanted you to know just how this whole thing started. If you don't want to see him, he won't push it, but he really would like a chance to explain the rest.''

Panic surged through Gina. She couldn't face Race—Rory—whatever his name was. It was one thing to suspect she had been tricked by him, but something else to know it for a certainty.

She felt so ridiculous for being taken in by him and his cartoon alter ego, and for allowing herself to be used to get at Bradley. Knowing that Diane's brother had taken his hoax to its ultimate length made her feel hot all over with shame. The last thing she needed was a reminder of exactly how and why she had fallen for his line. Or for him.

''No,'' she said in compressed tones. ''I don't think so.''

''Oh, Gina, you should see him for at least a minute. He feels like such a heel. You have no idea!''

''He should.''

''All he was doing was his job,'' Diane protested. ''And look what he did for you, how he shielded you. You could have been arrested with Bradley, you know, if Rory hadn't vouched for your innocence.''

So, it was Rory who had cleared her of wrongdoing, not Bradley. Actually, that was more logical, Gina realized; she might have known Bradley was not so altruistic. She said, ''I can't help that, and anyway, it makes no difference. Your brother and I have nothing more to say to each other.''

''You may not, but Rory has a few things to tell you.''

''Why should I listen? If I remember right, you warned me against him yourself that second time I phoned you.''

''I was afraid you might get hurt, I'll admit it. Rory has always been so single-minded about what he's doing, besides being wary of women who go ape over his looks and his money. I knew you were different, but couldn't be sure he would see it. But he did, he does. What can it hurt to give him a chance?''

Give him a chance. Etta had said she should want to do that, but Gina didn't, she couldn't. She was too embarrassed and humiliated. More than that, the possibility that he might discover how she felt about him was just too great to risk.

She had tried living dangerously, and look where it had gotten her. She had no heart to try it again.

Corey, watching them with close attention, got up from the love seat and came to stand in front of Gina. Looking up into her face in serious concentration, he said, "Don't you like Uncle Rory, Miss Gina?"

How could she explain it to a small boy when she wasn't sure she could sort out for herself the morass of fear and anger, aching need and pride that shifted inside her? "Not exactly."

"He wanted you to. He said he would try hard to make you like him."

Gina smiled a little, touching the boy's head, smoothing his hair with her fingers in an effort to soothe his worry. "Your uncle Rory did a good job; I did like him. But sometimes people do things that hurt other people's feelings."

"I know, and they have to say they're sorry. Then it's all right."

"Yes, but it doesn't always work."

Concern made wrinkles in his small brow. "Not even if they promise not to do it again? Not even when they kiss and make up?"

A firm footstep came from behind them. Hard on it came a low, masculine voice. "Great idea, sport. I think I can handle it from here."

Gina swung with a gasp to see Race—no, Rory—standing in the opening from the foyer. In tones that creaked with strain, she demanded, "How did you get in here?"

"Etta," he answered, holding up a pass key. "I got restless and threw myself on her mercy. You were taking too long."

"Come on, Corey," Diane said to her son. "I think this is where we make ourselves scarce."

"But I want to see them kiss and make—"

"Later, young man, say when you're about twenty years older." As Diane hustled her son out, she smiled over her shoulder at Gina and her brother. " 'Bye, guys."

The silence became stifling the instant the door closed behind the pair. Gina's lips tightened. She ignored Rory Donavan as she swung away, moving into the bedroom, where she closed her suitcase and locked it. Lifting it off the luggage rest, she set it beside the door. Her purse lay on a chair, and she reached for it and slid the strap onto her shoulder. Walking into the bathroom, she made a last check, then returned to the bedroom. She had everything. It was time to go.

Rory had come to stand in the bedroom doorway. His voice quietly implacable, he said, "You aren't leaving."

"No?" She barely glanced at him. "What makes you think so?"

"You have to go through me."

"That can be arranged."

"Fine. Try it."

He was bigger, heavier, harder; it was clearly impossible and he knew it. The urge to hit him swept over her with such force that she slowly curled the fingers of her right hand into a fist.

"Go ahead if it will make you feel better," he said, straightening and moving toward her. "Who knows? It might even help my feelings."

She watched his advance for a wary instant. Then she whirled away from him and clasped her arms across her chest. "What do you want from me? You got what you needed; I've agreed to cooperate with the investigation against Bradley. Can't we just leave it at that?"

"What I want, not to mention what I need, has nothing to do with Dillman."

"Oh, certainly not." The words carried a sarcastic edge of disbelief.

"Not by a long shot," he answered distinctly. "I didn't show up outside your door night before last to persuade you to anything, regardless of how it turned out. What I had in mind was making absolutely certain that you weren't up to your pretty neck in turning bad money into good."

"Thank you very much for your confidence!"

"You're welcome, since I hardly knew you at the time. You were handling Dillman's bookkeeping chores. You'll have to admit it looked suspicious."

She glared at him over her shoulder. "Everything I did was open and aboveboard. I can't help it if the only information I had was from summaries of daily income and deposits that Bradley brought to the accounting office.''

"But something didn't look right to you, all the same. Am I right?"

"After Bradley and I started going out, I noticed there never seemed to be as many customers at his Shreveport pizza franchise as I expected. When I asked about cash register tapes and supply invoices, he always put me off, so I paid a surprise visit. That was two weeks before the wedding." She gave a jerky shrug. "The register tapes showed sales of eight or nine hundred dollars per day on average, but Bradley was making daily deposits of over five thousand."

"A classic case," Rory said. "So you dumped him because you wouldn't put up with it. Which is the way you are. When I figured out that last part, I decided to stick around to be sure Dillman didn't try anything funny when he realized you could convict him."

She gave a short laugh. "You were protecting me from Bradley?"

"It was possible you might need it. The main reason Bradley planned a quick marriage and a honeymoon here was because he found out you were still registered and saw it as a way to get to you in a place where no one knew you. I decided to be on hand to discourage any rough stuff, or permanent solution."

Would Bradley have harmed her? It was impossible to say. She didn't like to think so, but she was glad, suddenly, that she had not been forced to find out. She didn't, of course, have to tell Rory Donavan so.

"So that's your excuse," she said with a shake of her head that was supposed to signal disbelief.

"But not the only one," Rory said, his voice dropping to a softer note. "There was also the small matter of being totally unable to drag myself away."

"Yes, well, it was a fascinating case, I'm sure."

"With a fascinating star witness, a woman I wanted from the moment I first saw her laughing through her misery while she joked about renting a bridegroom. I figured if a husband was what you had in mind, it might as well be me."

She refused to look at him. Voice raw, she said, "So you had the honeymoon without the bother of the wedding. Fine. Now you can have a separation without going to court. All you have to do is walk out."

Swearing in exasperation, he shoved fingers through the ruffled waves of his hair, then balled them into a fist. "I'm not going anywhere until you listen to me. I swear I never meant to lay a hand on you; all I had in mind at the start was a pleasant evening ending with an apology for the joke once you were cleared. Then I saw other possibilities and—I don't know what happened. Maybe it was this special suite, maybe it was the idea of being your husband, maybe it was just—just you. What I do know is that I wouldn't have missed a single thing about the past two days, up to and including last night. The only thing I would change is what took place before I set foot in this blessed love palace. And what I did this morning."

She turned slowly to face him. Moistening her dry lips, she said, "This morning, you left."

"This morning I ran out on you," he said flatly. "I ran because I was scared to death of what you were going to say when you woke up and found out that I had lied to you. I didn't want to see your face when you knew I was a fake. And you would find out; you had to because I had given the go-ahead to arrest Dillman. Everything was bound to snowball from there."

A soft sound of wonder left her. "You couldn't accept the risk."

"I didn't dare," he agreed, his eyes dark. "I found out about all these principles you live by, and also how much you despise being given the runaround. I admire and respect that about you, but I knew too well that you had dumped one guy already because of it."

"A different guy, on different principles."

"Yes, but I wasn't much better. So I did what any sane man does when faced with overwhelming odds. I called in reinforcements."

"Diane."

"And my buddy, Corey."

She gave him a sharp look of disbelief. "You coached that child!"

There was warm affection in Rory's smile even as he shook his head. "He did it all himself. But I owe the little guy, all the same."

She could not stop the smile that tugged at her lips. Then, taking her courage in both hands, living dangerously one last time for the sake of the chance she saw glimmering somewhere between them, she said, "But you were saying—you said there was something that took place before you first got to the suite that you would change?"

"There was indeed." His smile was whimsical, yet shadowed with regret, with censure, and yes, with longing. "I'd much rather have been showing up for my honeymoon. I wish I had been married to you."

She drew a sharp breath. "But can't—you don't want—"

"I can, and I do. Or would—will, if you can ever forgive me. What I mean to say," he continued on a deep breath, "is that I'd like to have the biggest, fanciest wedding you've ever seen, a real blowout. We can rope in a dozen bridesmaids, groomsmen galore, a flower girl in one of those little white dresses, Corey as ring bearer, the whole works. Afterward, there should be a champagne reception with a cake ten feet tall, lots of food, maybe a twelve-piece orchestra, and enough confetti and bird seed to fill a washtub. You'll throw your bouquet, then we'll make our getaway in a white limousine."

He moved closer and reached to touch her cheek with his fingertips before he went on. "We'll come back here to this suite. This time we'll have a candlelight dinner on the balcony and drink our pink champagne. You'll put on that white nightgown with all the lace and thousands of buttons. And then—" He stopped abruptly, as if afraid he had said too much.

Gina, watching the rich light in the depths of his eyes, thought of Etta. What was it the maid had said? *The golden rule of loving is to always believe that the one you love has your best interests at heart.*

She did believe it, beyond all reason.

Rory's mouth set in a straight line and he threw up his hands. "All right, all right, forget it. I can see the whole idea has you about ready to attack me again. Just forget I said anything. Forget any of this ever—''

''You think I want to attack you?'' she said on a soft laugh that was not quite even. ''It's an idea, all right. Especially when I let myself think of just what you might be wearing when I put on my nightgown.''

His face went blank. He studied the sweet yet faintly wicked curves of her lips with suspicion and a definite darkening of his bronzed skin.

When he made no immediate reply, she stepped closer to place her hands on his chest, smoothing her palms along the bands of muscles covered by his soft, pima cotton shirt, seeking the throb of his heart. ''Etta told me you sleep in your briefs, but somehow that doesn't seem very romantic. Is that what you always wear?''

He shook his head, a slow gesture. Voice husky, he said, ''Not always.''

''Then just what were thinking of packing for your wedding night?'' she prompted, veiling her gaze with her lashes.

''Nothing?'' The word was hoarse with its mix of hope and despair.

''Perfect,'' she said with soft satisfaction as she slid her arms around his neck.

He dragged her hard against him, lifting her from her feet as he swung her around in a slow circle. With his face buried in the shining swath of her hair, he whispered, ''God, you had me going. I love you, love you, and will never, ever lie to you again so long as I have breath in my body.''

''You can if you have good reason,'' she said in shaken tones. ''Just as long as you don't ever leave me again.''

''Never. Not for anything, ever. I promise.''

His grasp tightened to crushing force. Gina didn't mind. Murmuring softly of her own love, she pressed into him as if flesh and blood could be blended by desire alone.

It was sometime later that she lifted her head. With love and laughter bright in her eyes, she said, ''About this honeymoon you were planning?''

''What about it?'' The words were thick and a little rough.

"I think you were going to tell me what will happen after the bit about my buttons? I should wait to find out, but I'm not sure I can. You know the part I mean. It began, 'And then . . .'"

Rory gave a laugh of gladness and triumph that echoed around the room. Gina joined him even as she buried her face in his throat.

And then.

He demonstrated.

Checkout Time

Margaret Brownley

Chapter One

She was late. Not just late, but *late*. Two hours late! Rick Matthews paced back and forth across the marble floor of the lobby of the world-renowned Glass Garden Hotel in Dallas, Texas.

He'd lived with Dana for twenty-seven out of the twenty-eight years they'd been married, and never had he known her to be on time. He had only himself to blame for rushing to meet her at noon as promised. To add insult to injury, he'd made the three-hour drive from Austin to Dallas in record time and arrived a full thirty-two minutes early. Would he ever learn?

Come to think of it, she'd even been late for their wedding, leaving him to trace a nervous path between the altar and the parking lot. He remembered the horror of thinking she'd been in an accident, or had cold feet, or that something had happened to the baby she was carrying.

Surprised—and more than a little irritated—to find himself recalling their long-ago wedding day, he swung a wide circle around the lobby, passing the three hotel restaurants. On the outside chance he might have missed her, he scanned the area, his eyes taking in anyone that resembled, however slightly, his five-foot-two, blue-eyed, blond-haired, soon-to-be ex-wife.

The Glass Garden was filled to overflowing with the lunch crowd. Tourists were busily oohing and aahing as they craned their necks to look up at the three-story glass wall overlooking the lake, brick patio, and lush, full gardens outside. High overhead, green feathery ferns spilled from white wicker baskets. One matronly woman was determined to photograph the gardens from every possible angle, while her friends busied themselves throwing coins into the fountain, and placated her constant pleas to "Say cheese" with silly grins.

Returning to the lobby, he walked past the grand staircase and ended up in front of the gift shop, where he could keep an eye on the main entrance of the hotel. Catching a glimpse of his own grim face in the shiny glass window of the shop, he realized he was more worried than angry.

What if she'd been in an accident . . . ?

He glanced at his watch. Only a few minutes had passed since the last time he'd looked, but it seemed much longer.

She hadn't been in an accident those many times she'd been late in the past. So why was he so willing to believe today was any different?

She was simply being her usual time-dyslexic self.

Of course, it was quite possible she wasn't coming. Not that he'd blame her. Neither one of them would have agreed to spend this week together had it not been for their three grown children.

Just thinking about it made his blood boil. He and Dana had been damned good parents. Not one of their kids had been in trouble with the law or gotten into drugs. So how did the kids pay them back? By employing every low-down, guilt-producing tactic in the book to get their divorcing parents to spend one last final week together, that's how!

It was a bad idea. He *knew* it was a bad idea. Even Dana agreed. Come to think of it, it was the first time the two of them had agreed on anything in two years.

The divorce would be final in a few weeks' time. Everything that needed to be said had been said more times than he cared to remember. It was time to put the past aside and move forward. Both he and Dana tried to explain this to the kids.

But did they listen? They did not!

When guilt alone failed to achieve its goal, their two sons, Brian and Sean, and their daughter Debby and her husband Steve, pleaded—*ha, begged more like it*—and otherwise pulled every underhanded trick in the book to get their own way.

What was wrong with their oldest son, Brian? Did he really think he'd get away with that threat to appear on Geraldo's "Selfish Parents and the Children Who Love Them" show? Even his only daughter turned on him, hugging him and calling him Daddy Bear the way she used to when she was a little girl. If she hadn't pulled that trick— if she hadn't been pregnant with his and Dana's first grandchild—he would have turned her request down flat.

Damned kids. He and Dana never had a chance. He couldn't believe it. They had actually agreed to spend an entire week together! They hadn't even been able to get through Christmas dinner. Hell, they couldn't talk on the telephone without an argument.

Well, at least *he* kept his promise to the children and showed up at the hotel, he thought smugly. Let her explain to the kids why *she* didn't keep hers.

He had just about decided to call it quits and drive home when he spotted Dana dashing through the brass-trimmed double doors.

She was dressed in jeans that revealed the feminine curves of her slender hips and tiny waist. Her blond hair pulled back in a ponytail, she looked almost as young and frazzled as the day they'd first met, when she'd pulled into the parking lot of their high school and driven smack into the side of his car. She'd worn jeans on that day, too. He remembered it distinctly, for that had been the day he fell in love with her.

Dana spotted Rick as soon as she ran through the doors of the hotel. It wasn't hard to do. At six-foot-four, he had a way of filling a room, even one the size of this particular lobby. He was dressed in form-fitting blue jeans, cowboy boots, and a flannel shirt the same arresting blue as his eyes.

Somehow, during the four weeks since Christmas, he'd managed to acquire a tan. This was no small feat considering the entire month of January had, so far, been overcast. She wondered if the woman with the syrupy voice who had answered his phone earlier in the week also sported an unseasonal tan. The thought irritated her; was it asking too much for a man to whom she'd been married for twenty-eight years to wait until *after* the divorce before indulging in such vacations?

Chiding herself for caring about how he spent his time, Dana readjusted her shoulder bag and gripped her fingers tight around the handle of her suitcase.

Taking a deep breath, she braced herself and marched across the lobby. The grim look on his face told her he was furious. She knew he would be.

He hated her being late, and no matter how hard she tried to be on time, she never could quite manage it. Even when she allowed extra time, something unexpected always seemed to happen at the last minute. This morning it was the red warning light on the dashboard which started to flash halfway to Dallas.

"You're late!"

His hard cold voice sent shivers down her spine. She gritted her teeth and dropped her suitcase by her side. Had he shown the least bit of concern, she would have explained about the fuel pump. Who knows? She might have even managed an apology. Not now!

"I'm here, aren't I?"

"Don't think you're doing me any favors."

"Just think," she snapped, refusing to let anything he said hurt her, "after this week, you won't have to wait for me ever again."

"What will I do with all my free time?" He picked up her suitcase and headed for the reservation desk.

She stared after him, hands on her hips. She could think of a few things he could do with his time. Being that they were in public, she bit back the urge to tell him.

Seething, she followed him and dropped her overnight case on the marble floor in front of the reception desk, next to her suitcase.

She knew this week would be a mistake. They couldn't seem to be in the same room together without snipping at each other like two angry mutts.

Trying to ignore the hard knot in her stomach, she took

a deep breath and tried to steady her nerves. Agreeing to spend this week with Rick, even for the children's sake, was not only a mistake, it bordered on masochism.

Chapter Two

Only one desk clerk was on duty, and it seemed to take forever for the man ahead of them to straighten out the problem with his bill.

"You could have checked in," Dana said irritably, keeping her voice low.

"I didn't think you were coming."

"I said I was coming, didn't I?"

"You said you'd be here two hours ago."

"May I help you?" Neither one of them noticed the man ahead of them finishing his business and leaving.

Rick stepped forward and gave his name to the pretty young woman behind the counter. The desk clerk flashed a smile that was far more dazzling than the one she'd bestowed on the previous guest.

Zeroing in on the conversation, Dana felt her last thread of control snap. "Did you say the Honeymoon Suite?" she stammered.

The woman smiled again, but this time it lacked the bright spark that she'd flashed for Rick's benefit moments earlier. "Right on the fourth floor overlooking the lake." Her gaze returned to Rick, who was immediately rewarded with another dazzling smile. "It's soooo romantic," she cooed. "Especially at night when the city lights come on."

"Miss . . ." Dana glanced at the name tag that dangled in front of the young woman's chest like the pastie of an exotic dancer, and her irritation increased. ". . . Ashlee. Would it be possible to have another room? Perhaps something less . . . something smaller."

"Another room?" The woman managed to draw her attention away from Rick long enough to type onto the keyboard of the computer.

"We promised the kids to do it their way," Rick said impatiently, keeping his voice low.

"I didn't know we would be staying in the Honeymoon Suite." Their daughter, Debby, had made the arrangements. *The conniving little . . .*

Ashlee stared at the monitor and shook her head. "I'm sorry. It's the only suite that's available for a week. Unless of course you want the Presidential Suite, in which case, I'll have to speak to the manager."

"The Honeymoon Suite will do," Rick said.

Ashlee tried to reassure Dana with a smile, though it was clear she was puzzled by Dana's objection. "You won't be sorry, Mrs. Matthews. I promise you." She handed Rick a pen. "Sign here."

Rick signed and accepted the key without a word. "Are you coming?" He was addressing Dana, but he could have just as easily been talking to a stranger. His voice sounded distant and cold, but still managed to touch some deep and needy chord inside her.

Swallowing back the lump rising in her throat, she gave a curt nod and picked up her overnight case.

A young bellman dressed in a red and gray uniform hurried to her side. "I'll take that, ma'am." He added her case to the cart and led them to the West Tower elevator.

Inside the elevator the bellman's gaze swung back and forth between her and Rick as if to measure the physical and emotional distance between them. "Where you folks from?"

"From Austin." She replied politely, glancing at the name "Chad" on his name tag. She judged him to be about the same age as their son Sean, and relaxed. This young man would surely have better things to think about than why she and Rick stood on opposite sides of the elevator.

The elevator stopped with a gentle sigh and the doors slid apart with barely a whisper.

Chad led them from the elevator down a long elegant hall that jutted to the right. The Honeymoon Suite was at the end of the hall, next to the Diamond Suite. Their footsteps were muffled by the plush red carpet.

"You chose a good week to stay here," he said cheerfully. "You'll practically have this whole tower to yourselves for a day or two. January tends to be a slow month.

I guess folks are still recovering from the holidays. Starting next week, we're booked solid for the rest of the year."

Dana glanced at each door they passed, reading the bronze name plates centered beneath each peephole. She would have preferred to stay in any other room. The Ruby Suite, perhaps. Or the Emerald Suite.

The management had given their daughter and son-in-law a complimentary week at the hotel as a goodwill gesture. During a recent stay, Debby's wedding ring had disappeared, and Debby was positive it had been taken from her room. Devastated by the loss, she still hadn't cashed in the check from the insurance company. Nor had she let her husband, Steve, buy her a new ring. "It wouldn't be the same," she'd said.

Debby couldn't even bring herself to return to the "scene of the crime," so to speak, and had insisted that her mother and father make use of the hotel's generosity. It seemed to Dana that lately her brood subscribed to the "Why be miserable when you can make your parents miserable?" philosophy.

Scowling as she recalled how she'd been manipulated into spending this week with Rick, Dana glanced at her soon-to-be ex-husband and returned his murderous look with one of her own. If looks could kill, the Honeymoon Suite was about to become the scene of yet another crime.

Chad inserted a brass key into the ornate lock, pushed the door open with an exaggerated flourish, and flipped on the switch. A star-shaped light cast a warm glow upon an elegant foyer filled with potted plants and graceful statues.

The young bellman gave Rick a knowing grin. "Whenever you're ready."

Rick looked perplexed. "I'm sorry . . . ?"

"Don't feel shy. We're used to seeing our guests carry their brides over the threshold. I get a charge out of watching some of the old folks trying it."

Dana regarded the bellman with the same parental-type disapproval she'd recently shown her own offspring. *Old folks indeed!* Surely this young . . . whippersnapper wasn't suggesting that she and Rick . . . She chanced a glance at Rick.

He still maintained a strong, lean physique. There was no question in her mind that Rick could carry her across that threshold with ease, if he wanted to. Not that she would let him, of course.

"I wouldn't want to hurt my . . . Mr. Matthew's back," Dana explained.

"There's nothing wrong with my back," Rick said, looking indignant. As if to prove it, he surprised her by suddenly wrapping one arm around her shoulder and slipping the other arm around her knees, then swooping her off the floor. Before she could protest, he eased her through the foyer and carried her all the way to the elegantly furnished sitting room. Without further ado he stood her upright by the glass-topped dining table. He couldn't have been less emotionally involved had she been a sack of potatoes.

Even so, the impact to her own senses was akin to being overwhelmed by a tidal wave. He was right; there was nothing wrong with his back. Nor was there anything wrong with the powerful arms he'd wrapped around her or the crushing hardness of his chest.

She hated knowing that Rick could still affect her physically, if not emotionally. Not that it meant anything, of course. She wasn't exactly over the hill. She was still interested in romance and sex, and it had been a long time since she and Rick had been intimate or even shared the same bed. A very long time.

Feeling somewhat shaken, she walked to the French doors and stepped onto the balcony that overlooked Glass Lake and the lovely, tranquil gardens. Were it not for the rise of skyscrapers in the distance, it would have been hard to believe they were so close to the city.

It was a cool day. Big fluffy clouds skimmed across a deep blue sky, but the sun was bright and the recent rain had left everything clear and sparkling. She leaned over the railing and took a much needed breath of air before turning back to the suite.

The bellman had left by the time she stepped inside. The room suddenly seemed small and intimate, not because of any structural design, but because Rick always seemed to fill to capacity any room he entered.

She tore her gaze away from him and concentrated on the gas fire blazing warmly beneath the marble mantelpiece.

A bottle of champagne was chilling on the glass coffee table. Tiny orange flames danced lazily upon the polished silver surface of the ice bucket.

"Dom Pérignon," Rick said. He picked up a tiny envelope and read the card inside. "Love, your adoring children."

Dana groaned inwardly. All three of their children were trying to make ends meet. Dom Pérignon was not in their budgets.

She felt the worst possible case of maternal guilt wash over her. With the guilt came resentment. She'd never been one to interfere in her children's lives. Why did they insist upon trying to interfere with hers?

Rick popped the cork and poured the champagne into two crystal flutes he'd retrieved from the wet bar, with the same sense of purpose he used to pour oil into the engine of a car. Leave it to Rick.

He handed her a glass. "Is something wrong?"

"No. Yes. I don't want to do this, Rick. What's the point? Why give the children false hope?"

"It's only for a week." He took a swallow of his champagne and grimaced. "We put up with each other for twenty-eight years. I don't suppose another couple of days will hurt." He placed his champagne on the table and walked down the short hall leading to the sunken bedroom.

Stunned and hurt by his words, she lowered herself onto the white wicker love seat and stared into the blazing hot fire. Put up with each other? Is that what he thought of their marriage?

Had she been fooling herself all these years? Thinking they had a happy marriage, when Rick thought otherwise? Was it possible that their problems had begun *before* Rick had lost his job? Had she simply been too blind or too self-absorbed or too complacent to notice? It was a devastating thought and one that shook her to the core.

Dana took a sip of the champagne, but for all the satisfaction she derived, she might as well have been drinking city water.

She set her glass on the table just as the phone rang. It was Debby, sounding cheerful and breathless.

It was the breathless part that concerned Dana. "Is the baby . . . ?"

A moment's silence greeted her. "What?"

"Is the baby coming?" Dana asked.

"Mother, don't be ridiculous. The baby isn't due for another couple of weeks."

Dana breathed a sigh of relief. "Well, you never can tell."

"I'm fine, Mom, honest. Steve insists that I take it easy."

"I hope you're listening to him."

"Of course I am. I called to see how you like the room. Isn't that the most gorgeous room you've ever seen in your life?"

Dana scanned the room. The floral wallpaper, white wicker furniture, and lush green plants worked together to create the elegant charm of a Victorian garden. The rose and greens of the Aubusson carpet were repeated in the cushions adorning the wicker furniture. Moss-green draperies trimmed in rose framed the floor-to-ceiling windows in brocaded folds. "It's beautiful," she said, trying to sound enthusiastic. Her gaze lingered on the leather-bound old books that filled the recessed bookshelves on either side of the fireplace.

"And what about the champagne? Was it on ice like we requested?"

"I'm . . . we're drinking it now," Dana said. "But you really shouldn't have. . . ."

"Of course we should have!" Debby exclaimed. "Say hello to Etta for me."

"Etta?"

"The maid. You remember, the one I told you about who looks like Betty White? She really went out of her way to help after my wedding ring was stolen."

"Yes . . . well, Debby, I don't want you and your brothers to get your hopes up. My marriage to your father really is over and—"

"I've got to run, Mom," Debby said abruptly. "I just wanted to know that you and Dad arrived safely."

"Wait, Debby . . . we need to talk—" She stopped at the sound of the dial tone. *Of all the spoiled, ungrateful* . . .

Slamming down the phone, she glanced at her wristwatch. It was only three in the afternoon. What in the world were she and Rick going to do for the remainder of the day, let alone the rest of the week?

She glanced down the hall leading to the bedroom and felt her already taut nerves stretch beyond endurance. They were in the honeymoon suite. She was willing to bet that the regal Victorian-style canopied bed that commanded the entire width of the bedroom's double doors was the one and *only* bed.

Chapter Three

Rick finished unpacking his few belongings. His one suit looked lost in the oversized closet. Lord, what honeymoon couple would need such a gigantic closet? The king-sized bed would probably fit inside with room to spare.

The bed. It was difficult, if not altogether impossible, to ignore the bed, centered as it was in front of a full-mirrored wall. Even without the mirrored wall it was an impressive bed, with its gilt swags and black lacquered head- and footboard decorated with painted pink roses. He'd never seen such an impressive bed.

He hadn't thought about sleeping arrangements. His main concern was how he and Dana were going to get through the days without killing each other. He hadn't thought about the nights.

Fortunately, the bed was large enough for an army. Certainly, two reasonably mature adults could share it without getting in each other's way.

No sooner had Rick made this determination when he recalled the moment he carried Dana over the threshold. It had been a long time since he'd held her in his arms. She still felt as light as the day he married her.

A movement in the mirrored wall startled him out of his

reverie. At first glance Rick thought he'd traveled back in time.

Dana stood behind him, looking as young and uncertain as she had those many years ago on their wedding night. He never had figured out why the very act of marriage made them feel shy and unsure in each other's presence. But that's how he'd felt, and it hadn't been hard to determine that she'd felt much the same way.

Dana had kept him waiting long enough that night. It took her over two hours to get ready for bed. He finally had to pound on the bathroom door and demand that she make her presence known.

He would never forget the sight that greeted him when the door finally opened. She looked breathtakingly beautiful in a white negligee that floated around her lovely body in a silky white mist.

He remembered the futility of trying to get her to relax when his own nerves were tighter than a rubber band. But once they finally settled down and he had lovingly disrobed her, all the guilt and awkwardness that had been part of their earlier encounters in the backseat of his car disappeared, and it felt as if making love to each other fulfilled the very purpose of their lives.

He recalled that night so clearly, and all the wonderful nights that followed through the years; the countless nights they ripped each other's clothes off while in the throes of heated passion. The nights and even days when desire expressed itself more tenderly, but no less meaningfully. The other times, those cherished moments—not many, but some—when a tender kiss was all that was necessary.

He wondered if her memories of their love life were as sweet as his own.

He turned, not to ask her aloud, but to see if he could find the answer by looking directly at her.

He was momentarily shocked by the look of hostility and resentment on her face. Had she slapped him, he couldn't have stunned him more.

Dear God, don't let her be thinking about our first night together as a married couple—or any of the nights that followed. Her eyes were too hard, her face too grim. Maybe he was being an old fool, maybe he was being selfish, but he desperately wanted her to remember the good years they had spent together in the same warm way he remembered them.

Why didn't she? He watched her flip open her suitcase, and felt his already low spirits drop. Her every movement made it perfectly clear how much she hated being in this room with him—how bitter her own memories were in comparison to his own.

He wanted to take her by the arms and shake her. Make her admit, if only to herself, how good their marriage had been.

It had been a good marriage, dammit! Just because things went bad at the end was no reason to deny the rest.

"I'm going down to the lobby to get a newspaper." His voice was hoarse, coming from a part of him that was still affected by her. With a little luck and a lot of willpower, that part would no longer exist by the end of the week. Not if he could help it.

Dana stood in place long after Rick had stormed out of the suite. She felt as if someone had taken her heart and stomped on it. He'd hurt her deeply in the sitting room, and before she'd had time to recover, she'd walked into the bedroom, only to be hit with the memory of their wedding night. . . .

Why, oh, why did she have to think about that night, now, of all times, when she needed to keep her mind clear?

She knew why. It was because when she caught his face reflected in the mirror, he had looked so youthful and strong and vulnerable—just as he'd looked on the first night of their honeymoon. And she had been so tempted—so utterly and mindlessly tempted—to go to him, just as she had on that night.

Fortunately, she stopped short of making a fool of herself. Clenching her fists, she vowed he would never touch her again, not emotionally. Not physically. Not in any way.

"Lara's Theme" filled the air, and it took her a moment to realize the chiming tune was the doorbell. Thinking Rick had forgotten his key, Dana ran shoeless through the foyer, the marble cold beneath her feet. She opened the door and knew immediately from Debby's description that the clear blue eyes that stared at her from a friendly round face belonged to Etta, the maid.

"You must be Miz Matthews," the woman said in her Texas drawl. "Welcome to the Glass Garden Hotel. I brought y'all some spare towels."

"Thank you." Dana stepped aside to let Etta in.

"It's my pleasure to make certain everything's as it should be," Etta explained, seeming in no hurry to place the towels in the bathroom. She straightened a pillow on the love seat in front of the fireplace and stopped to fiddle with a lampshade.

"My daughter sends her regards. I don't know if you remember her. Her name's Debby Tobias. She and her husband—"

Etta's face lit up. "Tobias. My word. You're that sweet little thing's mother? What do you know! They spent their annivers'ry right here in this very room. Never saw a young man eat so much. Kept the kitchen staff busy and made a real hit with the chef. Nice couple. Yes, I can see the resemblance . . . the eyes. You and your little girl have the same pretty blue eyes."

"Debby's expecting their first child."

"Now ain't that nice. Your first grandchild, is it?"

"Yes, it is."

"You're gonna make a real nice gramma." She patted the oversized pockets of her frilly white apron as she ambled to the bathroom. She reappeared a moment later with a feather duster in hand, which she flicked around the frame of a Monet print.

"What a pity. About your girl's weddin' ring. I've worked here for ten years, and that was the first time anything like that happened."

"Debby is still upset."

"And who can blame her?" Etta shook her head. "We searched high and low. I organized the search myself."

"She's pretty certain it was stolen."

The maid looked doubtful. "Well now, honey, y'all lock up real tight. Just on general principles. You folks live far from here?"

"I . . . we live in Austin."

If Etta caught the slip of the tongue, she gave no indication. "I've had lots of nice couples from Austin stay in my room."

"Your room?"

"The Honeymoon Suite." The woman's face beamed with pride as she glanced around. "This is my special room. Take care of it myself, personally. Have for ten years. My word, they'll have to carry me out feet first to get rid'a me."

"It's a beautiful suite," Dana said. "And that's a beautiful necklace you're wearing."

Etta touched the heart-shaped pendent with her fingers. "I got a real weakness for heart-shaped jewelry. Most of it came from couples who've stayed in this room. You folks here for any special occasion?"

"Not really," Dana said slowly. It seemed easier to lie than to admit they were celebrating, if that was the right word, the end of a marriage. "The hotel was kind enough to give Debby a week's stay, along with the insurance settlement, to make up for the loss of her ring. She and her husband insisted that we use the week." *Bullied was more like it.*

"That's real nice. How long you folks been married?"

It was a simple question, one that should have been easy to answer. "T-Twenty . . . eight years."

"Twenty-eight years." Etta nodded knowingly. "That's one of those tricky milestones."

"Tricky?"

"You know what I mean. It's like the seven-year-itch. Somewhere around twenty-eight years, couples have to get used to each other all over again. Kids leave home. Things just sorta change."

Dana swallowed hard. She thought she'd been ready for those changes. She and Rick had talked about finally taking that European vacation, and maybe buying a motor home and touring the country. A lump rose in her throat as she thought of the many cherished dreams that died along with the marriage. Nothing seemed to survive a divorce. Not the past; not the future. "How . . . how do you know so much about marriage?" *And why, oh, why did I have to become an expert on divorce?*

"Why, honey, I read." Etta pulled out a paperback book from the deep pocket of her apron and held it up for Dana to see. It was a romance called *Silver Hearts.* "The couple's last child left home, and suddenly they had nothin' to talk about," Etta explained. "For twenty-some years they've related to each other as parents. Then, wham! They have to talk to each other as people."

"I suppose that can be a problem for some couples," Dana agreed. *But not for Rick and Me. We never lost sight of each other as individuals.*

Etta slipped the novel back into her pocket and swiped the coffee table with the feather duster. "Number twenty-eight is one of the tricky ones, all right." She shuffled toward the door just as Rick walked into the room.

"And this must be Mr. Matthews. I'm Etta. If you need anything, just holler."

Etta left and a moment's awkward silence stretched across the room as Dana tried to think of something to say to break the tension. "I haven't eaten since breakfast. Have you?"

"Not a thing." He glanced at his watch. "We can go down to the Crystal Room Tavern and get a bite to eat."

"That's a good idea. I . . . just have to finish unpacking."

"Take your time."

Rick sat down and opened the newspaper to the classified section. Dana recalled the years she had watched him turn first thing each morning to the sports page. But that was before he lost his job. Now the only part of the newspaper that seemed to exist for him was the classified section.

She walked into the bedroom, pulled her dress out of the suitcase and hung it on a coat hanger next to the white terry-cloth robes provided by the hotel. The robes served as a divider between her one dress and Rick's single suit.

It took only a matter of moments to stack her assortment of sweats and jeans into one of the large bureau drawers.

She returned to the sitting room to find Rick holding an enormous arrangement of brightly colored exotic flowers, the expensive kind that grow in Hawaii.

"Oh, Rick, they're beautiful!" she exclaimed. She couldn't remember the last time he gave her flowers. He was much more inclined to give her something more practical.

"They just came," he said. "Who do you suppose sent them?"

"I . . . can't imagine." She tried not to let her disappointment show. How foolish of her to think they might possibly have come from Rick. "Don't tell me. The kids again. First Dom Pérignon, and now this." She bit her lower lip to keep from prattling, as was her habit when she was trying to hide her feelings.

Rick set the flowers on the table and plucked the little white envelope from the center. "It's addressed to you."

"Me?" She took the envelope from him and pulled out the tiny card. *Thinking about you, Love Alex,* she read in silence. Alex was an attorney in the law firm where she worked as a receptionist. She and Alex had gone out to dinner on occasion, but she wasn't ready for anything more and she'd been honest about her feelings. But lately he was beginning to push for more, and had even gone so far as to invite her to go on a cruise with him. He accepted her rejection like a perfect gentleman. She only wished he'd been half as gracious upon learning she was going to spend the week with her soon-to-be ex-husband. The flowers were obviously meant as an apology.

Feeling Rick's curious gaze on her, she shoved the card back into its envelope.

"Aren't you going to tell me who sent the flowers?"

"They're . . . from a friend."

A muscle tightened at his jaw. "A friend?"

"Actually, they're from Alex." What was the point of being evasive? She had nothing to hide. "You remember Alex, don't you? He's one of the attorneys at the law firm?"

"The short balding one?"

"He's not short."

Rick watched her turn the arrangement to best advantage. "Is there something going on between you and this Alex?"

She straightened. "I'm not sure yet."

"What does that mean? You're not sure?"

"It means that I, at least, have the decency to wait until *after* the divorce is final before I become involved in another relationship."

"I would say by the looks of those flowers, you're very involved."

"How would you know? The last time you gave me flowers was . . . oh, never mind!" She grabbed her purse and started for the door. She wasn't about to get roped into another argument.

"Wait a minute." Rick grabbed her by the arm. "Are you saying that I never gave you flowers?"

"You gave me flowers. Once."

"Once?"

"Maybe twice. You were never . . . that romantic."

He looked offended or shocked, possibly both. Why he should take offense or be surprised, she couldn't imagine. It was the truth.

"I think I'm very romantic."

She almost laughed out loud, but managed to hold back. Barely. "You think you're . . . Is that why you proposed to me on the side of a busy highway while changing a flat tire? Because you're so romantic?"

"If you didn't like the way I proposed, then why did you marry me?"

"Because I—" She bit back the words *loved you*. It surprised her that the pain was still so close to the surface. Twenty-eight years had passed since that long-ago day. For the most part they had been good years. Still, the pain existed, even now, after all this time. "I've changed my mind. I don't feel like lunch. I think I'll lie down for a while."

Rick looked about to say something. Instead he grabbed his newspaper and stomped out of the suite.

Chapter Four

"How do you want to handle the sleeping arrangements?" Dana asked. The question seemed to hang in the air as if caught by a relentless current of wind. It was a question she had postponed asking or even thinking about for as long as possible. But it was getting late and she was tired.

Rick gave a careless shrug, as if the matter was of little or no consequence. He sat in front of the fire, his stockinged feet propped up on the coffee table. He had spent most of the afternoon reading a magazine on classic cars. Refurbishing old cars was a hobby of his or had been before he'd lost his job. "Do what you want."

She hesitated. What she wanted to do was forget this week and go home. "I'll take the bedroom, and you can take . . ."

She glanced at the inadequately sized furniture that filled the sitting room. The love seats. The cozy chairs. Everything was scaled to promote intimacy between couples. Not one stick of furniture would adequately accommodate her own reclining body, let alone Rick's.

"We could ask for a cot," she offered.

"We could do that," he said coolly. "I'm sure it would be a first for the Honeymoon Suite."

He was probably right. She could well imagine Etta or Chad's disapproving face if either one of them had to cart a cot up to their room. "You take the bed. I'll curl up . . ." She glanced around. ". . . on the love seat."

"We'll both take the bed."

"I don't think that would be a good idea. . . ." They hadn't slept in the same bed for nearly a year.

"Are you afraid of what might happen if we shared a bed?"

"Nothing will happen," she said firmly.

"You got that right. So what's the problem?"

She swallowed hard. The problem was that she was still feeling the aftershocks of being in his arms earlier. It had been nearly a year since they'd been intimate, and he was still the most attractive man she knew. He was also the most conceited, judging by the challenging look he gave her.

"There's no problem," she said. She would die rather than let him know she had any doubts to the contrary. "If you stay on your *own* side."

"I never go where I'm not wanted."

She could argue the point, but she wouldn't. Not tonight. Not ever. They had done their arguing. It was time to put the past behind them and get on with their lives. If nothing else came out of this week together, maybe some sort of closure would.

The phone rang and Rick's face grew dark. "Do you suppose it's your attorney friend?"

"He wouldn't call."

"Why not? He sent flowers. I'm surprised he hasn't joined us."

Glaring at him, she picked up the phone, this time the fancy gold and white French telephone on the wet bar. So far she'd counted six phones in the suite.

It was her eldest son, Brian, the traitorous one. The one who had taken her aside after she'd refused to spend the week with Rick and pleaded with her to "Do this one thing for me, Mom. Please." He better be enjoying this because it was the last thing she ever intended to do for him!

No sooner had she finished talking to Brian than Sean's wife, Abby, called, followed by Rick's mother, and their son-in-law, Steve.

By the time she hung up from the last call, Dana was so weary of trying to explain to everyone why spending the week with Rick was not going to work, she was almost ready to scream.

What she needed was a bath and a good night's sleep. She walked into the bathroom and switched on the light. The bathroom was clearly designed for lovers. The oversized pink marble Jacuzzi tub stood on a platform surrounded by three steps.

Scented bath oils were lined up on a glass shelf. She read the labels on the colorful bottles and chose the one marked Purple Passion. She hadn't felt anything remotely like passion for so long, she was curious about the fragrance of this particular bath oil. She unscrewed the purple cap, took a sniff and laughed aloud. The scented bath oil smelled like citrus.

Considering her sour disposition, it seemed appropriate. She dumped the entire contents of the bottle into the soft churning water. It was wasteful, but given her depression, necessary.

Moments later she sank into the luxurious hot water and blew the bubbles away from her chin. She was startled by the ringing of the telephone. Turning her head, she located the offensive instrument. A phone in the bathroom, for goodness' sakes.

Not wanting to be disturbed, she sank lower into the sudsy water, letting the massaging jets of water do their job. After the fourth ring, the phone fell silent. She wondered if Rick had answered it or the caller had simply hung up.

She closed her eyes. Somehow she and Rick had survived one day together. That meant there was only six more days left to endure. Six long days and six long nights . . .

How foolish of her to agree to spend this time with him. What was the point of digging up old hurts? Even thinking about happy times, like the day he proposed, brought her pain. Still, she couldn't seem to help herself.

She remembered every detail of that day as if it were yesterday. They had been en route to his parents' house for dinner. Why she chose that particular time to break the news of her pregnancy to him, she couldn't say. Maybe it was because she felt scared and very much alone. In retrospect, her fears seemed ridiculous. In today's society, no one seemed to think twice about pregnancy before marriage. But it was still a big deal in the sixties.

She and Rick had dated off and on all during high school. They hadn't gone "all the way," as they called it back then, until the day they graduated. It seemed like the world was theirs that night. Rick had just won a full scholarship to a prestigious eastern college, and she had just been accepted at Berkeley. Rick had promised to write and spend every holiday with her. It wasn't a declaration of love, exactly, but it was a commitment of sorts. To a young woman in love, it was enough. Youthful exuberance turned to passion that night—and two lives changed forever.

No sooner had she blurted out the news of her pregnancy as they drove along that country road, when, ironically enough, they blew a tire. Rick pulled the car to the side of the road. "Are you sure?" he'd asked.

"I'm sure," she said.

Without another word he climbed out of the car to change the tire. After a few minutes she joined him. She stood next to his side while he jacked the rear wheel up. "We'll get married," he announced.

"What about your scholarship?"

"Don't worry about that. I'll get a job. I can go to school at night. We'll manage." It seemed at the time that settling their future was easier than changing the tire. She supposed that was a good thing. She was too scared to seriously consider any alternative that didn't involve marriage. The truth was, she had been too young to know she even had alternatives.

Later, after they announced their engagement, her family gave a collective sigh. Everyone told her how lucky she was. Most men would have run the other way, her mother had reminded her on more occasions than she cared to remember. Her mother-in-law never did forgive her for "ruining her son's chances."

She *was* lucky, of course. Rick was a good and faithful husband and a wonderful father. Never once had he made her feel the pregnancy had been her fault or that he felt trapped into marrying her.

Still, there was the gnawing feeling that had she not been pregnant, things might have turned out differently. Rick would most definitely have graduated from that prestigious college and probably would have married someone else.

His dreams of becoming a lawyer were put on hold, as he liked to say in those early days, and after the second baby came along, were abandoned altogether. Rick was making good money in the aerodynamics field and there was plenty of chance for advancement. The industry was booming, and it never occurred to anyone that it wouldn't continue to prosper.

Mustn't think about the day Rick lost his job, she told herself, for that was the beginning of the end. She tried to concentrate instead on pleasant thoughts. Her first grandchild . . . Maybe she'd try her hand at making a baby quilt . . . perhaps sewing little pieces of fabric together for the happy occasion would help her through the remorse of her own fragmented life.

She emerged from the bathroom feeling warm and relaxed. The moment of well-being was a fleeting one. Rick was already in bed, the blanket up to his waist. This left his chest—his disgustingly firm, disgustingly youthful-looking chest—fully exposed in all its suntanned glory.

A flash of feminine approval swept through her, followed by alarm. Her reeling emotions quickly escalated to panic upon meeting his warm and seemingly penetrating gaze. Surely he wouldn't . . . he couldn't . . . Oh, dear God.

In all the years she'd lived with this man, she'd never known him to sleep in anything. He'd slept in the buff no matter what the weather; rain or snow, it made no difference. But surely under the circumstances . . .

She tore her gaze away from his and turned off the lamp on the dresser. Of course the lamps on both sides of the bed were still on, which meant there was ample light in the bedroom. More than ample.

She inhaled and took a moment to compose herself before turning toward the bed. If she made a scene or in any way looked upset, he might assume that his presence affected her in some way. Which, of course, it didn't. The unexpected feelings of awareness that she'd felt when he carried her over the threshold had been nothing more than . . . surprise.

Well, she wasn't surprised now; she was mad. All she wanted was for him to show common courtesy and wear some fricking pajamas to bed. Was that too much to ask?

It was hard to know where to look. She glanced to the right and saw the bronzed skin of his chest reflected in the glass mirrors on the closet doors. There was no getting away from it; the Honeymoon Suite was the telephone and mirror capital of the world.

Angry that he put her in such an awkward position, she decided she would not let anything he did upset her. She forced herself to look him straight in the face.

Their eyes locked for an instant before his gaze traveled down the length of her. Suddenly her flannel nightgown, bought solely for the occasion, felt every bit as unfeminine as a beer barrel. Not that she cared, of course, what she looked like. Or what he thought she looked like.

She plopped down on the edge of the mattress, her back toward him. She tried to calm her racing pulse. Just because he was bare from the waist up didn't necessarily mean he was naked all over. He was probably wearing pajama bottoms. That was it. Pajama bottoms. Wonderful, beautiful, and modest pajama bottoms.

She slipped between the covers and pulled the sheet to her chin. She normally read in bed, but she'd left her book in the other room. After a moment's consideration, she decided there was no way in hell that she was going to leave the safety of the bed. *Safety?* She almost laughed aloud at the thought. If that wasn't a paradox, she didn't know what was.

She turned on her side, facing outward. The bed *was* safe. There was at least three feet between them. All right, two.

"Good night," she said, her voice a masterpiece of cool formality. She turned off the light and lay her head on the pillow.

"Good night." If the two feet was worrisome, his voice certainly wasn't. It was colder than an icicle in a snowstorm.

She relaxed for one full minute before an annoying thought pried the cap off her carefully contained emotions. *He didn't own pajamas.*

Her heart started pounding so quickly, it felt as if the mattress came equipped with a built-in vibrator. Suddenly the two feet—or was it three?—between them seemed like mere inches. She was afraid to move, to breathe even. Angry at herself for getting all worked up about nothing, she tried forcing herself to breathe. When that didn't work, she considered the possibility that she was mistaken about the pajamas.

He could have purchased a pair sometime during the eleven months he'd lived in his own apartment. It was a comforting thought, but she didn't believe it for a moment. The man had never bought himself an article of clothing during their entire marriage. She doubted he would start at this late date.

Underwear. That was it. He had to be wearing underwear.

She was not normally the obsessive type. Tonight, she was obsessed.

It soon became clear that if she expected to get any sleep, she had better find a way to forget the naked man at her side. It became even more obvious that it would be easier to forget a rattlesnake in her bed than to forget Rick.

Maybe if she knew for sure what he was wearing. The problem was how to find out. She considered the possibilities. She could ask him outright what he was wearing. *Sure she could.*

She could also turn on the light and rip the covers off him.

It took several moments before she calmed down enough to consider yet another option; she could *accidentally* touch him.

Simple as that. Nothing to it, she told herself. Just a quick touch, mind you, nothing personal or intimate. Just an itsy-bitsy touch. If she waited until he was asleep, he'd never know.

She lay on her back and stared up at the dark ceiling. She kept herself rigid as a board as she listened to his breathing. Any moment now, he was bound to fall asleep.

Then she would know for sure.

Chapter Five

How could she sleep in that damn flannel nightgown? Rick lay ramrod straight on his back and stared at the ceiling. He tried to see something in the shifting light patterns that didn't remind him of his soon-to-be ex-wife.

The air conditioner hummed softly, but the room felt hot. Or was it just him?

For the last eleven months, one week, and two days, he'd slept on the twin bed in his bachelor apartment. No wonder he was having trouble sleeping. The reason he was afraid to move was because he was used to a narrow bed. He'd conditioned himself not to toss and turn. It had nothing to do with his bed partner. To prove it, he turned over and punched his pillow.

Satisfied, he lay his head down and shut his eyes. Almost immediately he felt himself drift off in a cloud of soft petals. His eyes flew open. What was that intriguing fragrance? Perfume? Shampoo? And what was she doing wearing it in his bed?

He flopped over on his other side, this time placing his back toward her. He could no longer smell the fragrance, but he could feel the warmth of her. He hoped to God she roasted to death in that damn flannel nightgown of hers! It would serve her bloody-well right.

Next to him, Dana continued to lay straight and rigid. She knew by all the subtle and not-so-subtle signs that he was not asleep. She was beginning to think he was never going to sleep.

And she was feeling . . . itchy. Was it possible to be allergic to flannel? She didn't think so, but then she couldn't remember the last time she'd worn flannel. Not since the separation. Not before . . . She caught herself just in time. She wasn't going think about before.

Besides, she was beginning to itch so much, it was hard to think about anything. Maybe it was prickly heat.

She pushed the blanket away. She felt cooler, but the itching grew worse. Much worse. *Agonizingly worse.*

Sitting up, she turned on the light. Rick rolled over to face her. It irritated her that he looked so calm and handsome, when she felt as if her skin was about to burn up.

"You did this on purpose," she charged. She felt so miserable, she wanted to scream. Blaming him was the next best thing. She jumped out of bed and practically pulled a bureau drawer out of its casing.

"Did what?"

"You know what!" She grabbed a T-shirt and charged into the bathroom, slamming the door behind her. She quickly pulled off her flannel gown. Her skin was red, flaming. She turned on the shower and ducked beneath the stream of soothing cool water.

After scrubbing herself with soap and water, she stepped out of the shower and dried off. She'd never suffered an allergic reaction, and had no idea what to do next. The itching was less intense, and for that she was grateful. Maybe now she could get some sleep.

She found Rick propped against the headboard, his legs drawn up beneath the sheets. He looked devilishly handsome, and this only added to her irritation.

"A cold shower?" he asked mockingly.

"It was *not* a cold shower!" she fumed. How like him to think he was so irresistible that she couldn't control herself around him. Well, she *could* control herself! Of course she could!

"You don't have to snap my head off. Now, would you mind telling me what it is I'm supposed to have done on purpose?" He looked at her closely. "What's the matter with you?"

"Nothing's the matter with me. The question is what's the matter with you? How dare you get into my bed without . . . naked?"

He looked genuinely puzzled. "I'm wearing the same thing I always wear."

She almost choked. "That's . . . that's the problem."

"I don't understand. You've never objected to my bedtime attire before."

"I think we should get one thing straight. What you are wearing is not bedtime attire. The word 'attire' means clothing, apparel." She held up her flannel nightgown.

He folded his arms across his chest. "I'm not wearing that nightgown and that's final!"

They glared at each other, she with her hands at her waist. "You could at least have the decency to cover yourself."

"I *am* covered."

"This is no time for jokes!"

"I'm not joking, Dana. Now would you mind telling me what you're so upset about?"

"You want to know why I'm upset? Well, I'll tell you! You and I are no longer living together as husband and wife. You have no right—no right at all—to get into my bed wearing . . ." She was so upset, she almost sputtered. "The only reason we are in this same room is because of the children."

"Is it because of the children that you wore that ridiculous granny gown?"

"It's not ridiculous!"

"And is that why you're now wearing that . . . that skimpy T-shirt?" His gaze dropped down the length of her legs.

The rush of hot blood to her cheeks was the final straw. Now her entire body felt like it was burning up. Rubbing her arms, she began to shake. "I think I'm allergic to flannel."

Rick sat forward, his face full of concern. "Allergic? Do you want me to take you to the emergency room?"

"That's not necessary. I'm sure I'll be all right. If only the itching would go away."

Before she could complete her sentence, Rick had jumped out of bed and was at her side. *Naked.*

Startled, her gaze froze on his long lean form, then took a daring dive down the length of his muscular chest and firm abdomen to his . . . *penis!*

The sight of him was enough to send her senses into orbit. She could barely think, let alone breathe, and neither difficulty had anything to do with her allergy. It was probably a good thing that she couldn't function; the Lord only knew what she would have done with her hands had she been able to get them to move.

Fortunately, he was too busy checking her arms to guess at her thoughts, or to notice where she had planted . . . uh, let her eyes wander.

It took her a while, but she finally found her voice. "Would you please put something on?" she hissed. In two minutes she was going to break down and cry. It was the itching, of course, and had nothing to do with Rick. Nor did it have anything to do with the sudden realization that she still found him sexy and desirable.

To his credit, he quickly donned one of the courtesy robes with the Glass Garden Hotel logo and tied it around the middle. The robe barely touched his knees, and the V-neck opening exposed more of his chest than she would have preferred, but at least a certain part of his anatomy was safely hidden.

"I have some first-aid cream here somewhere." He pawed through his belongings and held up a tube as if to display a prized trophy. "Lie on the bed and I'll rub this on you."

"That won't be necessary," she stammered. She might feel miserable from the rash, but she wasn't foolish enough to let him rub his hands up and down her body.

"Come on. It'll only take a minute, and this is guaranteed to stop the itching." Ignoring her protests, he put his arm around her shoulders and led her to the bed.

She sat on the edge of the mattress while he examined the red skin on her arms and legs.

"Looks like sunburn." His voice was soft with concern. "Are you sure your nightgown caused this?"

"What else could it be?"

He gave her a dubious look and unscrewed the cap. He put a dab of cream into the palm of his hand, then gently rubbed the soothing salve onto her burning skin.

At first his main concern was to relieve her discomfort. But no sooner had he rubbed his hand up one shapely leg, which still felt silky smooth to the touch despite the redness, when he felt a hot surge of desire race toward his groin. He hadn't felt desire like this since . . .

He jerked his hand away from her slender thigh.

She glanced up at him, her eyes soft with gratitude. "That feels so much better." She sounded unsure of herself. He decided it was because of the way he was staring at her. Or trying not to stare. Not that he could help himself . . .

"I hate to ask this of you. But my back is itching like crazy. Would you mind?"

He swallowed hard and watched helplessly as she turned her back toward him and lifted her T-shirt. He caught a glimpse of one lovely full-rounded breast and pressed his fingers hard on the tube of ointment. A stream of white lotion splattered on her back.

"Ow! That's cold!"

"Sorry," he muttered. He laid the tube on the end table and began working the cream up and down the length of her back. He'd forgotten how creamy soft her skin felt, how . . .

Clamping down on his thoughts, he pressed his fingers harder against her flesh, as if to push her away.

"Not so hard." She sat up and dropped the hem of the T-shirt.

"Sorry."

She glanced over her shoulder, and for an instant their gazes locked. Then just as quickly they looked away, she to check out the rash on her arms, he to reach for the cap to screw back on the tube of ointment.

Dana lay against the pillow and Rick covered her gently with the blanket. It was a simple kind gesture on his part, but she was nearly shattered by the many memories stirred by his action. She recalled in vivid detail all those other times he had tucked her into bed: the happy times, the loving times, the vulnerable times. Warm feelings washed over when she recollected the three separate times she had lain in a hospital bed after giving birth, and how he used to sneak into her room past visiting hours to tuck her in and kiss her good night.

His voice snapped her out of her reverie. "Try to get some sleep." He cleared the huskiness from his throat, and she couldn't help but wonder if he, too, was remembering those times.

She had her answer when he glanced at her lips, and a deep pain rose from the depths of her as yet another memory came to the fore; this was the first time he'd tucked her in bed without kissing her.

"Thank you," she whispered. She swallowed hard and fought against the stinging sensation in her eyes. She was not, absolutely not, going to cry!

"I'm going in the other room to read."

"Is . . . is everything all right?" she called after him. He sounded . . . strange.

He hesitated at the doorway, his back toward her. "Everything's fine."

He didn't read, couldn't read. He tried, but the words kept blurring together. All he could think about was the ache in his groin and the woman who put it there.

What was the matter with him? Why hadn't he been able to put his life back together? Let go of the past and move on? Why?

His buddies said he needed to get out and meet more people. What a mistake that had turned out to be. He had no idea that there were so many lonely women out there, all waiting for Mr. Right to come along to make their world perfect.

Not all women were as independent as his soon-to-be ex-wife. Marsha certainly wasn't. His friend Joe had talked him into going on a blind date with Marsha, who was described as having a knockout body. One thing to be said for Joe, he knew a body when he saw one. His failure was that he apparently never bothered to talk to his dates. If he did, he might have given more thought to a woman's intelligence.

Miss "Bod" was always showing up on his doorstep under one guise or another; once to look for an earring, another time to deliver a casserole. She had practically pleaded with him to take her along on a camping trip—citing all that stuff about how much she missed the great outdoors. "I love to sleep naked under the stars, don't you?" she cooed.

Lord, what was a man supposed to say to something like that? *No?*

What a disaster that weekend had been. He never considered himself a prude, but what other explanation could explain his lack of sexual prowess? Marsha pranced around him like a naked wood nymph, and the best he could muster was a disgusting case of fatherly tolerance. He remembered saying something totally out of character like, "You better put some clothes on before you catch your death of cold."

He had all kinds of excuses for what happened, or rather, what didn't happen that weekend. It was too soon.

The divorce wasn't final. He was getting older. To her credit, Marsha didn't take offense. She looked him square in the face and declared herself ready to try a more "mature" love. Whatever that meant.

He didn't stick around long enough to find out. Nor did he make the mistake of repeating that disastrous weekend with anyone else. If he'd lost it, he sure as hell didn't want the world to know.

He hadn't lost it. Not if tonight was any indication. The only thing that saved him from making a fool of himself was the hotel robe, and even that threatened to give his secret away, making it necessary to retreat into the next room.

He couldn't believe it; forty-eight years old, and he could still "cross the ocean without a ship," as the old saying went.

Normally, this would be a reason to celebrate. Not in this case, for now he was plagued by the possibility of another, more worrisome concern. Was it possible to be faithful to one woman for so long that having sex with anyone else was out of the question?

As unwelcome as this thought was, it was nowhere near as disconcerting as the one that followed: maybe his problem wasn't so much that those other women lacked something. Perhaps he was still hung up on Dana. How else could he explain the way she aroused him when Marsha with all her physical assets and willingness to please had failed?

Even dressed in that damned flannel thing Dana called a nightgown, she was still the sexiest woman he'd ever known.

Admitting this last truth to himself brought his thoughts to a mind-boggling, stupefying conclusion: he was a man with a full-blown case of the hots for his soon-to-be ex-wife. The question was, what the hell was he going to do about it?

Chapter Six

Dana awoke the next morning and groaned. Her head ached, her back itched, and she was in bed with Rick.

Granted, both had scrupulously respected the two-perhaps-three-feet-that-seemed-like-mere-inches between them. Still, she couldn't have been more aware of him than if he held her in his arms.

Rick rolled over and looked her over. "You need a doctor."

She sat up in bed and shook her head stubbornly. The early morning sun streamed through an opening in the draperies, and a golden ray danced upon the silver strands of his sleep-tousled hair. She recalled with a pang the many times she had run her fingers through those same disheveled locks.

He climbed out of bed and stood outlined against the window, wearing only his bathing suit. A compromise, he'd called it the previous night after donning it.

Some compromise, she thought, tracing an imaginary line around the intriguing manly bulge that jutted from between his thighs.

She couldn't seem to help herself, even now, after knowing the danger of giving in to such impulses.

He turned to lift his watch off the dresser, allowing her to study the width of his shoulders without censure. Unnerved by the realization that he still had a powerful hold on her, she threw back the covers and reached for a robe.

"Maybe the hotel will recommend a doctor," he said.

"I told you, I don't need a doctor. It's an allergy. It'll clear up in a day or two."

Rick drew the strap of his watch around his wrist, then reached for the jeans he'd tossed onto a chair the night before. "But the rash is all over your body."

"It's not *all* over," Dana said, irritably. There was no rash on her face, thank goodness.

When Rick insisted upon calling a doctor, she donned a robe and walked out to the sitting room, hoping to prevent an argument.

Rick followed her, tucking his shirt in his pants. "I don't know why you're so stubborn."

"And I don't know why you're making a federal case out of a little rash."

"What would it hurt to ask the hotel to recommend a doctor? Just in case we need one later?"

She hated when he resorted to logic.

Apparently thinking her lack of response was compliance, he disappeared through the louvered doors. After a moment his voice drifted from the foyer. Wondering whom he was talking to, Dana adjusted the robe she wore and retied the belt.

"Look who's here," Rick said, returning to the sitting room.

Etta followed him over to where Dana sat. "Mr. Matthews told me you had yourself a nasty rash."

"It's not that bad," Dana said, glaring at Rick.

Etta lifted Dana's arm and examined it. "You ever have a rash like this before?"

"Never."

"Looks like an allergy to me. Any chance you're allergic to somethin' in this room?"

"Anything's possible." *Even an allergy to a soon-to-be-ex.*

"She might be allergic to flannel," he said helpfully.

Etta looked offended. "We don't use flannel in this hotel. Everything here is first-class all the way." As if to emphasize how high those standards were, Etta leaned over the coffee table to reposition Rodin's statuette of "The Kiss."

"He was referring to my nightgown," Dana explained.

A thunderstruck expression crossed the maid's face. "You slept in a *flannel* nightgown on your honeymoon?"

She made it sound like Dana had committed some unforgivable sin. "It's not my honeymoon. It's—"

"My wife feels the cold," Rick hastened to explain.

Dana was surprised that Rick was so quick to defend her. Not that she needed defending, of course. Come to think of it, he was probably preserving his male ego. What man wanted to admit that a woman was inspired to wear flannel in his presence?

"You poor little thing." Etta patted Dana soothingly. "You could have a circulation problem. I read about such a thing once in a romance novel. The heroine was always dressed in wool, even in summer, and—"

The phone rang. Anxious to escape further scrutiny, Dana leaped up from her chair and hastened toward the bedroom to take the call in private. It was her eighty-three-year-old mother. "How did you know where to find me?"

"I talked to Debby last night. She said things are going great guns for you two."

"Don't get any ideas, Mother. Nothing has changed."

"You're spending a whole week together and you say nothing has changed?"

"We are here only because the children insisted. But it doesn't mean anything."

"Of course it means something," her mother said. "Everything we do in life means something."

"Speaking of which, how are *you* doing mother?"

"You're changing the subject."

"I've done no such thing. We're talking about life, and I'm asking you how yours is."

"Mine's fine. So when can I make the big announcement?"

Dana felt a tightness in her stomach. "What big announcement?"

"About you and Rick, of course. When can I tell my friends at canasta that the two of you have come to your senses?"

"Never, Mother."

"He's a good man, Dana. Most men would have run the other way all those years back when you told him you were—"

There she goes again. Praising Rick for marrying a poor, pregnant woman. "I've got to go, Mother. I'll call you later."

She hung up the phone and sat on the edge of the bed, glaring into space. Her mother's habit of taking every opportunity to credit Rick with unblemished virtue made her want to scream.

She curtailed the urge, but only because she could still hear Etta's cheerful voice in the sitting room. Instead she picked up the flannel nightgown where she had discarded it during the night and tossed it across the room.

She waited for Etta to leave before she walked back out to the sitting room. Rick was on the phone, ordering their breakfast through room service.

It annoyed her that he hadn't bothered to ask her what she wanted. On the other hand, there really was no reason he should. She ate the same soft boiled egg, English muffin, and fresh fruit breakfast every blessed day of her life.

"Do you think I'm boring?" she asked him after he hung up.

She hated that he seemed to take his own sweet time in answering, as if the question required consideration. "No," he said, and stepped through the French doors to the balcony.

She was sorry she'd asked. She was sorry about a lot of things.

Rick stepped to the railing, startling a pigeon. The man-made lake sparkled amid a grove of weeping willow trees. A child stood on the bank feeding the ducks. The tranquil scene made all the mixed-up feelings inside that much more difficult to bear.

Dana's voice drifted outside, and a few minutes later Chad, the bellman, rolled a cart with their breakfast onto the balcony.

Rick turned to watch the young man, who seemed to be rock-and-rolling to the sound of phantom music. "Where do you want it?" He sounded remarkably reserved, considering his body was going *yeah, yeah, yeah.*

"Right there's fine," Dana said. "That was quick."

"That's me, Fast Time Chad. Fast on the feet and . . ." His hand made a quick dart toward the bill that Rick handed him. ". . . fast on the draw." He did a fancy two-step across the balcony, then with a funny two-fingered salute disappeared through the open French doors.

Rick sat down at the table and drew a piece of paper from his shirt pocket. "Etta gave me the name of the doctor recommended by the hotel."

"I told you, I don't need a doctor. The rash is almost cleared up."

"Suit yourself." He slipped the square of paper back into his pocket.

Dana studied his grim face, wondering what had put him in such a bad mood. She handed him a steaming cup of coffee. "Maybe I'll take a walk around the lake later." It hadn't been meant as an invitation, but if he offered to join her, she would not object.

Rick grunted, but made no other comment. She should be used to the silences that had now become a habit with them. It never used to be that way. She could still remember how there never seemed to be enough time in a day to say everything they needed to say to one another. All that changed the day Rick lost his job.

Perhaps the loss of employment would have had less impact had the boom been lowered at some other time. As it was, she and Rick were already going through a difficult period in their marriage.

For the six months following Debby's wedding, Dana sensed some sort of tension between them that she couldn't understand. Uncertainty had crept into their relationship. They seemed overly aware of each other. Rick had started to question her about what she was doing with her time, where she was going, and this was so unlike him.

She in turn began to wonder about his day. At first she thought it was part of the adjustment period that couples must surely face after the last of their offspring left home. Perhaps they were going through the so-called empty nest syndrome. When the strain between them stretched into months, she began to suspect Rick was seeing another woman.

She almost felt a sense of relief when he came home and told her he'd been laid off. Although he denied knowing his job was in jeopardy, she was convinced otherwise. It explained everything; most certainly it explained why he'd been so edgy lately. There was no other woman. She'd never felt so happy in her life.

At first, neither of them was that concerned. They had each other. They also had a savings account, depleted somewhat after Debby's wedding, but adequate for their modest needs. They were convinced that Rick would find something else, another job, in a related field, perhaps.

What a laugh. There was no related field, and even if there had been, the competition was keen. Rick was in his forties, still young, but not as young as most of the other men competing in the ever-shrinking job market.

Rick refused to talk about his difficulties in landing a job. It was his problem, he told her whenever she tried to broach the subject, and he would handle it.

Had he plunged a knife in her heart, he couldn't have hurt her more. It was *their* problem. Couldn't he see that? They needed to talk about it. *She* needed to talk about it!

Reluctantly, she gave up trying to get him to confide in her. Her hope was that if she avoided the subject, he would eventually share his feelings.

The subject that no one wanted to talk about had a way of creeping into the most benign of conversations. No topic, it seemed, was safe. One day she mentioned the weather and he blew into a rage. "Why don't you just come out and say it!" he stormed. "It's a nice day. So why isn't the bum out looking for a job?"

She was shocked that he would accuse her of having such thoughts. "That's not what I was going to say," she protested. "I thought maybe we could do something. . . ."

Nothing she said could convince him that she didn't blame him for losing his job. After several more blow-ups unlike any previously experienced in their marriage, it became painfully clear that no matter how much they tried, they could no longer reach each other.

The silence that followed was the hardest to bear. Love, it seems, dies quietly.

Rick eventually left for California to look for work. He was convinced that he'd find something in what at the time was the aerodynamics capital of the world. Dana hated the thought of moving to California, away from their three children and her elderly mother.

"We'll take Mom with us," Rick had said. "Unless, of course, you don't want to go with me."

"Of course I'll go!" she'd exclaimed without a moment's hesitation. It was only after he'd left for the coast that she began to wonder if he wanted her to go.

He returned from California more solemn than ever, and more discouraged. The strain that she had first felt in their marriage following Debby's wedding had grown worse. They no longer talked. Not about anything meaningful. Not about anything at all.

Soon after Rick's futile trip, their marriage fell apart completely.

Shaking away the memories, she sat across from him and quietly stewed. The least he could do was be halfway sociable. Would it kill him to make conversation? To be pleasant, or at the very least, stop scowling at her?

She resented his attitude, as if she were to blame for their having to spend the week together. One would think he would try to make the best of things. But no, he was going to make things just as difficult as he possibly could. Well, two could definitely play that game!

She bit down hard on an English muffin and glowered back.

His mood growing darker with each passing minute, he grabbed the sugar bowl and put twice as much sugar as he wanted into his coffee cup. The least she could have done was to dress properly for breakfast. True, she wore one of the complimentary bathrobes provided by the hotel. But it barely reached her knees.

He had always enjoyed their breakfasts together. He especially enjoyed the times he could detect a satisfied gleam in her eyes, knowing he had put it there.

There was no such satisfied look on her face today, no warm glow.

Irritated by his thoughts, he purposefully searched for something about her that would make him forget those other times.

She could have brushed her hair. It was indecent of her to sit opposite him with her sleep-tousled hair. And makeup—couldn't she have put on lipstick? So that he wouldn't have to look at her naked lips.

Her soft, pink, naked lips.

He pushed his cup away. "The coffee's cold," he growled.

She could see the steam rising from his cup, but she wasn't about to argue with him.

Breakfast ended none too soon in Dana's estimation. After Rick left to get a newspaper, she fled from the balcony as quickly as a woman might leave the bed of an unwanted lover.

She took a leisurely shower. The rash was barely noticeable. She lifted her face to the heavy spray and closed her eyes. The warm water massaged her skin with gentle strokes, pressing, soft and feathery, like Rick's fingers had felt last night. . . .

She drew away from the stream of water and opened her eyes. Rick had not caressed her. He had simply rubbed liniment onto her rash. Nothing special about that.

Nothing!

She jerked off the water, opened the door and grabbed a towel.

She was still scowling a half hour later when she walked into the sitting room and found Rick on the phone, his voice hushed.

He replaced the phone carefully. "That was a . . . business call."

Business, indeed! Rick supported himself with odd jobs, mostly painting apartments and minor carpentry. So why was he acting so secretive? Unless . . .

He'd been talking to a woman. She'd bet on it. Probably Miss What's-her-name-with-the-sultry-voice. "There's no need to explain!" She hated sounding like a shrew, but she couldn't seem to help herself. Oh, well, if he could be in a bad mood, so could she!

"Apparently there is," he said, frowning.

She took a deep breath. "The least you could do is call your *girlfriend* from the lobby." Great! She went from sounding like a shrew to a jealous lover. What in the world was the matter with her? He could talk to whomever he pleased for all she cared!

"I was not talking to any girlfriend, and even I were, you're a fine one to talk."

"Me?"

"Yes, you. The least you could have done is ask your

boyfriend to wait until you got home to have his flowers delivered."

"He's not my boyfriend!" she snapped. *Yet!*

"You sure fooled me. He signed the card 'With love.' "

Her eyes widened in astonishment. "You *read* the card?"

"You left it on the table for everyone to see."

"That's because I have nothing to hide!" she shouted.

"Good, neither do I!" he shouted back.

They stood glaring at each other, practically nose-to-nose. "If you would be kind enough to keep your boyfriends out of our room, I will be happy to extend the same courtesy!"

"See that you do!" she said, for no good reason. For all she cared, he could bring his girlfriend to spend the week. Maybe that would keep him out of her hair!

"Very well." He turned and grabbed the flower arrangement.

"Where are you going with that?" she demanded.

He walked through the French doors to the patio and tossed the bouquet over the railing, sending dozens of pigeons scurrying around in a flutter of wings.

"How dare you!" she cried.

He turned, his face dark, his eyes forbidding. He stormed past her and out the front door. The door to their suite slammed with such force, the breakfast dishes rattled.

She stood frozen in place, her eyes blurred with tears. All the anger and all the hurt she thought she had worked through rose inside, every bit as potent as it had been during those first days of separation.

This week . . . was a mistake. She should never have agreed to spend it with him.

How in the world were they going to get through the next five days? The next five nights?

Chapter Seven

A knock sounded on the door followed by the jiggling of the lock. "Yoo-hoo, it's me, Etta."

Dana quickly wiped away her tears. "Come in."

Etta appeared at the doorway between the foyer and sitting room. "I saw your handsome husband downstairs. I thought it might be a good time to clean your room. If that's okay with you, honey."

"That's fine."

"How's that nasty allergy?"

Dana forced a smile. Thank God she had the allergy to blame for her teary eyes. "The rash seems to be going away."

"What an awful thing to happen, especially on your honeymoon. But don't you worry about a thing, honey. You'll find some nice things in the gift shop—nightgowns and such."

"What?"

"Your husband said you were allergic to flannel. In case that's all you got to wear to bed, you could buy something pretty in the gift shop."

"Oh." For no good reason, Dana felt herself blush. "I'll have to check it out."

"Need more heat in here? Or maybe some more blankets?"

"I'm sorry?" She couldn't seem to concentrate.

"Your husband said you feel the cold." Etta closed the balcony doors, shooing away the pigeons as she did so. "Darn pesky birds!" she muttered.

"That won't be necessary," Dana said. "The room is quite comfortable." She tried to think of a way to steer the conversation onto another topic. "That's a beautiful brooch you're wearing."

"Ain't it just!" Etta looked pleased. "I just got a letter from the dolls who gave it to me. Nice couple, real nice. Celebrated their fiftieth weddin' anniv'rsary in this very room."

"My goodness. Fifty."

Etta patted the oversized pocket of her apron. "That's one of those tricky years, you know. Fifty."

Dana couldn't help but laugh. Was there any time in a marriage that wasn't tricky? "You mean tricky like twenty-eight years?"

"If they make it past fifty, it should be smooth sailing until their sixty-third anniversary."

"Did you really learn all this stuff about marriage from romance novels?"

"You bet I did." She pulled her latest romance novel from the pocket of her apron. "Most folks don't understand the nature of marriage. When you get married, y'all don't become one. You remain individuals. It's like the sea and the land—there's this constant coming together and drawing apart. I read that in a romance called *Seagull Dreams*. About the sea and the land part, I mean."

Dana nodded. "If you ask me, it's the times couples draw apart that causes the most trouble."

Etta slipped her book back into her pocket. "Can't be helped. Things happen. Families grow up, people get older. Health fails. Married folks have to face these things as individuals first, before they can face them as a couple. That's what Dr. Hammill says."

"Dr. Hammill?"

"He was the marriage counselor in *Seagull Dreams.*"

"Your Dr. Hammill sounds like he knows what he's talking about." Dana fell silent for a moment. "I remember the time our daughter was hit by a car and we thought we'd lost her. It was like Rick and I withdrew from each other for a while, and then . . ."

She and Rick had sat at Debby's bedside all night long. They had spoken not a word to each other during that long, awful night. It was only later, after gaining strength as individuals, apparently, that they were able to cling to each other and share their fears.

"Is she the daughter I met?"

"Yes, Debby. The accident happened several years back. But what you said . . . about the land and sea—it makes sense. After we got through Debby's crisis, Rick and I were closer than ever. And until he lost his job . . ." Surprised to find herself confiding in someone she hardly knew, Dana bit back the surge of emotion that suddenly came to the fore.

"Losing a job is certainly a crisis for any marriage. The same thing happened in *Tomorrow's Promise*. The hero lost his job, and let me tell you, they had a real time of it."

Dana stared into the fire and said nothing.

Etta squirted the glass table with window cleaner. "Do you want this newspaper or can I toss it out?"

"Newspaper? Maybe." She took the paper from Etta. It was the classified section. One of the ads was circled. Dana felt guilty for having made a fuss over Rick's phone call. There was something about getting divorced that brought out the worst in people. During the last painful year, she had acted petty and bitter, demanding and unreasonable. It horrified her to discover that she was capable of so many undesirable traits. The separation had taken its toll. Not only had she lost a husband and a lover, it appeared at times that she had lost an essential part of herself, the part capable of tolerance and understanding.

"Mr. Matthews was tellin' me he fixes up old cars. My nephew collects cars from the twenties. He's always complainin' about how hard it is to find someone to restore them."

"Rick's very good at it," Dana said. To her knowledge, he'd not refurbished a car since losing his job. She was suddenly reminded of how little she knew about Rick these days and how he spent his time. Then recalling Miss *Sultry,* she decided maybe it was best that she didn't know.

Soon after Etta left, Rick returned, the *Dallas Morning News* tucked under his arm. He looked tired, his face drawn. "Dana . . . the flowers . . ."

She placed a bookmark between the pages of the book she'd been unable to read. "The flowers weren't important."

"I think they were. I saw your face when you received them. You looked . . ."

"How . . . how did I look?" He was staring at her with an odd expression, as if seeing something he'd not seen before. For a moment she feared he could read her mind; she didn't want him to know how disappointed she was the flowers had not come from him. She didn't want anyone to know.

He turned away, and she sighed with relief; her secret was safe.

"I've never been one for flowers and all those romantic trappings that women seem to like."

She studied his profile, not knowing what to say. She never thought much of the romantic fluff that some of her friends considered so important. With Rick, sharing a sandwich in the back of a pickup truck seemed every bit as romantic as a candlelight dinner for two in an expensive restaurant. "None of that mattered to me, Rick. The only thing I cared about was . . ."

He waited, and when she failed to finish what she'd started to say, he prompted her. "Go on."

"Never mind. It wasn't important."

He looked about to argue with her, then seemed to change his mind. Instead he glanced around the room as if he didn't know whether to sit or stand. "This week . . . is important to the kids. The least we can do is try to get along."

"I agree."

"I . . . I made reservations at the Terrace Restaurant at eight."

Normally, she would welcome the chance to dine in the hotel restaurant. "Do you think that's a good idea? I'm sure it's expensive, and . . ." As soon as she saw the dark look on his face, she knew she'd said the wrong thing.

"Is that all you can think about? How much it's going to cost?"

"No, of course not. I'm sorry, Rick. It's just . . ."

"Say it, why don't you? I don't have a job. Say it!"

So his call earlier had resulted in another dead end. She longed to rush into his arms, to comfort him and tell him . . . what? She didn't know and it didn't matter. He looked so distant, there was nothing she could say that would bridge the chasm between them. If there had been something, she would have said it long ago. "Don't Rick, please. We both agreed to try and get along. . . ."

He raked his fingers through his hair, leaving it to stand

up in such a way that it practically begged her to rearrange the locks. Recognizing the need to pull away, if only physically, she turned to stare into the fire. It was the only way she knew to gather strength.

"The restaurant is dressy," he said. If this was his way of trying to get along, he failed, for his voice sounded distant and cold.

They didn't speak for the remainder of the afternoon. Rick read the newspaper and watched TV. Actually, what he did was flip through the channels until a collage of unrelated products and images kept popping up on the screen.

Dana tried to read, but it was as if her mind was connected to its own remote control, and bits and pieces from the past kept up a steady intrusion.

Talking to Etta earlier about Debby's accident brought other such family crises to mind: the year her father had died, Rick's parents, his grandparents, hers. The day their oldest son left for the Gulf War, that frightening moment when their youngest son stopped breathing.

She recalled with startling clarity the numerous nights Rick had discovered her walking the floor, or she'd found him staring out the window in the wee hours of the morning.

It was as if they each sensed the precise moment when the other's time to be alone had passed, and were ready to embrace the special strength that could only come when the two of them faced a problem together.

She never thought of such times as being necessary to them both as individuals and to the marriage as a whole. She never thought about those times at all. It was preferable to dwell upon the glorious coming together, rather than the drawing apart.

She leaned her head against the back of the chair and closed her eyes. Why had their marriage been strong enough to bridge the chasm created by death and war but not the loss of a job? Why?

It was dark outside when Dana walked into the bedroom to dress for dinner. She stood by the French doors and gazed at the Dallas skyline.

She couldn't help but notice the black void separating

her from the bright city lights. She reached up and yanked on the cord. The satiny panels that made up the draperies came together with a whisper, blocking out the darkness but not her depression.

She pulled off her sweats and reached for her dinner dress.

It was a simple black sheath that showed off her still slender figure, the result of regular workouts and avoiding the employee lounge on "goody day."

She hadn't worn the dress in quite some time, and had forgotten how low the neckline plunged. She tugged the dress this way and that, but her cleavage was very much in evidence. She hadn't packed any jewelry, so she had no way of breaking up the expanse of ivory-white skin.

Etta solved the dilemma. The maid had arrived to turn down the bed. "See how this looks." She undid the necklace from around her own neck and handed it to Dana.

It was an exquisite antique gold heart on a black velvet ribbon—not something one would normally wear to work. But Etta seemed to live by her own rules.

"It's beautiful," Dana exclaimed. Indeed, it complemented the dress perfectly. "Are you sure you want me to wear it?"

"Now would I be offerin' if I didn't want you wearing it?"

"I guess not. Thank you." Dana stared at herself in the mirror. "Was this a gift from one of your couples?"

Etta smiled. "You're getting to know me pretty well, ain't you?" Etta turned down the bed on both sides and planted a foil-covered candy kiss on each pillow.

Rick walked out of the dressing room and into the bedroom, looking devastatingly handsome in his dark suit.

The maid nodded in approval. "My word. If you two don't look handsome enough to be on the cover of a romance novel. Have a good time."

"Thank you," Dana called after her. She turned to find Rick watching her with a look that took her breath away. Warm lights of approval glowed in the depths of his eyes.

"You look . . . beautiful."

Never had a compliment hurt or affected her more. For it only served to emphasize all the wonderful things they had in the past but had lost. The bitter taste of anger filled her mouth; anger at herself. Anger at the state of the economy and all the other forces that were responsible for Rick losing his job.

But mostly she was angry with Rick. She didn't want his compliments, nor did she want him to look at her the way he was looking at her. What she wanted—all she could handle, really—was civility.

"Thank you," she said, her voice politely cool, distant, coming from a part of her that was anything but cool and distant. "You look . . ." She almost choked on the word. ". . . nice." Handsome is how he looked, irresistibly handsome.

"Shall we?" He crooked his elbow, and she slipped her hand around his arm, hoping he didn't notice how much she trembled. Upon accepting his arm, she also had to accept a disturbing truth; he still affected her on some level—all levels. And if she thought there was the slimmest possible chance for them to put their marriage back together, she would be tempted to try. But there wasn't; the anger was still too great, the hurt too deep.

It would require an enormous amount of effort on her part, but she could do it. She could maintain the cool detachment that had gotten her through their separation. If she didn't look too deeply into his eyes. If she didn't stand too close to him, or too far apart, which might tempt her to try to watch him undetected. She must do it, otherwise she would have to start the long, painful adjustment to single life all over. And she could never again relive the last few months.

Chapter Eight

They didn't say a word during the elevator ride to the lobby.

Dana felt as if she were playing a difficult part on stage. Every move she made had to be carefully choreographed in advance, every word chosen carefully and scrupulously edited before delivery.

Mustn't let her eyes linger on him for too long, she

cautioned herself. For this reason, she kept them focused on the soaring ceiling of the Glass Garden and the wide array of tropical plants lit with tiny white lights.

She tried not to think about Rick's hand on the small of her back as they followed the tuxedoed maître d' to their table. Or the way their footsteps seemed to be in perfect sync, as if rehearsed.

The Terrace Restaurant shimmered with the soft, flickering glow of dozens of tall tapering candles. Mustn't think about the romantic light cast by the candles, she reminded herself, or the way the lights picked up the silver highlights in his hair.

Mustn't think about the lush ferns that reminded her of the foliage in the first apartment they shared, or the boats lit by colorful lanterns and filled with lovers that glided up and down the lake.

Mustn't think of the miniature lights twinkling from bare branches like diamonds tossed at random. For they reminded her of the wedding ring worn thin through the years, that she had tossed into a drawer, along with a splattering of tears.

Mustn't think of the crescent moon that seemed to mock the world below, for that was exactly how the moon had looked the first night they had made love. But the moon hadn't mocked them that long-ago night. No, indeed!

Her eyes met Rick's. He ran a finger along the collar of his shirt. He looked so uncomfortable, Dana took pity on him. "If you want to take off your tie, I won't mind."

She was acutely aware that his gaze had rested upon her lips. Oh, no, you don't, she protested in silence, rallying her every defense. She pulled back until she sat rigid on her chair and stared with grim determination at her menu.

She pondered the many delectable choices. All the while, she toyed nervously with the golden heart at her neck. Not a good idea, she realized upon noting Rick's gaze settle on her cleavage.

"That's a nice necklace," he said. "It . . . goes with the dress."

"Thank you. Etta loaned it to me."

She held her menu in such a way as to block her neckline from view. His eyes collided with hers for an instant before he glanced down at his own menu.

She lowered her voice so as not to be overheard. "Don't you think it odd that a maid would wear something like this to work?"

He shrugged his shoulders. "I don't know. I suppose so."

"Come to think of it, I've never seen one person wear so much jewelry. Have you noticed all the rings on her fingers, and the brooches?"

"So, she likes jewelry. What's the big deal?"

"Some of her pieces were given to her by hotel guests. I don't know . . . it seems strange."

"So what are you saying?"

"You . . . you don't suppose she stole the jewelry, do you?"

His eyes widened with surprise. "What in the world gave you such a crazy idea?"

"I know it sounds ridiculous. But look at this thing." She held the heart between her fingers. "Don't you think it's a bit too coincidental that Debby's missing ring just happened to be heart-shaped? Etta made a point of telling me that she collected heart-shaped jewelry."

Rick tapped his fingers together. "If she was a thief, the hotel would have figured it out by now. Others would have reported thefts, not just Debby."

"Maybe," Dana conceded. "But what if they thought they simply lost the jewelry? I've lost earrings and even a pin, and it never occurred to me they might have been stolen."

Rick looked unconvinced. "I don't know. If she really did steal that stuff, would she be wearing it for everyone to see?"

The conversation was interrupted by the waiter, who had come to take their order.

After the waiter left, Rick seemed reluctant to discuss the matter, and Dana let the subject drop. Try as she might, she couldn't think of another one to take its place.

Work would inevitably mean talking about Alex or bringing up the painful reality of Rick's situation. The past would only bring up bittersweet memories. The future meant having to talk about the impending divorce. That left the somewhat awkward present. It seemed a whole lot easier to eat in silence.

Still, it was a shock to Dana when she inadvertently caught a glimpse of their reflection in the window. Rick's face looked hard and dark, so unyielding and so unlike the man she so easily fell in love with those many years ago.

Her own reflection was every bit as somber. She lay down her fork and drew the soft linen napkin to her mouth as if to wipe away the grim look reflected on the window-pane.

How could this have happened? How could a couple become strangers after years of loving and sharing? Maybe strangers wasn't the right word. If Rick were a stranger, she could at least bring up the subject of the weather without remembering the walks they used to take in the rain and the times they shared picnic lunches in the sunshine.

She let her napkin drop on her lap. "The salmon is delicious." It was cooked to perfection in a succulent dill sauce.

"Not quite as good as Harvey's."

Their gazes met for an instant before she focused her eyes on her plate. Harvey's Fish House was one of their favorite restaurants.

Mustn't talk about the food. Or the weather. Or the soft violins playing the song they had danced to at their wedding. She moved her foot and her knee accidently brushed his. She quickly pulled her leg back. "I wonder if Debby will go full term." She lifted her voice in an attempt to drown out the music. Surely it was safe to discuss this, their first grandchild?

"I hope she waits until she gets to the hospital before having the baby. When I think what I had to go through to get you to the hospital on time. Remember when you went into labor with Brian and—" He stopped. A long moment of silence stretched between them. "Do you want some more wine?"

"I shouldn't." Two glasses was her limit. Nevertheless, he refilled her glass from the carafe and she made no move to stop him.

"We don't have to worry about driving."

He was right. They didn't have to drive; they only had to navigate around each other. Keep a proper distance. Watch what they said, where they put their eyes, their hands, their feet.

They lingered over coffee until the other diners had left. Neither, apparently, was anxious to return to their suite, where they would once again be forced to deal with the bedroom situation.

Rick had ordered another carafe of wine. Against her better judgment, or perhaps because of it, Dana started on yet another glass. Her thoughts grew fuzzy and she could no longer concentrate on the music. The candles blurred together.

The background began to fade into a hazy fog, but not Rick. Her vision of him remained sharp, and the little things she had once taken for granted grew more distinct, as if someone had turned a magnifying glass on him. Like the way his left eyebrow arched a millimeter higher than his right one. And the way the lines around his eyes deepened or grew less pronounced with each passing thought.

Her imagination took wings. The napkin she had placed at her side suddenly took the shape of the bathing suit he wore the night before, complete with his manly bulge. She remembered him telling her he'd wear his swimming suit as a compromise.

She giggled and hiccuped. His forehead creased as it did when he was worried. His hand moved across the table, stopping short of hers.

"Are you all right? Do you want some coffee?"

"I'm fine." She set the glass down and toyed with the stem. "I'm not fine. I'm miserable and I want to go home."

Rick swirled the last of his wine and wondered why he'd drunk so much wine when he despised it. He wasn't a wine drinker. He wasn't a drinker at all, although on occasion he did enjoy a bottle of ice-cold beer. "We promised the kids."

"Oh, yes, we mustn't break our promise." She hesitated for a moment, but only because her tongue seemed to have doubled in size, making it difficult to form her words.

"Bad things happen to parents who break their promises."
She lifted her glass, but he stayed her hand.

"I think we better go," he said. He took the glass from
her and set it aside. "We could do something tomorrow,"
he suggested. "That might help pass the time. We could
go sightseeing, go to the museum."

"You hate . . . mu-mu . . . whatever that is."

"I don't hate them."

"Yes, you do." She fought to regain control of her
senses. "Re-Remember the time . . ." Her mind went
blank; blissfully, peacefully blank. She giggled. "I don't
remember a thing."

He marveled at her. Never in all the years they'd been
married had he ever known her to drink too much. Of
course, he was a fine one to talk. His own head wasn't
feeling all that great, though he doubted the wine had anything to do with it. "Let's dance."

"You . . . you don't like to dance," she said.

She had that right, but it suddenly seemed imperative to
do something. Maybe if he got her moving, he could sober
her up. Besides, he was feeling slightly reckless, and if he
didn't get the hell away from that table, he was likely to
lean over and kiss her. "What better way to end an awkward evening than by doing something I hate?" He stood
abruptly and grabbed her hand. "Come on."

She tried to pull away, but his hold on her was iron-
tight. She'd have been in trouble had he not held her, and
apparently she knew it, for she grabbed his arm with her
other hand as he led her to the dance floor. "I don't think
this is a good idea." Her voice wavered as if she were out
of breath.

"Why not?" He made no effort to keep his voice low.
The music was too loud for private conversations. "Are
you still having a miserable time?"

"You know I am." She glanced around nervously. "We
better go. . . ."

"What's the problem?" He slipped his hand around her
waist and drew her closer than necessary, or even, as it
turned out, prudent. It was a fine time to discover that even
on the dance floor she could still light his fires. And if he
didn't do something quick, he was going to fully ignite.

He spun her around like a top, at a far faster tempo than the music and a good deal quicker than a man who didn't know the difference between a two-step and a Charleston should ever attempt to move on a dance floor.

She looked startled, and he could hardly blame her. The few times in the past she had managed to drag him onto a dance floor, he had held her in his arms and shuffled his feet around like a man trying to walk across a tightrope. He never did cotton much to the modern dances where the drums commanded the beat and partners were optional.

He twirled her around in one direction and then the other. "What are you doing?" she gasped.

"You want slow dancing? Is that what you want?" He pulled her dangerously close and buried his nose in her soft, fragrant hair. For a moment the pose offered him a respite. He could almost pretend things were how they used to be; he had his old job back. His marriage was intact. Later, he would take her home and make love to her. . . .

The music stopped. Stark reality hit him like a bullet to the heart; he wanted things back as they were before.

Dana pulled away from the circle of his arms and clapped her hands with the other couples, but it was obvious from the look on her face that she was furious with him.

He knew most men would know not to push their luck. But he wasn't thinking right. He was too busy noticing how the candlelight reflected in her eyes, on her lips—on her beautiful, soft, demanding-to-be-kissed lips.

He lowered his head and brushed her mouth with his own. She looked startled, but didn't pull back. Encouraged, he wrapped her in his arms and pressed his lips hard against hers.

Time stood still, but only for the instant before she pushed him away. The kiss had a sobering effect on him, and by the look on her face, had made a definite impact on her, though not the one he'd hoped for.

She turned and hurried back to their table to gather up her wrap and evening bag.

"Dana!" He chased after her, but by the time he reached their table, she was gone.

Chapter Nine

Rick scribbled his signature and room number across the check and rushed after her. Dana stood by the West Tower elevator, and when she saw him coming, she dashed through the door leading to the stairwell.

He followed her. "Dana! Would you wait?" He caught up to her on the landing between the third and fourth floors. He grabbed her arm and swung her around to face him.

"Why are you doing this to me?" she demanded. "Why?"

"What do you want? An apology? I'm sorry I kissed my wife. Does that make you feel better?"

Her eyes flashed. "I'm not your wife, Rick! Not in any real sense, and you had no right!"

"I said I was sorry!"

"You don't have to shout. Do you want the whole hotel to hear?"

"I want to make sure *you* hear."

"I hear you loud and clear." She pulled her arm from his.

He rubbed his chin. "What do you want from me?"

"Want? I'll tell you what I want. I want for this week to end so I can go home and get on with my life. It was a mistake . . . we shouldn't have let the children talk us into it."

"Are you here only because of the children?"

She looked so surprised by the question that any hopes he harbored to the contrary were almost dashed.

"You know I would never have agreed to this weekend had it not been for the children. Isn't that why you're here?"

"Yes. No . . . I don't know." He was almost as surprised by his own confusion as she looked. "Maybe we're here because we want to be here. Did you ever stop to think about that? We're pretty strong-willed people. Do you really think the children could have talked us into this week if we didn't want them to?"

"I never wanted to spend this week with you. I would have sooner spent the week in hell!"

"I'm sorry you feel that way. Even so . . ." He hesitated. He wasn't good at expressing his feelings. He wasn't good with words at all. "I want you to know I'm glad we had this time together."

Something snapped in her. He saw it in her eyes, in her face. The next thing he knew, she flew at him like a wildcat, pounding on his chest with her fists. "You're glad! You walked out on our marriage and you say you're glad for this time—"

He grabbed her by the wrists. "I didn't walk out, Dana. You're the one who wanted this divorce—"

"Me!" She pulled her arms away and they stood staring at each other like two bulls about to charge. "You blame me for this?"

"I'm not blaming you. I know I was hard to live with."

"You weren't hard to live with, you were impossible! You wouldn't let me help you."

"There was nothing you could do. There was nothing anyone could do."

"I wasn't just anyone. I was your wife. I wanted to be there for you. To comfort you. But you wouldn't let me. You wouldn't talk about it."

"Dana, please . . ."

She jerked away. "Don't touch me." She turned and ran up the short flight of metal stairs to the door.

His first instinct was to let her go. He knew better than to confront her when she was in such a state. Not that he'd seen her so angry before, and certainly never at him. The few times she'd been in such a rage, it was usually because of some terrible injustice that had been done to someone who was not in a position to fight back. Dana had taken up her share of causes throughout their marriage, and with great success.

But the rage he saw on her face moments ago wasn't about charitable causes and injustice. She had every right to be angry with him. He'd been a fool. Worse. But it wasn't the anger that shattered him as much as it was the raw and honest pain in her eyes. It was that pain that propelled him up the remaining steps, two at a time, to the fourth floor.

He had turned from her in his own time of need, but never, never could he turn away when it was so obvious *she* was the one in need.

He burst through the door leading from the stairwell, causing poor Etta, who happened to be pushing her supply cart down the hall, to cry out in alarm.

"My word! You scared the life out of me!"

"Sorry," he muttered, and kept going.

"Is everything all right?" she called after him.

"Yes." *No.* It was not all right, and it would never be all right again. His hand shook as he tried to put the key into the lock.

The sitting room was empty. "Dana!" He ran into the bedroom. "We need to talk."

She flung his canvas bag at him. "I think you better leave."

"Now calm down, Dana. We both had a bit more to drink than usual and—"

"A few glasses of wine does not give you the right to think you can kiss me anytime you darn well, please."

"It won't happen again, I swear."

"You're right about that!" She stormed into the bathroom, slamming the door after her. She was shaking so much she had a difficult time undoing the necklace and the zipper of her dress.

At last she stood in her bra and panties, undecided whether to take a hot bath to calm her nerves or a cold shower to cool her hot flesh. Damn it! It wasn't fair. After all these years, he could still work his magic on her. One little kiss—not even a proper one at that—and she was ready to melt in his arms and forget everything.

She picked up a towel and accidentally knocked over his aftershave lotion. A small puddle remained after she righted the bottle, but the fragrance lingered, bringing with it more memories, more pain, and more reasons to hate him.

The sooner she rid herself of both the fragrance and the man, the better. How dare he suggest she *wanted* to be here!

She turned the gold-plated handles of the bathtub faucets full force and dumped an entire bottle of Passion bubble oil beneath the stream of water.

By the time she peeled off her underwear and recalled in seething silence every last reason why she hated or should hate her soon-to-be ex-husband, the foamy bubbles rose from the depths of the marble tub.

He was in bed when she emerged fifty-some minutes later, his arms folded behind his head, a copy of *Classic Car* magazine on the mattress by his side. The upper part of his body was fully exposed, disrupting the nerves she had just spent the better part of an hour trying to calm.

Knowing him, he probably didn't even have the decency to wear his bathing suit! She only wished he would stop looking at her as if *she* were the one who was naked.

"I asked you to leave."

"I'm not leaving until we've talked."

"You never wanted to talk before, remember? During all those months before we separated?"

"I didn't want to talk about losing my job. And I still don't. I want to talk about us. About us and what happened downstairs."

"Nothing happened." She grabbed her pillow, sending the candy kiss flying halfway across the room.

She looked around for the blanket Etta had promised. Unable to find it, she grabbed her bathrobe and marched out of the bedroom. After she arranged the pillow on the love seat and turned off the lamp, she plopped herself upon the cushions and covered herself with her robe.

I want to talk. Rick's words kept repeating themselves in her mind. She would have given anything had he said those very words two years ago when he first lost his job and their troubles began. Or even later, when it was becoming increasingly evident that they were drifting apart, and she'd begged him to open up to her. Why now, after all this time, did he finally want to talk?

There was nothing he could say, no words to erase the pain and heartache she'd suffered these last two years. None!

It was hot in the room. Or maybe it was just her. Maybe it was the aftereffects of too much wine. Her overheated body had nothing to do with being in his arms or with his kiss. Nothing!

She folded her pillow in half, punched it, flipped it over, and retrieved it from the floor. She couldn't get comfortable. She was hot and feeling hotter by the minute.

Suddenly, she began to itch.

Chapter Ten

She tried not to wake him as she searched the dark bedroom for the tube of ointment. Her skin was on fire and she was itching so much she wanted to scream. Upon stubbing her toe, she *did* scream.

"Dana?"

The light flicked on.

"It's nothing, Rick. Go back to sleep."

He sat up. "Your legs are all red."

"I guess I'm not allergic to flannel after all. Do you know where the ointment is?"

"It's right here." He flung the covers back and she quickly averted her eyes.

Please, please, *please* be wearing something, she prayed.

"Let me help you."

"I can manage," she said hoarsely.

But he wouldn't hear of it. "Lie on the bed. For God's sake, Dana. I want to help you."

Only a desperate woman would accept an offer like that; thanks to the rapidly spreading rash, she *was* a desperate woman. Keeping her eyes downcast, she walked to the bed. He donned a hotel robe and followed her.

"Try not to scratch." He pulled the pillow from his side of the bed and arranged it behind her back. He then unscrewed the cap off the tube and pressed a dab of ointment into the palms of his hands.

His gentle fingers left a soothing trail on her arms and legs that felt as smooth as liquid satin. The relief was short-lived at best. The burning sensation left her skin, but another more worrisome feeling took its place—it felt alarmingly like need and want.

She tried to concentrate on something, anything but him. She closed her eyes. If she didn't see him, didn't have to watch sympathy play across his face as he worked his fingers into her flesh, she would be all right. But even with her eyes closed she could feel the intensity of him, absorb his essence, his scent. . . .

Her eyes flew open. "I just figured out what I'm allergic to!" she declared. "It's Passion."

Rick drew back in bewilderment. "Passion?"

"The bath oil I used. *Purple* Passion bath oil. That's what's causing this rash."

"I'm glad that mystery's solved." He continued working his fingers against her flesh. "Maybe I should call the doctor. . . ."

"I don't need a doctor." What she needed was a cold, cold shower.

"Have it your way. But will you at least roll over so I can do your back?"

He waited for her to settle facedown on the bed before pushing the hem of her T-shirt all the way to her armpits. He slathered her burning skin with ointment and worked soft, feathery circles up and down her back. He did the job quickly and efficiently, but even so, his hands on her back felt too much like a lover's hands for her peace of mind.

Tugging her shirt down, she turned over. Their eyes locked and his gaze drifted lazily to her parted lips. She inhaled slowly. The world seemed to stop. She took another deep breath and he lowered his head.

She welcomed his kiss with a muffled sob. It was as if a missing part of her had returned after a long absence. She felt whole again. It was like the coming together of the perfect words and the perfect melody to make the perfect song.

She worked her arms around his neck, and her fingers slid through his hair as they had so often in the past. He slipped his tongue into her mouth and she shamelessly urged him to deepen the kiss.

His hand slipped beneath her T-shirt and his strong, yet gentle fingers made a loving cradle for her breast. Arching against him, she tilted her head back and he ran his lips along her neck.

She gave a soft sigh as she luxuriated in the gentle touch of his hands and lips. Lord, it had been so long. . . .

Reality hit her. She didn't want it to; she fought it with everything she had. But the anger and hurt of the past came roaring back. Apparently sensing something had changed, he was the one who pulled away.

"Dana?"

She pulled down her T-shirt and fought her way upright. "I can't do this. I just . . . can't."

"I need you."

"Not the way I want to be needed."

"Dana, please . . ."

"Don't . . . just don't . . ." She stood and stumbled from the room, blurry-eyed and heavyhearted. Her body was burning, her skin on fire. Walking out of that room was the hardest thing she ever had to do. It was also the most necessary.

Rick stared after her. Now he'd done it. Acted like some adolescent boy in glandular overdrive. He paced the bedroom, making a frenzied trek between the French doors and the mirrored closet. So what did that make him? A criminal?

She didn't have to go running off as if her life depended on it. A simple no would have taken the wind out of his sails. Maybe.

All right, he admitted it. He still thought his wife the sexiest, most desirable woman alive.

And if he had half a mind, if he had a job . . . or a prospect of a job—or even a marketable skill, he would fight to get her back.

For the truth of the matter was that despite all the training and hard work, despite extensive experience in the aerodynamics field, he was a dinosaur. He wasn't so much without a job as he was without a profession.

He had no right to try and win her back, not when his future looked so bleak. No right.

Oh, but he wanted her back.

Wanted her back with every cell, every molecule of his body and soul, his whole being.

It was a hard thing to admit, even to himself, for that meant facing hard, cold facts. He had nothing left to offer her. Nothing! Not a job. Not damned thing! Maybe the best thing he could do for her—the best way he could show his love—was to step aside and let her have her fancy-dancy lawyer with his fancy-dancy flowers.

Chapter Eleven

Shaken by the encounter in the bedroom, Dana raced barefoot through the sitting room, ripped open the French doors and ran outside. Brushing against a potted plant, she grabbed hold of the railing in an attempt to steady herself. The night air was cool, nipping at the skin like a playful puppy. She took a deep breath, letting the sweet fragrance of the garden fill her lungs.

Why, oh why did he do this to her? Why was he still able to fill her heart with longing and desire? Why did it take only one kiss or one simple caress of his hands to make her body ache for him? Why did she let him do this to her? Lord, why?

She had no idea how long she stood on the balcony before hearing his voice. It seemed like hours, but it must have only been minutes, for her heart was still pounding and her lips still on fire.

When she didn't answer him, he called her name again. "Dana?"

She let out her breath and turned to face him. His eyes were in the shadows, but not the soft sensuous mouth that twice in a single night had turned her inside out, upside down, until she didn't know which way she was going.

"You were right. Spending this week together was a mistake." His voice sounded hard, cold, distant, and for that she was grateful. "I think we should leave tomorrow."

She gripped the railing with one hand. "I think that's best."

She swallowed the lump at her throat. She had hoped for some sort of closure so that she could put the past to rest once and for all. What she got was more heartache. "What shall we tell the children?"

"The truth." He sounded resigned.

She bit her lower lip. The truth was, she still wanted this man—wanted him with everything she had or ever hoped to have. How could she tell the children—or anyone—that indisputable truth?

He stepped back to the French doors and she spun around to once again face the city lights, to hide the tears that had sprung to her eyes.

It surprised her that this last good-bye felt as painful and devastating as it had the day he walked out of their house for good. Perhaps it was because in between the anger and the ill-conceived passion, there had been a moment of coming together that allowed him to recognize her need—and her to recognize his. But recognizing the need in each other was not the same as fulfilling it.

Behind her, Rick cursed. She half turned. "What's the matter?"

"The door's locked."

"What?" She rubbed the moisture from her eyes and joined him.

She peered through the glass of the French door and spotted a folded blanket on the love seat. "It must have been Etta. She didn't know we were outside. She must have thought we forgot to lock up."

"Isn't that just great?" Rick studied the frame of the door. "This is a safety door. There's no way I'm going to break through that glass."

Shivering, Dana ran her hands up and down her bare arms. The night air that had moments earlier offered a welcome respite now seemed cold and damp.

Rick crossed the balcony and stuck his head over the railing. "Anyone hear me?" The West Tower was situated on the most isolated part of the grounds. Even during daylight hours she'd not seen many people around.

Rick walked to the side and opened up a trellised gate leading to the next balcony. After a moment he returned. "No luck. The suites around us are still vacant." He lifted his foot onto the railing and looked ready to heave himself over.

Dana gasped and grabbed his arm. "What are you doing? We're four stories high."

"I'm going to try to climb to the balcony below. Maybe the door is open."

"You can't do that! You could fall and break your neck."

"What choice do we have? We'll freeze to death out here."

"Maybe if we keep yelling for help, someone will hear us."

"Who's going to hear us?" He heaved himself upward and straddled the railing, which suddenly seemed terribly flimsy.

"Careful!" she cried, tugging on the hem of his robe.

Rick almost lost his balance, and for a terrifying moment tottered on the edge. Dana cried out and grabbed his bare leg. "Don't, Rick! It's too dangerous."

He looked about to argue, but thought better of it after glancing at the ground below. "All right," he conceded.

He jumped down beside her, and she surprised him by flinging her arms around his neck. "You crazy fool! You scared the life out of me. Don't you know . . ."

She stared up at him and he stared back at her. A long moment passed before she dropped her arms to her sides and pulled herself away.

Rick shoved his hands in his robe pockets. She folded her arms in front of her to ward off the chill of the night. She was shaking, suddenly.

"You're freezing." He walked the length of the balcony, checking each window and glass door in turn. "Great! It's all security glass. It would take a sledgehammer to break through." As if to test the obvious, he picked up one of the potted plants and, cautioning her to move away, hurled the clay pot against a window.

The pot broke, sending pieces of crockery flying across the balcony, but the glass pane remained intact. "It looks like we're stuck here until morning."

He kicked aside the plant that had fallen to his feet. "Brrrr," he said. He jumped up and down to keep warm. "Now what are we going to do?"

"I don't know." What she wouldn't give for her flannel nightgown!

"If you hadn't gone running away like some scared adolescent child—"

"Don't you go blaming me for this fiasco, Richard Matthews! You're the one who got all—"

"Hot and bothered?" he finished.

"Pushy!" She flung the word at him as if she were hurling a rock.

"I see. And of course I had no encouragement."

"You took advantage of me. You knew I was feeling itchy and . . . Oh, never mind! I don't want to argue with you." She sank onto the outdoor carpeting and huddled against the wall. She had never felt so miserable in her life.

He sat down next to her. "I don't want to argue, either." Their shoulders were only an inch or so apart. They were far too close together for comfort, far too far apart.

He knew better than to bridge the tiny gap between them, but she was shivering so much, he could practically hear her teeth chatter. He really had no choice but to slip an arm around her shoulders.

She stiffened and tried to pull away.

"Don't, Dana. We can keep each other warm." It was a reasonable request, and apparently she agreed. For after a short time, she snapped her mouth shut and leaned her head on his shoulder.

"You feel like ice," he said, drawing his arms full around her.

She couldn't have disagreed more, for suddenly she felt warm and protected.

"Dana . . . I . . . just want to say one thing. I wish you every happiness. And if Alex is the one to make you happy, I'm not going to step in the way."

"And you know I feel the same way about Miss . . ." She almost said *Sultry*. "Whoever the woman was who answered your phone and called you on Christmas Day."

"My landlady?"

"What?"

"She called on Christmas Day to tell me about a fire on

the floor above mine. She wanted permission to check my apartment for problems.''

"And you didn't take a vacation with her?''

"What in the world gave you that idea?''

"Your suntan, for one.''

He laughed. "I spent a couple of days in Florida, checking out the job market.''

"That's it.'' Dana felt utterly foolish. "Why didn't you say so before?''

"I tried, but you wouldn't listen.''

He was right. She hadn't listened. Obviously, she needed the obstacle of another woman between them. She needed as many reasons as possible to stay away from him.

"And what about you and Alex?''

"We're just friends.''

"It's obvious he wants more.'' Rick paused for a moment. "He sends you flowers. I'm not good at those kinds of things. I don't understand why a bouquet of flowers makes a woman think she's special.''

"I know.'' She never wanted flowers. Not from Rick. Anyone could buy a woman flowers, but only Rick would buy a woman a gift from a hardware store and get away with it. "You'd sooner give a woman flares for the car.''

"You didn't like the ones I gave you?''

He sounded so surprised, she couldn't help but laugh. "Rick, flares are not something you like or dislike.''

"I was worried about you. I thought you should have them in case you broke down somewhere.''

"But did you have to give them to me for our anniversary? And what about the strap for the vacuum cleaner that you gave me on Valentine's Day three years ago?''

"What's so hard to understand about that? I was worried about your back. . . .''

"And the hard hat?''

"Safety helmet for when you go bicycle riding.''

She started to laugh. Maybe it was the ridiculous situation they found themselves in. Maybe it was the cold air affecting her brain.

"What's so funny?''

"Do you remember how you proposed to me?''

"Of course I remember.''

"Do you recall proposing to me on the side of the road while changing a tire?"

"Yeah? So?"

"Never mind."

He shifted his weight. "Now don't say that. We need to talk about this." He drew back so he could see her face. "Apparently you think my proposal was lacking in some way."

"Come to think of it . . . you said we'd get married. You didn't even ask me."

"I didn't think it was necessary. You were—"

"Pregnant," she finished for him. "Yes, I was. And you did the right thing."

"The right thing. Is that what you think I did?"

"It's what everyone thinks you did. Your mother, my parents. Everyone."

"And you?" he asked quietly. "What do you think?"

"I know you only married me because of the baby."

"Isn't that why *you* married me?"

She found the accusation so offensive, her mouth fell open. Several seconds of silence stretched between before she found her voice. "I *loved* you."

"You were desperate."

"Is that what you think? I was desperate?" She pulled away angrily. "You think I couldn't take care of myself if I had to?"

"And you think I married you out of obligation? I would have lived up to my responsibilities to our baby. Make no mistake about that. But I married you for one reason and one reason alone. I loved you. And I would have married you even if you weren't pregnant!"

Her heart stood still. "You would have?" Her voice was barely a whisper.

He frowned. "That was my plan all along. As soon I finished college. My only hope was that you would have me."

"Have you? Of course I would have you, but you never said anything about marriage. Not until I told you I was pregnant."

"You're a fine one to talk. You never told me you were

serious about me until you *got* pregnant. All you talked about was going away to college. . . ."

"But that was because I thought your only interest was going back East and . . ."

They stared at each other.

"Great!" His breath hissed through his lips. "It took us twenty-eight years to figure out why we married each other. How long do you suppose it will take us to figure out why we're getting a divorce?"

"I know why we're getting a divorce."

"Do me a favor. Tell me, so we'll both know."

"You're very funny."

"I'm serious, Dana."

"Tell me something first. The truth."

"It'll be the truth. I'm too damned cold to lie."

"Do you ever resent giving up that scholarship for me?"

"What kind of question is that? Why would I resent it?"

"You really wanted that scholarship. You partied all night after finding out you'd won it."

"I partied for a week after you said you'd marry me."

"Because of me you missed out on a wonderful opportunity. . . ."

"Because of you I had everything a man could want."

"Oh, Rick . . . What went wrong?"

"I lost my job."

"But why wasn't our marriage strong enough to survive? It survived all those other times. When Debby was injured and we thought she'd never come out of the coma . . . When Brian left for combat duty . . . Why not the loss of a job?"

"I don't know, Dana." He buried his nose in her hair. "I don't know. All I know is that after Debby got married and left home . . . I guess I always thought that once the kids were gone, it would only be a matter of time before you'd leave, too."

"You thought that?" She stared at him in astonishment and thought of all the time wasted trying to get him to talk about things that didn't matter. It wasn't the loss of his job that tore them apart; it was the last child leaving home that had made them pull away from each other. But only because they'd never really established the real reason that brought them together in the first place. "You thought I would just up and leave? Because the kids were gone?"

"Lots of couples stay together because of the kids. And as soon as they leave home . . . What else could I think? Your mother never let me forget for a moment why you married me in the first place."

"My mother!" She thought of all the times her mother had told her how grateful she should be that Rick had accepted his responsibility and married *her*. It seemed that wasn't all her mother said.

"Mother was wrong." She lifted a hand to touch his whisker-rough cheek. "I married you for one reason only, and that was because I loved you. The baby—our dear sweet Brian—all he did was change the timing."

He took her hand in his, her lovely soft hand, and held it against his mouth. "I married you because I loved you more than life itself." He'd never been good with words in the past, but tonight he knew exactly what he wanted to say. "I thanked God every day that Brian made an early appearance. That made my love for you that much more special."

"I feel so foolish," she whispered.

"No more foolish than I feel. . . ."

"We should have talked about this long ago."

"Maybe I was afraid to talk about it. Afraid that you would confirm what I already believed to be true. Maybe that's why I pulled away from you after Debby left home. . . ."

"And here I thought it was because you lost your job."

"That only made it worse."

"Oh, Rick." She melted into his arms. The honest feelings they'd just shared filled her with hope. She never thought it possible, but just maybe they could find their way back to each other.

Burying her face next to him, she ran her hand up his chest. "The past has a way of popping up, doesn't it? Pulling couples apart when they least expect it. Etta said that marriage was like the land and the sea. There's always something pulling the couple apart and bringing them together.''

His sigh sounded like a sob against her ear. ''What will it take to bring us together like we were before?''

''The cold?'' she said, only half teasing.

He chuckled softly and moved his lips onto her forehead. She lifted her face, and his mouth found hers, and this time there was no holding back.

She slipped her arms inside his robe and around his waist. Her earlier suspicions proved correct; he wore nothing beneath his robe. But rather than feeling threatened, she greeted the discovery with a shiver of anticipation. She ran her fingers down his sturdy thighs and dropped tiny kisses upon his chest.

He moaned aloud and murmured her name. ''It's been so long,'' he whispered in her ear, his hot breath washing over her, warming her.

''I know,'' she whispered back.

He moved his hands beneath her T-shirt to work his special magic upon her aching breasts. He kissed each rosy peak in turn until hot flames of desire made her literally cry out in need.

Murmuring her name, he ran his hand along the soft lines of her waist, her hips, and thighs until every womanly curve had been set afire.

He lay back, pulling her on top of him. She wiggled against him and was delighted to find that her body still seemed to meld next to his as easily as . . . well, the land and the sea.

''My God, look what you've done to me,'' he whispered. He was breathing heavily and his body seemed to pulse with vitality, as if something inside was ready to explode.

She pressed her pelvis against his hardness and a rush of heated yearning coursed through her veins, leaving in its wake a need so great she could hardly contain it. ''You're as good as ever.''

''But only with you, Dana. There could never be any other woman but you. And I'm not saying that out of any sense of responsibility.''

"There could be no other man but you." She knew that now. Perhaps she had always known that.

He rolled her onto her back with tender urgency. She let out a soft cry of happiness as he lowered his body onto hers. Opening up to him like a flower opens up to the morning sun, she pressed her fingers against his back and rose to meet him. He slid inside her in a way that was both familiar and new.

Their lips were the last to meet, locking their bodies together in every way possible. But it was the coming together of their hearts that closed the final distance between them.

Chapter Twelve

Rays of warm sunshine flooded the balcony. Dana's eyes flickered open. She was lying in Rick's arms and it was obvious that he been watching her sleep. "You all right?" he whispered, brushing her brow with his lips.

"I couldn't be more all right," she whispered back. She reached up and caressed the sweet roughness of his cheek. He took her hand in his and kissed it.

She stretched along the length of him, basking in the still warm memories of the night. She felt like a bride. She felt like she had fallen in love all over again.

Rick leaned over and kissed her tenderly on the mouth, and her heart began to flutter again in anticipation.

"I thought I was dreaming," he whispered in her ear. He stiffened suddenly. "Ouch. My back."

She uncurled herself and stretched her own sore muscles. "I guess it's my turn to rub first-aid lotion on you."

He grinned. "I look forward to it." He stood and tried to work the kinks out of his muscles. "How long do you think it'll take before Etta makes it to our room?"

"Soon, I hope." Dana glanced over the railing and scanned the area between the trees. Where was a jogger when you needed one?

"Dana . . ."

She turned.

"Last night. It was special."

"It was special for me, too," she said.

"I want to say something. I want to do this right."

There was warmth in his eyes, and love—the kind of love that was unbearably precious and needed to be protected at all costs. She shuddered at how close they had come to throwing it away. "What do you want to do right?"

He knelt on one knee and adjusted the inadequate robe as he tried to strike a classic romantic pose. This was so out of character for Rick that he looked like a bad actor in a melodrama. Were it not for the serious look on his face, she might have been inclined to laugh. Instead she gazed in wonder at the love and sincerity in his eyes.

"What do you say we—" He stopped, cleared his throat and began again. "Would you do me the honor of staying married to me? I'm not offering you much. I don't have a job. . . ."

Her heart began to beat so quickly, she could hardly stand still. "It doesn't matter. . . ."

"But I do have an idea . . ."

"What idea?"

"I'm not sure it would work. Actually, I got the idea from something Etta said. She noticed me reading a magazine on classic cars and told me about her nephew and the trouble he had finding someone to refurbish his 1926 Pierce Arrow Roadster. I got to thinking that maybe I should go into business for myself."

"Oh, Rick, that's a wonderful idea! You're so good at it. Why didn't we think of this before?"

"I don't know. I guess I couldn't imagine myself owning my own business. It would mean having to drum up some capital."

"We can do that. I know we can." She couldn't believe it; the two of them making plans and sharing dreams again, after all this time. Her excitement building, she could hardly get the words out fast enough. "We could mortgage the house and—"

He stood and touched his fingers to her lips. It was important that this time around there be no misunderstandings. "I'm probably never going to send you flowers."

"That's not important. . . ."

"And I want you to know there's only one reason why I want us to be together, and that's because I love you. . . ."

"Oh, Rick . . ." Her eyes filled with tears. "I love you, too." She moved toward him, but he held her back.

"This time I'm going to do it right." He glanced around as if looking for something. "Ah-ha!" He leaned over to pick up the straggly-leaf plant that had fallen out of the broken pot the night before.

"What are you doing?"

"I'm going to prove that I'm a romantic guy. I don't have flowers or diamonds. But I would be very happy if you would accept this plant as a token of my love."

She laughed appreciatively as he placed the drooping plant into her hands. "Oh, Rick, I shall always cherish this."

It was his turn to laugh. "As much as the hard hat?" He captured her face in his hands and kissed her soundly on the lips. As he did so, she dropped the plant and it fell between their feet.

"Oh, no!" she cried out. She scooped up the plant and cupped it tenderly. This was going into the trunk of mementos where she kept the tire iron from his first proposal. "Poor plant." She brushed the soil aside with a finger and felt something hard. Digging deeper into the clump of dirt, she retrieved a shiny object.

It took a moment to realize what she'd found. "Oh, Rick!" she exclaimed. "Look! It's Debby's ring!"

"What?" His eyes widened in disbelief. "Are you sure?"

"Positive." She held the ring up to the sunlight. "See inside the band? To D.M. love S.T."

"Well, I'll be. How do you suppose Debby's ring got into the plant?"

"I don't know. Wait a minute. Do you suppose a pigeon might have swiped the ring from their room?" And to think she had all but accused poor Etta. "I've seen pigeons forge around in these pots."

"I guess it's possible." He took the ring from her hand. "Do you think Debby would mind if we made use of this ring for a little while?"

"Make use? How . . . ?"

He slipped the gold band onto her ring finger, just as he had at the altar those many years ago.

Happiness filled her heart. At that moment she felt she could fly off that balcony all the way to heaven and beyond. "I'm sure she wouldn't mind."

"So, will you stay married to me?"

She threw her arms around his neck. "Yes! Yes! Yes!"

He held her tight and captured her lips just as the phone rang. They jumped apart and stared at a previously unnoticed phone box that was all but hidden by two chaise longues.

"Do you mean to tell me that we nearly froze to death and there was a phone here all the time?"

"I don't believe it!" Dana exclaimed. She opened the box and picked up the phone on the third ring. "Hello?"

"Mom, it's Steve. I'm sorry to bother you so early but I thought you'd want to know. Debby gave birth to a baby boy. . . ."

"A baby boy," Dana gasped, gazing into Rick's loving face. She hadn't seen him look so happy in a very long time. She tried to concentrate on what her son-in-law was saying. The baby was early but the doctor said everything was fine.

"You bet we're coming home." She squeezed Rick's hand. "Give Debby our love and tell her we have a surprise for her." Admiring the wedding ring on her finger, she added, "We have two surprises for her."

No sooner had she hung up, than Rick picked her up in his arms and whirled her around. "That makes you the world's most beautiful grandma," he said.

"And you the world's most handsome grandpa," she countered.

"Let's go home," he said.

They raced to the door before remembering it was locked.

"The phone!" Rick jumped over a chaise longue and grabbed the phone to call the front desk. In less than a minute he hung up. "Etta is on her way."

He wrapped his arms around her.

Dana smiled and nuzzled next to him. What a night it

had been, what a wonderful, wonderful night. "You don't suppose that Etta locked us outside on purpose? Do you?"

"Why are you always so suspicious of her? First you accuse her of stealing Debby's ring, and now . . . She's nothing but a nice lady with a romantic streak. She didn't know we were on the balcony." He dropped a peck on Dana's nose and was about to capture her moist, pink lips when a banging sound made him look up. Etta waved at them from the other side of the French doors.

There was something about the satisfied look on the older woman's face as she unlocked the door that made him frown in uncertainty. "Nah. She wouldn't lock us outside on purpose." *Would she?*

Wake-up Call

Ruth Jean Dale

Chapter One

Claire Kendall Elliott strode across the impressive lobby of the Glass Garden Hotel in Dallas like a woman with a mission—which she was. Wearing what used to be called a "smart little suit," carrying a no-nonsense leather brief-case and trailed by a bellman toting an expensive set of monogrammed luggage, she practically oozed authority and self-control.

"Mornin', Miz Elliott"; "Good morning, Mrs. Elliott"; "Nice to see you again, Ms. Elliott . . ." Every hotel employee she met greeted her by name and offered warm smiles of welcome. Claire responded with a certain reserve that bespoke her serious purpose.

Ashlee the desk clerk, pretty and perky enough to give Miss America hives, offered a particularly dazzling smile along with a room key. "Welcome back to the Glass Garden, Ms. Elliott," she said brightly. "We're all just so glad to—"

"Thank you, Ashlee." Claire took command along with the key. "Chad can carry my things right on up."

"Yes, ma'am." Ashlee's smile didn't waver. "Would you like me to—"

"No, thank you, Ashlee. I have everything I require for the moment." Claire was already moving away with the bellman, Chad, at her heels. No time for idle chitchat; a vague wave dismissed Ashlee.

With purposeful steps, Claire led the way to the elevator that would transport her to her destination in the West Tower. To her right lay the glorious garden from which the hotel took its name and its fame, but she ignored it. She'd seen it before and it was beautiful. Soothing. Beckoning. With a glass wall soaring three stories high, the garden provided an unparalleled view of Glass Lake and its year-round population of feathery freeloaders.

Later she would have plenty of time to sit within the tropical confines of that magic kingdom for adults and meditate on life's meaning. For the moment she had places to go and things to do.

Deliberately turning her back on all that serenity, she stepped into the posh elevator and waited with barely concealed impatience while the young bellman wrestled with the luggage cart. At last the elevator began its ascent. Chad gave her a whimsical smile which she did not return.

"Nice weather we're having," he said.

Why was he bothering her? Couldn't he see that she was holding herself together with spit and bailing wire, as her grandfather used to say?

Chad sighed and rolled his eyes. "I told Charlie that was no kinda ice breaker, but that dude's living in la-la land," he said in a confidential tone. "Don't tell him I said so, though. Wouldn't want to hurt the old guy's feelings."

Claire, from her many previous visits, knew that Charlie was "head dude" in the bellman's hierarchy. "For you, Chad," she said, "anything." She spoke wryly, wondering why on earth he might imagine her discussing him with anyone. Even at her most gregarious, she was a private woman who kept her own counsel.

The elevator glided to a halt and the doors slid open with well-oiled precision. Claire stepped out and drew a deep, steadying breath. She was almost there. She took off at a pace just short of a trot.

The door to the Honeymoon Suite stood slightly ajar, and she reached out tentatively to touch the brass nameplate with her fingertips before walking inside. As always, her heart gave a little leap of anticipation before settling into a pounding, anxious rhythm. Everything was as it had been: the mirrored foyer with blush-pink marble floor, a lush fern with graceful drooping fronds, and, in its own special niche, a marble bust of Mitsy Packard, beloved wife of the hotel's founder.

Obviously, a man who knew a good thing when he had it, Claire thought darkly.

Mitsy's husband, Diamond Mike Packard of Texas oil and cattle fame, had built the Glass Garden in 1921 for his adored wife. When the pale and waiflike Mitsy found the heat and humidity of Dallas a strain, Diamond Mike proceeded to create the Glass Garden itself, so his loved one could watch the lake from the protection of her own massive "greenhouse."

Portraits of Mitsy—blond, blue-eyed, patrician, and very, very sad-looking—hung throughout the hotel, as they had through the decades.

Hard to believe any man could dredge up that kind of faithful devotion.

Wheeling to the right, Claire marched through the doorway and into a splendid approximation of a romantic Victorian garden room. A floor-to-ceiling glass wall offered a breathtaking view of the Dallas skyline, and French doors opened out onto a private wraparound balcony designed and lavishly decorated to match the Victorian theme.

Claire knew all the special details. She knew about the Jacuzzi tub in the bathroom, on a dias atop three marble steps. She knew how it felt when, like Cleopatra, she let her filmy negligee drift to the floor before stepping serenely into the steaming water.

Yes, everything was the same, from the well-stocked wet bar to the arched marble-faced fireplace with its ankle-deep sheepskin rug . . . a rug of many uses. Recessed shelves held an assortment of old books and art, which she'd had time to thoroughly peruse over the years. Her least favorite piece was a prominent marble reproduction of Rodin's "The Kiss."

She'd put that sucker in a closet someplace.

Dropping her purse and briefcase on the wicker settee, she made a beeline down the hall toward the bedroom. First things first, and the first thing she always did was—

Run smack into the maid. Etta Hannibal looked up with a wide, welcoming smile from her position on the far side of the lavishly appointed bed. As always, she wore a pink uniform with a white apron; as always, she smiled literally from ear to ear. Although somewhere in her late fifties or early sixties, she wore her bright blond hair Texas-big, always with a heart-shaped ornament stuck in that bird's nest somewhere. She was also the possessor of what had to be the world's largest collection of heart-shaped jewelry, which she wore with liberal abandon.

"Welcome back, honey," Etta exclaimed in her broad Texas drawl. "Watch them stairs, now, ya hear?" She nodded toward the wide curving steps leading down into the sunken bedroom. "That third one's a lulu."

As if I don't know that, Claire thought, displeased—but not surprised—to find Etta here. Etta and the Honeymoon Suite sort of went together. The fourth-floor maid was in her true element here, for she was a hopeless romantic and proud as punch of her position as caretaker for those who ventured into *her* domain.

Gad, Claire thought with dismay; she's even more cheerful than she was last year. I may toss my cookies.

Chad halted at the top of the steps and surveyed the room, resplendent with scented satins and laces and polished woods. "Want me to throw this stuff on the bed?" he asked.

Distracted, Claire turned. "Just leave everything there and I'll—"

"Sure do," Etta sang out. "Drag it on down here, boy, and I'll have Miz Elliott unpacked in the blink of a gnat's eye."

Claire felt her control of the situation slipping away. "Please don't bother, Etta."

"No bother, honey! Why, I love doin' this for my *special* people." Etta's reproachful expression left no room for dissent. She flapped her hands. "You just relax yourself and let Chad there open one'a them bottles' a champagne I got chillin' in the refrigerator. Let us do for you, honey. That's what we get paid for."

Claire's composure took another nosedive, but what the hell? She was here. She'd made it. Let Etta take over now.

She walked back to the sitting room, dropped into the white wicker love seat and closed her eyes.

"Here you go, Ms. Elliott."

Chad held out a champagne flute with an inch or so of golden bubbles inside. Accepting the glass, she raised it in a mocking salute. "Cheers," she said, and tossed off the contents.

Oh, yes, that was it; she held out her empty glass and he refilled it. Wedging the bottle into a crystal and silver wine cooler, he set the whole thing on the smoky glass table before her.

"What else? You name it, you got it."

Ah, that it were true—she sighed. He really was a nice boy. Shame on her for being cross. "Not a thing, Chad. Thanks." She cleared her throat as if to account for her husky tone.

With a sloppy salute, he departed. A half glass of champagne later, Etta entered with offers of further assistance. Claire responded with a shake of her head.

Etta hesitated, solicitous as always. "You change your mind, you just holler."

Claire swallowed hard, almost afraid to trust her voice. "C-Could you put out the Do Not Disturb sign when you go?"

"You got it, honey. Anything else?"

Claire shook her head.

"It feel hot in here to you? I could turn up the air conditioner."

Claire made an unintelligible sound.

The maid took it as a negative, which it was. "If you're satisfied, I guess I gotta be." Etta took several reluctant steps toward the foyer. "You like a few snacks to go with that stuff you're drinkin'? You was supposed to have a fruit basket, courtesy of the management, but it ain't showed up yet. I could bring you up some nice—"

Claire shook her head again, this time vigorously.

"Well, if you're sure . . . ."

At last they were gone; they were all gone. At last she was alone.

Carefully placing her empty champagne glass on the table, Claire pulled the bottle out of the ice bucket, kicked off the red pumps that were a perfect match for her red suit, and stalked out onto the balcony overlooking Glass Lake and downtown Dallas.

Tears fell so fast that the fabled view was soon obscured. She lifted the bottle in a toast.

"Here's to the louse who ruined my life," she said in a fierce tone. And she took a swig of champagne straight from the bottle.

Claire slumped in a padded wicker chair a half hour later, her legs extended so she could rest her feet on the balcony railing. Her suit jacket lay on the floor beside her, and her white silk blouse was askew.

She didn't care. There was nobody and nothing to see her.

She'd drink to that. Lifting the champagne bottle to her lips, she was surprised to find it half empty. Damned stuff must have evaporated. Strange, considering how humid Dallas was. Musta changed in the year since she'd been here, turned to desert or something.

And got noisier, too. What in the world was that ringing and where was it coming from? Ah, yes, the telephone . . .

Climbing awkwardly to her feet, she looked around, trying to remember where the hell the balcony phone was located. The Honeymoon Suite had more telephones than —than a dog had fleas! She giggled at her own wit.

The telephone continued to ring. Concentrating hard, she followed the sound, finally arriving at an ornate wooden box artfully surrounded by ivy and begonias. Setting the bottle on the table, she fumbled with the little carved door to the box, finally getting it open so she could grab the handset and mutter an incensed, "Hello!"

"Hi, Claire," said an obnoxiously cheerful voice. "It's me, Glynn."

Claire groaned. Glynn Johnson was the thirty-year-old son of her boss at Tuff Tire Corp. of NYC. He was several other things as well, including her would-be lover and a genuine, dyed-in-the-wool, computer nerd—whole nine yards, including frameless eyeglasses and a pen leaking ink in the chest pocket of every shirt he owned.

He was also kind of cute, in a short-haired, sincere way. Unfortunately, he drove Claire absolutely crazy with his attentions, but he was so damned nice and accommodating about it that she couldn't even yell "Sexual harassment!" to get relief.

She could, however, be cross with him, and was—every chance she got. "What do you mean, calling me here?" she demanded.

"I just had to make sure you arrived safely," Glynn said, undeterred by the chilly reception.

"Why wooden sigh—I mean, why wouldn't I? Glynn, you've got to stop this. I can't have you—"

"Sure, Claire, whatever you say. Is there anything you need, anything I can—"

"No! Except stop calling me."

"In that case, maybe I could come—"

She hung up the telephone. Drat Glynn. Drat men. Drat J. D. Elliott.

Reaching for her champagne, she somehow managed to knock the bottle over. Fumbling for it, she propelled it over the edge of the table and onto the outdoor carpeting, where it landed with a dull thunk. The bottle didn't break, but by the time she got it upright, it was empty.

Muttering under her breath, she tottered inside to grab another bottle from the bar fridge. It wasn't easy, but she managed to bumble her way through the opening ritual: foil, wire bale, cork. Sparkly wine foamed over the lip of the bottle, and she licked it away quickly, determined not to waste another drop.

She needed all the false courage she could muster. Although not usually a drinking woman, today was August 12, and she had to work up her courage to face August 13. For it was on August 13 four years ago that she married John David Elliott, also known as the Louse, following what had truly been a whirlwind courtship.

They met on a ten-day Caribbean cruise. Claire was treating herself to a vacation because she'd just nailed a great job at Tuff Tire; J.D. was treating *himself* because he'd just completed a series about political corruption— which eventually won one of journalism's most coveted prizes: the J. Howard Welborne Investigative Journalism trophy.

She knew she was in trouble the minute she laid eyes on him, and steeled herself to resist. If there was one thing

Claire wasn't interested in, it was a vacation romance. She'd had one of those once, and it had turned out badly. She'd thought it was love and was not pleased to realize she'd been wrong.

After that she'd made a conscious decision to put her career first and all that moon-June stuff never. With single-minded determination she'd worked her way up in the corporate world, all the way from El Paso to New York City and an executive's office—with a window, yet. When she stepped onto that cruise boat, she was a woman who knew who she was and where she was going.

And she was *not* going to fall for Mr. John David Elliott, no matter how blue his eyes, how charming his smile, how sparkling his conversation.

Then fate—or something—stepped in. She upgraded her cabin at the last minute and ended up two doors from his. She chose second sitting for meals and ended up at the same dining table with him several times a day. She set out to earn enough of those damned Seaworthy Doubloons to get a free fitness T-shirt, and found herself striding around the deck with him every morning for a determined twenty minutes.

Proximity softened her up, no doubt about it. But if they hadn't run into a Caribbean squall with all its accompanying drama, she wouldn't have ended up in bed with him and that's for damned sure.

As long as she lived she'd remember with crystal clarity the events leading up to her downfall. The stage had been set by the majestic rise and fall of the great ship as she plowed through troubled waters. Claire hadn't felt seasick in the slightest, although others were falling like flies. What she felt was out of control, a rare condition that always frightened her. Her knees trembled and she couldn't find her sea legs; her head spun and she felt as if she might start sliding down the tilted decks and right on out to sea.

It seemed somehow inevitable that J.D. would materialize to slide a supportive arm around her waist. "Hey," he said, his tone filled with concern. "You okay?"

"N-No," she said. "I'm not okay." For her, that was an admission of enormous proportions. "Do you think you could . . . get me back to my cabin and lock me in until this is over?''

''For you,'' he said with a grandiose gesture, ''anything.''

She gave him a sour glance but was happy to lean on his strong arm and let him guide her down the wide staircase. With his help, she even managed to navigate the narrow hallway without careening from side to side. At her door she fished the key from her small evening purse, and he took it from her quaking fingers.

The door to her cabin swung open and she stumbled inside. Behind her, she remembered hearing him say, ''Is there anything else milady requires?''

Milady: the charming form of address of the friendly and attentive Jamaican crew. Hanging on to the edge of the dressing table, she attempted a smile.

At that precise moment the ship seemed to rise up, then fall into a hole in the ocean. The unexpected force of it sent J.D. hurtling inside the cabin and into Claire. Before either of them knew what was happening, they stumbled the length of her cabin to sprawl across her double bed, the door slamming shut behind them.

Claire wound up flat on her back with J.D. flat on top of her. She felt his chest strong against her breasts, his hipbones pressing into hers. Breathing hard, he lifted his head and looked down at her, his expression as stormy as the weather.

''I couldn't have planned it better,'' he murmured, moving his hips against her.

''Stop that.'' Wiggling to escape made it worse . . . or better, depending on how she looked at it. She wiggled some more and added as an afterthought, ''I don't need this!''

''No, of course not.'' He kissed the curve of her jaw. ''Who does?''

Apparently, she was going to have to get tough. ''I mean it,'' she said. She slid her hands around his neck and twisted her fingers through the rich brown hair curling at his nape. And hung on, aware of the roll of the ship, the pounding of her heart, the harsh sound of his breathing. ''I don't sleep around, in case you've got the wrong idea here," she added desperately.

"No, of course not." He slipped her silky dress off one shoulder and trailed kisses over her collarbone and down the curve of her shoulder. "Who does?"

She groaned. "Damn it, J.D., this is exactly what I've been trying to avoid the entire cruise. I'm not some easy lay—and if you say 'Of course not. Who is?' I'm going to kill you."

"God, Claire, there's nothing *easy* about you." The dress had stretched as far as it was going to; he began to work on the buttons. "You're probably the most difficult woman I ever . . . got personal with. Difficult and prickly and . . . and smart . . . and gorgeous . . ."

She remembered shifting to accommodate his clever fingers, although she hadn't meant to. In a twinkling the dress fell open to her waist and he stroked the upper curves of her breasts.

She gasped and closed her eyes. "But you live in California!" she cried.

"I know where I live," he muttered, his mouth seeking. "Mind if I don't say anything else for a few minutes? I can . . . walk and chew gum, but I'm not sure I can . . . talk . . . and make love. . . ."

As it turned out, he could and did—all the way to Puerto Rico three days later.

Where the cruise ended. Their relationship, however, didn't. They'd just found each other and couldn't bear to part. They spent their last twenty-four hours on board the ship wrapped in each other's arms, with a Do Not Disturb sign on the door, a damned poor way to search for the strength and courage to say good-bye. In fact, it was impossible.

That being the case, they picked a spot roughly halfway between New York and San Francisco, flew there and got married.

That spot was Dallas, where they honeymooned at the famous Glass Garden—and glorioski, was it ever great. Only on their last day did they get around to talking about their future.

They quickly discovered they didn't have one, wedding

license to the contrary. She said ee-ther and he said eye-ther, and that was only the beginning of their differences. She, supremely ambitious, was about to start her dream job in New York, while he, a mellow many-generations Californian, couldn't imagine living anywhere else.

They never really got past the bitter realization that neither would compromise on the issue of geography; it pretty much eclipsed the things they *did* agree on and put the marriage on the skids. They got together a few times after that, brief meetings that yielded little besides steamy sex—not to be scorned, but not enough, either. Six months after they tied the knot, they agreed to a "friendly" divorce.

Claire didn't actually feel very friendly about it, but pretended. Since then she'd tried desperately to get on with her life, but to little avail.

Knowing J.D., loving J.D., seemed to have pretty much ruined her for other men. Every male she met suffered by comparison. As what should have been her first wedding anniversary approached, she grew so melancholy that, on an impulse, she flew to Dallas. There, she spent five days alone in the Glass Garden Hotel Honeymoon Suite with the Do Not Disturb sign on the door, determined to confront her ghosts and put them behind her.

The effect was just the opposite; J.D. was more real to her each time she left than he had been when she arrived. But being a self-styled tough-as-nails career-type woman, she persisted. Each year since, she'd spent her "anniversary" alone at the Glass Garden, boohooing into her champagne and swearing that this time would be the last.

Maybe she ought to give Glynn Johnson a chance, she brooded, glaring at the champagne bottle. When he tried to talk her into letting him fly to Dallas with her, maybe she should have said yes.

Or maybe she shouldn't have come herself.

This is it, she vowed. *This is the absolute very last time I'm going to do this.* Enough was enough; it was time she got a life. Her biological clock was ticking—hell, at thirty-four it was running amok.

Even the hotel help seemed to sense her new resolve, because not one of them had asked hopefully if Mr. Elliott would be joining her. This year, unlike the previous ones, no one had even mentioned his name. Good!

Sniffling and carrying her bottle of champagne, she stumbled into the bathroom and turned on the water in the Jacuzzi. This time it was going to work.

This time when she left the Glass Garden, she'd have forgotten she ever *knew* Mr. John David Elliott.

Meanwhile, Mr. John David Elliott was checking into the Dallas Glass Garden Hotel with an agenda of his own.

Chapter Two

J.D. looked around the lobby of the Glass Garden with something akin to awe. It was exactly the way he remembered it, and he remembered it more clearly than he did the San Francisco apartment he'd called home for almost a decade. Some things never changed, apparently.

More's the pity.

The business suit at the head of the line completed his transaction and moved away. J.D. stepped up to the counter, whereupon he was favored by a warmly professional smile from the blond, blue-eyed Miss Texas–type on duty.

"Ashlee," announced her name tag. One of the many chi-chi *ee* names: Ashlee, Courtnee, Kellee, Kristee, and J.D.'s personal favorite, Chutnee.

"Hi ya, Ash," he said, hiding his trepidation with more good cheer than he felt. "I've got a reservation, name of Elliott."

"Oh, Mr. *Elliott!*"

If he thought she was smiling before, he didn't know what smiling really was.

She gushed on: "We've been expecting you. Welcome to the Glass Garden, Mr. Elliott." She snapped her fingers. "Chad!"

A long-haired and sun-bleached young man in a bellman's gray and red uniform stepped promptly to J.D.'s side. He was the kind of goofy kid you'd find at any California beach or mall.

"This is Mr. *Elliott,* Chad," Ashlee said, bearing down on the name as if it were indeed a great recommendation. "If you'll sign the register, Mr. Elliott, Chad will take your things right up."

Chad grinned. "Hey, man," he said to J.D. "Welcome to the Glass Garden. Yo!" He gave a funny little two-fingered salute.

J.D. vaguely remembered the staff as friendly, but this was ridiculous. Of course, during the course of his one and only visit here, his attention had been otherwise occupied.

After a brief hesitation, he signed the register *Mr. and Mrs. J. D. Elliott, San Francisco,* hoping God would forgive him for lying.

Okay, he was weak, but it wasn't entirely his fault. Women had always pursued him—all except his ex-wife. Maybe her determination to avoid a relationship was what first attracted him to her. After the breakup of his marriage it got worse, with prospective replacements lurking around every corner. None, however, had caught him, even briefly: i.e., he hadn't slept with a woman since his divorce —which felt as if it must have been twenty years ago, at least.

Helluva way for a grown man to live, he brooded, full of self-pity even as he laid down the pen and accepted the key from a still-smiling Ashlee. That state of affairs was about to change, thanks to the perseverance of Ramona Daniels.

Ramona had hit on him relentlessly since she joined the editorial staff of the *San Francisco Evening Star* two years ago. As the dreaded August 13 anniversary approached, J.D. made a cold-blooded decision to let her catch him, but in a way guaranteed to obliterate memories of Claire for all time.

That's why he'd booked the Honeymoon Suite. That's why he'd invited Mona to join him in it tomorrow. That's why his hand shook when he signed the register.

J. D. Elliott was about to make his move. Take that, memories!

* * *

Chad deposited the bags in the foyer of the Honeymoon Suite, accepted a healthy tip and departed. J.D. stood there for a moment, looking around with a sense of wonder.

Everything was precisely as he remembered, from the mirrored walls to the marble bust of Mitsy Packard, a sad sack if he'd ever seen one. He took a hesitant step. Yes, everything was the same . . . except he found no warm and willing woman waiting to be swept into his arms. Maybe it hadn't been such a hot idea, checking in a day ahead of Mona. Too much time to think . . .

But then he rallied. He was a man of iron will. He'd keep busy. He wouldn't mope around. Grabbing his single bag, he carried it into the sitting room and dropped it on the green and rose Aubusson rug. With brisk decisiveness, he dialed the desk to request a wake-up call for six the next morning.

Yeah, he'd keep busy. He'd run around Glass Lake a few times before breakfast; he'd work in a few games of handball before lunch; he'd swim laps before dinner. He'd take Mona dancing every night and they'd trip the light fantastic until the wee small hours—

The muted but unmistakable sound of footsteps on lush carpet startled him from his reverie. Swinging toward the sound, J.D. froze at the sight that greeted his eyes—

Claire, standing in the doorway, wearing a white terry-cloth hotel robe that ended well above the knee, dangling an open champagne bottle in one hand. Short, wet hair framed her face; utter amazement radiated from her wide brown eyes.

Even in his shock, he thought she looked better than ever: sexy and soft and womanly.

Those last two were not qualities he normally would have attributed to her.

"What are you doing here?" they demanded simultaneously; *"I asked you first!"* they responded in unison.

Claire, the champagne glow knocked out of her by the unexpected appearance of the man who'd broken her heart, stared at him with a yearning she was unprepared to confront. He looked wonderful: six feet of tanned California sex appeal, with tousled brown hair and sexy blue eyes that melted every resolve she'd ever mustered.

The whole situation was too ridiculous. Her emotions, lubricated by the bubbly, lay so uncommonly near the surface that she was either going to laugh or cry.

Being Claire, a woman who considered tears a sign of feminine weakness to be eschewed, she chose to laugh.

Now she knew why none of the hotel staff had inquired about J.D., as they'd done incessantly each previous year; they all believed that *this* year he was coming! So why had he?

Suddenly all too aware that beneath the robe was nothing but bare skin, she stopped laughing and pulled the belt tighter. "What the hell are you doing here?" she choked out.

"I . . . well, that is . . . I thought . . . it seemed like a good idea at the—" He mumbled to a halt, frowning. "Wait a minute, what are *you* doing here?"

"I asked first."

"That's beside the point. First, second, what's the difference?"

"Why, it's—I don't see . . . that's none of your—" Completely flustered, she whirled and started toward the bedroom.

He came after her, which brought her swinging around. "Where the hell do you think you're going?"

"With you. How are we supposed to get this straightened out if we're in different rooms?"

"Oh. In that čase . . ." She pivoted and headed back to the sitting room, head down to avoid looking at him. That simply put her at too much of a disadvantage.

Placing the wine bottle on an end table, she dropped into the wicker chair, curling her legs beneath her. Terry cloth slid apart over her thighs and she tried to draw the edges of fabric together, without much success.

Looking up, she found him staring at her exposed legs with the most peculiar expression: she interpreted it as part disbelief and part lusty memory. Still, since there was little she could do, why bother trying? He'd seen more, he simply hadn't seen it recently. She lifted her chin a notch, refusing to back down.

He cleared his throat, dragged his gaze up to meet hers, shrugged as if he knew she'd caught him looking and didn't give a damn. Dropping onto the settee, he reentered the fray. "You were about to tell me what you're doing here," he reminded her, his tone slightly hoarse.

"Oh. Well, there's nothing to tell, actually. I . . . that is, I . . . I like Dallas, always have. I like the hotel—"

"You like honeymoon suites in general or this one in particular?"

"I like privacy," she said, feeling a touch of heat in her cheeks. "I *thought* I'd get it here. In fact, there's supposed to be a Do Not Disturb sign on my door. So what's your excuse?" A sobering thought—a literally sobering thought —hit her in the gut. "Have you remarried?" she blurted.

He looked down at the toes of his leather sports shoes. "Well, no," he admitted, drawing it out, "but . . ."

Understanding dawned, bringing with it shock and dismay. "You're meeting another woman here . . . where we spent our honeymoon?" She jumped to her feet, paying little heed to the flap of terry against her thighs. "How could you be so insensitive?" She pushed her hair back from her face, using both hands. "Talk about adding insult to injury!"

"Now, don't jump to conclusions." He shifted uneasily on the flowered cushion, looking greatly offended. "Give me a break here. What kind of man do you take me for— don't answer that."

"Then why are you here?"

"I . . . I'm . . ." He swallowed hard. "I'm on assignment."

She sank back down, weak with relief despite almost immediate doubts as to the veracity of his claim. "Assignment?"

"Yes, that's right, I'm on assignment. For the paper. And the hotel's full-up—big conference going on, big. People all over the place."

"Really? I hadn't noticed any particular—"

"Oh, yeah, big crowd, very big. People stacked to the rafters. Nothing was available except this suite—"

"It's not available, either!" She leaned forward, real-

ized the robe wrapped across her chest gaped open to the
waist and tugged the pesky garment safely closed again.

"Well, I thought it was." He licked his lips. "Obviously what we have here is a failure to communicate. The
hotel probably thought we"—he wiggled his forefinger to
indicate the two of them—"were together, or maybe they
never knew we were apart. I sure as hell didn't tell them,
did you?"

"I don't go around sharing details of my personal life
with hotel employees," she sputtered.

"You don't share much of anything with anybody, as I
recall."

That was hitting below the belt, so she hit back.
"You're only saying that because you're a professional
snoop. Privacy means nothing to you."

"In your case, it's not privacy, it's secrecy."

It dawned on her that they'd degenerated into petty
bickering. And it further dawned on her that his excuse for
being here didn't hold much water. "On assignment, you
say?" she prodded.

"That's right." He lifted his head, fixing her with his
most sincere expression.

The one he used just before urging some benighted
source to "trust me," she supposed. "Liar," she muttered.

He jerked as if she'd spit in his eye. "No name calling,
please," he requested with dignity. "My reason's more
reasonable than yours. At least I'm here in the line of
duty."

She no more believed that than she believed the moon
was made of green cheese. He *was* meeting another
woman, and she'd be *damned* if she'd let him get away
with thinking that she cared. They could pull out her
tongue before she'd admit how much it would hurt to see
him with someone else, even after all this time.

"Actually," she said with a grim tilt to her chin, "I'm
meeting . . . someone myself. A . . . friend."

"A man?" He darted a glance around the room as if he
expected someone to be lurking behind the potted ferns or
the heavy draperies. Finding no one, he turned on her with
a curl to his lips. "Yeah, right."

How dare he not believe her! "It's true," she said, pressing her lie. "He'll be here tomorrow. Hey, when you and I split up, I didn't slash my wrists or enter a nunnery. My life is a mad social whirl, if you must know, but n-now I think I've finally found Mr. Right."

He wasn't buying it, she knew that even before he gave an incredulous bark of laughter.

"Mr. Right, is it? Give me a break! The only mad whirl you ever got involved with was to the top of the business world, not the social ladder. You never had time for romance—hell, I only got in on a pass. Are you telling me that's changed? Ha!"

"I'm telling you it's immaterial to me whether you believe me or not."

"Oh, yeah?" His jaw jutted out at a pugnacious angle. "Convince me," he taunted. "Who is this man among men you've deigned to honor?"

Yeah, who? "He's . . ." Floundering, she bit her lip, stalling. "Why should I tell you?" she finally burst out. "You're harassing me."

"Me? Harass *you?*"

"In a New York minute." She slumped against the cushion, trying to gather her thoughts to defend her lie.

"Gosh," he said ingenuously, "why am I having trouble believing this? Let's see, what could bring you here? I've got it—you're interviewing for a job. What're you up for, queen of Texas? I can't imagine you'd leave the Big Apple for anything less."

Damn him! He had no right to barge in here and practically force her to tell all these outrageous lies. But since she had to defend herself, she said, "His name is Glynn Johnson and he's my boss's son. He's a very—"

"A-ha!" J.D. sat upright. "Boss's son—a clear case of sexual harassment in the workplace if I ever heard one. I've done a couple stories on that and I know what I'm talking about. Did Daddy dangle you in front of Junior as a sexual toy? Or did he—"

"I'm nobody's sexual toy," she said, getting huffy about it, "and no one would *dare* dangle me anywhere. Glynn doesn't even work at Tuff Tire. He's an engineer with a big firm that specializes in—"

She stopped, glowering at her ex-husband. "I have no obligation to explain any of this to you. Suffice it to say that since our divorce I've been besieged by men. I picked Glynn. He's coming tomorrow. We'll spend a glorious vacation together. Then . . . well, we'll see where it leads."

"Do you love him?"

"That's none of your business!"

"Then you don't. I'm shocked, Claire," he said, looking it, "well and truly shocked to find you about to shack up in our honeymoon suite with another man you're not even in love with. And you say *I* lack sensitivity."

"You weren't supposed to be around to see it!" She threw up her hands defensively. "Look, since you're going to have to find another room anyway, why not make it in another hotel and spare us both?"

"I don't see why I should be the one to—"

"Be reasonable, J.D." She couldn't believe she was pleading. "Neither of us could possibly be comfortable in the same hotel."

He looked as if he were about to protest, but didn't. "Fine," he said, "if that's how you feel about it." He jumped to his feet, his blue eyes stormy. Bending with supple grace, he snatched up his carry-on bag and took an angry stride toward the door.

Claire held her breath. He was going. Despite her panicked reaction to seeing him again after all this time, she'd kept her head and she'd won. *Thank you, God—thank you, thank you, thank you. . . .*

J.D. stopped short. "Wait a minute." Dropping the case, he squared his shoulders and turned back, his brow wrinkling like a man just coming to his senses. "I'm not going anywhere. This is the room I reserved and it's the room I want."

"I was here first!"

"So what's your point?"

"My point is, get out!"

"Why should I? What's in it for me, except the hassle of finding someplace else to bunk? Naw, I think I'll stay."

She felt near to tears, emotionally overwrought and vulnerable. Shouldn't have drunk all that damned champagne;

that was it, the champagne. Not the man; please, not the man! "John David Elliott," she said in a quivering voice, "you're no gentleman!"

"Which makes us even, since you're no lady, Claire Kendall Elliott. I have as much right to our little love nest as you do."

She groaned; they'd hit an impasse and it had only taken them minutes. A fitting simile for their marriage.

They stared at each other across the narrow space separating them. In actual fact, the things that separated them had always been minor, she thought, but at the same time, powerful. Especially for two stubborn people who had never learned to bend.

They might have stood there indefinitely, gazes locked, had not the doorbell gently pealed the arrival of a new contender. Claire flinched; the doorbell at the Glass Garden didn't merely say "ding-dong" like doorbells the world over, it rang the opening notes of "Lara's Theme" from *Doctor Zhivago*, a blatant attempt at emotional manipulation.

Which never failed to work. Quick tears sprang to her eyes and she blinked mightily to discourage them.

J.D.'s gaze narrowed. "Whoever it is, I'll get rid of them so we can thrash this out." He disappeared into the foyer.

Claire let out her breath in a great whoosh. Every muscle in her body trembled with strain. Why had she lied to him? She hated lies, never told them unless her back was to the wall, then told them badly.

But how could she have confessed her true reason for being here? She couldn't tell him that she'd never gotten over him, that she came back to the scene of the crime annually in a desperate ritual designed to rip him from her heart and memory.

He, on the other hand, was no more truthful than she. On assignment, my eye, she thought savagely. *He's meeting some little bimbo or my name isn't—*

"Miz Elliott, look what I got!" Etta Hannibal, a Texas tornado in pink uniform and lacy heart-shaped hankie pinned to her left shoulder, burst into the room. In one hand she clasped the handle of an enormous basket of fruit; in the other hand she transported an equally impressive arrangement of flowers, primarily birds of paradise.

"Courtesy of the management," she announced, plunking both baskets down on the coffee table. She placed her hands on ample hips, positively beaming. "My word, I can't tell y'all how tickled I am to see the two'a you here together again."

J.D. shuffled his feet, looking as ill at ease as Claire felt. "Etta, right?" At her eager nod, he continued. "Etta, it's not exactly what you—"

"Honey," the maid interrupted, "I been in the honeymoon business long enough to know that the sea of love ain't always smooth sailin'—"

"That's right," Claire inserted eagerly. "And when two people—"

"—really love each other, there ain't no stoppin' them." Etta leaned over to poke at the flowers, propping up a bird of paradise that threatened to topple. "Honey, relax and go with the flow. When your marriage begins in my Honeymoon Suite at the Glass Garden Hotel, you are guar-an-danged-*teed* a lifetime run. And that's a promise."

Don't I wish, Claire thought around the sudden constriction of her heart. If only it were that simple.

"So what can I do you for?" Etta pressed on, her soft drawl eager. She glanced at her heart-shaped wristwatch. "Gettin' on toward six. How 'bout I make you dinner arrangements? Y'all goin' out or eatin' in?"

Before either could respond, Etta struck her temple a lightly glancing blow. "Silly me! You wanna eat at the Terrace like you did on your first honeymoon. Lemme make a quick call."

First honeymoon? Claire's panicky glance met J.D.'s and he shrugged helplessly. Calling it a "first" honeymoon implied they were here on a "second" one, and nothing could be further from the truth.

Memories of that "first" honeymoon brought with it feelings Claire had never wanted to confront again. Damn that J.D. for showing up where he wasn't wanted. This really was all his fault.

Etta covered the telephone mouthpiece with one be-ringed hand. "The Terrace is so intimate, just right for a romantic tayat-à-tayat." She turned back to the telephone. "That's right, Mr. and Miz J. D. Elliott. The best table, Ty-*rone*. They're in the Honeymoon Suite and prob'ly won't be lingerin' over the canopies, but let's make it nice while they're there."

She hung up, smiling at the stunned couple. "All fixed, folks. Table'll be waitin' for you in a half hour so you best hustle."

"Oh, dear." Claire glanced at J.D. for guidance: *What do we do now?*

He didn't look as if he had any better handle on the situation than she. He sucked in a deep breath. "Why not?" he asked in an I-give-up tone. "We've got to eat, right?"

"Well, now," Etta said with gusty approval. "That's the spirit. You wanna eat the rest of your meals in this very room, I'll be pleased to take care of it. But this first night, go on out." She grinned at Claire. "Let him court you all over again, is my advice. And you . . ."

She swung on J.D. "You think back on how it was in the beginnin', and romance the little lady like you done then." She clasped her hands together in apparent ecstasy. "Oh, this is gonna be great, absolutely great!"

The beleaguered couple stood there staring blankly at each other while Etta departed. Claire, remembering their courtship, felt her cheeks burn with mortification. This wasn't why she'd come here; this wasn't what she wanted at all.

J.D. broke the silence, his voice brimming with reproof. "Etta's going to be bitterly disappointed when old George shows up in a day or two."

"Glynn—and let me worry about that."

"Hey, it's your life." He looked around the room as if in search of a focal point—and finding none except her. "So what do you think? She made the reservations. We have to eat sooner or later. Should we risk it?"

"I suppose we're stuck." She tightened her hold on the terry-cloth robe.

"Maybe it's for the best. We do have to talk."

"About what?"

He looked pained. "About the mix-up, of course. About who's going to get this suite and who moves out."

"That," she said, "is not open for debate."

His expression grew cool. "Don't push me, Claire. You always knew how, but you don't really want to do that now."

She lifted her chin. "I—" She stopped. "You're right," she said, more humbly than she'd intended. "We can discuss this over dinner, like two civilized people." The phrase *civilized people* was like ashes on her tongue. They'd had a civilized divorce, or so they'd agreed, and it had practically ripped her heart out.

J.D. looked a little white around the mouth. "Then get dressed and let's get this over with," he snapped, turning away as if he could no longer bear the sight of her.

Which he couldn't, without doing something he'd regret. Something like . . . grabbing her and kissing those soft lips, ripping that robe open and—damn!

He heard her angry footsteps marching down the hall and called himself all kinds of a fool.

She really *did* know how to punch all his buttons, probably because most of them still had her name on them.

Chapter Three

The Glass Garden offered three opportunities for the drinking and dining pleasure of guests, and as newlyweds, Claire and J.D. had tried them all.

Montague's specialized in good ol' down-home Texas cookin': barbecue and steaks, corn bread and chili, biscuits and gravy—that sort of thing. The Crystal Room Tavern offered a lunch and dinner buffet with a fixed menu of barbecue chicken, ribs and brisket with all the fixin's— and a giant television screen, dedicated to the Dallas Cowboys first and other sporting events a distant last.

Then there was the Terrace . . .

Plush, under-lit, overstaffed, and totally posh in every detail, the Terrace offered five-star dining for the most discriminating.

Or, in the case of Claire and J.D. Elliott, who'd shared

their first meal as husband and wife there, the least discriminating. To this day she didn't remember what she'd eaten at her wedding supper. She remembered that it was good, but not as good as looking at the handsome man with whom her life would forever after be entwined.

What made her think she could come here with him now and resist the pull of that happier past?

The maître d', crisp and debonair in his tuxedo, bowed low. "Ah, Mr. and Mrs. Elliott. Tyrone has instructed us to do everything in our power to see that your second honeymoon is as . . . delightful as your first." He spoke blandly, with a glance that said he knew damned well the success of their honeymoon didn't depend on him, but what the hell, he'd go along with that fiction.

Ill at ease yet again, Claire followed him through the dusky labyrinth, too aware of J.D. right behind her. She was relieved to reach an intimate booth upholstered in jewel tones of blue and green, high-backed for maximum intimacy. She slid in one side, J.D. on the other, and they sat there like statues while their guide lit the delicate crystal-encased candle in the middle of the table before shifting the fresh flower arrangement so it wouldn't impede conversation or lingering glances. He departed with a promise that their waiter would arrive in an instant.

J.D. looked at her, his expression blank. "Tyrone?"

It took her an instant to recall the maître d's reference. "The concierge. You must remember him—a handsome old gentleman with a southern accent?"

His blank expression didn't waver. "He must have made more of an impression on you than he did on me."

Oops! "Apparently." She'd have to watch it—couldn't let him know the reason she remembered the hotel and staff so well was because she'd become a regular. "This whole place made a real impression on me," she said, too defensively. "I—I always wanted to come back. I knew it'd be a great place for a regular vacation."

He gave her an enigmatic look. "It wasn't half bad for a honeymoon, either—and here's our waiter now. Care for a drink?"

"Champagne," she said without a moment's hesitation, longing for a return to her earlier glow.

He nodded and turned to the waiter. "A bottle of your best champagne," he said grandly, "and two glasses."

"When did you start drinking wine?" she asked in surprise. He was a beer drinker ordinarily, or at least, had been.

He gave her a wry smile. "When you walked into the middle of *my* suite wearing nothing but a robe and a confused expression," he admitted. "God, Claire." He drew a shuddering breath. "It's been a long, long time since I've . . . had a surprise like that."

"Amen."

Memories . . . enclosing them in an almost liquid warmth of good times past. They'd been so happy four years ago, so in love. Or so in something; whatever it was had barely survived the honeymoon.

"Tell me," she said brightly, her voice brittle as crystal, "how's life been treating you?"

"Fine." He toyed with his silverware. "Professionally, never better. My editors seem to like my work."

She pursed her lips and shook her head. "You always were too modest. I know all about that big prize you won."

"Yeah, the J. Howard Welborne. I didn't deserve it, but I took it just the same. Keep thinking there'll be a knock on my door any time now and they'll take it back."

"J.D., you're good. You earned it."

"Thanks for the vote of support, even from someone who didn't read the series that won."

"But I did." *Oops again!*

"Now how would a New Yorker know anything about what's in a San Francisco newspaper?"

She gave him a sheepish smile. "If you must know, I'm a subscriber."

"A . . . ?" He leaned back against his seat, his expression incredulous. "I can't believe what I'm hearing."

Good, she thought; don't. Because she'd subscribed right after they were married. At least in some small way, however impersonally, she could keep tabs on him.

The arrival of the wine steward spared her from making a further response. The champagne was presented with great ceremony, followed by a waiter to take their dinner order: a steak for her, fish for him.

The waiter left, and J.D. caught her flustered glance up short. "Same thing we ate our wedding night," he observed with no particular inflection.

She caught her breath on a gasp; she honestly hadn't remembered, or had convinced herself she didn't. Damn! She didn't like all these reminders. They made her more uneasy than ever.

Until she looked at him. God, she loved the way he looked, the brown hair tumbling over his forehead just as she remembered, the keen intelligence in the blue eyes, even the laughing curve of his mouth.

J.D. found excitement in everything he did. His curiosity knew no bounds, and his interest in people was completely genuine. Where she was often stiff and uncomfortable in purely social situations, he was completely at ease.

"He never met a stranger," her mother would have said of him, and it was true.

Now he lifted his champagne flute. "Cheers," he said softly, holding the pose until she joined in.

They sipped, still staring into each other's eyes. Claire wished he wouldn't look at her in that intent, probing way. It made her all . . . hot and melting inside.

"So tell me about you," he said. "I . . . hope life has been good to you."

"Oh, it has," she chirped. "I've had several promotions at work and another one is coming up."

"Work." His mouth curved down.

Her single-minded dedication to her career had been a source of friction between them "And I've got a new apartment," she added defensively.

"Good one?"

"Oh, great." Okay, great was a bit strong. It wasn't a lot better than her old place, but it was closer to work—which somehow wasn't quite as important as it used to be. Rents in New York were sky-high, but she didn't need much. "Do you still live in the same place?"

As if she needed to ask. He was more devoted to his

classy San Francisco apartment than she was to her job—another source of friction way back when.

"Yes." He waited until the waiter had served the salad and departed. "So you say you've become a social animal since our . . . breakup?"

"Well . . ." Claire stared at the crisp greens and bright chunks of radish and tomato. "I may have overstated that the tiniest little bit."

"Really. Then explain Mr. Right."

Wouldn't give her any slack, would he? "About that . . . I've dated a couple of guys, but nothing really serious."

His brows rose. "Nothing *really* serious?"

She slapped down her salad fork. "Okay, nothing even halfway, remotely serious. You can't be satisfied until I say it, can you?"

"Only if it's true." He thrust out his jaw. "How about this George guy?"

"Nothing about him—and the name is Glynn. He's just a guy."

His disapproval was clear. "Come on, Claire. Do you expect me to believe you're meeting a guy here tomorrow and you're not even serious about him? You may have changed, but you sure as hell haven't changed *that* much."

"I have—I mean, I haven't. I'm not." She closed her eyes and drew a painful breath, feeling the truth sneaking up on little cat feet. "Don't confuse me. I have changed, but not the way you mean. And Glynn isn't coming in tomorrow. I'm not meeting anyone. I'm here all alone for a little well-deserved R-and-R."

"Sure you are." He gestured toward a silver dish. "Pass the butter."

He didn't believe her. Suddenly it was important that she convince him. "No, really, I'm not meeting anyone. I just said that because—well, you made me mad."

"Swell, but I still need the butter."

She passed it gracelessly. "You never did recognize the truth, even when it kicked you in the shins," she grumbled.

"That's what makes me such a dandy reporter," he

agreed with a half grin. "You can level with me. I've got
no hold on you anymore."

No? He—or the memory of him, which was the same
thing—had destroyed every relationship she'd tried to es-
tablish in the past three years. Yeah, he still had a hold on
her.

Her grim smile nearly cracked her face. "I'd rather talk
about you. Living with anyone?"

"I am *way* too smart for that."

Good! "Date much?"

He shrugged. "A little." He shifted his gaze back down
to his salad. "To tell you the truth—"

"And why would you lie?" She laughed; it was one of
their jokes.

He joined in somewhat sheepishly. "True. Why would
I? So to tell you the truth, I've had—I had a little trouble
getting back into the social swim myself, after our . . ."

"The D-word's kind of hard to say, isn't it?"

He grinned agreement, and she found herself wondering
why a handsome and highly eligible man with a glamorous
high-profile job would have such a problem. Her dubious
gaze locked with his. Sparks sizzled between them, jolting
her back in her seat.

He'd missed her; she saw it in his face. Just as she had
longed for him, he'd longed for her. If they weren't sitting
politely with a dining table between them, he just might
show her how much. She licked her lips, aware of a sudden tightening in the pit of her stomach—

"Madame, may I remove your salad?"

God, yes, take it! What she wanted wasn't anything that
could come out of a restaurant kitchen. . . .

She felt faint with excitement. Maybe the Honeymoon
Suite won't be wasted after all, she thought wildly.

This dinner was as much a blur to her as the first one in
the Terrace had been. J.D. was charming, attentive, and
cautious; Claire was swept away before she ever had a
chance to defend herself. Champagne flowed; gradually
their respective guards slipped; and soon they were laughing and talking, although not as openly as they'd once
done.

Just as she drained the last drop of champagne from her glass, the waiter approached. Leaning over the table, he spoke in a confidential tone. "You have a call, Mrs. Elliott. Shall I bring a telephone to the table?"

She blinked in surprise and thought fast. It had to be Glynn; no one else would track her down this way. Considering the sexy and exciting man across the table from her, she knew she didn't want to take the call here, didn't want to talk to another man in front of him.

"May I take it up front?" she asked.

"Certainly."

J.D. rose as she did, stopping her flight with a quick hand on her shoulder. "I'll wait here for you," he said. "We still haven't talked about . . ." He glanced at the waiter, who was engrossed in contemplation of a crystal chandelier.

She knew what he meant; they still hadn't settled the matter of the suite. Somehow that seemed less of a problem to her now than it had earlier.

She shivered beneath his light hold and gave him a tentative smile. "Wh-Why don't you go on up to the suite and wait for me there?" she suggested a bit breathlessly. "You're right, we do need to . . . talk."

He watched her walk away, not knowing what to think. Woodenly he signed the check, woodenly he rose from the table, woodenly he stood there trying to get a grip.

Woodenly he walked out of the restaurant. He had to think. Without making a conscious decision, he veered into the Glass Garden.

He found a wrought-iron bench near the fountain and sat down. He'd stared at the fountain sculpture for several minutes before he realized it depicted the "Seven Labors of Hercules." Seemed appropriate—some poor slob trying to do the impossible.

And then he told himself he had to stop thinking what he was thinking: thoughts about lust and love and loss. It didn't help to realize all over again that no woman had ever turned him on the way Claire did—*did*, present tense, not past tense—but damn it, that was only the frosting on the cake. Okay, she was a workaholic, but nobody was perfect. She was also bright and articulate, funny and fearless.

Was there a chance for them to try again?

Caught completely by surprise at the thought, he shuddered. She'd hurt him once . . . but he had hurt her, too. Maybe . . .

He knew that he had changed greatly in the past four years. Missing her had done that to him. A dozen—hell, a hundred times he'd reached for the telephone to call her, and each time stopped. She was the one who'd wanted the divorce, after all. Why set himself up for another fall?

But maybe she'd changed, too. Before, she'd been a workaholic with an attitude, a woman who shot from the lip and let the bodies fall where they would.

Of course, she also laughed at his humor, however lame, and made him laugh at hers—and sometimes at himself. Not too bad a thing for a man who excelled at a career that bred arrogance.

For a while she'd made him feel he was the only man in the universe for her. In the end he'd concluded that no man could compete with her ambition—himself included.

Rising, he fished around in his trouser pocket and pulled out a coin. Walking at the edge of the pool in the middle of the garden, he paused to watch water bubble from the top of the fifteen foot edifice. A few other guests strolled past, and he could clearly see diners at the edges, overlooking the jungle lushness, but he still felt alone.

He'd felt alone for a long time now. He was damn sick and tired of it. He turned the penny between his fingers, wondering . . . hoping.

Deciding. He stuck the penny back in his pocket and hauled out a quarter; why take a chance? He'd call Ramona; he'd call her tonight and tell her not to come tomorrow. He'd tell her he wasn't worthy of her—the truth, obviously, because he was throwing her over for a long shot, the longest shot of his life.

Hell, he'd tell her he had the plague, anything. He closed his eyes and tossed the quarter with more force than the task required.

"I wish—" he began.

"For me, I hope," purred a voice behind him. "Darling, I couldn't wait!"

Ramona Daniels stepped around in front of him, threw her arms around his neck and planted a big one square on his numb lips. Frozen with horror, J. D. Elliott could only stand there, a doomed man.

Inside the Terrace Restaurant, Claire was surprised, but not unpleasantly, to find the telephone line dead. Great! She was eager to get upstairs for her . . . talk with J.D.

Hanging up the telephone in the manager's office, she stood for a moment with her eyes closed, willing herself to be rational about the situation in which she so unexpectedly found herself.

It was too soon to jump to conclusions, but there did seem to be a slight, ever so slight, chance they could "talk" this out—oh, who was she kidding? They always did their best communicating in bed.

After that, was there a chance for them? She didn't know about J.D., but she had changed greatly in their years apart. Her job, she'd finally admitted, was no longer the end-all and be-all it had been back then. She'd proven herself in business but found her victory hollow.

She wondered what had ever made her think she was different from any other woman. She wanted a husband and family with every fiber of her being, and at thirty-four was all too aware of the inexorable ticking of her biological clock—a cliché, sure, but one that cut to the heart of what she was feeling.

She was tired of being alone. She wanted J.D. back, damn it; if not him, then she'd force herself to settle for second best. But she'd never forgive herself if she didn't take this one last, desperate risk.

Or maybe it wasn't so desperate. Maybe he'd learned the art of compromise himself. Maybe he'd missed her as she'd missed him. Maybe he was even sorry he'd asked for the divorce.

Smiling to herself, she hurried out of the restaurant, a woman with a brand new purpose. Tonight, perhaps she wouldn't be alone after all.

Which was the fastest route to the elevator, past the front desk or through the Glass Garden? For a moment, she hesitated, trying to decide. . . .

Chapter Four

The garden would have to wait; Claire was in a *serious* hurry. She couldn't get to the suite fast enough.

Only to find J.D. wasn't there yet. Disappointment quickly gave way to anticipation. He'd arrive soon, and when he did . . . Warmed by erotic thoughts, she stood in the middle of the sitting room, hugging herself and grinning.

She was just about to kick off her shoes when he came roaring in as if he had the devil on his heels. Mildly surprised, but too wrapped up in her fantasies to be unduly concerned, she simply smiled . . . a long, slow, *sincere* smile.

He skidded to a halt. "Oops," he said. "You beat me."

"Yes." Bracing herself with a hand on the back of the settee, she raised one leg and dangled a slipper from her toes before letting it fall onto the luscious green and rose rug.

He stared as if mesmerized while she repeated the process to remove the other shoe. He swallowed hard and looked away. "Oh, yeah, anyway," he mumbled, "I ran into someone I thought I knew in the lobby and got held up."

"No problem." She took a couple of steps toward him. The thick carpet tickled her feet deliciously, sending new shivers of excitement through her. "I was just about to slip into something more . . . comfortable, as they say."

"Wh-Who says?" He looked practically wild-eyed.

She laughed low in her throat; she had him. She took another teasing step. "Jean Harlow, Mae West, someone like that."

"Uhhh, yeah, that's right." He swallowed hard. "You think you should?" he burst out. "I mean . . . what you've got on looks comfortable to me." He made a feeble gesture toward her conservative white crepe dinner dress.

Her level, promising gaze met his shifty, uneasy one. She smiled, watching him squirm. "Sweetheart," she murmured, "you ain't seen nothin' yet."

J.D. might still be confused by this sudden turn of events, but she wasn't. Going to him, she slid her arms around his neck, rose on tiptoe and gave him a passionate kiss.

Or started to. She'd no more than touched her lips to his than, with a groan, he enveloped her in his arms. His mouth covered hers, hot and hungry, and he leaned into her, bending her back before his unbridled enthusiasm.

She was just getting into it when he let her go as suddenly as he'd grabbed her. For a moment she swayed, dizzy with a multitude of feelings she'd never thought she'd have to confront again.

Faculties returning, she blinked twice, gave him a pointed glance that promised the moon, then turned and sauntered toward the bedroom.

J.D. stood there like a stump, with all his old feelings reborn—in spades. He was in shock, unable to believe what had just happened. She was going to try to seduce him! Try? Son of a bitch, she was going to *do* it unless he told her the truth about Ramona.

In which case he'd be up that fabled creek without a paddle. He groaned.

But maybe he could salvage the situation. Pacing from one end of the room to the other, he examined his options with frantic urgency. It all came back to the same thing: What in the hell was he going to do about Ramona?

It had taken a lot of fast talking on his part to buy a little time with her. First he'd had to convince her there'd been a hotel mix-up, that they wouldn't be getting their suite right away. Then he'd added insult to injury by telling her that he was on his way out of the hotel to the police station, yeah, that was it, the police station. He was doing a ride-along. Jeez, he hadn't done a ride-along since he was a cub reporter grasping at bylines.

Fortunately, Ramona worked in Lifestyles and had no

idea what real reporters did. Would he be gone all night? she'd asked with a pout.

Oh, hey, yeah, all night for sure—bummer!

He had to run, he'd told her, talking fast and trying to avoid clinging arms and puckered lips. She'd have no trouble getting a nice room in the East Tower, he assured her; he'd stressed *East* Tower. That's where he'd look for her tomorrow, but right now, duty called.

He'd dodged that bullet, but now found himself striding around the Honeymoon Suite wondering what in the hell he should do next. Obviously he had to tell Claire about Ramona, but how? And just when things were going so well between them—think, damn it!

A faint tapping on the door finally caught his attention, a sound so timorous that he wasn't even sure what it was since "Lara" usually announced visitors with her theme. Etta, he supposed, wanting to turn down the bed or do some other damned thing. That, he didn't need. He had enough troubles.

Standing in the middle of the sitting room, he glared at the doorway leading to the foyer. And as he did so, a horrible apparition rose before him in the form of Ramona Daniels, peeking around the door frame, her shoulder-length brown hair brushing her cheek and her hazel eyes wide and wary.

"Sweetheart," she exclaimed, "it is you! I wasn't sure —the door just sort of swung open."

My life is over, J.D. realized. Now's the time for lightning to strike or a meteor to fall on top of me. Because failing that, one of these women is going to kill me dead.

Ramona approached with *yes-yes* in her eyes while J.D. stood stiff as a post. She stopped in front of him and proceeded to give him a thorough once-over.

His brain began to function—not a minute too soon— and his survival instincts forged to the forefront. All was not yet lost; if he could just get her out of here before Claire—

"Mona," he said in a strangled voice, "there's something I need to tell you. There's been a mistake—"

"A wonderful mistake. We got our suite after all. Darling! Let's not waste a minute!"

And she flung herself against his chest just as Claire, wearing nothing but a sexy black teddy, came slinking into the room.

"Who is that woman?" two voices shrieked as one.

"I can explain!" J.D. ran backward out of Ramona's embrace, raising both hands in supplication. His harried gaze swung between the two women, who seemed equally paralyzed by shock.

Ramona recovered first. "Oh, gosh," she exclaimed, her expression contrite. "There's been a terrible mistake." Her glance ran up and down the form of the woman in the revealing teddy. "You were obviously expecting someone else. We can't apologize enough for intruding. You see, we were supposed to—"

"J.D., do something!" Claire shuddered. "Say something!"

"Oh, yeah, sure. But, uhh—would you like to get dressed first?"

She gasped and crossed her arms over her breasts. Her face went white.

Ramona frowned. "You know this woman, J.D.?"

It suddenly occurred to J.D. that a true sophisticate could probably pull this off. What would Cary Grant say? Pulling himself together, he attempted a nonchalant air.

"Mona, I'd like you to meet my ex-wife, Claire. Claire, this is—" He caught a glimpse of her face and knew that if looks could kill, he'd already be dead. Which knowledge made him stumble. "Th-This is . . ." He swallowed hard. ". . . a c-coworker."

"Does this 'c-coworker' have a name?"

Her tone gave him chills. "Of course she does," he responded indignantly. "It's . . . it's . . ." Jesus, what *was* it?

"Ramona, but my friends call me Mona." She gave him a lightly chiding glance. "Ramona Daniels, to be exact. I work in the Lifestyles section of the—"

"Well, *Miss Daniels,* I'm sure you'll excuse me while I put on something a little less comfortable."

Claire's parting glare felt like acid on J.D.'s skin. He stared after her helplessly, knowing she'd put on that black thing for him and now he'd screwed up and would never see it again, never have the pleasure of stripping it away from that firm and fancy body.

He groaned.

Ramona gave him a sympathetic pat on the arm. "It's all right, sweetie. Really, it is." She squeezed his hand. "I understand exactly what happened."

"Y-You do?" He regarded her suspiciously. Only she seemed unperturbed by the situation.

"Sure. This mix-up is obviously the hotel's fault—"

"You can say that again."

"—and you're trying to get your ex out of here so we can move in." She turned an adoring face toward him. "Is this a weird coincidence or what? I think it's darling of you to want to shield me and all that, but it's not necessary. I understand these things."

"Y-You do?"

"Sure! Hey, I was stuck in a ski lodge once with an ex-boyfriend and his current girlfriend. Stuff happens. We can't let it bother us, right?"

He couldn't have said "Right" and meant it if his life depended upon it, especially when Claire reappeared. She was swathed in terry cloth and an expression that could peel the hide off a buffalo.

"God!" she exclaimed. "Are you two still here?"

"We're going," Ramona said kindly. "J.D.'s explained everything."

"This I'd like to hear."

Ramona nodded. "About the hotel mix-up, and the way they double-booked this suite, and how he came here to try to talk the other party into letting us have it."

Claire looked on the verge of apoplexy. "The other party!"

"Well," Ramona said reasonably, "he couldn't know it was you, now could he? I mean, is this a coincidence or what?" She looked from one to the other for confirmation.

If he didn't do something quick, his ex-wife was going to attack his would-be paramour with anything she could get her hands on, including but not limited to the basket of fruit she toyed with. He could just see her stuffing that orange—

"Ramona!"

At his strangled cry, both women turned toward him.

He swallowed hard. "Mona, why don't you go down-stairs and wait for me in the lobby? I'd like to talk to Claire privately for a few—"

"In your dreams!" Claire faced him with arms rigid at her sides, hands balled into furious fists. "I've got nothing to say to you, you philandering—"

"Of course, sweetheart." Ramona's expression held only pity, pity for J.D. having to deal with a crazy woman. She started toward the door, then hesitated. "It was nice to meet you, Claire," she said earnestly. "Really."

She left.

J.D. took a step toward his seething ex-wife. "Claire, let me explain—"

"Explain? Explain!" She stamped a bare foot. "Don't bother. I wouldn't believe a word you said if you wrote it in blood."

"But—"

"You lied to me! You rented my Honeymoon Suite for a sordid affair with another woman! What was dinner, a shot at softening me up so I'd move out and let you conduct your cheap affair in *my* suite?"

"No, of course not. You've got it all wrong." He shook his head wearily, well aware that nothing he could say would make any difference to her, but unable to suppress the need to try. "Claire, five minutes with you and I forgot Ramona even existed, and that's the truth."

Her lips curled into something akin to a sneer, those same lips he'd kissed so hungrily just minutes ago. "I'll give you some truth," she flung at him. "Hell will freeze over before I let you have this suite or anything else that's mine. You might as well go give your playmate the bad news, because it ain't gonna happen."

"I don't give a damn about the suite," he said impa-tiently. "I'm only concerned with—"

"Yourself, as always, which isn't such a bad idea. Be-cause you're going to pay for this, John David Elliott. You're going to pay if it's the last thing I . . . ever . . . do!"

"Just a damned minute!" He shoved both hands

through his hair, agitated enough to speak first and think later. "Okay, I admit I asked Ramona to meet me here, but so what? How about you and George?"

"Glynn! And I told you I made that up so you wouldn't realize—" She stopped short, staring at him, wide-eyed.

"Oh, really? Then how'd you happen to have such sexy lingerie handy if your love life's so dull?"

Her face went white. "You jerk," she whispered. "*You* bought it for me on our honeymoon."

She whirled and ran down the hall. The big double doors to the bedroom slammed, followed by a banging and scraping which suggested she was wedging furniture against the doorknobs in case he tried to follow.

If he'd had a hope in hell of accomplishing anything by going after her, he'd have taken a shot at it. But he'd seen Claire's temper in full flower before, and he knew that this time he'd really messed up.

Biiig-time.

Ramona, naturally, was waiting for him in the lobby. She took one look at his dejected expression and patted his cheek reassuringly.

"Don't let her get to you," she advised, ever supportive. "Maybe that's the way all ex-wives act." She rose on tiptoe to kiss his throat.

Embarrassed by such a public display and feeling like a two-timer—although God knows, he shouldn't have, J.D. reminded himself self-righteously—he tried to avoid her groping hands. "Yeah, well, that's real nice of you, Mona, but she's so mad now that any chance of getting the suite is out the window."

"Who cares about that old Honeymoon Suite, anyway?" She gave him a sultry look and slid her arms around his waist, pressing her body against his. "*Where* isn't nearly as important as *what* and *who*. Come to Mona, baby, and I'll make you forget all about—"

"Ah, hell."

"Now what?"

He busied himself trying to remove her clinging hands, which snaked over and around all his attempts to escape. "An ill-chosen expression of regret," he improvised. "I'd love to, ah—I'd love to accept your invitation, but I . . . I can't."

She frowned. "What are you babbling about, J.D.? What do you mean, you can't? That's what we came here for, is it not?"

He finally managed to extricate himself and step back. "Yes, of course, but I've got that ride-along scheduled with the cops—"

"Can't you put that off until tomorrow?" Her hazel eyes narrowed, but at least she quit trying to grope him.

"Damn, you don't know how much I wish I could. But it's for a special series—last minute stuff, important." He glanced at his watch. "I'm late now. Really got to get going, but first I'll help you get a room." *As far away from Claire's as possible.*

Her satisfied smile made his stomach knot like a pretzel. "No problem," she purred. "We're in luck for once. I've already taken the Emerald Suite, right next door to the Honeymoon Suite. Is that great or what?"

J.D. felt faint. His only response was a strangled moan.

Ramona didn't seem to notice. "Actually, that's how I learned there was a Mr. and Mrs. Elliott booked into the Honeymoon Suite. When the bellboy took me up, he mentioned it, which naturally made me curious. Then when I found that door ajar—well, you know the rest."

He did, to his sorrow. But there was nothing to be done except escort her to her door, try (with limited success) to put her off with a quick kiss on the cheek, then escape back into the elevator.

Shortly after midnight, he slunk back to the Honeymoon Suite and let himself in. It was the only way; he'd sleep on the settee, the floor, anyplace other than with Mona. He felt like a damned adulterer and couldn't figure out why, since he'd been divorced from Claire for years and had never slept with Mona—hell, he hadn't slept with anyone since his marriage went south. He'd turned into a damned monk.

The suite was dark and deathly quiet. For a long time he sat in a chair with his head propped on his hands, miserable and trying to figure a way out of the hole he'd dug for himself.

Barefoot, he crept down the hall and into the bathroom. Jesus, this place! For a moment he just stood there, staring at the circular Jacuzzi and the glass-walled rain forest that backed the tub, not soothed by the trickling waterfall. Memories pummeled him and he closed his eyes.

Scented candles, soft music, hot bubbling water and the woman he loved—his wife—turning toward him with a smile that said it all. Her breasts gleamed below the roiling surface, and she held his gaze while she rose to her knees, straddled him. . . .

"I love you," she whispered, leaning closer so she could speak directly into his ear. "I want you . . ."

He remembered how her breasts had felt when he'd cupped them in his hands, could almost hear her soft little sounds of approval. Her flesh had been hot and smooth, firm and resilient beneath his greedy, flexing fingers.

She'd begun to lower herself over him, wiggling a little to get the angle just right . . . lowering herself, taking him inside her—

Jesus Christ! He threw cold water on his face, managing to splash the gold-plated fixtures and the marble countertop and make a general mess. He'd convinced himself that he'd put their marriage behind him, including the sensual aspects. He'd accepted the fact that the kind of sex he'd found with her was not something that came around more than once in a lifetime, and he'd further convinced himself that he could live with that.

And damn it, he could have, if he'd never laid eyes on her again. Now he was firmly mired once more in the kind of sexual heat that drove otherwise sane men to drink.

—she'd begun a gentle rocking motion, offering him her all, welcoming him into her velvety depths. Her head fell back on her slender neck and she murmured her pleasure, gasping when his seeking mouth closed over one quivering breast.

"Yes," she'd whispered. "Yes! I love you, John David . . . Never stop loving me, darling, never stop. . . ."

And God help him, he hadn't. To this very day, this day of ultimate disasters, he hadn't.

Knowing she was only a doorway beyond was more than he could handle. She was there, just out of his reach, sleeping in a bed they'd shared. Naked, probably. They'd both slept naked in those days, although he'd later taken to wearing pajama bottoms. Funny; he didn't know why, he just had. . . .

She'd be all warm and drowsy. When he touched her, the placid rhythm of her breathing would accelerate and she'd turn toward him blindly. He'd caress her breasts, drag his fingers intimately down over her belly while she quivered and murmured his name in her sleep.

He'd slide his hand between her thighs and massage the warmth he'd find there. That's when she'd open her eyes, her thighs. That's when she'd beg him to take her—

J.D. Elliott was sweating bullets. Maybe he should make one last attempt to . . . reason with her. Heart in his throat, he turned off the bathroom light and crept to her door on silent, eager feet.

And found it locked.

He called her name, very softly; he patted the door with a flat hand, holding his breath.

No response. None whatsoever. Apparently she'd meant what she said: that she hated him and wanted nothing further to do with him.

Could he leave it at that?

Could he *possibly* leave it at that, when mere thoughts of her got him so steamed up that he wanted to bang his head against the door and howl?

Chapter Five

Claire heard him outside her door. Lying stiff and sleepless in her lacy bower, she squeezed her eyes tightly closed and held her breath until he went away—out of her suite, her hotel, her life.

Her humiliation knew no bounds. Alone in the night in what had been her bridal bed, she had finally been forced to admit an inescapable fact: if *that woman* had not turned up when she did, Claire would have slept with that louse!

What had she been thinking? What had *he* been thinking? Had he intended to make love to his ex-wife tonight and to his girlfriend tomorrow?

Ohhhh! She could kill him for this, strangle him with her bare hands!

But he'd pay. She'd get even, no matter what it took. She'd begin by digging in her heels; she would be *damned* if she'd vacate these premises one single second before her allotted time. She would be *damned* if she spared him another even halfway friendly thought.

Okay, be calm, she tried to soothe her raging psyche. It hadn't been a pleasant scene, but to be honest, she'd needed just that kind of wake-up call.

Now, for sure, she'd find a way to get on with her life. She'd go out and find somebody to love. She could do it; sure she could. All she had to do was get focused and stay focused.

She'd date. A lot. She'd go where men were, and do what she had to do to attract them.

Not that she needed a man to validate her existence, of course. She could be perfectly happy alone . . . if she worked at it. And if the urge for maternity continued to grow, she could always adopt.

Climbing wearily from her lonely bed, she wandered over to the floor-to-ceiling windows and drew the draperies, completely opening one wall to a panoramic view of Glass Lake. Tiny lights twinkled among the limbs of the shadowy trees, turning it into a magic fairyland.

Life is good, she tried to rally herself, pressing her forehead against the cool glass wall. She was content.

She stifled a sob. Really, she was.

If there was anything Claire hated—and there was—it was going to sleep late and being roused early. Which, of course, is exactly what happened the next morning. The telephone beside her bed rang about a half hour after she'd finally fallen into an exhausted sleep—or, at least, it felt like thirty minutes, max.

"Good mornin', Miz Elliott," sang out a voice so cheerful it would try a saint. "It's six o'clock and this is Mr. Elliott's wake-up call. Welcome to another glorious day at the Glass Garden Hotel. If there's anything we can do to make your stay even more wonderful, y'all don't hesitate to—"

Claire groaned and hung up, collapsing back on the tangled bed. An awful day threatened to follow an awful night.

Never let it be said that Claire Kendall Elliott was the kind of woman who put off facing unpleasant chores. Clutching her terry robe about her, she stumbled out of the bedroom and into the sitting room. Yawning prodigiously, she headed toward the small refrigerator beneath the bar, praying she'd find a jug of orange ju—

The hair on the nape of her neck prickled a warning and she stopped short. Slowly, she turned, half afraid she'd find a burglar digging through her purse or a flasher on the balcony.

What she found was far worse: J.D., sleeping half on, half off the white wicker settee. And judging by his anguished expression, not very damned comfortably.

All her rage came roaring back. "You!" she shouted.

"Huh? What—Who . . . ?"

She watched him struggle to rise, to open his eyes, to untangle himself from the elaborately fringed afghan, to maneuver his feet around and onto the floor. With a complete lack of sympathy, she grabbed a pitcher from the bar, filled it with cold water, marched up behind him and emptied it over his head.

Gasping and sputtering, he finally found his feet and jumped up, swearing. Shaking himself like a wet dog, he flung drops of water in a glittering cascade before finally finding his voice. "God damn it! What are you trying to do, drown me?"

"Yes!" She gave him a malicious smile. "And then I'm going to have you arrested for trespassing! You've got some nerve, sneaking in here in the dead of night and—"

"Shut up and let me apologize." Her mouth fell open in shock, and he continued. "When you're right, you're right. I never should have lied to you about meeting Mona in the lobby. But you've got to realize, seeing you—"

He shoved his wet hair back with both hands. He had on the same clothes he'd worn to dinner last night, but now they were wet and wrinkled. In a word, he looked like hell. She smiled an evil smile.

He responded with a grimace. "Seeing you caught me

completely by surprise. I didn't know what I was doing. I
plead temporary insanity."

"I don't care if you plead terminal stupidity. You can't
just waltz in here and—" She stopped short, realizing that
she was handling this all wrong. He expected her to be
angry. Therefore, she would change her tactics.

"Yes?" he urged. "Go on, bawl me out. I deserve it.
Let me have it with both barrels and then we can go on
from there." He dropped his arms to his sides, squared his
jaw and prepared to take it on the chin. "I can't just waltz
in here and . . . what?"

"Let it go." She turned her back on him and walked to
the refrigerator. "It doesn't really matter, does it?"

"What do you mean, it doesn't matter? Last night—
hell, sixty seconds ago you were ready to kill me."

"I reacted strictly out of habit," she said blandly. "The
truth is, I no longer care what you do or who you do it
with, so why don't you run along and—and do it?"

"Well, I'll be damned."

"In all likelihood," she agreed, still reeling from the
lies flowing past her lips. "Did I hear you say you were
leaving now?"

"No, but if you listen close you'll hear the shower running."

Instantly alarmed, she protested. "Not here! Go away
and let's just forget we ever knew each other. I won't have
you wandering in and out of my suite and in and out of my
bathroom and in and out of my life—"

He was no longer around to hear the litany of things she
wouldn't have. The next sound she heard was that of a
running shower.

Now what was she supposed to do? Maybe she'd think
better after a cup of coffee. She picked up the telephone,
but before she could reach room service, "Lara's Theme"
interrupted. It was a waiter. "Your husband placed the order last night," he announced cheerfully.

Seething, she let him wheel in the serving cart, set everything up on the balcony, and depart. He'd brought
enough food and drink to satisfy three strong men and a
pack of hungry dogs, but she'd be damned if she'd enjoy
it! Pouring orange juice from a crystal pitcher, she drank

deeply, then sat down in a wicker chair with a sigh of defeat.

What in the name of heaven—

"Why, hello there," piped a cheery voice. "Is this a beautiful morning or what?"

Claire knew she had to open her eyes and face this new threat, but she could only do so by inches. The first thing she saw between almost-closed lids was the ornate fence separating this balcony from the one next door. Opening her eyes a fraction more, she saw the rose-covered trellis designed to provide a privacy screen.

Opening her eyes completely, she saw Ramona, peeking around a hinged section of trellis and fence that served as a gate—my God, was nothing sacred? Claire bolted upright and prepared to utter a tart reproof.

Before she could get it out, Ramona plunged ahead. "That coffee smells just heavenly, and I see you've got a whole bunch of extra cups."

The nerve of the woman! She swung the rosy gate wider and walked through, chatting up a storm.

"Gosh, is this a great hotel or what? I'm in the Emerald Suite right next door. Have you ever seen it? It's wonderful—not as big or fancy as the Honeymoon Suite, of course, but fabulous. Do you know that maid, Etta? Is she a kick or what?"

Ramona sat down and poured coffee without missing a beat. "You know, I've been really curious about J.D.'s ex-wife. Just because I have the hots for him doesn't mean we can't be friends, don't you agree? I mean, you had your shot, am I right?"

Claire realized her jaw was hanging open, and she snapped her mouth shut.

Ramona reached for a croissant. "I knew you'd agree. I'm really tickled we're all being so civilized about this. Just for the record, I don't chase married men. I wouldn't be here if J.D. wasn't available. Married men are nothing but trouble, I always say, and with so many other fish in the sea—but of course, you know that, being single yourself. Don't you find it irritating, the way men are always trying to hit on us? It gets to be such a drag, fighting them off when you know most of them are only after one thing.''

''Oh, well, sure,'' Claire lied, thinking there must be something seriously wrong in her own life. If this little flake was fighting men off with a stick . . .

But that wasn't really fair. Sitting there with Ramona, Claire was stunned to realize that the girl was actually . . . *likable.* Not J.D.'s type, or at least not the type that used to be his type, but likable nonetheless.

Under other circumstances, she and Claire might actually have been . . . not enemies.

Claire leaned forward. ''Ramona,'' she said sternly, ''there's something I need to explain to—''

The French doors flew open and J.D. walked through, wearing jeans and nothing else. He was toweling his wet hair with vigorous strokes, and his arms and torso were a mass of rippling muscle. ''Coffee,'' he said. ''I smell— Ramona? *What the hell are you doing here?''*

With minor exceptions, J.D. could imagine few scenarios worse than walking half dressed though a door to find his ex-wife and his would-be lover sharing a friendly cup of coffee and an intimate chat. This boded ill, it sure as hell did.

''J.D.!'' Ramona looked totally confused. ''What are *you* doing here?''

''Yes, J.D.,'' Claire echoed smugly. ''Tell Ramona what you're doing here.''

Digging holes in the outdoor carpeting with his bare toes, J.D. tried to concentrate on Mona; if he looked at Claire, he might not be able to resist the temptation to wrap his hands around that lovely neck.

''See, this is what happened,'' he said earnestly. ''I thought everything over and decided that my best bet was to sleep on that damned little sofa in there.'' He jerked his head to indicate the room behind him.

Ramona frowned. ''But why?''

''Why.'' J.D. pressed his lips together. ''Why. Well . . . because it's my suite.''

''Our suite,'' Ramona corrected helpfully.

''*My* suite,'' Claire inserted.

He ignored Claire. "That's what I meant," he said to Mona. "Our suite. I—We've got as much right to it as *she* does, and I'm not budging. There's a principle involved here."

"You got that right," Claire snarled.

He finally had to face her. "Yeah, well, if you'll be reasonable, we can work this out to our mutual satisfaction. But I'm not going to let you throw me out when I've got as much right to be here as you do. That's final."

"Is it?" She rose from her chair, her movements taut and graceful. "There's nothing to work out. I'm warning you, John David Elliott—stay out of my way!"

He waited until she'd stomped off the balcony before turning back to Ramona. "I swear, it's true," he said. "I wouldn't want you to think there's anything going on between—"

"Silly boy!" Chuckling warmly, she rose and started toward him. "I believe you."

"Y-You do?"

"Sure! Why on earth would you waste your time on that prickly pear when you've got your very own little ol' honeysuckle rose just waitin' for a chance t'twine all over you?"

Before he could get over his amazement at her goofy approximation of a Texas drawl, she slid her arms around his neck and ran her fingers seductively through his wet hair. He resisted the urge to glance over his shoulder to see if Claire was watching.

He resisted the urge to run screaming from the balcony.

He resisted the urge to fling himself over the edge, but it wasn't easy.

She *would* have fun, Claire swore to herself. Under no circumstances would she allow J.D. and his sweetie pie to ruin *her* vacation.

So she spent the day in dogged exploration of the Glass Garden Hotel. There was certainly plenty to explore, and all of it wonderful: Glass Lake with its island and gazebo; the Glass Garden itself, filled with exotic plants and magnificent statuary; the beautifully landscaped grounds; the photo gallery of Glass Garden history.

Everywhere she went and everything she saw, she remembered seeing it with *him*. That was not a new problem; she'd always had trouble with that aspect of her annual vacation. Only this time it was much worse, because she also saw *him,* in the flesh, with Ramona clinging to his arm and gazing at him with unmistakable admiration.

A little bit of that went a long way, Claire discovered. In fact, it soon became too much. She gave up. In desperate need of a happy ending, she bought a romance novel in the gift shop, hurried back to the suite and settled down for a good read—with a guaranteed happy ending. Talk about fantasy!

That's where Etta found her in mid-afternoon, ostensibly weeping over her book. At first Claire tried to brazen it out, but upon finding herself wrapped in those motherly arms, she proceeded to sob out her woes.

Etta listened with sympathetic little murmurings and supportive comments. When the eye of the hurricane had passed, she administered a series of "There-Theres" and a couple of pats on Claire's still-quaking shoulders.

Claire swallowed the last of her hiccupy whimpers. She'd made a total ass of herself, but strangely enough, she felt better after confiding the basics of her situation: she and J.D. were divorced, she was still wasting her vacations mooning over him, and now he'd brought another woman to profane what they'd once shared.

"It's hopeless," she concluded. "Now I won't even be able to remember the good times without feeling like he's stabbed me in the back."

"Honey, never say die," Etta advised. "I figured there was some kinda problem, what with him never joinin' you on your visits here. Not divorce, though." She shook her head with conviction. "You two got too much goin' for that. I knew it the first time I saw y'all."

Etta unpinned the heart-shaped hankie attached to the bosom of her pink uniform and offered it to Claire, who accepted gratefully and dabbed at wet eyes.

"*He* wanted the divorce," she choked out, "so what could I do?"

"You coulda told him no!" Etta looked astonished that

Claire didn't realize this. "Honey, men don't know what they want until some woman tells 'em. Like that little gal in the Emerald Suite."

"Ramona?" Claire sank deeper into self-pity.

"That's the one. She's tellin' him loud and clear what it is he wants."

Claire felt her lips tremble. "Is this supposed to make me feel better?"

"I dunno." Etta's eyes were wide and innocent. "All I know is, she's sellin' hard, but he ain't buyin'. Not yet, anyhows."

"You mean it?" A spark of hope flickered in Claire's secret soul.

"I'd bet the farm on it." Etta glanced at her heart-shaped wristwatch, gasped and jumped to her feet. "I gotta go, honey. If you're feelin' better, that is."

"Of course." Claire stood up a little uncertainly. "I—I don't know how to thank you, Etta. I may not know what to do, but at least I'm feeling better." She gave the maid a quick, shy hug.

Etta beamed. "A'course you know what to do," she said in mock-scolding tones. "Just do the right thing—and keep smilin'!"

Ah, that it were so easy.

Hours spent hiding in her suite eventually brought Claire to the realization that there was nothing whatsoever to be gained by further moping. Dressing to the nines in a red-sequined sheath, she went downstairs to dinner.

With many a puzzled glance, the maître d' showed her to the last available table in the Terrace Restaurant. Once seated, she realized she should have lent more credence to his peculiar manner.

For there, only a table away, sat Ramona and J.D. To J.D.'s credit, he looked as unhappy to see Claire as she was to see him.

Not Ramona, though; she gave a cheery wave and started to rise. Only J.D.'s restraining hand kept her from rushing to greet her boyfriend's ex-wife.

So much for a pleasant meal. Tempted to turn around

and walk out, Claire instead lifted her chin and gritted her teeth. She'd show him—

"Haven't we met?"

A man, a pleasant-enough-looking man, paused beside her table and smiled down at the cleavage revealed by the red dress.

She frowned, trying to remember, then suddenly realizing it was nothing more than a pickup line. About to give him her usual abrupt brush-off, she caught herself and batted her eyelashes.

"I'm sure I'd have remembered," she said, striving for a flirtatious tone. "Perhaps you've mistaken me for someone else."

"Seems impossible," he said smoothly. "I'd like to buy you a drink later so we can talk about it."

"Perhaps," she agreed, hoping J.D. was watching. She couldn't resist stealing a glance in his direction.

Unfortunately, he had his head in the oversized menu and had apparently missed the entire encounter. So much for inspiring jealousy.

"Oh, go away!" she snapped at her erstwhile admirer. "We never laid eyes on each other before and you know it as well as I do."

"Well, ex-*cuuuse* me."

Before he was even out of sight, Claire was sorry she'd brushed him off. The best way to get J.D. out of her mind and heart was to let someone else in. She wanted to attract, not attack. The sooner she started, the better. If J.D. happened to be around to see her do it, it was all right with her.

So it was no accident that she left the Terrace a mere step ahead of J.D. and Ramona. And it was no accident when she marched straight over to the Crystal Room Tavern and found a seat at the bar. Ordering a glass of wine, she crossed her legs so that the tight red dress slid up to mid-thigh, then looked around for a man to flirt with.

She found slim pickin's; most of those in the sparse crowd were already paired up. Swinging back to the bar, she reached for her goblet of white zinfandel.

Someone reached for her at the same moment, and a male voice murmured in her ear a tentative, "Surprise!"

She was surprised, all right, and more so when unidentified arms closed around her in a big bear hug. The glass in her hand tilted. "Hey, watch it!" she shouted, but too late, as the contents splashed over the rim.

And over her. The impact of cold wine hitting her breasts above the scoop neck of her dress ripped a shriek of surprise from her. But before she had time to gather her wits or offer further protest, her hugger was ripped away with such violence that he nearly dragged her from her bar stool.

Catching her balance, she looked up into the face of J.D. Elliott, trained observer of—as opposed to participant in—the human scene. She'd never seen that kind of fire in his eyes before. He held his victim with one hand wrapped around his throat and a fist drawn back at the ready.

"The surprise," J.D. said from between gritted teeth, "is on you."

And he let fly a roundhouse right.

Chapter Six

Claire flung herself off the bar stool too late; Glynn, good old nerdy Glynn, dropped like a stone. J.D. stood over the body as if he were the U.S. Cavalry to the rescue.

"What do you think you're *doing?*" she screamed through the confusion erupting around her. She beat on his chest with her fists. "How dare you create a scene! Haven't you humiliated me enough? Now you've got to start fights in public places!"

J.D. grabbed her flailing arms at the wrists. "Stop that! I was defending you. Do you enjoy having strange men sneak up from behind and maul you?"

She aimed a murderous foot at his shins. He yelped and shoved her away. "What are you, crazy? All I did was—"

"I saw what you did, you brute, and don't think I'll ever forgive—"

"*You, everybody—back off! Give him air!*"

It was the bartender, a muscular and commanding young woman in a Dallas Cowboys T-shirt, elbowing her way through the mob.

And effectively reminding Claire that in her outrage over what J.D. had done, she'd completely overlooked Glynn, supine upon the floor. Filled with guilty remorse, she turned—

—to find Ramona on her knees, cradling the fallen man's head on her lap while she stroked his brow and uttered soothing little assurances. Glynn looked unconscious; omigod, what if he were really hurt? What if J.D. had . . . ?

Glynn's eyelids fluttered and he opened his eyes, or rather, he *sort of* opened his eyes, since his eyeballs rolled around without focus and his lids blinked crazily. He groaned and raised a quivering hand to touch the side of his face. "What hit me?" he inquired plaintively.

A sharp burst of relieved laughter escaped Claire's lips. Her unseemly reaction earned her a scowl from the bartender.

"I've called security," the woman warned. "Don't anybody move!"

"But it's all a mistake," Claire exclaimed, regaining her composure. "It's nothing more than a case of mistaken identity."

The bartender's expression did not soften. Kneeling beside Glynn, she touched his shoulder gingerly. "You all right, guy? Anything broken? I'll call an ambulance if you need medical attention."

"Jesus, no." With a little help from Ramona, Glynn struggled to a sitting position. Working his jaw with his hands, he seemed to reassure himself that he was still in one piece. He looked up, saw Claire standing there, and appealed to her: "What happened?"

Before she could reply, J.D. thrust his way into the innermost circle. White lines of strain bracketed his mouth. He gave Claire a scathing glance. "Don't tell me—let me guess. This is George, right?"

"No! This is *Glynn!*" In her frustration, Claire swung her clenched fist against his shoulder. "You almost killed him, you animal! I hope they haul you off to jail and throw away the key! I hope—"

Glynn's voice rose above her tirade. "Hey, nothing's

broken. Maybe we should give the man a chance to ex-pla—"

"Security! Security! Clear the way—security!"

"Over here! Some guy's tryin' to start a fight!"

"The hell I am! I'm defending the lady's honor."

"My honor is none of your business, J.D. Elliott, not anymore!"

And above the general tumult, at last a voice of reason: Ramona's. "Come on, people! Let's act like grown-ups. Don't you think we can work this whole thing out over a friendly drink?"

Friendly? *Friendly?* J.D. sure as hell wouldn't call it friendly, although he appreciated the sentiment and Ramona's presence of mind in making the suggestion. It was sufficient to calm everybody down long enough for George—check that, Glynn—to determine that he wasn't seriously injured, and to promise that he wouldn't be suing the hotel or his assailant or anybody else.

Ramona, now—good old Mona had come through like a champ. She'd helped Glynn to his feet and to a table where he now slumped, a wet bar towel pressed to the side of his face.

Claire continued to glare at J.D. from across the table, as if he were somehow at fault. J.D. glared back.

He'd had nothing but her best interests at heart, he thought indignantly. How was he to know she let this Glynn guy manhandle her at will?

His gaze dropped to the dark stain marring the front of her slinky red dress, lingered for an inordinate amount of time on the swell of her breasts above the glittery sequins. Claire was one classy-looking babe—

He was completely unprepared for the toe that slammed into his shin. "Ow! What was that for?"

"For punching first and asking questions later," she blustered, but bright spots of color glowed on her high cheekbones.

He rubbed his bruised leg. If that Glynn guy wasn't bent out of shape about taking a shot in the jaw, why was she? He had apologized, J.D. thought. He'd humiliated himself in front of a roomful of strangers to do it, so what was her problem?

Mona smiled at one and all. "Now, now, let's act like civilized adults. No reason we can't all be friends, is there?"

Claire groaned.

J.D.'s sentiments exactly.

Glynn produced a cautious smile. "Works for me," he said, giving J.D. a wary once-over. "It's a natural mistake . . . I suppose."

Claire slumped down so she could cover her face with her hands.

"Hey," Glynn persisted, "I'm glad someone was around to look out for you, Claire."

"Isn't he sweet?" Ramona piped up, patting his arm. "A lot of guys wouldn't understand if they got their lights punched out by their girlfriend's ex-husband. Or why said ex-husband is sharing a Honeymoon Suite with said girlfriend."

"They explained all that." Glynn's anxious glance was only a tiny bit askew. "Hey, I trust them." He frowned at Ramona. "Don't you?"

Ramona nodded with enthusiasm. "Oh, sure, what's not to trust? The way they go at each other tooth and nail, the only thing we have to worry about is that one of them'll kill the other before they can get this double-reservation business straightened out."

Glynn glanced from Claire's scowling face to J.D.'s. His smile brightened. "I see what you mean."

For a few minutes they sat there in a silence more depressing than tense. Again it was Ramona who filled the void.

"So now what?" she inquired.

Glynn shrugged. "I suppose I should do something about getting a room."

Ramona patted his hand. "That's true. You can't very well stay with Claire while J.D.'s underfoot," she sympathized.

Claire looked up, startled. "Now hold on just—" A quick glance at J.D. seemed to alter her course. "Do something!" she snapped.

"Don't look at me." J.D. declined responsibility. "You don't like me for a roommate, you're free to move out anytime you feel like it."

"See?" Ramona arched her brows. "They're stubborn. But I've got an idea, Glynn. Since my boyfriend—"

J.D. winced.

"—is sleeping on your girlfriend's couch—"

Claire winced.

"—you're welcome to bunk on *my* couch."

Glynn recoiled. "I couldn't put you out."

"You won't. I've got a lovely suite right next door to theirs, with plenty of room." Her smile turned pixyish. "On a clear day, I can hear them screaming at each other. Come on," she coaxed, "fair is fair. We can at least keep each other company while our significant others duke it out."

"My God," Claire murmured in a faint voice. "I don't believe this."

Neither did J.D.

Standing uneasily in the hall between the doors of their two suites, Ramona kissed J.D. good night while Claire suffered Glynn to give her a peck on the cheek. Then Glynn and Ramona went in one door while J.D. and Claire entered the other.

She stomped into the sitting room and kicked off her shoes before firing the opening volley. "I hope you're happy! You made fools of us both."

"No, I didn't."

She swung around to face him. "The hell you didn't! Brawling like a common—"

He grinned and his dimple flashed. "Temper, temper. You know where that gets you."

She did. To her sorrow, she did. She changed her tactics so abruptly it even confused her. "Okay, I'll beg. *Pa-leeze* go away and leave me alone. If you do, I'll never ask you for another favor as long as I live."

He stopped smiling. "You're that eager to get old George in the sack?"

"No!" She caught her breath. "Yes!" She closed her eyes. "Maybe. What difference does it make to you? I'm not trying to run your life, so why are you trying to run mine?''

''Are we talking 'life' or 'love life,' here? Not that it matters, since I'd have to be a brainless idiot to believe anything you said to me anyway.''

Her shoulders slumped. ''That's not fair.''

He walked to the small refrigerator and withdrew a beer. ''You lied to me. You swore you weren't meeting a guy here, and climbed my tree because of Mona.''

''I only lied to you because you lied to me first. What I really said was, I *was* meeting another man, only that was the lie because I wasn't—''

She stopped short, realizing that she was talking herself into a corner. If she told him Glynn's arrival was as much a surprise to her as it was to him, he'd never believe her— but if he did believe her, it'd be worse, for then how could she explain what she was doing here at the Glass Garden alone? And not only alone *this* year, but last year and the year before that?

She couldn't, so she gave up. ''Have it your way. We lied to each other. I'm going to bed.''

''So am I.''

They'd reached a stand-off, and Claire suddenly found that she could no longer breathe. He'd unbuttoned his pale blue shirt and it hung open over his tanned and toned chest, but that wasn't what stopped her cold, not primarily, anyway.

It was his expression, his hungry expression of need. She'd seen it before. A ripple of apprehension ran down her spine, quickly followed by a fire that started in the pit of her belly and fanned out until every inch of her burned. Her breasts tightened, nipples peaking beneath the wine-soaked bodice of her dress.

He spoke raggedly. ''I still might decide to . . . fight you for the bedroom. That thing over there that passes for a couch is like sleeping on a bed of nails.''

That's what he said: *fight*. But she knew that wasn't what he meant. He mean *share*. He wanted the bed, all right, but he wanted her in it with him.

Or maybe he wanted Ramona but was willing to settle for—

"In your dreams, mister. I was here first, and possession is a tenth of the law!" She yanked free of the spell he'd cast and flounced down the hall, head high.

"That's nine-tenths of the law," he called after her, "but who's counting?"

And then he said her name in a completely different tone, so different that it stopped her cold with her hand already on the doorknob.

"It's August thirteenth. Happy anniversary."

His voice came from directly behind her; he'd followed her to the bedroom. Prepared to hurl bitter words of rebuke at him, she whirled—right into his arms. Before she could protest, he kissed her.

The passion was still there in the touch of his lips on hers, but she tasted something else as well, a kind of tender regret. All day long she'd run from the realization that this would have been the celebration of their fourth year together, instead of what it was; a memorial to their failure. Now he had forced a confrontation . . . a sensual confrontation which she would have to lose to win.

Her head urged her to resist, but her heart and body melted before a thrill of desire. She felt the probing of his tongue against her lips, and with a sigh of surrender, allowed him entry. At the same moment, his hands touched her hips, lifted her narrow skirt enough for him to slide his leg between her thighs.

Against her will, she melted into his hard form. Body aching for his possession, she responded to his kiss and the stroking motions of his hard thigh with a reckless abandon she'd all but forgotten. Tried to forget . . . for this was the man who'd breached her defenses in a way no other had, or ever would. With him, she'd been so vulnerable it had frightened her.

She dared not let that happen again! Bracing her hands on his shoulders, she pushed him back, twisting her head to one side to break the kiss. Her breath rasped in her throat and her body still blazed with excitement, but in one desperate move she was free.

For a moment they stared into each other's eyes in the dimly lit hallway. She was breathing hard, but so was he, and she saw a dangerous glint in his narrow eyes.

He was going to grab her, she thought with stunning certainty, and what would she do then? He was going to grab her and carry her inside and dump her on the bed, and then he was going to make love to her and she—she, heaven help her—was . . . going to meet him more than halfway. Her eyes widened and she caught her breath on a little sound that was half sob, half invitation.

He shoved his hair back with one hand and looked away, breaking eye contact. "Ah, hell," he said, "get some sleep." He turned and walked down the hall, his back stiff.

And that was the unkindest blow of all.

A group breakfast downstairs at Montague's the next morning did little to ease the tensions of the previous night. Claire found herself responding in monosyllables, and eventually noticed J.D. doing the same.

It seemed preferable to the alternative: fighting. After that shocking encounter of last night, which had left her aroused and angry and sleepless, she dared not allow her hostility toward him to soften.

Ramona carried the conversation, as usual. After an awkward beginning, Glynn seemed to decide his best course of action was simply to follow her lead, so he did.

Even Ramona's supply of small talk eventually ran dry, and they settled into another uneasy silence, finally broken by J.D.

"Can somebody please pass the jam?"

Since the jam jar was at Claire's elbow, she handed it over. "You know my name," she sniped at him. "Aren't you satisfied with what you pulled on me last night? Do you have to—"

Too late, she realized how that must sound. Her cheeks burning, she tried to cover her tracks. "We had another fight before we went to bed," she explained, "and—"

God! She'd made it worse. Glynn looked positively shocked, although Ramona seemed unperturbed.

J.D. turned a hateful smile on her. "Wanna go for three?"

"No, I want to go for your throat! Why are you doing this to me? Everyone knew what I meant."

"You don't even know what you meant. Jeeze, Claire, at least you used to—"

"—at it again. Tell me, is this your first trip to Dallas?" Ramona was saying in the background.

"—keep your wits about you in a fair fight."

"—lived in New York City all my life," Glynn responded in an undertone.

"That's because you don't fight fair, J.D. You never did and you never will."

"—never been to this hotel before. Would you like to see Glass Lake? I understand it's—"

"The hell I don't. Haven't you ever heard that all's fair in love and war?"

"I've heard it, I just don't believe it." She threw down her napkin. "And I don't have to sit here and take this from you. Glynn! Why don't we—"

Glynn was gone. So was Ramona. Claire blinked and turned to J.D. for an explanation, but he seemed equally surprised.

"Well, how do you like that," she muttered, looking around the busy restaurant but seeing no sign of the missing couple. "They didn't even say good-bye."

J.D. picked up the check. "How can you be sure?" He fished his wallet from the hip pocket of his khaki shorts. "We weren't exactly paying a lot of attention to them, now were we?" He threw down several bills and stood up. "They're not getting away with it. If they think I'm going to deal with you alone, they're out of their minds."

She glared at him; he glared back. And waited. And waited.

Finally he said, "Well, are you coming or not?"

She was.

They spent the rest of the morning and part of the afternoon chasing after the elusive Ramona and Glynn. Over a late lunch, Ramona explained that neither she nor Glynn had the least interest in refereeing any more fights, arguments, or differences of opinion between the formerly-weds; she said this completely without rancor.

Claire and J.D. apologized profusely, between darting furious glances at each other, and swore they'd be more considerate. If they could have spent five minutes together without finding something to jump on, it would have been a major victory.

"How did you two ever get together in the first place?" Ramona wailed. "If I ever saw a less likely couple, it's you guys. J.D.'s a liberal—"

"And Claire's a conservative," Glynn came in as if on cue.

"J.D. comes from big bucks—"

"And Claire had to work her way up the corporate ladder."

"J.D. is—"

"Not enjoying this conversation." He shoved his virtually untouched Caesar salad away.

Neither was Claire. They *were* different in just about every conceivable way. He came from old San Francisco society, while she'd grown up on a farm in South Texas. He was whimsical, and she was practical; he was optimistic where she was cynical. He'd gone to Stanford, while she'd struggled to make it through business school, then had earned a degree at night school.

She stared down at her half-eaten hamburger, dismayed. What *had* J.D. ever seen in her?

She didn't figure she'd ever know. Whatever it was, she'd obviously lost it somewhere along the way.

Slapping at mosquitoes in the Victorian gazebo on Glass Lake's small island several hours later, Claire and J.D. discovered simultaneously that Glynn and Ramona had disappeared yet again.

"Those two are harder to keep a handle on than—than the national debt," Claire groused.

"I'll say."

"What drove them away this time? I thought we'd been getting on rather well . . . for us."

"Those two have no staying power."

"Well, we obviously do. Shall we track them down, the cowards?"

"After you."

With a sweeping bow he indicated the walkway connecting the man-made island with the hotel grounds. Together they followed the path beneath drooping cypress and leafy magnolias. Peacocks and guinea fowl wandered freely, adding to the exotic atmosphere.

The lushness of the grounds gave her a quick rush of pleasure. This was a beautiful, elegant establishment, not meant for estrangements or other unhappiness. J.D. stepped up beside her and took her arm as they walked onto the patio outside the Glass Garden itself. She shivered and tried to pull her elbow away.

"Did you know," she said breathlessly, "that they have to build special scaffolding to wash all that glass?"

He tightened his grip, steering her on. "As a matter of fact, I didn't." His tone sounded very tongue-in-cheek. "How often do they do it, once a decade?"

"Four times a year." They entered the garden. "This is really an interesting place." She indicated the tall fountain that had become a de facto wishing well, probably on the day it opened. "Have you ever thrown in a penny and made a wish?"

Was that a groan? "Recently. It didn't come true, unfortunately."

She gave him a puzzled glance. "All the coins are donated to the Red Cross, so I guess it's worthwhile even if you don't get your wish."

"I expect to get my wishes." He punched the up arrow for the West Tower elevator with more violence than the task warranted. "That fountain let me down, major bigtime."

The way he looked at her made her wonder if he was talking about the fountain or about her.

They rode up to their floor in uncomfortable silence. While J.D. tried to rouse an answer at the Emerald Suite, Claire hurried into the Honeymoon Suite to see if the missing pair had left any messages.

They hadn't. When J.D. joined her, he was frowning.

Claire pursed her lips. "Now what do you suppose—"

"Who the hell knows?" He flopped onto the settee. "I'll call down and check for messages at the desk."

"Our—My phone message light would be flashing."

"Then *you* think of something."

She puzzled it over for a minute. "Do you suppose they'd leave the hotel? If they did, we'll never find them."

"They'd have to come back sooner or later."

"That's not good enough. I have no intention of—"

"Lara's Theme" interrupted the debate. Claire's shoulders slumped in relief. "There they are now."

"I'll let them in, and then we've got to settle this thing once and for all." He looked at her impassively. "Agreed?"

"Agreed." He was right. She couldn't spend another day like this one; it was far too emotionally draining. Would she be willing to give up and move out of the suite if he stood firm?

Decision time. She turned to greet Glynn and Ramona, but that's not who walked in.

Chapter Seven

Etta rolled her overburdened cart to the middle of the room and looked at Claire expectantly. "Want me to set this up on the balcony, honey? It's mighty pretty out there, this time'a day."

Claire frowned at the assortment of silver and crystal dishes, a wine bucket, an elaborate floral arrangement, and candles. Confused, she turned to J.D., who rolled his eyes and shrugged.

"There must be some mistake," she ventured. "What is this stuff?"

"Just what the doctor ordered," Etta assured her. "And this is just the beginnin', the first course. I got champagne and strawberries and caviar and a whole buncha good stuff here. When you're ready, I'll be standin' by to serve you steak and lobster with all the trimmin's, and we got baked Alaska for dessert."

"We didn't order this," J.D. said flatly.

"Somebody did," the maid retorted. "Y'all quit standin' there gapin' and let me set this up."

"But—"

But nothing; Etta was gone, through the French doors and onto the balcony. With conspicuous efficiency, she whisked out white linen and proceeded to arrange the table:

J.D. turned to Claire. "You didn't order this, did you?"

"Certainly not. Why would I? *When* would I?" Affronted, she turned her back on him.

"Okay, okay, I apologize. But if you didn't and I didn't—" He snapped his fingers in sudden inspiration. "Ramona and Glynn. I'll bet they think we can work everything out over a nice dinner."

"Ramona and Glynn," Claire agreed unhappily. "They probably couldn't face another meal with us sniping at each other."

Etta came back inside. "There," she announced with satisfaction. "Y'all just go on out there, set yourselves down and *enjoy.*"

"I suppose we might as well," Claire conceded.

J.D. gave a short nod. "Yeah. This will probably be our last chance, Claire. Let's give it one more try. What have we got to lose?"

Etta recoiled. "Bite yore tongue!" she exclaimed in mock horror. "I swear, sometimes I think you young people don't have the sense God give a goose."

Sometimes Claire didn't think so, either, although she wouldn't have phrased it quite the same way.

They dined extravagantly while a million stars twinkled down, a million city lights twinkled up. It all seemed so magical; a sense of déjà vu that swept over her. She'd been here before with this man. She'd looked at him across the table with the same love and longing.

She forced herself to give due consideration to the melting ice cream and meringue on her plate, while she pondered how her plans could have gone so far astray. She'd come here to forget; instead, he'd reestablished his utter supremacy in her heart.

J.D. put down his dessert spoon with a clatter. "We're delaying the inevitable," he said.

"I know." Her spoon joined his on the crisp white linen. "I have to admit, I'm loath to rejoin the fray."

"Yeah, me too."

"Can't we ease into it instead of jumping in with both

feet?'' she asked plaintively. ''All kidding aside, it's . . . it's wonderful to see you looking so . . . fit. I suppose you still like working for the paper?''

He looked out over the lights of the city and spoke pensively. ''Yes, but . . .'' He hesitated, as if uncertain how much he should confide in her. ''I've been offered a chance to write a syndicated political column based in Washington.''

'':D.C.?'' Claire gasped with pleasure. ''That's wonderful!'' Without thinking, she touched his hand where it lay on the table. ''J.D., I'm so happy for you. Not surprised, you understand—happy. You're a wonderful journalist. Congratulations—and I mean that sincerely.''

He was looking at her with his head cocked and his eyes searching, as if her response puzzled him. ''Thanks, but congratulations may be premature. I haven't made up my mind to take it yet.''

''You're kidding. Isn't this what you always wanted— your own syndicated column?''

''Yeah . . .''

''Then what is it? Not the challenge, surely. You've never shied away from a challenge.''

He shook his head, his face devoid of expression. ''I'm probably going to turn it down because I'd have to leave the West Coast.''

''You have got to be kidding!'' Claire recoiled, her grip on his hand tightening.

He gave her a lopsided smile. ''Don't act so shocked. I used to think I could only be happy in California. At least I've widened my scope to include the entire West Coast.''

She sighed. ''J.D., happiness doesn't depend on surroundings, it depends on attitude.''

His mouth dropped open and he gaped at her. ''Wait a minute, wait a minute. Is this Claire talking? I don't recognize this new and more mature you. Are you sure you mean *attitude* and not *job?*''

She laughed sheepishly. ''The truth of the matter is, my job is no longer my number one priority.''

J.D.'s mouth turned down. ''What is? Glynn?''

A crossroads yawned before her. The truth—that she regretted choosing her work over him more than any decision she'd ever made in her life—would lead her into emotional quicksand. A lie—that Glynn was more to her than an irritation—would at least let her off the hook with- out embarrassment.

She looked at J.D., searching for a spark of encourage- ment to tell the truth. All she saw was skepticism.

So of course she tried to hedge her bets. "Glynn . . . well, maybe." She added brightly, as if it didn't matter to her, "And what about you and Ramona?"

"Who knows? Stranger things have happened . . . I guess." He yanked his hand from beneath hers and plucked the champagne bottle from the ice bucket. It was empty. "I'll just grab another," he said, and bolted from the balcony.

Claire waited, growing more melancholy by the second. She *had* changed, she realized with a finality heretofore missing. All she really wanted out of this fiasco was to see J.D. happy. If Ramona could do that, then she stood ready to step aside.

Tears stung Claire's eyelids and she blinked furiously. Was that what real love meant, putting the happiness of someone else before your own?

Jumping up, she strode to the wall separating the two balconies. If the missing couple had returned, she'd put her money where her mouth was.

Opening the gate, Claire slipped through. This was the right thing to do, she told herself, a *far, far better thing than she had ever done*—

Ramona and Glynn were there, all right, locked in an embrace so passionate that Claire's knees went weak. Half dressed, they grappled on the couch with complete aban- don, the entire scene revealed by wide-open draperies.

Shock brought Claire to a trembling halt and thrust all homilies from her mind. She jumped back, heart pounding and breath labored. My God, she thought wildly, Glynn and Ramona? How can this be?

Then she knew how it could be. She'd all but made this happen. She'd kept Ramona and J.D. apart; yes, she had! She'd come between them, and she might as well admit she'd done so deliberately. She hadn't been able to bear thinking of her ex-husband with another woman.

And Glynn—how had Claire returned his selfless devotion? She'd done her best to discourage it, treated it with something little short of contempt. Yet it had never occurred to her that he might transfer those feelings to another.

Berating herself, she hurried back to her own balcony and closed the gate. What a mess she'd made; what a horrible, terrible mess!

Should she tell J.D. what she'd seen?

Yes, because then he'd send that tramp on her way; no, because such news coming from his ex-wife would sound like the worst kind of sour grapes.

If J.D. really cared for Ramona, he'd hate her even more for being the bearer of bad tidings. But didn't he deserve to know what kind of woman she was?

What to do, what to do . . . ?

J.D. returned with an open bottle of champagne in his hand. He took one look at her, then perused the balcony as if expecting to find an intruder behind one of the many flower urns.

"Something the matter?" he asked, pouring the wine.

"N-Nothing," she said, too quickly. Grabbing her glass, she swigged down the contents, saw his dubious expression and choked. Finally in control again, she forced a smile. "T-Tell me, J.D.—if you don't mind my asking . . ."

"Ask away." He looked almost as if he were anticipating her question.

"Are you . . ." She was finding this difficult to say. "At the risk of belaboring the obvious, how serious are you about Ramona, *really?*"

His expression grew cool and distant. She'd managed to ask her question, but knew at once she'd gone too far.

"That depends on how you define serious," he all but snapped.

His hostile expression unnerved her, but she'd gone too far to turn back now. "I'll spell it out for you. A-Are you in love with her? Because if you are—"

She bit off her words: *If you are, I'll keep my mouth shut and move out of this suite in a flash. That girl isn't worthy of you, but you'll find that out for yourself.*

He tossed off his wine in a single angry gulp; they were both throwing down the expensive champagne like cough syrup.

He refilled their glasses, his movements jerky and somehow intense. "If you're about to give any potential union your blessing, don't waste your breath. I don't need my ex-wife's approval."

"No, of course not. I was just—"

"I know what you were just." He sounded thoroughly irate. "Look, I understand why you want me off your hands—so you can be with lover-boy. Tell you what, I'll pop next door, and if the missing twosome has turned up, I'll invite them over for a drink. We'll settle this suite business once and for all."

"No!"

"Huh?" He paused in the act of rising.

"Don't!"

"Why the hell not?"

"Because—Because we can work it out more quickly between the two of us. B-Because . . ." She cast around frantically for reasons, excuses, anything that would stop him. She grabbed a belt loop on his shorts. "Because I still have things I want to tell you. Please, J.D., don't—"

His hard expression stopped the incoherent tumble of her words. "I don't think I want to hear anything else you have to tell me," he said slowly, capturing her clutching hands with his.

"Probably not," she admitted, "but—"

He shoved her hands away. "I'll only be a minute."

What more could she do? She sank back in her chair and closed her eyes, praying that the couple next door had taken their show on the road—the road to the bedroom, where they couldn't disillusion anybody else.

J.D. didn't have a voyeuristic bone in his body, but he couldn't help staring at the couple entwined on the couch in the Emerald Suite. No matter how he looked at it, they were in a decidedly compromising position.

Maybe there was an explanation.

Yeah, and maybe Sharon Stone's acting ability made her a star. Now that he had a chance to think about it, Ramona sort of reminded him of Sharon Stone, at least her most acclaimed attributes.

But that sonuvabitch with her—

Grinding his teeth, J.D. charged through the connecting gate to the Honeymoon Suite balcony and slammed it closed behind him. That bastard wasn't worthy of Claire, but she wouldn't take kindly to having that pointed out by her ex-husband. It would be a hard lesson, but she'd have to learn it herself. He couldn't take the pain for her— although he realized with a start that if he could, he would.

Claire's head swung up and she stared at him, brown eyes wide and concerned. J.D. figured he must look like some kind of madman to elicit that response.

He realized he'd bared his teeth in a snarl and forced himself to relax, tried to exact a smile but wasn't sure he got past a grimace. "Nobody's home." He flung himself back into his chair.

"Oh?" She blinked as if surprised, then visibly relaxed. "Oh!" She smiled.

"I've made a decision," he announced hoarsely. "I'm moving out so Glynn can move in. You win. The Honeymoon Suite is all yours."

"But you can't!" She jumped up, leaning forward with her hands on the edge of the table.

"The hell I can't!" He also stood up, and braced himself on his palms.

She faced him bravely. "You don't understand. *I've* decided to let *you* have it. I'm the one who's moving out."

"The hell you are!" He was yelling but he didn't care. "Let me do this for you!"

She was shaking her head and she thrust out her lower lip, a stubborn habit that used to make him smile. There was a time when he'd got his way by kissing that lip, and the rest of her, too.

That time, alas, was past.

Her response matched his in volume. "I don't want this suite or this hotel or—or this damned state! I'm out of here, the quicker the better!"

"What's the matter with you? You won! I'll move out, your boyfriend can move in and—"

Her eyes flew wide with such shock that he stopped

shouting and swung around to see what had provoked such a response. Glynn and Ramona stood in the opening between balconies, wearing matching terry-cloth robes with the GG logo and matching Cheshire cat smiles.

That did it, as far as J.D. was concerned. In a half-dozen infuriated strides he reached the traitors. Grabbing Glynn by the front of his robe, J.D. hauled the smaller man forward.

"You son of a bitch," he roared. "I'll show you you can't treat Claire this way!"

Ramona shrieked and threw herself on J.D.'s back, scratching and clawing. Claire grabbed J.D.'s free arm and hung on, while Glynn struggled to escape the iron hold dragging him inexorably to his doom.

Everybody clamored for attention at once, words overlapped by cries and whimpers:

"We can explain!"

"Explain hell! You're dead—"

"J.D., if you'll just listen!"

"Haven't you done enough to him? Get *away!*"

And then a usually soft Texas voice, raised in alarm: "What's goin' on here? Y'all lost your *minds?*"

They all tried to answer Etta at once, everybody speaking at the top of their lungs. Clustering around, they jostled for position and for a chance to show where their loyalties lay. Etta waited until everyone paused for breath at the same time before clapping her hands sharply to get their attention.

"Lemme get this straight," she said. "Miz Elliott is mad because Ramona broke Mr. Elliott's heart."

Claire nodded with sharp condemnation.

Etta continued. "And Mr. Elliott is a'fixin' to kill George here—"

"Glynn!" Ramona cried indignantly.

"Glynn," the maid corrected herself. "Irregardless, Mr. Elliott's a'fixin' to kill him for betrayin' Miz Elliott, did I get that right?"

J.D. snarled agreement and took a menacing step toward the other man. "Killing's too good for him."

Glynn swallowed hard and retreated. "What're they so mad about? Mona and I are the one's who've been stood up. While those two share the Honeymoon Suite, what're we supposed to do? We were just coming to tell them that—''

''That's weak,'' J.D. sneered, ''really weak, Johnson. Did you or did you not come to Texas to be with Claire? When she's otherwise occupied, do you always hit the sack with whoever's handy?'' He flexed his fingers as if they ached to curve around somebody's throat. ''Why the hell she ever invited you to—''

''She didn't invite me, I just came. In fact, she told me *not* to come, but I did anyway.'' He slid one arm around Ramona. ''If it wasn't for Mona, here, I'd figure it was the biggest mistake of my life.''

Claire stepped forward to confront the woman in Glynn's arms. ''Ramona Daniels, you should be ashamed of yourself! Glynn is unencumbered, but what about you? Bed-hopping that way—''

Ramona rose on her toes and strained forward, her face filled with outrage. ''You don't know anything about it!''

At the same time, J.D. curved his arms around Claire's waist and drew her snugly against his chest. ''Don't,'' he said in a thick voice. ''They're not worth it.''

Etta took charge again. ''Wait a minute, wait a minute,'' she ordered. ''I don't see any evidence of broken hearts or terrible betrayals here.''

Claire turned on the maid. ''Haven't you been listening?''

''Yep, but I've also been watchin'.'' Etta raised both eyebrows. ''Did it ever occur to y'all that there's a possibility—heck, I'd call it a danged good likelihood—that you're paired off just the way you oughta be?''

Claire was in J.D.'s arms, Ramona in Glynn's.

Slow smiles blossomed on every face. Claire turned in the tight and loving circle of J.D.'s embrace. ''Time to tell the truth, the whole truth, and nothing but the truth so help us God?'' she challenged.

He nodded, his smile warming her to the core.

''Glynn is nothing more to me than a friend. He never was. He came here over my objections, but I let you believe what you wanted because I couldn't afford to let you learn the truth.''

"Which is?"

She didn't want to tell him what a fool she'd been, but this was last-chance time. "I've come back to the Honeymoon Suite every year on our anniversary, trying to get over you."

"You're kidding." He looked stunned.

"Would I kid about a thing like that? I swear, John David Elliott, you've spoiled me for anybody else, and I might as well admit it. It's you or nothing."

She tried to tear her gaze from his, but he cupped her chin with his hand and made her look at him. "Let's try again," he burst out in an anguished tone. "I mean, marry me again. I love you, Claire. I never stopped loving you. Yes, I reserved the Honeymoon Suite and arranged to meet Mona here, but I only did it because I was so damned desperate to forget you."

"Do you mean it?" She gazed at him through teary eyes. "You better be sure! I still say ee-ther and you still say eye-ther—"

"Sad but true." A smile tugged at his lips.

"And I'm still politically conservative and you're still a liberal—or have you seen the light?"

"No way!" He was laughing now.

"Ever since Ramona brought it up last night at dinner, I've been racking my brain to figure out what you ever saw in me."

"Are you kidding?" He caressed the side of her face with a hand that trembled slightly. "You're smart and strong and savvy and you keep me on my toes." He frowned. "But in all honesty, I'd probably love you if you were dumb and weak and naive. I love you 'cause you're you. Go figure."

What could she possibly say to that? No one could explain love; it either was or it wasn't, and all the declarations or denials in the world couldn't change that.

He must have misunderstood her silence, for he frowned. "Not good enough? Okay, try this—I'll take the job in Washington and you can commute to work in New York until we figure out a better—"

"Commute, hell!" She shook herself from a state of near-paralytic happiness, rose on her toes and wrapped her arms around his neck. "I'll quit that job and get another—as a lobbyist! Can't you just see us, Mr. Liberal Columnist and Mrs. Conservative Lobbyist? We'll be great! And by the way, I love you, too, and my answer is yes."

Lost in each other's arms, they belatedly remembered that that they weren't alone. As one, they turned warily to face Glynn and Ramona.

Who, as it turned out, couldn't have been happier.

Ramona blew J.D. a kiss. "Nobody can say I didn't try," she informed him cheerfully. "I almost got you where I wanted you, admit it."

J.D.'s cheeks darkened. "C'mon, Mona," he begged, rolling his eyes toward Claire, "have a heart."

"Close only counts in horseshoes and hand grenades," Etta sang out. "My word, this is so perfect it near makes me break down and bawl."

Glynn's grin was as wide as Ramona's. "Best of luck to you both," he said. "I mean that."

Claire believed him; she'd never felt such fondness for him as she did at that moment. Watching them return to their own balcony, she called out, "Thanks for ordering that elegant dinner for us. It was perfect."

Glynn glanced over his shoulder; he and Ramona hadn't taken their hands off each other since the contretemps was settled, and they didn't now. "Glad you enjoyed it, but we didn't do it. We . . . had other things on our minds."

They disappeared behind the rose-clad gate. As one, J.D. and Claire turned on Etta.

"Hey," she said defensively, taking a step backward. "Somebody hadta do somethin' to get you two in a decent mood."

"Well," J.D. said, "I've only got one thing to say to you, Etta Hannibal—thank you! Thank you, and good night."

"That's two things," Etta said, but they weren't listening.

J.D. scooped Claire up into his arms and strode inside, pausing just inside the door to glance back at the chortling maid.

"Make it three things," he called. "Cancel my wake-up call tomorrow."

"Honey, I'd say you already had your wake-up call," she observed happily, watching him carry Claire down the hall. Them two—why'd it take 'em so doggoned long to admit they were meant for each other? Etta knew it the first minute she laid eyes on them four years ago.

Humming a happy little ditty, she let herself out of the Honeymoon Suite. She hung a Do Not Disturb sign on the doorknob . . . and another on the door of the suite next door.

Got me two with one arrow that go-round, she thought proudly, adjusting the Cupid's pin that held the heart-shaped hankie to her bosom.

That ain't half bad, even for me!

Lost and Found

Sheryl Lynn

Chapter One

"This isn't an executive suite." Sandra Campbell followed the bellboy into the sitting room. She dropped her briefcase and it struck the carpet with a muffled thud.

Turning in a slow circle, she absorbed the green-and-rose Victorian atmosphere: brocade draperies, wicker furniture, wallpaper patterned by tiny roses, and a marble fireplace. She'd never seen anything like it in her life.

She lowered a sour gaze on her traveling companion. Martin's nonchalant acceptance of the situation irritated her. For a plant engineer, he was awfully slow to recognize emergencies. "It's—It's . . ." How in the world could she describe this place? "It's a love nest!"

As if fearing the delicate furniture might collapse, Martin eased onto the white-wicker love seat. "Don't let your little old heart pitty-pat. Much as you might find me irresistible, this is strictly business."

A lot of women considered Martin Stonehouse irresistible, but only because they were too dumb to resist the big, broad-shouldered, long-eyelashed, green-eyed, curly-haired, stuck on himself and completely insufferable type. In the year he'd lived in Bugle Creek, he'd swept through the single-female population like a sweet-talking tornado. Even worse, no one seemed to realize what an irresponsible, love 'em and leave 'em playboy he actually was.

Except for Sandra. She knew his type and she didn't like it. If it weren't for the fact that Martin kept the machinery running in her uncle Wally's recycling plant, she wouldn't have anything to do with him at all.

Now he'd weaseled in on her first business trip. *Pitty-pat!* She gave him a glare capable of withering the wallpaper roses. "I can't give my sales presentation here." She clamped her hands on her hips. "I'll be a laughingstock."

"Nobody laughs about the Honeymoon Suite, ma'am." The bellboy unloaded the luggage cart with practiced efficiency. "Place is drowning in ancient history, ya know? That foxy lady statue in the foyer, that's Mitsy Packard. This was her suite."

Sandra paced and despaired. An image of her uncle's sweet face swam before her, and all too familiar anxiety gave her a bellyache. Folks in Bugle Creek thought Wally was a terrific businessman, but she knew better. Wally chugged along, stuck in his old-fashioned, handshake-and-a-promise ways, content with barely scraping by. He was getting old, though, and deserved a worry-free retirement. If she handled sales, she could ensure his financial security. Now that he'd finally given her a chance, she'd planned meticulously for the sales meeting to end all meetings: a presentation guaranteed to knock the socks off potential customers.

Nothing, *absolutely* nothing, had gone right. She sank onto a chair, buried her face in her hands and groaned.

Thunder boomed, making her jump. Even the weather conspired against her. A deluge of rain and hail had stretched the easy four-hour drive from Bugle Creek to Dallas into a tense six-hour, white-knuckled, eye-straining, nerve-wrenching road survival test. The weather news promised more of the same.

Which was nothing compared to what they'd found when they reached Dallas. She still couldn't believe she'd lost her executive suite only to end up floundering in pink marshmallow.

"Ah, come on now, darlin', it's not all bad."

Sandra bristled. "Don't call me darlin'. I hate that."

"Sorry, slip of the tongue." Martin didn't sound sorry.

The bellboy continued his cheerful prattle about the romantically tragic life of the beautiful Mitsy Packard and her mysterious illness, which had caused her oil and cattle baron husband to build the Glass Garden Hotel for her pleasure.

Cute kid, Sandra thought, wondering if there was an elevator shaft she could push him into. Martin, too, since he sat there nodding and pretending interest.

She jumped to her feet. "Excuse me"—she read his name tag—"Chad. I'd like to be alone."

The bellboy gave Martin an exaggerated wink and a thumbs up. "No, problem-o, man." He managed to bow and hold out a discreet hand for his tip at the same time.

At the door, she fingered the old-fashioned-looking brass lock. "Excuse me, Chad." She kept her voice down.

"Chad's the name, getting the goods is my game. At your service, ma'am."

"How about a pot of cocoa?" She checked to make certain Martin wasn't paying attention. "This hotel—it's safe, isn't it?"

The young man scratched above his ear, rumpling the only neat patch of hair on his head. "Safe?"

Through the sitting room, beyond the French doors, the Dallas skyline with its multicolored lights and oddly shaped skyscrapers reflected the lightning storm. "It's such a big city. There's a lot of crime here."

He looked at her as if her face suddenly sported blue polka dots. "The old Glass Garden is safe as kissing Granny."

She locked the door behind him and put on the chain. Big cities crawled with murderers, rapists, muggers, and thieves. Any fool knew that.

In the sitting room, she studied Martin, resenting his unflappability. "I am positive," she said, measuring each word, "if you try really hard, you can find another hotel."

"We were lucky to find this one." He propped his size twelves atop the coffee table. "Besides, I like it here." Stroking his thumbs along imaginary suspenders, he closed his eyes. "Yes, darlin', I could grow real used to this kind of comfort. If you don't like it, *you* find another hotel."

When he laid on the country accent, it always made her grit her teeth. He only did it to make her aware that when she was under stress—like now—her East Texas twang boiled to the surface. "You're the excess baggage on this trip. I don't even know why Uncle Wally made me bring you."

"You brought *me?*"

His laughter took another big chomp out of her tattered nerves.

She shrugged out of her corduroy jacket. "That's right, brought you. This is business, the big B. Costs, marketing, profit projection. Stop me if I'm talking too fast for you to keep up." She hung her jacket on an ornate brass-and-ceramic coat rack.

"Well now," he drawled, "being as how I'm jist a dumb ol' country boy, maybe you oughten educate me." He rolled his eyes like a moonstruck calf. "We could start with figgerin' and work our ways up to ciphering my name."

"Is Uncle Wally aware that in the middle of a crisis you turn sarcastic?" She paced furiously. Buyers from the largest paper manufacturer in Texas expected to meet with her in an executive suite. A big walnut table, catered lunch, an overhead projector! Now this? She stopped before a bookshelf containing leather-bound copies of classic romances. Unbelievable.

He clucked his tongue. "We have to make a few changes. Big deal."

She whirled on him. "It is a big deal!" Slapping off fingers for emphasis, she said, "I had every detail planned. The entire itinerary mapped out to the minute." She flung out her arms. "Now look at this! And you, you think this is funny."

"Make a few phone calls and let everyone know we're in a different hotel. It's not a big deal."

"I can't call Mr. Taylor. What will he think if I change everything at the last minute? He'll think I'm an idiot."

Martin cocked his head. His long fingers tapped a languorous tattoo on the back of the love seat, and the toe of his boot swayed with the rhythm. She knew he was laughing; he always laughed at her. No doubt he couldn't wait to get back to Bugle Creek to entertain everyone with stories about her fiasco.

He stretched and worked his shoulders. "Not that I'm an expert—"

"That's for sure!"

"—but Wally usually meets buyers in a restaurant or a bar. We're selling recycled paper products, not crown jewels." He swung his head side to side. "All the fancy-pants stuff is nice, but you've got to stick to the point."

"I don't need lectures from you."

He arose, his body unfurling with gracefulness that belied his bulky shoulders and long limbs.

Sandra caught herself backing away and it annoyed her. Martin did that to her, always invading her space, making her feel physically insignificant. Something about him caused an indefinable little itch deep under her skin.

"It's been a rough day. Picking a fight with me isn't going to smooth it out."

"Don't flatter yourself."

He wandered the room, trailing his fingers over furniture and pieces of art. Prickling with awareness, Sandra watched him; air in the room felt too thick.

He turned the full force of his brilliant green eyes on her. Her breath caught in her throat. In all her careful planning, she hadn't foreseen being sequestered in a pink-and-green fantasy palace with Martin Stonehouse.

"I know you don't want me here."

She flipped hair off her shoulders. "What gave you your first clue?"

One eyebrow rose and his smile showed teeth. "If you want to do grown-up business, you best grow up. Learn how to roll with the punches."

Heat tickled her cheeks. "Who do you think you are?"

"I'm an engineer, trying to do my job. Why that gives you conniptions, well . . ." He showed the palms of his hands.

"I'll tell you something else, darlin'," he continued, "I've put up with about as much huffing, puffing, griping, and sniping from you as I can stomach in one day. So quit acting like a kid, and we'll get along fine."

Her face felt ready to burst into flame. Nobody talked to her like that—nobody! Certainly not this Oklahoma born, corn-fed oaf. She flopped onto the love seat and tugged off her boots. He put up with her? He had that backward. This was her business trip, her sales presentation; she'd done all the legwork and made the contacts. It was *her* uncle Wally's financial security at stake.

His soft-spoken, "huffing, puffing, griping, and sniping" clung to her and burned.

Working her bare toes against the velvety wool rug, she approached the French doors leading to the balcony. The lake behind the hotel danced with reflections burst into prisms by silvery sheets of rain. As much as she hated to admit it, it was a breathtaking view.

From the corner of her eye she saw Martin pick up her boots and socks and set them next to the fireplace. She started to tell him to keep his cotton-pickin' hands off her belongings, but the possibility of another stinging comment stopped her. *Grow up?* He was only four years older than her twenty-four years. He sure didn't qualify as a sage.

"I bet the concierge can arrange for us to use one of the meeting rooms in the hotel." He showed her a brochure. "Looks like they have plenty available."

Chimes pealed a vaguely familiar tune. Sandra looked around for a hidden speaker. "What is that?"

"The theme song from *Dr. Zhivago,* if I'm not mistaken. It's the doorbell."

Roses, perfume, plush . . . now sentimental songs? *I can't stand it.* She allowed in a waiter pushing a tea cart. At the sight of a bottle of champagne and a large basket filled with fruit, her eyes widened.

"Compliments of the management, ma'am, sir," the waiter said. "With best wishes from the Glass Garden staff."

The artfully arranged apples, oranges, and bananas made Sandra's mouth water. It had been a long time since lunch.

The waiter twirled the champagne bottle in its bucket, making the ice cubes tinkle like music. "Shall I open this for you, Mr. Stonehouse?"

Rubbing the back of his neck, Martin grinned. "Why not?"

The waiter popped the cork with a luxurious *whop.*

Martin accepted a delicate crystal flute bubbling with champagne.

Before Sandra could close the door behind the waiter, another hotel employee bustled inside. She wore a pale pink housekeeper's uniform, a starchy apron, and sensible white shoes, and she carried a large wicker basket. With each bouncy step her cascading heart earrings tinkled against her shoulders. Her thousand-watt smile sparkled.

"Good evening, folks! Welcome! I'm Etta, and the Jewel floor is mine." She counted off on fingers glittering with heart-motif rings: "There's the Diamond Suite, the Emerald Suite, Amethyst, Carnelian and Ruby suites. But this is my very favorite, the Honeymoon Suite. That doesn't sound like a jewel, but trust me, this is the crowning glory. My word, aren't you a handsome couple." She patted Sandra's arm. "Very handsome, and that's for sure! Aren't you a lucky girl? Young love just makes my heart flutter!"

Sandra exchanged a puzzled glance with Martin.

The woman swept through the room. From the basket she pulled delicate bowls filled with potpourri and foil-wrapped candies which she arranged artfully on the tables. "Like it says in *Wildest Dreams of You,* all the world's a castle when we share our love. All water is champagne and the meanest bread is ambrosia. 'Course now, nothing mean at all about the food here. We have the finest chef in Texas, and don't he know it, too! Now, if—"

"Miss Etta?"

"Yes, honey?" She noticed their luggage and gave a little start. "My word, you just got here." She dazzled Sandra with a smile. "You're a pretty little thing. Mr. Stonehouse, you are one lucky fella! Have you had the tour?"

Catching Sandra's elbow, Etta led her around the room. With enthusiasm borne of unmistakable pride, she pointed out how to use the gas-powered fireplace and the wet bar with an ice maker in the refrigerator.

Hands in his pockets, smiling like an idiot, Martin followed them down the short hall and into the bathroom.

Etta pointed. "That's a whirlpool bathtub. Got jets and bubbles. Just the ticket for rest and relaxation." She tugged Sandra's arm, urging her to climb a marble step. "That spigot there in the middle is no accident, honey. The tub's built to seat two nice and comfy. That bathtub's launched more than one couple on the proper road to wedded bliss."

Martin threw back his head and laughed. Etta blinked quizzically at him.

Martin said, "Hate to disappoint you, ma'am, but we're not married."

"Thank God for small favors," Sandra mumbled. In her escape from the blush-pink and gold bathroom, she gave Martin her dirtiest look.

"Not . . . married?" Etta said. Her lips pursed.

"Afraid not, ma'am, we're not on our honeymoon," Martin explained. *"Yet."*

"My word."

Sandra shot him a glare. "We're on a business trip. *Strictly* business."

Martin jerked a thumb at Sandra. "She's playing hard to get."

"I see." Etta sounded terribly disappointed, and Sandra felt vague shame about bursting her bubble.

"She'll come around," Martin drawled lazily, as if spouting a mundane truth. "Soon as she realizes I'm the best thing since Skippy peanut butter."

Did he always have to play the clown? Sandra wished she wore her boots so she could give his foot a good stomping.

Etta lost some of her sparkle and Sandra's shame deepened.

Sandra accompanied the housekeeper to the foyer. The woman looked past the louvered double doors toward the sitting room. "If you don't mind me saying, he's a right handsome fella. Haven't seen a head of hair like that since Mel Gibson broke my heart. Pleasant-talking, too."

He might charm everyone else, but he didn't fool Sandra a lick. Her and Martin Stonehouse—a couple? When the Texas prairies sprouted palm trees!

"It's only business."

"Strictly business, hmm?" Etta's blue-powdered eyelids lowered. "There's magic in this suite. True love built it. Ask Mitsy there." She pointed to the elegant bronze bust perched in a corner of the foyer. "She knows."

That almost sounded like a warning.

Chapter Two

Martin watched Sandra help herself to a cup of cocoa. Her eyes snapped blue lightning, signaling yet another storm.

"It's bad enough being in this stupid suite without you pretending we've got something going. Quit embarrassing me."

Martin knew he should stop baiting her. He assumed an expression of appropriate contrition.

He fingered maps and colorful brochures on the tabletop, but kept a covert eye on her. As she paced, muttering, she reminded him of a high-strung thoroughbred, crackling with energy and tension, yet innately graceful. He followed the swing of her hips and studied the play of lamplight on her coppery hair. He repressed a sigh.

She didn't like him, she blamed him for everything that went wrong in her life, and she never appreciated his help. In fact, the nicer he was, the more she acted as if he were her worst enemy. Who needed the headache? Not him, and it was high time he did something about it.

Which was the *only* reason he'd agreed to Wally's suggestion that he accompany her to Dallas. This trip was shock therapy. He'd get over whatever the hell it was that made her so fascinating. Three days and two nights of nonstop Sandra should be a big enough dose to knock her out of his system.

Not much ever bothered him—until that day a year ago when Sandra Campbell dropped into his life. Beautiful and fiery, excitable and exciting, she drew him like a moth to a flame. A man in his right mind would be sick and tired of getting his wings singed.

Unfortunately, *right mind* and *Sandra* rarely coincided.

She flopped onto the love seat and picked up the telephone. She dialed a number, waited a moment, listening, then said, "Uncle Wally! Well, we made it, but you won't believe what we had to go through." She nodded. "The car is fine, but the weather is horrible. And when we got to the Marcourt Hotel, they'd shut it down. An asbestos hazard! To top it off, there are about twenty-five conventions in town. Every hotel in Dallas is booked to overflowing. It took the Marcourt people hours to find us this place. And I'm about starved to death."

Martin handed her a hotel brochure folded back to reveal the telephone number so she could give it to Wally. "The Marcourt people are springing for half the tab here," he reminded her. "We're saving a few bucks."

She turned her back on him.

He returned to the table and focused on brochures. If this weather ever let up, he'd go sightseeing. Dallas was a fun town, with lots of night life and plenty of beautiful women. He'd not only knock Sandra out of his head, he'd erase her.

Getting rid of an obsession was like getting rid of a fear. Admit it, face it, get over it, then drive on.

Starting now. No watching her hands dance while she talked. No daydreaming about how nice her hair and skin smelled. No wishing for one of her rare and beautiful smiles, or admiring her stubborn determination, or allowing her infectious—if generally misdirected—energy to charge him with enthusiasm.

Sandra sighed, loud and martyred. "I'll see if I can tear him away from the liquor cabinet."

Martin looked up. She thrust the handset in his direction. He took it.

Wally said, "The trip isn't going well."

"Could be worse." Martin watched Sandra select an apple. She bit into it, lowered her eyelids and lifted her chin. Her long throat worked smoothly; he followed the line of it to the delicate hollow revealed by the vee neck of her shirt.

"She's just hungry." Wally sounded anxious. "Take her to dinner and she'll be right as rain. She's always cranky when she's hungry."

Or when things weren't going her way. Which was most of the time.

"See if you can unruffle her feathers, Marty. I know

she's a tad difficult, but as hard as she's worked, she deserves to do good.''

Distracted by Sandra's white teeth sinking into the apple and her full lips gleaming with juice, he half listened to Wally's tips about the care and feeding of his niece. After Wally hung up, Martin couldn't resist. He kept the phone to his ear and raised his voice. "Oh don't worry about her, Wally. Skinny redheads with big mouths are perfectly safe with me. I promise, I wouldn't touch her if I had a piggen string and a branding iron." Then he hung up.

Sandra gasped. "I'm not skinny."

"I notice you don't deny the big-mouth part."

She gestured at him with the apple core. "I have to talk loud and long to be heard over your conspiracies!"

This was a new one. He drew his head aside. "How's that?"

"You're always shooting down my budgets. What do you call that?"

Her indignation threw him for a loop. He often discussed budgets with her and hashed out the details, but shoot them down? When had business-as-usual turned into a conspiracy?

She snatched up her bags and stomped out of the room.

Good, stomp away. Let me see you at your petty, demanding, spoiled-brat, I'm-the-boss's-niece-and-don't-you-forget-it worst.

His real problem was that every time he convinced himself to stop fantasizing that he had a chance with her, she'd get tangled up in her big ideas or pull a knuckleheaded stunt that made the plant workers threaten mutiny. Then he'd soften and help her—not that she ever appreciated it.

Not this time. He was a man with a mission. This time he intended to let her push him hard enough, and he'd get mad enough to finally face reality.

Sandra appeared, head high, hands planted on her hips, and eyes flashing. "Stonehouse, are you aware this suite only has one bedroom?"

It figured she hadn't paid any attention to the desk

clerk's description of the suite. He crouched before the
hearth. "Yeah, so?"

"There's only one bed."

"Enjoy yourself, darlin'. I already asked for a roll-
away." The fireplace logs, formed of some kind of rock
threaded through with the gas lines, intrigued him.

"I really think you ought to find another hotel."

He risked a glance. If looks could kill, he needed a
grave digger. "Put away your big guns. I don't know why
you've got it in your head that I'm the bad guy. Considering you're about the nuttiest lady I've ever met, I don't
want to know. But until we get through this trip, I suggest
a truce."

She crossed her arms.

Shut up, he warned himself. He wanted her on her worst
behavior. He wanted to see those warts. Still, he said,
"Cease fire?"

She stomped away again, this time slamming a door. He
flinched. At least he didn't have to worry about her throwing herself at him.

When he heard the shower running, he relaxed. He
started a fire, then actually concentrated on the hotel brochure. What a place: restaurants, entertainment, a sauna
and workout room, and a pool, of course. He removed his
boots and stretched out on the love seat, which despite its
flimsy appearance made for comfortable seating.

Lulled by the crackling fire, his eyelids drooped. Driving all day in a thunderstorm had worn him out. His stomach grumbled. He debated whether he should shower and
join Sandra in one of the restaurants—where she obviously
meant to eat—or give in to laziness and order room service.

Join Sandra. Ha! He'd asked her out several times in the
first few months he'd known her. Her answer had always
been a flat no. What had he ever done to make her hate—

Sandra screamed.

Martin burst off the love seat and barked his knee
against the coffee table. Trying to grasp his knee and run
at the same time, he hobbled to the bedroom door. Locked.

"Sandra?" He pressed his ear to the door and heard
incoherent, high-pitched, panicky noises.

He rattled the doorknob. Horrible images of her writhing in agony filled his head. He ran back through the sitting room and onto the balcony.

Rainwater soaked his socks and icy wind grabbed his breath as he hurried to the French doors leading to the bedroom. Don't be locked, he prayed. He burst inside.

He expected twisted limbs or blood. He didn't expect to see Sandra wearing only a fluffy white towel, standing in the middle of the bed, looking as if she wanted to be clinging to the ceiling. He stopped short.

Clutching the towel in one hand, quivering, she pointed toward the balcony. "Rat," she gasped. "B-B-Big rat! Behind you!"

He rubbed the back of his head. He breathed deeply in an attempt to slow his racing heart. "What?"

"Giant, *huge* rat! Out there!" She danced frantically from foot to foot and the bedsprings squeaked ominously.

He looked through the open door. A rat in a place this nice? On a fourth floor balcony? He found the light switch.

A mournful coo caught his attention. In a corner against a wall, a pigeon preened its bedraggled feathers. Martin pressed his knuckles to his mouth.

Once sure he wouldn't bray laughter, he said, "It's a pigeon, darlin'."

"A what?" She crept a few inches closer to the edge of the bed and strained to see past him.

"A bird." He closed the door.

"Are you sure?" A flush climbed over her cheeks. She sank to her knees and tugged self-consciously at the towel. "It looked like a rat."

"Looks like an old wet bird to me. 'Course, I'm just a country boy. What do I know? Could be a big city rat. With wings."

Her lips compressed and her brow lowered. She jerked the towel higher over her breasts.

The bed finally dawned on Martin and his mouth fell open. Eight small children or four good-sized adults could sleep comfortably on its wide mattress. He blinked, then blinked again, taking in the black-lacquered frame painted with roses and curlicues and carved gilt swags. He lifted his stunned gaze to Sandra. She'd tamed her wild curls into a fancy braid and duded up her face so her eyes were enormous and her full lips gleamed soft coral. Against the backdrop of voluminous draperies hanging behind the bed and surrounded by lace and satin pillows, she looked like a fairy princess awaiting her prince.

More than anything in the world, he wanted to gather her sleek body, glowing pink from the shower and the excitement, into his arms. He wanted to soothe her and . . . He needed to get out of here.

Head down, heart pounding, he beat a hasty retreat.

Martin slammed the door. Sandra winced.

A pigeon!

She'd find another hotel. Even a roadside, eight-dollar-a-night flea trap was better than staying here with Martin.

As soon as she thought it, she got angry all over again —this time at herself.

If he ran her out of the Glass Garden, it would be another joke for him to share with the workers at the plant. *She'd* be a joke. Ha ha, guys, should have seen her, hair standing on end, screaming like a damned fool because of a pigeon.

Well, it had looked pretty ratlike to her.

She climbed off the bed.

Forget Martin, she told herself, and opened her garment bag. She pulled out her new dress. Made of electric-blue silk, it had a softly draped bodice and a tight, straight skirt that ended six inches above the knee. She hadn't owned a dress this nice since college homecoming.

Who knows, maybe some rich oilman or international playboy waited in one of the restaurants downstairs, hoping to meet a woman like her. A little flirtation was the salve her bruised ego needed. Nutty, skinny redhead . . . what did Martin know! She slathered lotion all over her naked body, then stepped into wispy silk panties and fastened on a garter belt. Once her stockings were in place, she slid her feet into silver sandals.

Oh Lord, even if she didn't meet a man, this was nice. Bugle Creek was a great place to live, but glamour wasn't a strong suit, or even in the running. Parading before the mirrored closet doors, she pulled back her shoulders and arched her rib cage.

Martin Stonehouse didn't know what he was missing. Dumb goat-roper. All that hokey charm might work on the naive girls back home, but it didn't affect her. Uh-uh, never her. His eyes, his voice, those ready smiles and that *aw shucks* helpfulness—she never even noticed.

The dress slithered onto her body like a second skin. She patted her hair and grinned at her reflection. She'd show him a skinny redhead.

Martin lounged on the love seat, staring at the fireplace as if some secret revealed itself in the flickering flames. Clearing her throat, Sandra lifted a flute of champagne. Most of the bubbles had dissipated, but it was the gesture that counted.

He glanced over his shoulder, looked back at the fire, then straightened and dropped his feet to the floor. He turned on the cushion, his lips parted and his eyes wide. A muscle leapt in his jaw.

She sipped delicately at the champagne. "See something green? What's the matter?"

"Ah, you look nice. Dress . . . like it."

"This old thing?" She sniffed. "Those restaurants look pretty fancy."

His cheek twitched again.

Sandra arched an eyebrow. He acted like a bull socked between the eyes with a two-by-four. If she didn't know him so well, she'd say he was impressed. Ha! He was too conceited and impressed with himself.

She drained the champagne. The remaining bubbles tickled her nose and she sneezed. "I might get lucky and meet somebody interesting." Giving him a good eyeful of her swinging hips, she left the suite.

At the elevator she pressed the down button. While waiting, she checked her handbag. Key, wallet, mini-canister of Mace, lipstick—the doors slid open and she stepped inside.

She immediately regretted it. A man occupied the car.

Dressed in a black suit with a white shirt and dark tie, he wore eyeglasses with shaded lenses.

The elevator went up.

Sandra pressed the button for the lobby, then noticed all the buttons were lit. The man turned his head slightly before facing front again. His rigid presence made her think of bodyguards, or gangsters.

She'd heard about men accosting women in elevators. Suddenly her sexy little frock seemed like a very bad idea. She pressed against the polished steel wall and focused fiercely on the door.

They reached the penthouse. No one waited there for the elevator. The man put a hand against the door edge and leaned out, looking around—for what? Witnesses? Sandra stealthily opened her handbag. The doors slid closed and a whirring sound announced their descent. The elevator stopped again. Again there was no one there, and again the man held the door while he looked around the hallway.

Sandra walked out of the elevator as quickly as her spiky heels allowed. A soft ding made her look back. The doors shut on the empty hallway. She sagged against the wall, pressing a hand against her pounding heart.

In Bugle Creek criminals were as rare as albino catfish, but she read newspapers and watched television. She knew what kind of vile, horrible things criminals did to innocent people who let down their guard.

Pushing through a heavy door, she found the stairwell. All dull-gray concrete and metal stairs, it smelled of dust and old paint. She wrinkled her nose. Trying as hard as she could to keep from sounding like an army on the march, she went down the stairs. On the next landing the door was marked For Employees Only. She went down another level. This door was marked To Mezzanine. She went down another turn.

On the landing below she saw a body.

Chapter Three

Glowering at his blurry reflection in the steamy bathroom mirror, Martin dried his hair. Where had Sandra found a dress like that silky blue marvel? Not in Bugle Creek, that's for certain. Vivid images of her surrounded by smooth-talking admirers tormented him. Worse was the idea of her smiling back at them, lowering her eyelids, fluttering her lashes, showing off those elegant legs—

Stop! Obsessing over Sandra was exactly what he wasn't supposed to be doing. He'd go downstairs, but not to join her. He'd meet someone else, a nice woman . . . he knew lots of nice women. In Bugle Creek he never lacked company for dancing at the Pinto Pony Saloon. He had plenty of lady friends, and quite a few had hinted that if he ever wanted more than friendship . . . he did, but the one woman he desired acted as if he were the reincarnate of Adolf Hitler. Who needed it?

Faintly, barely noticeable above the sound of the blow dryer, he thought he heard Sandra calling his name. The bathroom door burst open.

Sandra practically fell at his feet. She caught herself on the vanity. Her eyes widened in wild shock.

He flicked off the blow dryer. "Ever think about knocking?"

She did an abrupt about face. He wrapped a towel around his waist. Her seeing him buck naked didn't bother him nearly as much as her ragged breathing and trembling.

"What the hell is going on now? Find another rat?"

"Dead guy." She dragged in a long, shuddering breath. "Murdered. Dead." She waved her hands back and forth.

She'd come up with some doozies before, but this beat all. Martin crossed his arms and cocked a hip against the marble vanity. "Murder?"

"Stairwell." She whirled. Grabbing his shoulders, she shook him with surprising strength. His head bobbed. "There's a dead guy in the stairwell! He's been murdered! He's dead! We have to call the police!"

He caught her elbows and backed her forcibly out of the bathroom. At the door, he changed his grip to her upper arm and led her to the sitting room. He sat her down and gave her a glass of water. If this were anyone else, he'd consider it a joke. Sandra, however, hoarded her sense of humor as if letting it loose meant using it up.

"You're not making a lick of sense," he said. "Calm down."

"I can't calm down." She pressed a fist to her chest and her pulse beat birdlike in the hollow of her throat. "He was lying there all broken and still and—and—it was just awful!"

He urged her to drink the water.

"You're shaking like a cat in a dog kennel." He sat beside her and put his arm around her shoulders. No joke, she was terrified. He set his resolve aside—temporarily—and concentrated on soothing her. "Calm down, you're safe. What did this man look like?"

"He looked dead!"

Hard to imagine a murder happening in a place like this hotel. Looking dead and being dead were easily mistaken, he supposed. "Maybe he was resting."

"In a dirty stairwell? On a concrete floor?" She shuddered violently. Martin took the glass before she spilled water on her skirt. "He must have been shot or stabbed. Or strangled! Oh God, we've got to get out of here!"

He tightened his hold on her shoulders. The clean, fresh scent of her hair made his jaw clench. "Have to admit, you've got a bad habit of jumping to conclusions—"

She bristled with indignation. "Are you calling me a liar?"

This was so typically Sandra. Like the time she convinced herself the plant was being broken into at night, so she campaigned to hire armed security guards, and Wally had had to confess he let some workers hold their weekly poker parties in the office. Or the time she'd hoarded an IRS letter for a week, unopened, working herself into a panic over an impending audit when it was actually a notice about a change in tax forms.

Or mistaking a storm-blown pigeon for a rat.

Typically, he felt the softening like a wave of warm syrup replacing his bones. White knightism, his fatal flaw. Even knowing it, he couldn't help rubbing her satiny shoulder and murmuring, ''Before we get all excited, we should make sure you didn't misinterpret—''

She shoved him away. ''Stop with that logical crap! I saw a murdered man callously dumped in the stairwell. I'm calling security!''

Sandra calmed down, sort of. Finishing off the champagne helped a little. Martin getting dressed, in something besides a towel riding low on his hips, helped even more. In between downing champagne and pacing, Sandra made a sizable dent in the fruit basket contents. She nervously wiped apple juice off her fingers.

Finally, the security chief arrived. She was alone, which surprised Sandra, who expected, at the very least, the entire hotel security staff.

Holding a notebook in one hand and a pen in the other, the security chief introduced herself as Ms. Watters. She said, ''You claim you saw a body in the West Tower stairwell, Miss Campbell.''

''I did see him. Didn't you? Where are all your people? Looking for the killer?''

Ms. Watters arched a thin eyebrow. ''Where exactly was this alleged body?''

Sandra pointed down. ''I told you. The landing right before the lobby.''

''Can you describe the body?''

''Go look for yourself! He's a dead guy! He's not going anywhere.''

The interview went downhill from there. Ms. Watters was very polite, in a brittle, no-nonsense sort of way. She had checked the stairwell. No, she was not going to call the police, *or* issue an all points bulletin for the killer.

After the security chief departed, Sandra clamped her arms over her breast. ''She thinks I'm out of my everlovin' mind.''

Martin scratched the back of his head. ''Well now, darlin', you do have quite an imagination. Maybe you saw something that looked—''

''It was a body! An old man with white hair and . . .'' Scowling, she tried to dredge up details, but in her initial panic all she'd gotten was a glimpse. Details escaped her.

"What were you doing in the stairwell in the first place?"

She shrugged. "There was a man in the elevator." She darted an under-the-eyelash glance at Martin. "A scary-looking man."

Martin rubbed his mouth and jaw, hard. His eyes sparkled with repressed laughter.

"Why would I make this up?"

"I'm not calling you a liar."

"Then will you look? There has to be something. A clue or—or—blood."

He held up his hands. "All right, all right. Then we'll go to dinner. There are still a few rough spots to work out of your presentation."

He reached for her arm, she jerked away. "You don't believe me." She snatched up her purse. "I'll prove it to you." She flounced out of the suite, head high, shoulders back, and muttering to herself. How dare he patronize her?

She stopped at the door leading to the stairs. The glowing exit sign looked alien and out of place near the coved and sculptured ceiling.

Martin caught up to her. Wearing black jeans, a red and blue western shirt, and cowboy boots, he was big and sure of himself. For once she was glad he was an oversized hulk. He opened the steel door.

She peered cautiously over the metal railing, trying to see down to the lobby landing. Wincing and gritting her teeth against the noise, she unsnapped her handbag and pulled out her Mace.

"Put that away," Martin said.

"Shhh!"

"Now you're being silly."

"Oh, I am, am I?" she whispered. "There's one dead guy too many around here. I don't intend to be victim number two." With her finger on the canister trigger, she crept down the stairs.

By the time she reached the mezzanine level, she could barely breathe. Her heartbeat pulsed in a deafening roar against her eardrums. She pointed. "There."

Martin leaned far over the rail and twisted in an attempt to see. "Don't see nothing." He started down the stairs.

Sandra drew several long, steadying breaths. Unable to face possible blood—the mere thought made her ill—she squeezed her eyes shut and groped blindly down the stairs.

"Right here?" Martin asked.

She opened her eyes.

A few dust kitties and a cigarette butt littered the landing.

She crouched and ran her hand over the floor. A small amount of dust dirtied her palm, but nothing wet or bloody. "I swear, Stonehouse, he was right here. All twisted up and pitiful. He looked broken." She lifted her gaze in a mute plea for him to believe her.

He extended a hand. Ignoring it, she got to her feet. "I saw him. I did."

He looked toward the basement then up toward the guest floors. He studied the heavy-duty, fireproof door before shifting his gaze to the lightbulb high on the wall. "The light is real funny in here."

"I didn't see a trick of light. Or a shadow."

He waggled a finger. "Now hold on, I'm not saying you're hallucinating. I'm saying the light is funny. You might not have gotten that good a look." He cocked an eyebrow and his eyes gleamed under the stark bare bulb overhead. "Did you touch him?"

Shivering under a sudden onslaught of goose bumps, she hugged her elbows. She didn't want to admit she hadn't gotten any closer than the next landing up. "No."

"There you go. He wasn't dead."

"But—"

"There's a lot of liquor in a place like this. Could have been drunk and taking a nap."

She stamped a foot and listened to the echo. "Maybe the murderer heard me. Sheesh, you can hear everything in here. So he hid, and when I ran upstairs, he moved the body."

Sandra went up and down the stairs, seeking even the tiniest drop of anything remotely resembling blood. There had to be something—killers always left clues.

Arms crossed, Martin leaned a shoulder against the wall. "Wally says you have a fondness for horror movies. And mystery novels."

"I'm not taking this from you." She headed for the door.

Before she could pull it open, Martin put his hand on the door over her head. The smell of shampoo and clean maleness washed over her. Seams pulled on his shirtsleeve. His eyes were very green.

An image of him naked popped into her head. She'd been too scared to notice—or so she'd thought. Funny how much she remembered: the heavy ridge of his clavicle, the solid sculpting of long muscular thighs, the sleek back, powerful shoulders, and the appealing angle of his neck.

Her mouth went dry.

"There's nothing here."

She didn't want to trust him, but she did. She didn't want his low-pitched drawl to be the voice of reason and comfort, but it was. "Do you think I'm . . . seeing things?"

His eyebrows twitched and his lips acquired a peculiar softness. "Anybody can see something and think one thing when it's not that at all. I'm sure you saw a drunk."

Could he be right? Again, details about the body eluded her. Embarrassment replaced her fear. How did she *always* get herself into these messes? Why did Martin Stonehouse, of all people, *always* have to be around to witness it?

Why was it so hard to breathe?

His eyes fascinated her. Women in Bugle Creek had a running debate about whether he wore contact lenses to give them their jewel-like color. Up close, Sandra knew nothing stood between her and the pure emerald depths of his irises.

"You've had a long day," he said. "The drive down from Bugle Creek, all that hee-hawing around with the Marcourt. That's enough to skew anybody's perception." He pushed away from the door.

His movement snapped her back to reality. He wasn't attractive! He wasn't . . .

She shrugged her shoulders and patted her hair. "No murder, then," she said through her teeth. She hated giving up, but what choice did she have? "No body."

"So forget it. Let's go eat." He opened the door and made a gallant gesture for her to go first.

The longer she considered Martin's reasoning, the more it made sense. Maybe it was stress.

In the main lobby she turned to Martin. "I ought to talk to the concierge first. About the meeting room."

"Good idea." He kept looking at her with an intensity that made her previous fright acquire dreamlike proportions. He distracted her.

Even the hotel distracted her.

The glass garden took her breath away.

A glass wall loomed three stories. Twinkling lights, like stars, twined through the lush banks of foliage and around a tall baroque fountain, giving the dining terraces a fairy-tale quality. Sandra half expected the guests to suddenly begin singing and ballroom dancing as if in a 1940s musical extravaganza.

Martin took Sandra's elbow as they ascended the grand staircase to the mezzanine. Remembering in time that he hadn't laughed himself sick over the missing body, she bit back a sharp comment about male chauvinism.

"Ever seen anything like this?" he asked.

"Not me." She never even imagined anything like it.

He stopped at the top of the staircase and looked back at the glass-enclosed garden. Talk and laughter made the air hum. Hidden somewhere among the greenery, a pianist played a waltz.

"Isn't this something?" Martin whistled, low and appreciative. "I can see why folks want to honeymoon here."

She stepped back and looked up at his face. "I didn't figure you for a romantic."

He lifted a shoulder in a lazy shrug. "There's more to life than gear ratios and lubricant levels. Don't you think this is romantic?"

She hemmed and hawed. "Well, sure. It's pretty and . . . sumptuous and . . ."

"Sexy?" he said with a friendly leer.

Trust him to bring sex into it. He'd dated every unattached woman in Bugle Creek; no doubt he'd slept with all of them, too. He better not have any ideas about adding her to his list of conquests. "You'll never know what I think is sexy, Stonehouse." Head high, she went in search of the concierge.

Hands in his pockets, Martin strolled after her. Sandra grew exceedingly self-conscious about the way she walked on the high heels. The harder she tried not to slink, the slinkier she felt.

At the concierge desk she waited for the gentleman to finish talking on the telephone. Around sixty or so, he was the most elegant man Sandra had ever seen. His jacket looked fresh-from-the-laundry crisp, and his shirt was spotlessly white.

Martin rested a hand on the small of her back and whispered in her ear. "Looks like that fella from *Dynasty*. Wonder if he's got Joan Collins stashed someplace."

"Stop trying to make me laugh," she hissed over her shoulder. Stop touching me, she thought, but refused to give him the satisfaction of hearing her say it aloud.

The concierge, whose name tag read Tyrone, hung up the telephone and placed both hands on the desk. "How may I help you folks this evening?" For such a big man, he had a surprisingly small voice.

Martin stepped to the fore. "This is Sandra Campbell, I'm Martin Stonehouse. We're the folks who lost our suite at the Marcourt. We need a meeting room, sir."

"Ah yes, I see."

"For my business meeting," Sandra said. "I need it for four hours tomorrow. Can you help me?"

"Of course, of course. There are no problems in the Glass Garden, there are only situations in search of solutions." From beneath the desk he pulled out a large, wine-leather-covered ledger. He opened it. "And the time?"

Sandra explained what she needed. Reading his ledger upside down dismayed her. If the amount of black ink was any indication, she had yet another problem. This was the business trip from hell.

Tyrone tapped his pen against his lower lip. He made sounds like a mechanic looking under a car hood, serious and somehow expensive. He looked up with a fatherly smile. "Please, leave everything in my hands. Your room number is . . . ?"

"The Honeymoon Suite." Martin worked his fingers along Sandra's spine until he reached bare flesh. "Real nice place."

Sandra stepped out of reach. "That's all that was available. This is strictly business."

"Of course it is," Tyrone agreed. "Never fear, Miss Campbell, my full attention shall be focused upon meeting your needs."

"Thank you, sir."

She managed to keep quiet until she and Martin were around the corner. "Do you have to tell everybody in the world we're in the Honeymoon Suite?"

He blinked innocently. "What else can I tell them? There's no room number."

Why did she bother arguing logic with an engineer?

They descended the magnificent staircase. Sandra imagined the carved banister would be a lot of fun on which to slide. Hair flying, screaming in exhilaration, the wind rushing past her ears.

As if reading her thoughts, Martin whispered, "Want a boost?"

She threw him a look askance.

Heavenly aromas of barbecued meats and baking bread tempted her. On the right side of the garden the diners wore formal attire; on the left side, people were dressed casually.

She pointed to the left. "Let's go to Montague's."

Headed for the restaurant entrance, she glanced back the way they'd come. The man she'd seen in the elevator was descending the grand staircase. Same dark suit, same dark glasses, same hard-jawed, sinister sternness. He turned his head and his glasses reflected the light. She knew he stared directly at her. Her breath caught in her throat and she stumbled.

Martin caught her arm. "All that champagne catching up to you?"

"Keep walking," she whispered from the side of her mouth. "Don't turn around."

He started to turn and she elbowed him hard in the ribs. "I *said* don't turn around. It's the scary man from the elevator. He's following me!"

Chapter Four

The intimately dark interior of Montague's boasted high-backed booths and banks of foliage. Candlelight illuminated the tables, bathing diners in rosy glows. Sandra peered into dim corners and kept looking behind her while insisting to the hostess that she wanted a table out on the terrace.

Her antics made Martin roll his eyes—did she honestly believe a killer would sneak up on her inside the restaurant?—but he kept quiet. Maybe she was one of those excitement junkies he'd read about in a magazine. Every day had to be an adventure or she wasn't happy.

The hostess seated them at a table in the garden. Pleased by their proximity to the central fountain and the panoramic view of the storm raging outside, Martin looked over the menu.

A busboy filled their water glasses and then a young woman asked if they cared for cocktails. Sandra and Martin declined. Their waiter appeared. He described the evening's special: babyback ribs, slow-grilled over mesquite and basted with Montague's world-famous barbecue sauce.

The waiter's enthusiastic use of adjectives made Martin's mouth water.

"Yeah, yeah, that's fine," Sandra said, and handed over her menu. Wind howled against the glass wall. Girders groaned. She tensed and shivered.

As soon as the waiter left, Martin leaned close to her. "You're acting jumpy as a cricket in a chicken yard. Quit."

"He was following me. You saw him, too."

He leaned back on his chair and flipped open his napkin with a snap. "You wouldn't let me turn around." He laid a hand over hers. "If a man is following you, it's not because he's setting up an ambush."

She jerked away her hand and rubbed it. "Give me one good reason."

Don't start this. Here's proof right in your face that she's crazy as a June bug and you ought to shut up. . . .

"Maybe it's because you're the prettiest little heifer roaming this range."

"Don't be absurd." Alluring color rose on her creamy cheeks. She took a hasty sip from her water glass. "You can't miss him. He's wearing dark glasses and a black suit." She darted her eyes right and left.

He looked over her shoulder. "Like that fella over there?"

In her haste to turn around, she nearly fell off the chair.

"Ha, made you look." Martin chuckled deep in his throat.

"You are a sick individual," she muttered and retrieved her napkin from the floor. "I'm not going to eat with you if you insist on making fun of me."

"Ah now, life can't be so serious all the time. No wonder you're seeing bodies."

"What is that supposed to mean?"

"Have to admit, you put yourself under a lot of stress. You never slow down. The world won't come crashing to a stop if you have a little fun. Or at least relax a bit."

"I should follow your example and run off to the fishing hole every chance I get?"

"Why not?" He looked around at their glittering surroundings. "The Marcourt's bad luck is our good luck. Even you admit this is a great place. So slow down, have some fun, listen to the music."

Her lower lip trembled ever so slightly. "My job is a big responsibility." Defensiveness made her words twang with the accent she usually tried to control. "Payrolls, keeping the tax records straight, managing the contractors. You don't have any idea what I go through. This is *not* a fun trip. It's business."

Uh-oh. Those big blue eyes, all shimmery and wounded, tore at his heart. "All I'm saying is there's more to life than working. And running around like a headless chicken all the time."

She flinched. "You just don't get it."

Shut up, shut up, shut up. Look at the pretty ladies, listen to the piano player, figure out how much pressure it takes to operate the pump inside the fountain . . . don't look into her eyes and try to wheedle a smile out of her.

"Do you think I do it for myself?" She shook her head emphatically. "I do it for Uncle Wally. He saved my life."

Don't bring Wally into this. In spite of her faults, she loved her uncle. She doted on him, fussed over him, and genuinely adored him. "He did?"

"You've probably heard the gossip about my parents."

Martin had heard plenty. Folks around Bugle Creek considered the long-departed Campbells fair game. As small as the town was, he thought, the gossip must get back to Sandra. He wondered if she cared, or if it hurt her feelings.

"Every word is true. My father took off with that cocktail waitress from Oklahoma City. Mom moved to Las Vegas to be a blackjack dealer. They abandoned me." She snorted. "Major mid-life crises. They're both out of their minds."

Despite her it-doesn't-matter-a-bit tone of voice, pain dulled her eyes.

"I was only sixteen. Ready to drop out of high school." She lifted a shoulder. "Ready to elope with the first fella who treated me nice. Uncle Wally took me in."

An insight struck him: she was scared, and not of rats or bodies or mysterious scary men. She might not realize how scared she was or even have a name for it, but her fear went right down to her bones. No wonder she was such a ding-a-ling.

"He gave me a decent home, made sure I stayed out of trouble. He sent me to college. My folks don't even call on my birthday, but Wally is always there for me." She clamped her lips shut and toyed with the cut-glass salt shaker.

He didn't want to make excuses for her nuttiness, or offer a stable anchor for her stormy psyche. That was the point of this trip. Get her out of his system, forget her, find someone else. Still, the siren call of hopefulness echoed in his mind.

As if his brain disconnected from his mouth, he said, "Wally is a good old boy."

"The best. That's why I have to do the very best for him that I can. Everything has to run perfect so he doesn't

have to worry about anything. He's an old man, you know,
almost sixty. He needs me to take care of him.''

Wally had more life in him than six men half his age.
As for needing anybody's care, Martin figured anyone
who insisted Wally needed coddling was in for one of his
rare displays of temper. "Is that why you're so hell-bent
on taking over sales?''

"You thought I was doing it for myself? I'm not even
taking a commission.''

That surprised him. He realized it shouldn't. She drove
a rattletrap pickup truck and lived frugally in Wally's
house. The silk dress she wore was the first extravagance
he'd ever seen in her.

The waiter brought their salads and a basket of warm
corn bread and sourdough rolls. Sandra accepted the
waiter's offer of freshly ground black pepper on her salad.

Between mouthfuls she said, "There's such a thing as
too generous. Wally's a prime example. He's always forgiving debts and increasing salaries, not to mention the
bonuses. Every hard-luck case shows up on his doorstep.''

She gestured with a chunk of bread. "Consumer acceptance of recycled products is growing. I have to get Wally
in on the boom.''

Martin studied her closely. One thing about Sandra, she
was honest. Wrongheaded, usually, but always sincere.

She honestly believed herself on a rescue mission.
She'd do anything for Wally . . . all that energy, excitement, and wild enthusiasm offered without reservation for
the one she loved. Martin's insight clarified so sharply he
heard words inside his head: Wally was the one person
who had never abandoned her, and she was determined—
no, make that desperate—to keep it that way.

"Do you think I'm wrong?'' she asked.

He shook his head and focused on his salad.

"You're thinking something. What is it?'' She dropped
her fork and it clattered on the china bowl.

Annoyance tightened his forehead. Having dinner with
her was a mistake—this entire trip was a mistake. He was
supposed to get her out of his system. He wasn't supposed
to let his stupid, hopeful heart brim with understanding. "I
was wrong about you, that's all.''

"Wrong how?"

"Doesn't matter." He hoisted his fork. "This is good salad. What did he call this dressing? Honey and something. Got some mustard in there—"

"Don't change the subject! How were you wrong about me?"

He couldn't figure out which was worse: her bullheaded blindness toward how he felt about her, or getting roped into this conversation in the first place. "You know if this storm breaks, we can do some sightseeing. We'll have a few hours free tomorrow, so we can check out the Museum of Art or go on over to Fort Worth."

She tapped her fingers on the tabletop, making the flowers in the centerpiece quiver.

He knew better than attempting to sidetrack her. Once Sandra had the bit in her teeth, she never gave up. Why all of a sudden did she give a tinker's damn what he thought?

He slammed down his fork. "All right, you want the truth, then here it is. I figured you for a spoiled rotten brat, bound and determined to have your way about everything. I thought this fancy sales meeting of yours was just showing off." He scowled and his voice dropped to a mumble. "I was wrong."

He expected her to storm away from the table. Or yell at him. Or freeze him with an icy glare and a frosty shoulder.

He didn't expect tears to glaze her eyes. Too late he realized he'd zapped her where it hurt most. Crawling under the table tempted him.

Her long throat worked and she dabbed the napkin at her face. "Is that what everybody thinks about me?"

"It don't matter what everybody thinks." He wanted to stop dreaming about her, but he never meant to hurt her. He turned a forced smile toward the main restaurant. His cheeks ached. "Our ribs are coming. I can smell them from here."

"I have to pay Uncle Wally back for everything he's done. I want him to be proud of me."

"He is proud of you. Every time he talks about you, he about busts a gut he's so proud." He leaned back to give the waiter room to place a platter of steaming ribs and rice pilaf on the table.

"That's why you're along on this trip. Wally sent you to make sure I don't do anything stupid. He's just indulging me, patting me on the head. He's shutting up the spoiled brat."

Cutting the air with a sharp downstroke of his hand, Martin exclaimed, "Now there you go again, jumping to conclusions. You don't know Wally as well as you think you do. Nobody pushes him into anything. So you're here, you're going to do a good job, Wally will be proud of you. That's all there is to it."

Please shut up and quit looking at me with those wounded eyes. Stop making me feel like I kicked your feet out from under you.

As if reading his mind, she concentrated on her food.

Uneasy with the awkward silence, Martin pointed out interesting passersby and speculated about the amount of steel and glass that went into the construction of the three-story-high glass wall. She refused to look at him. Apologies clawed at his throat. Apologize for what, though? The truth?

By the time they finished dinner, he felt mighty sorry for himself. Exhaustion weighted his shoulders. The Glass Garden's opulence lost its charm. He felt provoked, abused—and like a world-class jerk.

In silence they headed back to the suite. All he wanted was sleep.

As they left the elevator Martin muttered, "I've swatted cats with newspapers that don't sulk half as bad as you do."

She stopped in her tracks. "I never sulk."

"Yeah, right." He dug in his pocket for the key. "You're the one who wanted to know what I think. You pushed me, I didn't offer."

"You made it perfectly clear how you feel about me. Just shut up."

Too much! He waggled a finger in her face. She scowled and backed away until she reached a door marked Linen.

"I told you what I thought. I didn't say a single blessed thing about how I feel."

She gulped and clutched her elbows. "There's no difference."

"There's a big difference." A miserable universe-sized difference. A pitiful inner voice said he'd never stop feeling what he felt for her. Maybe he should leave Bugle Creek and start over someplace else. Get as far away from Sandra Campbell as humanly possible. China maybe, or Australia. He stalked down the hallway and turned the corner.

Sandra trotted after him. "What is that supposed to mean?" She caught his arm and dug in her heels. "As long as I'm stuck with you, Stonehouse, I'd like to know where I stand."

"No you don't."

"Yes I do." She tugged his arm until he faced her. "You've been a thorn in my side ever since I started working at the plant. Either you're laughing at me or arguing with me or undercutting my authority."

She had that so backward, he was torn between laughter and fury. He was the only person at the plant who supported her one hundred percent. Always. Even when she was dead wrong. Even when it meant having plant workers grumbling about how soft-spined and knot-headed he was where the boss's niece was concerned.

Still she pressed him. "We should get everything out in the open."

So she could really knife him in the heart? Not on her life. He reached for the doorknob.

The door stood open about three inches. Hand and key extended, he froze. The brass key fob swung gently.

Sandra caught the back of his shirt and crowded his heels. "It's the killer," she breathed. "He's waiting for me."

Chapter Five

Martin swiped at Sandra's hands as if brushing a fly. "There's no killer."

"You shut the door. Didn't you make sure it was

locked?'' She looked about wildly for a telephone. Seeing a fire alarm box, she lunged for it.

Martin caught her around the waist and swung her off her feet. ''Quit! You set off that alarm, you'll get us both thrown out.''

She struggled mightily, but he was as strong as his size indicated and he kept a firm hold until she stilled. Crushed against Martin's chest, her breasts tingled. Her mouth tasted as if she'd been sucking pennies.

His eyebrows reached for the ceiling, then lowered into a puzzled frown. He set her on her feet but kept his arm around her waist. He said, ''I'll check it out.''

Her hands fluttered aimlessly. ''What if he's got a gun?''

''Nobody has a gun.'' He gave her a look of warning and slowly pulled his arm away. ''Stay away from the alarm. I mean it.''

He eased open the door and peeked into the suite. Head cocked, he listened for a moment before creeping through the foyer. He laughed and beckoned for Sandra to enter.

In the sitting room, the housekeeper straightened from her task of making up the roll-away bed. She gave them a bright smile.

Sandra's knees wobbled and she caught the door frame for support.

''Howdy, folks! Sorry I'm running so late. My word, I don't think I've ever seen the hotel this full. One hundred percent occupancy, can you believe it? Of course, we're usually pretty full anyway. This is the finest hotel in the entire Dallas–Fort Worth area, even in the state of Texas.'' She gave a plump pillow a final pat. ''In the morning I'll just slide this in the closet out of your way. Should be nice and comfy.''

Sandra wondered if Etta worked twenty-four hours a day. If so, how did she stay so cheerful? She looked even more chipper than she had before.

Etta bustled into the bedroom. Sandra watched the woman turn back the bed covers with an experienced flick of her wrists. ''We've got a good storm blowing. Shall I close the drapes, honey?''

Remembering the pigeon, Sandra nodded. "Do you live in the hotel, Miss Etta?"

"Me?" A smile wreathed her face. "I wish. I'm like Marianna in *True to the Dream,* living in the shadow of luxury. If you're wondering why I'm here so late, well, there's always some little thing. We have staff out sick with that awful flu going around. I don't trust temps with my floor." She pulled the draperies closed over the bank of windows and French doors. "Are you all right, honey? Look a little peaked." She sorted through her basket and brought out a tea packet. "How about some chamomile? Good for what ails you."

"No, thanks, I'm fine." Sandra glanced toward the sitting room and sighed. She still smarted from what Martin had said at dinner. The worst part was, it was her own fault.

No, the worst part was, he spoke the truth.

Etta squinted one eye and tapped her chin in a knowing way. "A pretty little thing like you shouldn't have all these problems."

"What problems?"

"Now, honey, I've been around a day or two." She patted her spun-sugar bouffant hair. "Taking care of folks the way I do, well, I notice things. Take that young fella in the next room for instance."

"Martin?" Growing uneasy with the sense that this woman could see right through her, Sandra's cheeks warmed. "What about him?"

"I see the way he looks at you. You'll feel right as rain when you stop playing hard to get."

A surprised laugh burst from Sandra. If Martin looked any way at her, it was with disgust. He'd said as much at dinner. "Pardon me?"

"Playing hard to get is old-fashioned. Honesty is the key to good relationships."

"He doesn't even like me!" Sandra blurted. "He thinks I'm a spoiled brat."

"Are you?"

Sandra had to think about it. "No. Maybe . . . I don't know. But he doesn't care about me." And that, she knew, was the dead-on truth. He wasn't the type who could ever care about any particular woman for more than a date or two. He proved it by dating a different girl every weekend.

Swishing past, Etta patted Sandra's arm. "You care about him, so there's no problem. Sleep good, honey. Call housekeeping if you need anything."

Troubled and bemused by Etta's words, Sandra undressed. Did she care about Martin?

A knock on the bedroom door made her snatch up her robe and shove her arms into the slippery green satin sleeves. She opened the door.

Martin's face was drawn and his eyelids drooped. He'd done the driving today; after she'd fallen apart at the Marcourt, he'd negotiated finding new accommodations. He was exhausted, and she made it worse by flaking out at every squeak and shadow. Shame tightened her rib cage.

"The concierge left a message on the telephone. The meeting rooms are full-up. He says if you speak to him in the morning, he'll see what else he can do." He chuckled. "No problem, he says. Never any problems at the Glass Garden."

She saw herself holding the sales meeting in the Honeymoon Suite. While she presented costs, the buyers would be staring at statues of naked people. Her vision blurred.

"If all else fails, we'll meet in one of the restaurants. . . ." His words trailed and his eyes widened.

Sandra followed his gaze down. She still wore the garter belt, stockings, and silver sandals. Her satin robe barely reached the tops of the stockings. She shut the door.

Martin called, "Sleep tight."

She tried.

A hint of roses clinging to the sheets made her restless. The beautiful bed was too big, too lonely and strange. She tossed and turned, wrestled with the pillows, kicked off covers and pulled them back on. When she shut her eyes, she saw images of Martin naked and felt ghostly traces of his big arms holding her tight. When she opened her eyes, the words "spoiled brat" played like a broken record inside her head.

She sat up and wrapped her arms around her knees.

God knows, she wasn't spoiled. She'd worked hard for everything she owned. All she wanted was to do her best for Uncle Wally, to repay his kindness and prove he hadn't wasted his time with her.

With such good intentions, how was it she was so miserable all the time?

"Hey, Stonehouse."

A soft hand grasped his shoulder, shaking him. "Huh? What?" He blinked and weak light peppered his eyes. Dreaming, had to be dreaming. He squeezed his eyelids shut. It was way, way too early for morning.

"We have to talk."

The roll-away bed sagged and covers slipped off his shoulders.

Sandra—the woman was a plague! Bad enough she drove him crazy, but did she have to interrupt his sleep as well?

She sighed. Dramatically. Miserably.

"Jesus, Sandra," he mumbled, "we'll find you a meeting room in the morning. Go away."

She shook him. "Am I that horrible? I keep thinking about what you said and how I act and . . . I don't mean it. I just want everything perfect. I don't want Wally to think he's wasting his time with me. I have to take care of him."

He rolled to his back and opened one eye. She gave a small start and grasped the lapels at her throat.

His heart skipped a beat. What the hell was she thinking? She'd turned on the light over the wet bar. Her skin gleamed like translucent ivory—a lot of skin with those long coltish legs exposed. Her scrubbed face and a mass of curls hanging over her shoulders made her look very young and vulnerable.

And beautiful.

If she didn't beat it right now, he'd end up embarrassing both of them.

She stared at the floor. "Maybe I'm a little jealous. You and Wally are always laughing and going fishing. All he talks about is how terrific you are. As far as he's concerned, you walk on water." She darted a glance at him.

Martin fought the groan building in his throat. His aching hands made him aware of how tightly he clutched the covers. "Darlin', go to bed."

"He says I'm too hard on you. I think he's right. I've never made an effort to be pleasant or to try to get to know you. You seem so . . . sure of yourself. I feel like you're always laughing at me."

She wasn't going away. She was going to sit there like some kind of demented angel, tormenting him. He must have lived a very bad previous life. He sat up and drew in his knees.

She scooted around to face him. "I know you don't like me. I haven't been very likable. Sometimes I think Uncle Wally doesn't like me very much, either."

Maybe he was dreaming. No, in that case they'd be in the other room, rolling around on that fantasy bed—and she wouldn't be talking.

"Come on, Stonehouse, talk to me," she said. "I can't do better if I don't know what I'm doing wrong."

No dream, not a chance. "There's nothing wrong with you. You're smart and a hard worker. All you need to do is slow down a bit. Stop turning everything into a life and death situation."

"Well, maybe so . . ."

"The world won't end if you work less than fourteen hours a day." The silky sheets rustled as he shifted position. He rested his head on his folded arms. "Most times, sitting around shooting the breeze gets better results than a formal meeting."

"Is there something wrong with my meetings?" Her lips pursed. "An awful lot of emergencies do tend to come up when I schedule something. Even Uncle Wally makes excuses not to attend."

At the sight of her stricken expression, his resolve melted. "You're eager, and people appreciate it. But no, nobody cares for the meetings."

She slowly straightened and turned her head to look him fully in the face. "Now that I think about it, you're the only who always makes the meetings."

So what was he supposed to say? The sensible thing? As plant engineer he felt duty bound to attend all meetings.

Or the truth? He couldn't bear it when she worked so hard only to face an empty room.

"What else do people hate about me?"

"Nobody hates you."

"What else?"

Why did people who insisted on stupid conversations always insist on having them at stupid hours? Why did the sexiest woman in the world have to sit on his bed to do it? A slit up the side of her short satin robe made him think there wasn't much underneath except lots of luscious Sandra. A low, slow burn began in his groin.

"Answer me."

"Putting the lunchroom off limits to the truck drivers." Frustration tightened his jaw. He tore his attention away from her legs. "Bad move."

She gave a start. "But the insurance . . . they're not authorized personnel. . . ."

"Those drivers are old friends. People like to catch up on the gossip. Not letting them in is unfriendly. I know in school they taught you all about costs and benefits, but there's more to business than rules, charts, and five-step plans."

He placed a hand on her shoulder and looked her in the eye. Touching her reminded him of her fancy stockings and those long, long, *long* legs. He jerked his hand away. "Nobody hates you. But there are a few folks who'd like to see you slow down some."

"Wally, too?"

He hesitated. He threatened to stick his foot in his mouth all the way to the ankle—but she asked for it. He nodded.

Turning her head, she pinched the bridge of her nose and made pitiful little snuffling noises. "And my taking over sales? What does Wally really think about it?"

"You need to talk to Wally."

"Come on, I'm asking you to be honest."

Honestly, he was head over heels mad about her. As much as she irritated him, the last thing he wanted to do was make her cry—and sitting here with a raging erection was getting damned uncomfortable. He fiddled with the sheets, twisting fabric between his fingers.

"I get it," she said. "He's just letting me do this to shut me up. That's it, isn't it?"

"Do we have to talk about it right now?"

"Please."

"You want the truth?"

She braced herself and lifted her chin. "Yes."

"All right. I don't think you're experienced enough." The words emerged in a hoarse rush. "I think you read too many business magazines and don't pay enough attention to what's actually happening around you. You write too many reports, make too many charts and way too many rules. You act like employees are necessary evils instead of good, decent human beings who want to put in an honest day's work. You yak about the way things ought to be, but you don't have a clue about how things are."

She sucked air over her teeth. Those big eyes got bigger —and darkened with pain. "Why didn't anybody tell me this before?"

"You don't listen."

Her chin quivered. "Uncle Wally agrees with you?" Now her voice was rough.

The sound of it broke his heart. "He thinks once you gain some confidence, you'll settle down."

"I've made a real fool of myself."

He stopped himself from reaching for her. "You need to forget all that theory and bottom-line stuff they taught you in school. Wally's a good businessman. You can learn a lot from him. I have."

"So you've been, uhm . . . humoring me. I've really been stupid."

"Sandra . . ."

She clamped her arms over her breasts. "I guess I'm just Uncle Wally's charity case after all."

Annoyance flipped into anger. She had no right to do this to him. He tried to control his temper—under any other circumstances, with any other person, he could control it—but he snapped. "It's just like seeing that guy in the stairwell. You don't think, you react. Your enthusiasm is real admirable, but going off half-cocked about everything isn't. You act like a nitwit. There! Is that what you want to know?'' He fell back and pulled a pillow over his face.

Go away, he pleaded silently. Get out of here. Let me suffer in peace.

''You do hate me,'' she said in a tiny voice.

Snorting and grumbling, he sat up. ''It's the middle of the night. Go to bed.''

''I guess Mr. Laugh-a-minute is just an act. You're a real grouch.'' She sniffed.

''Do you want an apology? Fine, I apologize. I am deeply, truly, and sincerely sorry. Now go away.''

''You're right. I do act like a . . . pushy spoiled brat. But I can change. Do better.'' Chewing her thumbnail, she watched his face. ''I get scared. If I don't do the very best I can, Uncle Wally will . . . he won't want me around.''

He couldn't win. She never listened, so why try? The world was full of agreeable women who didn't snap his chain and make him act like an idiot. If he'd forget about Sandra, he could find one. He slumped with his eyes closed.

''I know we got off to a bad start. I came home from college expecting to be Uncle Wally's right-hand helper, but there you were. It was like he had you for his best buddy and he didn't need me. I've said things I don't really mean. Can't we forget it and start over? I'll try if you try.''

He didn't want to feel sorry for her. He didn't want to understand—he sure as hell didn't want to continue feeling as if she were the only woman in the world for him. He ground his teeth.

''Please, Stone—Martin?'' Hesitantly, she rubbed a hand over his forearm. A smooth, silky hand that burned wherever she touched.

''Jesus, Sandra, I'm only human!''

''What's that supposed to mean?''

He flung an arm around her shoulders and jerked her tightly against his broad chest. She stared into his eyes. ''You really are clueless,'' he said, and kissed her.

Too startled to react, Sandra froze, unable to protest or resist as his supple lips claimed and captured hers. His scent, sleep-musky and intoxicatingly warm, drowned her.

His muscles tightened, pressing her breasts against his chest. His hand clasped the small of her back.

She couldn't breathe.

Everything focused on the thrust of his tongue; the flex of his fingers against the sensitive place just above the cleft of her bottom; the possessiveness of his arm around her shoulders.

She couldn't think.

He teased her response, drawing forth the tentative touch of her tongue. The sweeter-than-wine taste of him sent tremors through her midsection. Heat flooded her groin and shivery weakness gripped her knees. He plunged his fingers through her hair.

He released her as suddenly as he'd grabbed her. His eyes were burning, smoldering. His great chest heaved.

She wanted him.

And that scared the bejesus out of her.

She didn't realize she'd moved until she heard the sharp crack, felt the sting on her palm and saw the mark of her hand upon his cheek.

Leaping away from the bed, she gasped in horror. She'd never in her life struck another human being.

He fingered his cheek and grinned. "Somehow, I knew you were gonna do that. Go to bed." He lay down, rolled his back to her and jerked the covers high.

Apologies lodged in her throat. Her thoughts refused to coalesce into anything coherent. Panting, she stared at his implacable back. She cried, "If you think putting the moves on me will get you in good with Wally, you are sadly mistaken."

"Go away," came his muffled reply.

Chapter Six

Sandra burrowed from beneath the layers of bed coverings. For a long moment she studied the silvery light shining around the edges of the draperies, trying to figure out why shapes seemed all wrong. Finally she remembered where she was and how she got here.

She made her groggy way to the sitting room. The roll-away bed was empty, and so, apparently, was the suite. A porcelain mantel clock read eight-thirty A.M.

"Stonehouse?" Wind slicing against the bank of windows was the only reply.

Hugging herself, she went to the windows. The world was gray. Mist curled off the lake and shrouded the trees, while low clouds made the tops of distant skyscrapers look fuzzy and out of focus.

Everything Martin had said last night haunted her. It was true, every bit of it. All she ever wanted was to make the plant run efficiently for Uncle Wally, and instead she'd made herself a laughingstock.

Had she truly accused Martin of kissing her because he wanted to make points with Wally? What a laugh. Martin was a good engineer who kept the plant machinery running smoothly, and Wally liked and trusted him. Everybody liked and trusted Martin, so he didn't need to make points with anybody. So not only was it the stupidest accusation she could make, it was unfair and mean-spirited.

Which didn't explain why he'd kissed her. Or why she'd sat there and kissed him back.

Or why kissing him again held such appeal.

Martin strolled into the suite. He carried a tray holding a coffee carafe and cups. He wore a pair of skimpy gray shorts and a T-shirt with the sleeves ripped off. A fine sheen of sweat gleamed on his skin, and veins rose prominently on his taut biceps. High color flushed his smiling face.

His gaze dropped to her bare legs and his smile faded. The ruddiness deepened on his face. "Here's some mud to jump-start your battery."

Reason said her robe was perfectly modest, but she felt naked. Or maybe only her thoughts were naked. With her leg muscles so tight they threatened to cramp, she edged toward the bedroom. "Where have you been?"

"This place has a great workout room. Weight machines. A sauna." He set the tray on the coffee table. "If you want to shower first, go ahead." He poured coffee in a cup. His hand trembled.

"You can go first. You're all sweaty." Not to mention

sexy and gorgeous, his hair curling damply around his ears and neck. The shorts clung to his high buttocks.

Neither of them moved. Awkward energy crackled through the air.

"Ah," he said. "About last night—"

"No!" She flinched and her cheeks burned. "I mean, let's forget it."

"Sandra, I—"

"No." She made herself look up at his face. "I made you talk to me. I wanted honesty and you were"—she gulped—"honest. I appreciate it. But I don't want to talk about it."

"Yeah, well, we should—"

She raised a hand. One more word and she'd end up throwing herself into his arms. "We cleared the air. That's important, since we have to work together. So we . . ."

Why was he looking at her like that? His eyes were deep and soulful and perhaps slightly pained. Unable to stand it, she made herself leave the room. She shut and locked the bedroom door.

Martin knocked. "Open up."

She did. He handed her a cup of coffee.

He said, "I won't be long in the shower."

Unable to meet his eyes, she took the coffee. He'd dressed it up with cream to a caramel color, exactly the way she liked it. When had he noticed how she liked her coffee? Her embarrassment deepened.

Along with embarrassment came a deep, molasses-slow, foggy wave of desire. Horrified at herself, she shut the door.

"You're welcome," he called.

She paced and sipped coffee. What in the world was wrong with her? She stopped before a small table dressed with a ruffled skirt and topped by an old-fashioned lamp. It was this suite, that was it. Nobody could keep a cool, calm, objective head when surrounded by rose-and-green froth, mirrors, and paintings depicting lovers. And that bed —every time she looked at it, she saw Martin and how perfectly he'd fit its luxurious dimensions.

Maybe she lusted after him, but she couldn't possibly *want* him. He went through women like other men went through socks. The very fact that she'd never known him to have had a steady girlfriend proved he was incapable of commitment.

Still, for the first time she had to be in the same place at the same time with Martin, no escape, no excuses. She had to acknowledge him as a person.

She saw him as a man.

More so, she saw how unfairly she'd treated him—how shabbily and spitefully. Why? No amount of pacing or agonizing produced an answer . . . except for a tiny, uncomfortable idea that blaming Martin for everything wrong in her life was easy because he was safe, secure, always there for her no matter what happened, and she trusted—

Knocking on the bedroom door made her jump. Martin called, ''Shower's free.''

She showered—trying not to notice the alluring scent of aftershave permeating the bathroom—then went to the bedroom to dress in her business suit. Of light gray wool, the tailored jacket fit snugly and the slim skirt stopped a modest two inches above her knees. She fastened a jet-and-garnet bar pin under the blouse collar.

In the sitting room, Martin waited for her. He lowered the *Dallas Morning News*. ''You look nice.'' His voice had an unusually cautious quality. ''Very professional.''

She made sure the pins holding her hair in a coil were secure. ''Thank you.'' She ran her gaze over his jeans and casual shirt. ''Aren't you going to wear a suit?''

''Don't worry, I brought one, but I'm not wearing it until I have to.'' He folded the newspaper neatly. ''I hear they serve a great breakfast buffet in Montague's.''

''I'm ready.''

While he locked the door she said, ''I promise.'' She crossed her heart. ''No dead bodies, no killers.''

The corners of his mouth twitched. ''About last night—''

She pressed a finger against his lips. ''Forget it. Please.'' Touching him felt too good. While she was willing to be friends with him, she couldn't risk anything more. She jerked her hand away. ''I'm turning over a new leaf. No more jumping to conclusions. I swear.''

He shrugged.

"You'll see," she insisted. "I'm very determined. You know I am. I can change."

On the way downstairs Martin tried twice to broach the subject of last night; both times she cut him off with a firm, "Forget it."

Except, each glance from him made her nerves sing in husky yearning. As if her rational mind had no say whatsoever, her body willfully found reasons to touch him. A brush of her shoulder against his arm when she took her chair; a light prod with her fingers on his hand as she reached for the salt; an electrifying accidental caress of his knee with hers under the table.

How she made it through breakfast without disintegrating into a gibbering puddle she did not know. Martin talked, but words made no impression. His wide, generous mouth distracted her. His lips were beautifully formed, chiseled, yet supple.

Martin paid the bill. He gave her the receipt. "Let's get cracking."

"What?"

He stepped back. A line appeared between his eyebrows. "Didn't get enough sleep last night?" he asked wryly.

"Huh?"

He snapped his fingers. "Earth to Sandra. Wake up, darlin'. Are you coming down with something?"

"I'm fine." Pulling back to reality, she concentrated on the task at hand. "Okay, you see what you can do about a meeting room, I'll make the necessary calls."

"I thought that's what I just said."

Once Martin was off running his errands and she was alone in the suite, she called the buyer for the paper company. She reached his assistant.

"Oh, Miss Campbell, I'm so glad you called," the assistant said. "I haven't been able to reach you."

"We had to change hotels. Is there a problem?"

"It's this weather. Lightning struck a transformer. We had one of those never-happen-in-a-million-years kind of accidents. The whole thing blew up! It destroyed computers all over the building. It's pure chaos here, and to top it off, half our staff is out sick with the flu.''

''Oh my.'' Sandra had a sinking feeling the paper company's disaster meant disaster for her as well.

''We've got all our key personnel assessing damage and data loss. I won't go into the details, but Mr. Taylor can't get away today. Tomorrow morning, perhaps? He can only spare an hour, but he is eager to meet.''

An hour. She'd prepared a four-hour presentation. ''Uh, sure. What time? We're at the Glass Garden Hotel.''

''That's a beautiful place. I went there for a Valentine's Day ball.'' Paper rustled in the background. ''How about a breakfast meeting? Eight o'clock?''

''That'll be perfect,'' Sandra said through gritted teeth. One hour. ''I'll call you back shortly and let you know the exact location.''

After hanging up the telephone, she stared at her portable file box and briefcase. An hour. What about her visual aids, costs analysis, charts, graphs, and proposals? How was it that she tried so hard and worked so hard and gave everything she did one hundred and ten percent and still came up zero?

What would Martin think about this? A statuette of Rodin's ''The Kiss'' caught her eye. The naked lovers roused disturbing memories and her flesh tingled with heat.

''Lara's Theme'' chimed. She hurried to answer the door.

Chad the bellboy peered around an arrangement of pink roses. ''Miss Sandra Campbell of Bugle Creek, Texas? My favorite kind of delivery, ma'am.''

''For me?'' She accepted the flowers, which came inside a plastic vase tied up with a large pink satin bow. ''Thank you.''

Chad gave her a jaunty tip of the hat. Hands jammed in his uniform pockets, he whistled as he strolled away.

Sandra carried the roses to the sitting room. A smile teased her lips. Martin must have sent them. Maybe he didn't hate her so much. Maybe he didn't hate her at all.

She searched through the stems and leaves for a card. Nothing. She pulled off the big pink ribbon and shook it out. Still nothing.

Martin would have sent a card.

She backed away from the arrangement. Flowers spoke a special language. If she remembered correctly, red meant love and passion, white meant sympathy, yellow meant . . . something strange—what in the world did pink mean?

Chad's greeting echoed in her mind: *Miss Sandra Campbell of Bugle Creek, Texas* . . . Martin would have never told the bellboy to say that.

The man in the dark glasses! He must have sent these, which meant he knew her name, where she stayed, where she lived—he knew she'd seen the body.

Pink roses must be like the dead pigeons hit men sent to snitches. A warning, an omen. She raced to the telephone. Who to call? Ms. Watters? She'd never believe any of this. The police? That's it, she'd call the police and tell them everything: the body, the man, the roses.

The outside door rattled. Her heart skipped and she staggered.

"Hey, darlin', everything is perfect. Okay, maybe not perfect. We have to change the meeting time and the room is small, but we can get—"

Sandra came as close to swooning as she ever had in her life. Rubber-legged, she wobbled, fighting the urge to scream at the top of her lungs.

Martin stopped in the middle of the room. His brow wrinkled. "Are you coming down sick? Your face is dead white."

She sprang against him and wrapped her arms around his neck. "Martin!" she cried. "He's going to kill me!"

Chapter Seven

"That's the stupidest thing I ever heard." Martin peeled Sandra's arms from around his neck. "Who's going to kill you?"

She lurched in an aimless circle, wringing her hands. "The man in the dark glasses. He sent flowers. *Pink* flowers!"

Martin frowned and pulled at his jaw. Some smart aleck

must have gotten a good eyeful of her last night and awakened this morning with a head full of ideas. Let him get his hands on the sorry so-and-so trying to move in on her. He drew a steadying breath. "This is right peculiar."

"We have to get out of here," she whispered. "He must have been in the stairwell when I found the body. He knows I saw it. He knows I know it's him. We have to go, we have to—"

Killers again. Didn't she know what a heartbreaker she was? Even in her usual jeans and boots, she was more beautiful than any magazine model. Any man who didn't think so was either blind or brain damaged. "Thought you said he was in the elevator."

She caught her lower lip in her teeth.

"Sounds more like you picked up an admirer." *And just let Mr. Admirer poke his fat nose around here.* "You looked real fine last night."

"Don't be ridiculous! This is a death threat." She pointed at the offending flowers. "They're pink!"

He covered a laugh by leaning over and cupping a rose in his palm. He sniffed it. Why hadn't he thought of roses? "Seems to me pink flowers aren't much of a threat."

"What kind of proof do you need? Seeing me all bloody and dumped in a stairwell? This is the business trip from hell. Stephen King couldn't have come up with anything worse. I'm going home."

She marched into the bedroom.

Martin blinked stupidly at her back. She meant it. He hurried after her and snatched a cosmetic case from her grip. "Now hold on—"

"You hold on. You think I'm jumping to conclusions or making it all up. I'm not and I'm scared and I'm going home."

She'd never believe some smoothie had sent her flowers. He tried reason. "Come on, you've worked hard on this. You can't quit."

"Are you mad? Deranged? Stupid?"

She tried to grab the pink and gray case. Martin held it out of reach, refusing to budge. Maybe if he kissed her again . . . she hadn't slapped him all that hard.

"I saw a dead man and nobody believes me. A man

follows me and nobody believes me.'' She gestured wildly toward the sitting room. ''He sent me a warning and you still don't—''

''I sent the flowers.'' Martin dropped the case on the bed. He folded his arms over his chest and thrust his jaw forward. The lie was out; he couldn't take it back.

She stumbled a step. ''You?''

He gazed at the windows. Rain spattered the glass in fits and spurts. ''There's a florist in the lobby. I bought them there. I thought it would cheer you up.''

She moved right and left, trying to make him look in her eyes. With stiff head movements he eluded her. The lie rested uneasily in the pit of his belly.

''You didn't send them.''

''Sure I did.''

''Why didn't you send a card?''

He lifted his shoulders. ''I thought you'd get a kick out of a secret admirer.'' *Think, you idiot!* ''I, ah, meant it as sort of an apology for last night. I didn't think you'd take it so wrong. It was dumb, I'm sorry. Should have brought them up myself.''

''Cross your heart, hope to die, promise you sent them.''

He raked a finger diagonally across his chest. ''Honest.'' He shuffled a half turn toward the door. ''Now this is embarrassing. I did a dumb thing and I'm sorry. So let's drop it.''

Her eyes lost their storminess. She fiddled with her jacket lapel. ''Thank you.''

''Don't mention it.''

She sank onto the bed and slumped with her elbows on her knees and her chin on her fists. ''There I go again, jumping to conclusions. I'm hopeless. What am I going to do?''

He sat on the bed next to her. Leaning forward, he matched her posture. Why couldn't she be like this all the time? Soft, with a smile teasing the corners of her mouth, and able to laugh at herself. ''Ah, now, you aren't hopeless.''

''Yes, I am, and it gets worse. I talked to Mr. Taylor's

assistant.'' She told him about the telephone conversation and the change in plans.

"Hmm."

"I can't give my presentation in an hour. This entire trip is a waste of time and money. What am I going to tell Uncle Wally? He'll never let me handle another sales presentation or a trip or anything. I wouldn't blame him if he fired me."

"Nobody says you have to go the full eight seconds every time you leave the chute. Sometimes just getting on the bull is good enough."

She grimaced. "What is that supposed to mean?"

"It means we'll meet with Mr. Taylor, introduce ourselves, and we make a good contact. He agreed to meet with you because he's interested in what we have. That's ninety percent of it right there."

"But my visual aids . . . my proposals . . ."

"Mr. Taylor wants breakfast, let's take him to breakfast. We'll put together a sample for him, write him up a delivery schedule, then that's that."

He straightened and the bedspread rustled under his jeans. She straightened, too, and met his gaze. "I really went overboard," she said.

"You can't know something won't work until you try it."

Her smile blossomed, capturing her entire face—and his heart.

Martin grinned. "Here's my suggestion. Let's rework the presentation." He glanced over his shoulder. "If we're lucky, the worst of the rain will have stopped by the time we're finished. They've got an exhibition of Mayan art over at the museum. We can spend the afternoon there."

"Do you mean like . . . a date? Oh no."

Here it goes again. He turned his grin on the floor. "You always say no when I ask you out. Let's call it an afternoon at the museum."

A blush rose on her cheeks. "I only say no because . . ."

He waited a beat. "Because why?"

Her breast rose and fell in a heavy breath as she caressed the satin bedspread. "You know, I'm Wally's niece and—''. Her voice dropped to a mumble. ''No, that's a lie.'' The blush turned hot.

He touched his little finger to hers. Electric desire coursed through his veins. ''So what's the truth, darlin'?''

''You said I'm nutty. In fact, you said I'm the nuttiest woman you've ever met.''

He chuckled. ''But I never said you weren't interesting. That's not why you said no.''

She crossed and uncrossed her legs. She fiddled with buttons on her jacket. Emotion flickered in her lively eyes.

He wanted more than anything to know what caused her reluctance, but instinct said don't press too hard. He scrunched fabric between his fingers rather than give in to the urge to touch her.

She surprised him with a light kiss on his cheek.

She clamped her hands on her knees and stared fiercely at them. ''There. You can slap me now and we'll be even. Then we can be friends.''

Friends? He had lots of friends, but there was only one Sandra. He placed a fingertip on her chin and urged her to look at him. ''Darlin','' he said, ''I can think of plenty of things more fun than slapping you.'' He fingered her smooth cheek. The swell of her pupils, turning her eyes luminous, made him want to pound his chest and roar.

''Like what?'' she whispered.

''Yoo hoo?'' Etta sang from the sitting room. ''Anybody home?''

Sandra leaped to her feet. Martin imagined he saw relief on her face, and his hopefulness drained away. ''I'll go on down and talk to Tyrone about canceling the meeting room. You call Mr. Taylor. Breakfast in Montague's will work.''

She nodded without looking at him.

His good feelings wisped into smoke. Maybe she plain didn't like him. Maybe it had nothing to do with her fears and everything to do with his lack of appeal. On the way out of the bedroom, he said, ''Call Wally and tell him about our change of plans. He'll have some suggestions.''

Sandra waited until he left the room before falling limply back on the bed. Contemplating the sculpted swirls and ripples on the ceiling, she agonized over her conflicting wants and needs. She wanted Martin. She'd been a fool to ever tell herself otherwise.

She needed more, though. His big gentle hands weren't enough. His handsome smiles and soft, drawling voice murmuring sweet talk weren't enough. The way a mere look could shift her so deliciously off balance was not enough. She needed forever, and Martin was not a forever kind of man.

Etta bustled into the room and stopped short. "Beg pardon! If you're—"

Sandra pushed off the bed. "It's okay. Go ahead with what you need to do." She went to the sitting room to make her calls. She tried the plant, but Wally was out. He wasn't at home, either. So she called Mr. Taylor's assistant and arranged for the buyer to meet her and Martin in the morning at Montague's.

Unbuttoning her jacket, she wandered back to the bedroom.

Singing an enthusiastic if off-key rendition of "Love Is a Many Splendored Thing," Etta dotted the bed pillows with pink-foil-covered, heart-shaped candies.

Sandra said, "You really like your job."

Etta gave her a knowing smile. "It's not just a job, honey, it's my life. I always feel kind of sorry for folks who hate what they do. Can't hardly drag out of bed, can't find anything good about their boss or coworkers. Me, I'd rather go hungry than do that." She handed Sandra a cork-stoppered bottle filled with something granular.

"What's this?"

"Bath salts. Good for your skin, good for your soul." Her expression turned impish. "And not a man living can resist the scent."

Sandra tried to smile. And failed. She tried to give back the bottle, but Etta refused. Shaking her head, Sandra said, "I don't need this, Miss Etta."

"Unload what ails you, honey, that's what I'm here for."

Sandra followed the housekeeper out of the bedroom. "It's not exactly a load. It's just . . . Martin isn't . . . it could never work."

Etta replaced damp towels with fresh ones in the bathroom. "Never say never, is what I always say. What's the problem?"

"It isn't a problem." She stared in dismay at the pretty bottle of bath salts, doubting if resisting a woman had even occurred to Martin. "He's a nice guy and all. *That's* the problem, he's too nice! To everybody. Especially to women."

"You don't say?"

Etta's skepticism made Sandra bristle. "He dates a different woman every week. Well, mostly every week. He must be sleeping around. I absolutely cannot get involved with a love 'em and leave 'em kind of guy."

Nodding, Etta made a knowing sound. "All the signs are there, hmm?"

"Signs? What signs?"

"He eyeballs other women when he's with you."

Sandra had to think about it. No matter how hard she tried, she couldn't recall a single instance when she and Martin had been together when his attention hadn't been fully on her. In fact, he watched her so closely, sometimes it seemed he could read her mind.

Etta said, "And he's high and mighty, pestering women and calling them ugly names."

Sandra almost laughed. Martin Stonehouse was one of the politest men she'd ever met. Sure he teased her, but no one could ever accuse him of being crude. "Well, no—"

"When he's with other men, he talks dirty." Etta grimaced as if the very idea pained her. "Talks about women like they're chicken parts."

She had often overheard Martin in conversation with male plant workers. They'd always been discussing fishing or sports or cars. "Of course not—"

"Setting one woman against the other. Playing them like cards. Got a slimy reputation."

That didn't describe Martin at all. He liked people, women included, and everyone liked him. Nobody even talked poorly of him because he was from Oklahoma, much less because of his dating habits. "Miss Etta, he's not—"

"And bet he drives one of those slippery foreign cars. Red and mean, or I'm not Texas to the core!"

Sandra's mouth fell open. Where was Etta getting all this? The only thing that saved Martin from the distinction of owning the most rattletrap rust bucket in town was that she herself drove the most rattletrap pickup in town.

The woman gave Sandra's arm a motherly pat. She threw a sly glance at the bouquet of roses. "Sounds like a real dangerous fella. Could be he dates because he likes the company and 'cause the girl he wants is unavailable, but why take the chance? Yep, got to heed those signs. They never lie."

Numb, sensing she'd been outmaneuvered, but unsure exactly how it had happened, Sandra murmured, "I'll remember that." Long after the housekeeper had departed, Sandra stood staring at the bottle of bath salts.

If nothing else on this trip, she'd learned she'd been wrong in her thinking about some things. All right, most things. Could she be wrong about Martin, too? Mulling over those elusive signs, Sandra undressed. She pulled on her jeans. While she searched for her boots, the telephone rang.

She answered the nearest phone. It was her uncle, wanting to know if there was a problem.

She opened her mouth to recite a litany of her travails and remembered. "Uh, no, not really. Just some changes in my plan." She explained about Mr. Taylor's problems with the computers and how her meeting had been rescheduled and condensed. She tensed in apprehension.

"I see," Wally said slowly. "I imagine you're upset."

A yes almost popped out, but she caught it in time. "Stuff happens. Have to roll with the punches. Like Martin says, we show Mr. Taylor what we have and see if he wants it. Everything else is just window dressing. I'll do the best I can. We'll make the sale. Are you . . . mad at me?"

"Like Martin . . . ?"

"I'll do it better next time, Uncle Wally. I promise."

"Did you mean . . . our Marty? You two are getting along?"

He didn't sound upset, but he did sound confused, which confused her. "Uh-huh."

Wally chuckled. "By golly, I was right."

"About what?"

"I knew you'd get along. Now, Marty, he was dead set against going with you, but I was right."

"Wait a minute. Do you mean he didn't want to come on this trip?"

"He was saying it wasn't a good idea 'cause you'd be all distracted and upset, and he thought you'd do a better job without him along. But two's always better than one in my book. Glad to know I was right."

She sank to a chair. Martin had thought she'd do a better job without him? He could have told her instead of letting her complain and accuse him of weaseling in on her glory.

Except . . . Martin rarely complained about anything —or disabused her ridiculous notions.

Wally continued, "I knew you and Marty could get along if you had to. By the by, did you get my flowers?"

She bolted upright and snapped her head about. She stared at the pink roses.

"Sandra? Still there?"

"Uh, yes, I did. Thank you." Why that . . . how could he lie about sending her flowers? He'd seen his opportunity to soften her up and—and—

"My way of saying good luck. I know you'll do just fine. Sure do miss you. Can't wait till tomorrow. . . ."

Wally warned her to be extra careful on the drive home and told her how Bugle Creek had suffered through a tornado watch for most of the night. She half listened, thinking instead about Martin's lie. How dare he take credit for a thoughtful gesture? Of all the cheap, sleazy, no good, low-down, dirty dog tricks, that was the worst. He must be laughing his fool head off, imagining how she was so impressed with those dumb roses that she'd fall right into bed with him.

By the time she finished talking to Wally, her stomach ached.

She stood with her hand on the telephone, wondering about the best way to get even.

Martin returned to the suite. His mouth dropped open and his eyes widened.

She remembered she'd been in the middle of getting dressed when she answered the phone, so she wore only jeans and a bra. Not any old bra, either, but a peach-colored confection with half cups and peekaboo lace.

Martin executed an abrupt about face.

Startled and embarrassed, she covered her chest with her arms. As soon as she did, anger surged through her. She dropped her arms to her sides and raised her chin. Let Mr. Martin Big-fat-liar Stonehouse see exactly what he was missing.

"I just talked to Uncle Wally. He says hello."

"Good," Martin said tightly.

She sauntered across the room. Arms akimbo, shoulders back, she said, "I told him about the meeting. You were right, he's not upset. He understands how things can go wrong."

Martin peeked over his shoulder.

The simmering desire darkening his eyes knocked her off balance. Her anger faltered and the words she meant to say began flitting nonsensically in her head, eluding capture. Like a deer trapped in headlights, she sensed the danger, but it fascinated her anyway. She touched her tongue to her suddenly dry lips. He stared at her mouth with something akin to pain.

Rain against the windows made a ruffling sound that echoed Sandra's heart. Her nipples swelled and burned, thrusting against the peach-colored lace.

As if tugged by a string, Martin turned around.

"Wally says . . . uh, he says . . . good . . . luck." Her words emerged with a smokiness that rasped her ears. Her throat and chest filled with wool.

Hot wool.

Fresh from the dryer, cuddle-it-close-and-let-the-heat-burn-to-her-bones wool.

Martin took a stiff-legged step toward her. "Guess we ought to work on that presentation, then. Gonna take some doing. Pare it down to an hour."

"Hard . . . work," she breathed.

Another step. His eyes positively gleamed—glittered

and sparkled and glowed. They loomed closer, filling her vision.

In her head she saw herself primly enter the bedroom, shut the door, get dressed, then work on the presentation. In reality her eyelids drifted downward. Her lips parted. Martin touched her arm and grazed her flesh with the barest whisper of fingertips.

"Sandra," he murmured.

She shouldn't be doing this. He had lied to her. He wanted a one-night stand so he could put another notch for conquest on his belt.

Oh, but she wanted him. As his hand grew bold, skimming over her biceps and shoulder, lingering on the lace-edged bra strap, turning tender against the side of her neck where he rolled wisps of hair against her skin, she wanted him even more.

When he lowered his head, she raised hers. Her nostrils flared, inhaling the darkening scent of his skin. He kissed her, sweetly, gently.

"First time we met . . ." His words were soft as a sigh.

He kissed her again. He smoothed his hand over her back and pulled her against him. She fitted perfectly, line to line, curve to rise, mound to crevice. He kissed her hard, the thrust of his tongue demanding, the taste of him erotic and hot.

She worked her hands around to his back, blazing a trail of exploration over the bands of hard muscle along his ribs, the sharp jut of his shoulder blades, and the sinuous indent of his spine. He explored her arm, his fingers testing and teasing, outlining slender muscle and drawing ever closer to her shoulder. His other hand clasped the nape of her neck in a possessive grip that stripped all strength from her limbs, all thoughts from her head.

Desire filled her, overflowed . . . *Was she out of her ever-lovin' mind?*

She broke away. He tried to hold her, but she slammed her hands against his chest and shoved. He stumbled.

Panting, trying her damnedest not to look at his eyes or notice his excited breathing or smell his compelling scent, she hugged her elbows. "Uh, Wally also wanted to know if I got his flowers."

"His what?" Martin's voice was choked and raw.

She tossed a challenging glare at the pink roses. "Isn't it funny? Your flowers arrived, but his didn't. He sent them to wish me luck. Should we call the florist and find out what happened?"

He cocked his head one way and the other. Flowers, apparently, were the last thing on his mind. But Sandra knew if her words bothered him, it was only because he needed time to embellish his lie.

Time she had no intention of giving him.

Chapter Eight

Martin pounded his fist against the bedroom door. "Dammit, Sandra, open the door!"

Nothing, not a peep. Of all the knot-headed, idiotic things . . . Bad enough she'd pushed him into a lie, but to catch him in it and then get mad? She couldn't have possibly expected him to play along with her "killer" theory.

He stalked onto the balcony. Rain rat-tat-tatted against his face and soaked his shirt before he reached the bedroom door. Fighting the draperies on the inside and against the gusty wind on the outside, he pushed into the room.

Sandra yelled, "Get out of here!" She lay on the bed, her hands hooked behind her neck, her feet crossed, while she scowled at the ceiling.

He finally got the door closed. "Why the hell are you so mad at me?" He swiped water off his face.

She sat upright and shook a finger. "I've heard lust makes men do slimy things, but that is so—"

"What has lust got to do with anything? You were fixing to blow this joint. I had to say something."

Her mouth opened, her raised finger quivered as if announcing an impending sermon, but no words emerged. Anger and confusion clashed on her expressive face.

The effect was so comical, laughter built steam in Martin's throat. He cleared it and said, "But no, you can't believe a man thinks you're pretty. It has to be a killer. I'm sorry I lied. I was sorry as soon as I said it, but you wouldn't believe anything else.''

Her gaze drifted to the ceiling, the bed, the floor, and the walls—everywhere except at him. Her long throat worked convulsively.

''What's this crap about lust? I always reckoned your opinion of me was low, but I didn't know it was that low.'' He plucked damp fabric off his chest. Why did he bother? Making headway with Sandra meant one step forward, then fifty back. He headed for the door. ''I didn't mean any harm, but I'm sorry anyway.''

In the sitting room, while he finished putting on a fresh, dry shirt, the telephone rang. He answered.

Sandra crept into the room. Head down, her expression sheepish, she fetched her boots from beside the fireplace.

After a short conversation, Martin hung up the phone. ''That was the front desk. There's a problem with the bill.''

Sandra pulled on a boot. ''It figures. What kind of problem?''

''Didn't say exactly.'' But he knew exactly what he wanted to say to her. He wanted say his sun rose and set in her, and he wanted to kiss her again and hold her forever and never let her go. But her running hot and cold was killing him.

She reached for the back of her head as if to let down her hair, but paused. Her arms dropped to her sides. ''Guess we better go straighten it out.''

''Wally will have a heart attack if he has to foot the entire bill.''

''That, too.'' She suddenly twisted on the love seat. ''I'm sorry. My opinion of you isn't low, but—but I don't know what it is! I'm the one who's sorry. You've always been nice to me, and I'm rotten, but you're nice and I don't know why I say such stupid things and I sure don't know why you take it.''

Stunned, he raked damp hair off his face.

''I'll stop jumping to conclusions. I promise, but it's so *hard.*'' Her lower lip trembled. ''Stuff just pops into my head and I start . . . reacting. I always feel so stupid afterward.''

He chuckled softly and swung his head side to side.

"Can I have another chance?" she asked in a tiny, tremulous voice.

No more chances, reason said. If he couldn't love her exactly the way she was, then he had no business loving her at all. "That's up to you, darlin'." A nonanswer that didn't seem to satisfy her; it sure didn't satisfy him.

On the elevator ride downstairs, Sandra found it difficult to look at Martin. The best she could manage were sideways, under-the-eyelashes glances. The soul-shattering effect he had on her made the truth as evident as a black horse in a snowfield: his faults, real or imagined, didn't bother her, but she was scared to death he'd see *her* faults and find her lacking.

Letting down her guard meant trusting him. What if she trusted him, gave him her heart and her love, and he left her?

That terrified her.

The elevator doors swished open. Martin led the way toward the lobby. His silence bothered her.

She'd almost worked up the nerve to speak, when she noticed the crowd in front of the front desk. The lobby teemed with families, couples in casual clothing, and business people in crisp suits. Bellboys deftly maneuvered laden luggage carts across the marble floor. Behind the desk, harried clerks locked their gazes on computers and printers, processing the guests checking in and out.

Sandra's chest tightened with familiar impatience.

"At least," Martin said, his boot heels clicking on the polished floor, "it's consistent."

Complaints rose in her throat, but she choked them down. This was a test. A chance to prove she owned the ability to rise above petty inconveniences. The effort of forcing a smile made her light-headed.

They took a place in line.

A happy-sounding commotion caught Sandra's attention. A bride posed before a tall, gilt-framed portrait of Mitsy Packard. The bride's attendants, rustling in jewel-toned taffeta, straightened the bridal gown's trailing skirts. Off to the side, the groom stood beaming, while a photographer waved his arms and called out instructions.

The murmuring in the lobby shifted in tone from impatience to amusement. Soft laughter trickled through the crowd. Children, especially little girls, jostled for a better view.

"You know," Martin said, "I reckon there's only two impossibilities in this world—a baby that isn't cute and a bride that isn't beautiful. Isn't she something?"

Sandra started to agree when, from the corner of her eye, she noticed a man. His dove-gray tuxedo meant he belonged to the wedding party, but he didn't look happy. He slumped against a marble column and swayed as if his legs barely supported him. His skin had a distinctly greenish pallor, and his white hair rose in tangled spikes.

Sandra's mouth fell open. It was him, the man she'd seen in the stairwell—*the body*!

A woman had her arm hooked firmly with the man's. She turned a bright smile toward the photographer and called out suggestions; she whipped her head about to face the man and scowled, talking low. The man winced, flinched, and grimaced as if her words physically battered his head. She smiled again at the bride, called a few more suggestions, and resumed haranguing the man.

Close to Sandra's ear, Martin said, "Looks like that fella started celebrating the wedding reception early." He whistled. "And I'd say mama's not too pleased about it."

He'd been right, she'd seen a drunk, after all. Closing her eyes, she called herself twenty kinds of fool. She saw herself running up the stairs in those darn spiky high heels, bursting in on Martin in the bathroom—no wonder Ms. Watters had looked at her as if she were crazy.

When they finally reached the desk, the clerk had them sign some papers sent over by the Marcourt Hotel. Reading and signing took all of three minutes. Sandra refrained from a single huff, puff, snipe, or gripe.

"That wasn't too bad." Martin darted wary glances at her.

She straightened her shoulders and held her head high. "In fact, if you think about it, this much business means a booming economy, which means lots of paper. That's good for us. Right?''

"That's an interesting way of looking at it.''

Was that puzzlement or approval she saw in his smile?

They wandered to the glass garden. The storm had worsened, with black clouds shrouding the hotel and blotting out the view. Booming thunder made the glass vibrate.

Martin urged her to follow. Bemused, she trailed him down the marble steps to the central fountain. In contrast to the raging storm outside, the fountain trickled and giggled.

Martin handed Sandra a penny.

"What's this for?''

"Can't pass up a fountain without making a wish.'' He showed her a nickel.

"How come I only get a penny?''

He tossed the nickel in the air and caught it with a down swipe. "I need some extra wish power.'' He closed his eyes for a moment, then tossed the nickel. It sank to the algae-streaked bottom and glittered along with countless other coins. "Your turn.''

"What did you wish for?''

Solemnly, he shook his head. "Your turn.''

She stared at the penny. *I will do better, I can do better, I wish for a fresh start.* She kissed the coin and flung it at the fountain.

The penny struck a verdigris water lily, bounced off the sinewy shoulders of a man wrestling with a horse, and rolled onto the rippled back of a dragon.

Martin lowered his head and his shoulders shook with silent laughter.

"I can't even make a wish right,'' she grumbled. "Does, it count if it doesn't hit the water?''

"Don't rightly know.'' He gave her another penny. "Try again.''

Rolling her eyes and feeling foolish, she extended her hand over the basin and dropped the penny. "There.'' She turned around.

At the top of the grand staircase stood the man in dark glasses.

Sandra's heart leaped into her throat. In the nick of time she stopped a squeal. In the nick of time she remembered not to jump to conclusions or assume the worst.

Martin said, "There's a little store over yonder. I want to grab a couple things."

Be logical . . . How could the scary man possibly be a killer when the "corpse" was nursing a hangover and holding up a column in the lobby? The man in black was a businessman or a conventioneer, and she, Sandra Campbell, was a nitwit.

A laugh burst from her mouth. She clapped both hands to her face.

Martin glanced over his shoulder. "What's funny?"

Me, but I'm a lot more embarrassed than finding this funny, so I can't possibly explain—yet. "I'll tell you later. I promise."

At the small gift shop, Martin went inside while Sandra window-shopped. The hotel boasted several concessions, including a clothing boutique, a jewelry store, and an art gallery. She studied a display of Austrian crystal jewelry. As she moved to the side, the window caught the light at such an angle it turned into a mirror. People moved around behind her, but none wore a black suit and dark glasses. Someday, when she felt ready to accept a well-deserved "I told you so," she'd be able to tell Martin about her ridiculousness; for the time being, she contented herself with silent laughter.

"Hey, darlin'." Martin looked between her and the display case. "See something you like?"

"Just dreaming. Pretty stuff."

"We've about blown the morning." He patted his flat stomach. "It's either all this luxury or the weather, but I'm hungry again."

"Me, too," she said. "Let's order room service and we'll work on the presentation while we eat—"

Martin interrupted her with a shake of his head. "When I eat, I eat. When I work, I work."

"I eat at my desk all the time. It's efficient."

He took her hand in a firm grip. "You can't enjoy your food and you get grease on your papers." He cocked his head, his expression mild. "Your job would be a lot easier if you'd join the fellas in the lunchroom. Amazing what you can learn when folks are talking for no good reason.''

A hundred reasons for eating lunch in her office rose in her mind. A hundred excuses . . . Dropping her gaze, she confessed, "They don't want me there. They don't like me.''

Hooking his arm with hers, he led her down the carpeted walkway. "When Wally hired me, a lot of folks figured he'd lost his mind.''

"But why?''

"Only twenty-seven years old, from out of town. From out to state, to boot. That made me a pretty suspicious fella.'' He flashed a conspiratorial grin. "But I had an edge.''

"What's that?''

"Six older brothers and sisters. We grew up on a ranch in the middle of nowhere, so I had no one to complain to even if I wanted. I survived them. Having my desk glued shut and salt in my coffee was nothing.''

"The employees played jokes on you?'' Was it good or bad no one ever pulled a prank on her? Bad, probably.

"When they saw I knew my job and I had a sense of humor, they accepted me.'' He led her into the Crystal Tavern. "Give them a chance and they'll accept you, too. Trust me.''

A jukebox played a rollicking tune. Television sets mounted in corners showed football games. Waitresses, holding beverage trays high, worked their way through the crowd like experts on an obstacle course. The tangy scent of barbecue sauce made Sandra's stomach growl.

Martin nodded at the menu board. "All-you-can-eat buffet. I bet we can break the bank.''

They paid in advance, then moved through the buffet line. Sandra piled her plate with barbecued brisket, broasted chicken, green salad, corn bread, and fried potato skins. She and Martin took a table near a window with a view of the circular drive and gardens in front of the hotel.

Watching the rain, Martin waggled his eyebrows. "If we start seeing critters walking two by two, we're in trouble.''

After lunch they returned to the suite. The prodigious amounts of food she'd eaten, the weather, and the lack of sleep last night made Sandra so logy she couldn't stop yawning.

Martin nudged her toward the bedroom. "Take a nap."

Shaking her head, she faced the stacks of papers and bound proposals on the table. "Too much work to do. I really blew it, didn't I?"

Martin fiddled with the fireplace. "You haven't blown anything." He sat back on his heels and regarded her. "If you had it to do over again, what would you do?"

Good question. For a long moment she chewed her inner lip and shoved away the grandiose notions that had landed her in this mess in the first place. "I suppose . . . I should have set up a series of appointments with as many customers as I could possibly meet in two days, then met them informally with prepared samples." She picked up a transparency and held it toward the light. It would have been so impressive illuminated on a big screen. "Do you think Uncle Wally will ever let me try this again?"

Martin sat and patted the cushion beside him. "Let's talk about Wally and you."

She hugged herself and drew in her chin.

"Nothing bad," he assured her. "But there are some things you need to understand."

Reluctantly, she joined him. She sat stiffly, facing the fire.

"Wally loves you."

She didn't doubt it for a minute. He'd always been the rock of stability in her unstable life.

"But he worries about you."

That surprised her.

Martin picked up her hand and examined her fingers, tracing them and encircling them with his fingertips as if he wanted to burn the shape and feel of them into his memory. "He thinks you're unhappy working in the office."

"I love working for him!"

"Actions speak loudest, darlin'."

Protests built steam, but he was right. She closed her fingers over his. "I try too hard."

He agreed with a rueful smile.

"I don't know what else to do. His finances—"

"Are solid as a rock. He deals in cash. He's got no debt."

"But he's old."

Martin laughed heartily. "If you'd go fishing with him sometime, you'd change your mind. The man could run a mule to the ground. As for him retiring, that won't happen. He loves the plant. He'll keep working until the day he drops."

"He needs me to take care of him," she said, but couldn't raise much conviction in her thoughts or her voice.

"Sure he needs you. You're his family and he loves you. He doesn't need a million bucks or the biggest plant in Texas." He looked around at the opulent surroundings. "He thinks you're unhappy because you're always trying to change things."

He tugged her hand until she looked at him. "You do a lot of things real good. The paychecks are always perfect. Not one complaint in that department. You've got the computer system down pat."

A smile teased her lips.

"And you've got those EPA fellas right where we want them. Before you took over, Wally used to spend days at a time trying to figure out the forms. You took a big load off his back."

His genuine approval shone through. It made her realize he paid a lot more attention to her than she ever had to him. That would change, she vowed, starting right now.

If he meant to give her another chance.

"Do you want to make Wally happy, darlin'?"

She nodded eagerly.

He eased a stray tendril off her cheek, his big fingers gentle against her skin. Smiling tenderly, he searched her eyes. "Slow down. Have a little fun. Stop taking everything so serious."

"I'll try."

He shook his head. "Trying doesn't count. Do it." He tickled her lower lip. "Smile more. You're beautiful when you smile."

She drew a deep breath. Changing her ways, slowing down, fighting the anxiety plaguing her—massive tasks.

"I'll do it . . . Martin." She took another deep breath, willing the strength to ask the one thing she never imagined herself asking of him. "Will you help me?"

Chapter Nine

"This is it?" Sandra said. "This is all we need?" She shifted her gaze between the thick pile of prepared reports and overhead projector slides, and the thin sheaf of papers making up the new sales pitch.

Martin braced himself for a storm. She'd put her heart and soul into the original presentation—he couldn't blame her for wanting to hold on to it.

She picked up a dark red binder, sighed, and clutched it to her breast. "My report? I could . . . just give it to him?"

He shook his head. "Preaching to the choir. Mr. Taylor knows exactly what the market response is to recycled products."

Her expressive face ran the gamut of emotions—dismay, anger, and sadness, before settling on resignation. She placed the red binder on the big stack, scooped up everything and dropped all of it into her briefcase. She snapped the case shut.

Martin's heart went out to her. He believed she meant what she said about curbing her wild impulses.

She tossed her head and her eyes flashed. "If all I have is an hour of his precious time, then it'll be the best hour he ever spent." She shrugged. "At least we'll get a good breakfast."

"Atta girl. Find the silver lining." He'd started out looking for the final straw to break her hold on him. Now he observed what his stubborn heart had known all along —the Sandra he could love. "Now, go on, take a nap. You look beat."

"What about you?" She shuffled papers. Her voice dropped to a mumble. "I know you didn't get much sleep last night."

Was that an invitation? His body shouted an eager yes. His mind couldn't decide. These newfound feelings were fragile things. "I'm going to find a weather report. I need to figure out if we drive home tomorrow or hire a boat."

She looked around. "Tomorrow . . . just when I'm getting used to this place."

"No one says you can't come back. Someday." ·

She gave him a funny, measuring smile. "Well, I'm not counting on someday. I'm going to try out that fancy bathtub."

That raised some interesting images in his head. Images that grew more colorful and erotic as the sound of running water came from the bathroom. He started a fire, but instead of soothing him, the crackling flames made him think of dark nights and Sandra in his arms. He watched television, but the flickering images couldn't compete with the turmoil of his thoughts.

"Martin?" Her shout held an anxious note. "Martin!"

What now? A spider? Her toe stuck in the faucet?

Grinning, reckoning life with Sandra would always be like living in an *I Love Lucy* show, he ambled to the bathroom to find out what she was up to now.

"Martin!" Sandra sank lower into the concealing bubbles. "Please open the door. I need help."

The door opened a few inches. Martin's curly dark brown hair appeared by fractions, then one eye. "What's wrong?"

Despite the hot water and shield of foamy bubbles, she shivered in embarrassment. "I had an accident. Come in."

He stuck his head inside the bathroom. His nose twitched and wrinkled.

"It's bath salts. I dropped the jar." She pointed at the shattered glass and soapy crystals littering the marble steps around the bathtub. "I was reading the label and went to set it down and then . . . it slipped. Didn't you hear it? It was like a bomb." Musky rose attar filled the steamy bathroom. "Now there's glass everywhere and I'm trapped."

He made a funny, strangled noise.

"Go ahead and laugh. I know you want to."

With a washcloth folded into a tight square, he whisked broken glass and bath salts onto a towel.

She studied the flex of muscles pulling his shirt and the

way light gleamed on his hair. "I feel like a real dummy. I almost caught it . . . almost."

"Accidents happen, darlin'."

Emboldened by his amusement, she rose enough to rest her arms on the side of the tub. She watched his quick hands. "Smells kind of pretty, though."

He blew a sharp breath. "Pretty and strong."

She agreed with a laugh. "I've been thinking . . . a lot. You're always pulling me out of some kind of mess."

He lifted his face and his green eyes sparkled. "Might say it's a habit of mine."

"A good habit or a bad habit?"

He lifted a shoulder and made a noncommittal sound.

"Why? I'm awful to you, and you're . . . never terrible to me." She touched the side of his face. "I don't know how you can stand me."

He dampened the washcloth. Running the cloth over the marble, he picked up any remaining slivers of glass.

"Why, Martin?"

He sat on the top step and rested an arm over a raised knee. "Guess I keep hoping you'll realize we aren't enemies."

"Like now?"

Brow lowered, he paused thoughtfully. "Yeah."

He gave no indication he wanted to leave. The situation discomfited Sandra, but she didn't want him to leave either. "Can I ask a dumb question?"

"Go for it."

"How come you don't have a steady girlfriend?"

He gave a start and his eyes widened. She guessed she'd asked a really dumb question—but she was dying to know. He fidgeted and combed his hair with his fingers.

"You date a lot," she said. "I see you with different women all the time."

"They're not real dates." His shoulders twitched. "I like dancing, but I'd look like a fool out on the floor by myself. It's more like, I go out with friends."

Signs, Etta had said. The signs don't lie, and neither, Sandra sensed, did Martin. "So there's no one . . ." She searched for the right word. ". . . special?"

"Sure there is," he said, studying his boot. He bounced

his hand atop his knee to some unheard rhythm. "But I don't think she likes dancing. She always says no when I ask her to go. Doesn't seem to care for movies, either. Reckon she doesn't want me to know what she wants." He turned his head enough to see her. "Or maybe *she* doesn't know. Any advice?"

"She sounds stupid."

He shook his head. "I'm pretty frustrated. Keep waiting for her to come around, but I don't know if it'll happen. Do you think I'm fooling myself?"

Ashamed, knowing she was guilty of attributing every conceivable motive to Martin *except* that he cared for her, Sandra bowed her head.

He moved his head in her direction, pulled back, looked away, then smiled and kissed her. A nice kiss, friendly and sweet. "Am I fooling myself?"

Sandra saw her choices: say yes, and lose him forever; or say no, and take the chance of finding love. Both scared her down to her toes.

She found the answer in his kind, patient eyes. His expression was one she'd been seeing ever since the first day they met. In them she saw how wrong she'd been—he was *not* a love 'em and leave 'em man.

She looped a wet arm around his neck and kissed him. His lips parted and a tender duel of tongues turned urgent. Embers of desire burst into flame, filling her groin with liquid heat. Her hips ached and her breasts seemed to swell. She couldn't resist rubbing her nipples against the slick tub surface while wishing it was Martin touching her.

He slid his hand around her neck, his fingers tangling in her piled hair.

He pulled away suddenly. His pupils were black pools ringed by emerald fire. "Good answer, darlin', but best stop while I can."

Looking at him threatened to blind her. Not looking proved impossible. "Do you want to stop?"

"Uh-uh." The reply emerged husky and low. His throat worked heavily up and down.

"Will you hand me a towel?"

He arose from the step with less than his usual grace.

Steeling her nerves, she released the drain. He turned around, holding a large white towel in both hands.

The water drained quickly. Bubbles slithered off her breasts and across her belly and down her hips and thighs. She shivered, but not from cold. Why didn't he say something? Do something? Gulping, knowing the next move belonged to her, she grasped the sides of the tub and stood.

"The towel please?"

One side of his mouth pulled into a drunken grin. He lifted a boot to the top step and held the towel spread like swan's wings, ready to receive her. She stepped into its fluffy softness, and Martin wrapped it around her body. He held her for a moment in his embrace. Sensing more than feeling it, she knew he trembled.

He buried his nose against her hair. For the first time she could remember, she felt completely safe and cherished. He guided her down the steps and onto the fluffy mat. There, he began rubbing away bubbles and water. Nearly melting under the slow, firm strokes against her hot skin, she sought his mouth and his delicious kiss. She also sought and found the buttons on his shirt. By the time he'd dried her shoulders and back and worked his slow way to her derriere, she'd bared his chest.

A low, helpless noise fluttered in her throat as she tugged his shirt free of his jeans. He lowered himself to one knee to dry her hips and legs.

He raised one arm, then the other, to help her remove his shirt. His skin was dark against hers. Where she was sleek, he rippled with chiseled muscle.

What he could do with his hands!

He dried every inch of her body, leaving her panting and blind, dizzily yearning for more.

She was ready to sink to the floor. He tenderly wrapped her in the towel before leading her out of the bathroom. At the doorway to the bedroom he stopped and held up a hand for her to wait.

Clutching the towel around her shoulders, she hungrily absorbed his every move as he removed his boots and socks. Greedy as a child on a visit to a toy factory, she didn't know where to look next: the corded flexing of his forearms, the intriguing play of muscle along his shoulders, or his handsome face, as hot and smiling as hers must be.

He swept an arm in a grand gesture toward the massive pink-and-lace-covered bed.

"Aren't you forgetting something?" she asked.

He frowned a moment. To her surprise, he strode away. She listened in bemusement as he opened drawers. "Ah ha!" he said. On the way to the foyer he flashed the Do Not Disturb card for her to see.

When he rejoined her, she giggled. "Good idea, but I meant your britches." She unbuckled his belt. He wore button-front jeans, and as she worked free each metal button, he tensed and quivered. His jaw tightened and his gaze grew distant. She worked his jeans down his hips, revealing long, hard thighs. Beneath his briefs strained an erection that should frighten any woman with sense . . . which for once in her life she was glad she didn't possess.

When she finally had him freed from his clothing, she couldn't look. She did look.

God, but he was beautiful. No other word could describe him.

"Darlin'," he whispered in a graveled drawl, "I keep thinking about that bed."

He caught her hands in both of his and backed through the doorway. The towel slithered off her body. When he reached the bottom of the three curved steps, he shifted his grasp to her waist and lifted her, swinging her off the steps in a wide, exuberant circle. Once again on her feet, she laughed. He tugged pins from her hair, flinging them away with abandon, while he danced her slowly toward the fantasy bed.

The back of her knees struck the satin side of the bed, and there was nowhere to go but down into its welcoming lushness.

He followed her, resting his arms on either side of her, studying her face with anticipation. The hot eager shaft pressing her belly made her squirm.

"Kiss me," she urged. "I love it when you kiss me."

He curled his hands in her hair and kissed her the way she'd only thought possible in dreams. He kissed her

cheeks and her eyelids. His lips burned fiery trails across
the line of her jaw and down her throat.

Wriggling with the sheer joy of it, she curled one leg
around his hips and dug her other foot against the velvety
rug. He kissed the tender hollow of her throat and nibbled
caresses across her collarbone.

By then she knew her breasts would burst. If he didn't
touch her . . .

He slid his hands to her arms and urged them higher so
he could stroke her sensitive inner arms. When he reached
her sides with his bold caress, she gasped. He caught a
nipple between his lips. A violent shudder gripped her
body and the fire turned molten, filling her veins. He
kissed her breasts, long and lovingly, suckling until a cry
of pleasure escaped her. He kissed every inch of flesh on
her belly, building her anxiousness, stoking the fire. The
scent of him, musky and dark, filled her head.

He left her abruptly. His beautiful eyes were dark and
glazed, hidden by shadows. In the stormy gray light
through the balcony he was her shadow lover, all planes
and mystery and shivering arousal. He lifted her bodily
and set her in the middle of the bed.

"Now, Martin, please . . . I can't stand it." She knew
she begged shamelessly, but didn't care.

"I haven't finished kissing you," he replied wickedly,
and lifted her foot to his lips. He kissed the instep and the
tickling made her giggle. His long fingers encircled her
ankle. He kissed a teasing line up her calf. "I'll never
smell roses again without thinking of you."

"Oh, God . . ." She gave up and gave in, reveling in
the feel of his lips and the questing purposefulness of his
fingers as he tested every inch of first one leg and then the
other.

By the time he reached the juncture of her thighs, she'd
lost all control of her knees, and all she could do with her
hands was scrunch the bedspread. Exquisite agony tightened every muscle.

He gave her the sweetest kiss of all, and sweetened it
more with his clever fingers.

She burst. An explosion. She caught his hair in both
hands, clinging to him as the waves of pure pleasure

racked her from head to toe. Was that her making those noises—those squeals and throaty moans? She didn't care.

Smoky-eyed and smiling rakishly, Martin watched her face. He backed away from her, off the bed, his eyes never leaving hers.

"Where are you going?" she whispered. She couldn't move. She couldn't have moved if the bed were on fire. Dull panic weighted her chest. "Don't leave me. Come back."

He waggled an admonishing finger, and hurried out of the room. He soon reappeared, brandishing a small red and black box. She struggled to prop herself on her elbows. Realization dawned, and she knew what he'd bought downstairs in the store.

"Always, prepared, huh, Stonehouse?"

"I try, darlin'." He glanced at the close sky outside and the rain creating lacy patterns against the balcony glass. "Don't think we'll be doing much sightseeing." He tossed the box of condoms at her and it bounced next to her hip.

She picked it up and examined it. "There are only five. Think it'll be enough?"

Stalking toward the bed, he lifted a shoulder in a lazy shrug. "Guess we'll find out."

Chapter Ten

Sandra entered the sitting room. She wore the neat gray suit and had tamed her hair into a braid. Martin swallowed hard and worked a finger under his shirt collar. He wore a suit and tie in deference to her business meeting, and all of a sudden the tie choked him.

She looked prim and pretty, far removed from the fiery redhead with whom he'd spent all of yesterday afternoon and most of the night making love.

She glanced at the fireplace and color blossomed on her cheekbones. Martin grinned. The thick rug before the hearth had proved as soft as it looked, far softer than the whirlpool tub, and almost as interesting. His only regret had been that it was too cold to give the balcony a try.

As her tense silence wore on him, he began to wonder if

she had regrets. She acted so stiff and uncertain, she almost seemed embarrassed.

She straightened her shoulders and wiggled her back into an erect posture. "My bags are all packed. Did you call the desk?"

"The bellboy will come for our luggage around ten-thirty."

She picked up her briefcase. "I'm ready. Let's go dazzle Mr. Taylor."

Martin wanted to shout: What's wrong, how did I make you mad this time? Anxiety made him itch; his tongue felt too big for his mouth. Her refusal to look at him gave him a pain so deep and sharp, his knees wobbled. For the first time in his life he lacked the self-confidence to ask a simple question.

"We better go, I don't want to be late." She headed for the door.

On the ride down in the elevator, she fiddled with her jacket lapels, straightened her skirt, raised and lowered her briefcase, and sighed several times. Her clear-skinned face was paler than usual. A dozen times Martin started to ask her what was wrong; a dozen times fear of having her say that last night had been a mistake held him back.

By the time they reached their table, her face had lost all traces of color.

Martin pointed at the glass wall. "Looks like we'll have good weather going home." The sun shone through a widening break in the clouds, and water drops glittered on the glass wall like diamonds. The lake behind the hotel was smooth and dark, dotted by ducks, geese, and black swans. Sandra barely glanced at the view.

She opened her briefcase on a chair and pulled out her notes. Feeling invisible, Martin slumped. What had he done to offend her now? Only hours ago they'd fallen asleep in each other's arms. Only hours ago he'd been atop the world, so in love he'd felt capable of slaying dragons and leaping tall buildings.

She couldn't be the use 'em up and spit 'em out kind of woman. Not Sandra—could she? She sure didn't seem to want anything to do with him now.

Eight o'clock came and went. By ten minutes after eight

the skin around her mouth and eyes had grown taut. At
fifteen minutes after eight Martin gave up trying to make
conversation and suggested they order breakfast. Guests
were filling the tables and it wouldn't be too long before
the place was packed, slowing the service. She looked at
him as if he'd suggested they sacrifice a chicken on the
tabletop.

At twenty-five minutes after eight a waiter brought a
cordless telephone to the table. "Miss Campbell? A call
for you."

Martin didn't need to hear the other side of the conversation to know who called and why. All he had to do was
watch Sandra's face.

She drew in a shuddering breath. "I understand. Oh no,
I'll contact him in a week or so. Thank you for calling."
She placed the phone on the table.

"He canceled?"

"That was Mr. Taylor's assistant. Mr. Taylor called in
sick this morning with the flu." Her lower lip trembled
and her eyes shimmered. "Well, that does it!" She fumbled papers back inside her briefcase.

He reached across the table and took her hand. "It's
okay, darlin', it happens."

She jerked away. "It *happens?* Only to me! I've been a
nervous wreck. My stomach hurts. I've never sold anything in my life and I've been worried sick I was going to
make a fool of myself and he doesn't even have the decency to show up!"

Stunned, Martin leaned back on his chair. She wasn't
mad at him. It was the sales meeting—her attack of nerves
had nothing to do with him at all. Flooded with relief, he
laughed.

Flinging up her head like a spooked horse, Sandra
gasped. "It's not funny!"

He flashed an apologetic grin at nearby diners. "Stop
shouting. I'm not laughing at you."

"You are, too, laughing, I just heard you." She pushed
her chair away from the table and bounced to her feet.
"This isn't funny at all! It's—It's—It's a tragedy!"

Before he had a chance to compose calming words or an

apology, she stomped away. Shocked speechless for the second time this morning, he watched her go.

The waiter appeared. If the young man noticed anything unusual about Sandra's behavior, he didn't show it. "Are you ready to order, sir? Or would you like the buffet?"

Martin studied his empty coffee cup. "No, thanks. I'd like the bill for the coffee."

The waiter wrote up the ticket.

Martin arose and looked around for Sandra. He spotted her at the top of the grand staircase. Judging by the set of her shoulders and the way she swung her briefcase, he figured her anger was increasing by the second. Why did he have to go and laugh? Of all the dumb—

He noticed a man on the staircase, about nine or ten risers below Sandra. He wore a black suit, and when he looked over his shoulder, his dark glasses caught a ray of sunshine. The man swept the glass garden with an unreadable gaze before hurrying up the steps two at a time. He turned right, following Sandra.

Martin dug frantically in his pocket. That man couldn't be following her. Even thinking it was ridiculous, ludicrous . . . He flung a five dollar bill at the waiter.

Every table was full and people carrying laden plates filled the narrow walkways. Pushing through the crowd, Martin mumbled, "Pardon me, excuse me, pardon." He bumped into a waiter and the man deftly rescued a brimming coffee carafe. Martin barely glanced at him.

He took the stairs three at a time, grasping the banister and hauling himself to greater speed.

He reached the mezzanine level in time to see the back of the man's black jacket disappear through the doorway leading to the West Tower meeting rooms.

Where the hell was Sandra?

"What in the world is wrong with me?" Sandra muttered. She sat on a velvet-covered bench, glumly watching people stroll through the mezzanine.

Put on a pleasant face, she ordered herself, and go eat breakfast. Martin was right to laugh. This wasn't the business trip from hell, it was a Marx Brothers movie. A smile tugged her lips and a soft laugh bubbled in her throat. Bad weather, closed hotels, blown-up computers, drunks in stairwells—she laughed out loud.

She spotted Martin. He tore up the grand staircase as if a pack of dogs were chasing him. The sight of him, coming to rescue her from the doldrums, roused sensual memories and her knees trembled with hot weakness. He definitely had been right to laugh, and if she was ever going to do better, she better learn to laugh, too—especially at herself.

Forget breakfast. They had hours until checkout time, and the suite, with that marvelous bed, was paid for until—

Martin hurried past. She leaned to see around a lush shefflera and called to him, but he neither glanced her way nor slowed.

She picked up her briefcase and followed.

Martin reached the wide, double doors leading to the West Tower meeting rooms and banquet halls. He broke into a fast trot. Sandra knew he liked exercise, but this was ridiculous. When she reached the doorway, she cupped a hand by her mouth and called, "Martin!"

Without slowing, he looked over his shoulder—a man stepped from an alcove, directly into Martin's path. The men collided.

At the same time, across the hallway, doors clanked open and a crowd of business people streamed out of a meeting room. Martin flailed his arms and skidded, making a valiant effort to stay on his feet. The other man struck a large potted ficus tree. Both men hit the carpet. The ficus tree struck a woman squarely atop the head. She shrieked and fell into the arms of another woman. The ficus followed both women to the floor.

Sandra touched her hand to her mouth. "Wow," she breathed.

Fearing Martin had been hurt, Sandra hurried as quickly as her tight skirt and high heels allowed. He was in a crouch when she reached him, and she grasped his arm to help him the rest of the way to his feet.

"Are you all right?" she asked, running an anxious hand over his face.

He caught her in a bear hug that made her squeak.

People helped the hapless victims of the ficus tree. Aside from mussed hairdos and injured dignities, both women assured the gathering crowd that all was well.

The man Martin had hit still sat on the floor. With dazed eyes he studied a pair of mangled sunglasses as if trying to figure out how he'd get the twisted earpieces to fit his head.

Sandra pushed and squirmed until Martin loosened his crushing grip. She asked, "Why were you running down the hallway?"

Martin flung an accusing finger at the man on the floor. "You were right! He was following you. I saw him right behind you."

That caught the attention of every person in the crowd. Sandra tried a smile. "Uh . . . nobody was following me."

A man and a woman pushed their way through the crowd. They wore black suits; the man sported dark glasses. "Hotel security, please step aside." The woman crouched next to the man on the floor. "You okay, Roger? What happened?"

Sandra recognized the male newcomer as the man from the elevator. Hotel security? Uh-oh.

Martin gave her a look of pure horror and sprang away. He extended a hand to the man on the floor. "I'm sorry. All my fault, I was moving too fast and couldn't stop. I sure didn't mean to hit you, sir. Are you okay?"

The man shook himself, and allowed his coworkers to help him to his feet. He waved a hand, indicating he was all right.

Martin raked both hands through his hair. "You see, my —Sandra thought a man was following her. Only I didn't believe her, but when I saw you on the stairs, it looked like you were following her and I thought . . . it seemed . . . it looked—"

Poor Martin, Sandra thought, he looked so confused, so thoroughly bewildered, she knew she had to say something. Her throat convulsed with the effort of tamping down a laugh.

Martin whipped his head about. "Sandra, help me here."

If she opened her mouth, she'd lose it. She clutched her midsection. All she could manage was a choked *huh-huh-huh*. Tittering started to the left of her. The woman who'd been felled by the ficus plucked a leaf from her hair. Giggles rose in volume. A masculine laugh rang out.

Martin held out both hands, beseeching Sandra. "Tell them about the dead guy!"

Gulping hard, forcing her facial muscles under control, she said, "There's no dead guy, Martin, there never was," and she lost it. She laughed so hard, she staggered and caught the wall. She laughed until tears rolled from her eyes. Every time she found control, somebody else laughed, or she'd notice the fallen ficus, or the woman would pull another leaf from her hair, or the knocked-about security man would try fitting on his broken glasses, and she'd start laughing all over again.

By the time she stopped laughing finally and for good, Martin was gone.

She found Martin in the Honeymoon Suite. He paced through the sitting room, holding the telephone cradled on his arm and with the handset jammed between his shoulder and his jaw. His stormy face—red and scowling and furious—stopped her in her tracks.

"Who are you calling?" She'd never seen him like this, never realized he had this much anger inside him.

Mouthing a curse, he slammed the telephone onto the table. "I'm trying to call Wally, but they can't find him and—ah, hell! I'm not going back to Bugle Creek! Drive yourself! You tell Wally why I quit."

She staggered, catching the love seat for support. "Quit . . . What are you talking about?"

Shaking a fist at her, he shouted, "You set me up, but *good!* I've never been so embarrassed in my life! I can't believe I ever thought I was in love with you. Jesus, how long have you been planning this?"

"You're in love with me?"

"Trust me, darlin', I will get over it. So get out of my way and get out of my life."

"You liar. If you loved me, you'd never leave me." Tears scratched her eyes and her throat tightened.

"I don't know what kind of stunt you were pulling with that security man, but I'm not your whipping boy. No more." He swept the air with both hands. "I've had it!"

Her back snapped into a rigid line and she balled her fists. "And you say *I* jump to conclusions?"

"What kind of conclusion should I reach? You're the one who started it. I thought he was trying to kill you. But no, you can't even admit there was a dead guy. First you scare me half to death, then you let me stand there babbling like an idiot while everybody laughs at me. *You* laughed at me."

She saw him in the way he must see her most of the time: flustered, angry, confused, excited, and unreasonable. Not a pretty sight.

"Let me explain." She reached for him, but he turned an icy shoulder to her. Her forehead tightened with a rise of temper, but she squashed it. The urge to stomp away pulled her, but she resisted. She'd finally found a man she could love and trust, and she didn't intend to lose him because of her stupid impulses.

"At least listen. If you don't, you're as bad as I am."

He glared at her.

"Five minutes."

Head down, mouth pulled into a scowl, he sat. He crossed his legs and arms, and his jaw jutted pugnaciously. She cautiously joined him on the love seat and folded her hands on her lap. "Do you remember the bride in the lobby? And the man with the hangover? That's the dead guy."

Confusion twisted his brow. "What are you talking about?"

Laughter built pressure in her chest. If she let loose now, she'd lose him for certain. "You were right. I saw a drunk in the stairwell. No bodies, no killers. Nobody was ever following me."

His shoulders relaxed, a little. "You knew that yesterday?"

She flinched. "Well, I saw him and saw how stupid I'd been acting, and I was too embarrassed to tell you. I didn't want you to say I told you so."

He sat still and silent long enough to worry her. She

chewed on a thumbnail, shifted on the cushion and tried
not to listen to her fluttering heart.

Unable to bear the silence, she said, "You were going to
save me. I know you care about me."

"I never denied it." He slumped forward and dangled
his hands over his knees. "Reckon I did jump to a conclusion."

Her heart slowed. "Don't leave me, Martin. If you
really love me, give me another chance. I need you." She
stared at her hands. "I love you." She squeezed her eyes
shut.

He made a soft sound. It took several seconds for her to
realize he laughed. She peeked. He bent over with his
elbows on his knees and his broad shoulders shaking.

"Will you really get over me?" she asked.

"No." His laughter burst free. It came straight from his
belly, hearty and full-blown. He laughed until he ended up
clutching his stomach and tears formed at the corners of
his eyes. At last he choked out, "Reckon I'd never get
over you, darlin'. Never known anyone who can shake me
up the way you do. You're always one surprise after another."

Sandra caught his hand and pressed it between her
breasts. "Give me another chance. I do love you and I am
trying not be crazy and—and—and you're the one who
jumped to conclusions, so that means you're as nutty as I
am!"

He lifted an eyebrow.

"Okay, okay," she conceded. "But you do have your
moments. Do you really and truly love me?"

He smiled wryly. "I love you with all my heart when
you're at your worst. Don't stand a calf in a feed lot's
chance when you're at your best." He looped an arm
around her shoulders and pulled her close.

"I do love you, Martin, I do."

"Me, too, darlin', always and forever." As if words
weren't enough, he kissed her.

Etta Hannibal picked a hairpin off the Honeymoon Suite
bedroom floor, and another and another, following a trail
of pins to the bed. Grinning, she dropped them into her

apron pocket. She inhaled deeply the sweet scent of roses. All the signs said Sandra and Martin would return to the Honeymoon Suite, but business would be the furthest thing from their minds.

And the signs never lied.

Royd Camden is a prisoner of his own "respectability." But when he sees beautiful Moriah Lane—condemned by society and sentenced to prison for a crime she didn't commit—he cannot ignore her innocence that shines through dark despair. He swears to reach the woman behind the haunted eyes, never dreaming that his vow will launch them both on a perilous journey that will test her faith and shake his carefully-wrought world to its foundation. But can they free each other from their pasts and trust their hearts to love?

Evergreen

by Delia Parr

"A UNIQUELY FRESH BOOK WITH ENGAGINGLY HONEST CHARACTERS WHO WILL STEAL THEIR WAY INTO YOUR HEART."
–PATRICIA POTTER

ANITA MILLS
ARNETTE LAMB
ROSANNE BITTNER

*Join three of your favorite storytellers
on a tender journey of the heart...*

Cherished Moments is an extraordinary collection of
breathtaking novellas woven around the theme of mother-
hood. Before you turn the last page you will have been swept
from the storm-tossed coast of a Scottish isle to the fury of
the American frontier, and you will have lived the lives and
loves of three indomitable women, as they experience their
most passionate moments.

THE NATIONAL BESTSELLER

CHERISHED MOMENTS

CHERISHED MOMENTS
Anita Mills, Arnette Lamb, Rosanne Bittner
_____ 95473-5 $4.99 U.S./$5.99 Can.

Award-winning author of *Creole Fires*

GYPSY LORD
He was Dominic Edgemont, Lord Nightwyck, heir to
the Marquis of Gravenwold. But he was also a dark-
eyed, half-gypsy bastard...
_____ 92878-5 $4.99 U.S./$5.99 Can.

SWEET VENGEANCE
Rayne Garrick had found Jocelyn Asbury among a
band of cutthroats—and now he would do anything to
have her...
_____ 95095-0 $4.99 U.S./$5.99 Can.

BOLD ANGEL
Saxon beauty Caryn of Ivesham was once saved by a
mysterious Norman knight—but even that wouldn't
make her marry him.
_____ 95303-8 $4.99 U.S./$5.99 Can.